Full Circle

Full Circle

Full Circle

Skyy

ww.urbanbooks.net

Urban Books, LLC
78 East Industry Court
Deer Park, NY 11729

ISBN 13: 978-1-60162-385-0
ISBN 10: 1-60162-385-2

First Trade Paperback Printing June 2013
Printed in the United States of America

10 9 8 7 6 5 4 3 2

Distributed by Kensington Publishing Corp.
Submit Wholesale Orders to:
Kensington Publishing Corp.
C/O Penguin Group (USA) Inc.
Attention: Order Processing
405 Murray Hill Parkway
East Rutherford, NJ 07073-2316
Phone: 1-800-526-0275
Fax: 1-800-227-9604

Dedication

This book is dedicated to all the weirdos, nerds, geeks, and people who are just different. Be you. It's so much fun being different.

Acknowledgments

Ah, and now we have come to the end. Yes, people, this is the last book of the series. I know, I know. It sucks, but, hey, all good things must come to an end, right? As usual, I must pick the perfect song to play while I write these acknowledgments. I've chosen "Don't Rain on My Parade" because right now no one can rain on my parade.

Years ago I was at a very low point after a breakup, and of the character Denise began to talk in my head. I wrote what she said, and from there *Choices* was born. I love these characters, and I'm so thankful and grateful that you have grown to love them as much as I have, but it's time to let the characters rest, and I'll let you guys make up your own conclusions as to what happens for the rest of their lives. It's time to move on to new projects and to new characters that are also speaking in my head. I just hope you enjoy the book and don't completely hate the direction in which I took the characters.

There are so many people I want to thank, and I just hope I don't forget anyone.

First, I want to thank Robin and Sha of Kings Crossing Publishing. These two wonderful women were the first to take a chance on *Choices* and me, and if it wasn't for them, there wouldn't be a fourth book to write acknowledgements for. I also need to thank Carl Weber and Urban Books for assisting in taking my books to

Acknowledgments

the next level and helping to get them to a broader audience.

Michelle, thanks for sitting at my computer and telling me that you thought *Choices* was as good as the last E. J. Dickey book you read. If it wasn't for your comments, *Choices* would still be a file on my computer.

Dana, aka Oohzee, who holds the record for most books purchased by a single person, you've always supported me and given me amazing advice over the years. I'm so glad you came into my life.

Meshanna "Shunta" Jones, or my "Gayle," thanks for being my bestie even when I'm stuck in emotional Cancer moments. And also, Shawn, my best good-guy friend, you mean the world to me, sir! And, Bimbim, you drive me crazy, but my life would suck without you.

I also have to thank my friends who have talked me down off the bridge on more than one occasion. I have had so many moments where I was just fed up, but they help me remember why I do what I do. I don't need to name all the names as you all know who you are.

And most importantly, I have to thank all the fans of my books. You are the most amazing, crazy, insane, dedicated, and impatient people, and I swear you make my life so much better. Without you, again, there would be no need for this final book.

And finally, I have to thank the asshole who broke my heart all those years ago. Thank you, thank you, thank you for being such a horrible girlfriend. Without you, there really would be no books at all. I hope you all enjoy the book.

Chapter 1

Darkness. Lena didn't know what was going on. All around was pure darkness. She took a step forward. She could feel sand covering her feet. Suddenly, the sound and smell of the beach took over her senses. Lena squinted her eyes, hoping she would be able to see something. How did she end up on the beach?

"Hello?" Lena called out, but no one answered. She cautiously took a few steps forward. "Anyone here?"

There was no answer, just the sound of the ocean.

"Turn around," said a vaguely familiar woman's voice.

"Who's there?" Lena called out.

Instantly, a wave crashed into her, covering her legs with cold water. Lena jumped back. She turned around quickly.

Suddenly, Lena was standing in her dorm room. Everything was the same: the beds were perfectly made up, and her mother's taste was all over the room from when she decorated Lena's freshman year. Confused, Lena looked up. In her hands were the curtains that she was in the middle of taking down.

Lena's chair began to wobble. She gasped as she felt the chair give way under her.

"Denise!" Lena yelled. Where was Denise? She was supposed to catch her, but no one was there. Lena could feel herself falling. She screamed as her body began to tumble to the floor.

***

Lena's eyes popped open as she took a deep breath. She turned over in her plush king-size bed. She rubbed her eyes, her heart still beating fast from the unusual dream. She covered her eyes with her hands. She was used to her dreams, but this one was different and she had no idea what to make of it.

Reality set in as the annoying sound of a running vacuum cleaner and the blaring television in the living room reached her room. Lena looked over at her clock. She knew she had to talk to Jessica about her need to use the loudest gadgets at seven in the morning.

Lena finally forced herself out of the bed. She tiptoed into the bathroom, leaving the door cracked, trying not to make a sound. Lena stared at herself in the mirror. She brushed her frizzy edges back and pulled her hair, which had come undone during her peaceful slumber, back into a ponytail. She could hear DJ Lance Rock's voice coming from the other room. Lena rolled her eyes. She couldn't understand why her daughter was obsessed with the one television show she truly couldn't stand. She didn't know what it was, but something about a grown man in an orange leotard rubbed her the wrong way.

Lena knew taking a shower would ruin any chance of her getting in another hour of sleep. The hot water ran out of the large rain showerhead. The water felt good, waking up her last sleeping body parts. She decided to enjoy the time, knowing it would be the last moment of peace she would have. Lena washed her long hair just to take extra time.

Lena's eyes opened when she heard the small but loud voice echoing through the bathroom. Over and over again her name was being yelled at the top of her toddler's lungs. A gust of cold air hit her; her daughter had opened the bathroom door, letting the steam out. Lena grabbed her towel and wrapped it around her body.

"Yes, dear?" Lena said as she stepped out of the shower. She looked at her beautiful daughter, who was attempting to brush her long hair in the mirror.

Bria turned around and smiled. "Mommy!" Bria ran into Lena's arms.

Lena sat down on the chair in the bathroom, and Bria climbed on her lap. "Girl, what have you done to your hair?" Lena smiled as she gently brushed her daughter's wild mane with her fingers.

Bria shrugged her shoulders.

Lena couldn't do anything but laugh. No matter how good the ponytails or braids she put in Bria's hair before she went to sleep were, the next day her hair was a messy disaster.

There was a knock at the door. Bria jumped out of her mother's lap as Lena gave the okay for Jessica to enter.

"I'm sorry, Lena. I told her not to bother you." Jessica looked down at Bria, who blushed, knowing she had disobeyed.

"It's all right. I was just enjoying a longer than normal shower." Lena stood up and followed the two out of the bathroom. Lena opened the doors to her walk-in closet. It was organized to perfection, thanks to Jessica. Jessica was a godsend to Lena. She had been through a few different nannies and housekeepers but had hit the jackpot when she found Jessica.

"I am going to get little miss here ready. What time did you want to leave?" Jessica asked, causing Lena to pause. Jessica shook her head. "You forgot, didn't you?"

"Of course not. Of course I remembered that. . . ." Lena looked at Jessica and smiled.

"Lunch with your mother and father."

"Shit . . ."

"Oh, Mommy!" Bria put her hand over her mouth.

"Yes, Mommy knows she said a bad word. I won't do it again." Lena kissed Bria on her forehead.

A loud noise came from the TV. Obviously, the annoying characters did something that caused Bria to run out of the room quickly and park herself back in front of the big screen.

"Don't worry," Jessica assured Lena. "I'll get her ready, and there are muffins on the kitchen counter."

Lena mouthed "Thank you" as Jessica nodded and walked out, closing the door behind her. Lena's idea of throwing on a pair of oversize jeans went out the window. She pulled out a nice pair of jeans and one of her many designer shirts. She pulled out her makeup bag and began to paint her face. She remembered why she didn't like leaving the house. The days of taking time to look beautiful were behind her.

Her cell phone began to ring. It was Carmen's special ringtone. Lena smiled as she picked up the phone. "Hey, Carmicita."

Carmen rolled up the window to her car. "So, yesterday I was sitting in class, looking at those badass kids, and realized I couldn't take it anymore."

Lena's eyes widened in shock. "You quit your job?"

"Ugh, no." Carmen rolled her eyes. "But a bitch came down with a sudden illness and had to take the next few days off. I'm in the car on Seventy-eight and headed to Atlanta."

"Oh my God, you are crazy." Lena laughed to herself. She knew when Carmen decided to be a teacher that she wouldn't last long. Carmen had a very low tolerance for teenagers. "I told you not to teach eighth grade."

"Girl, who you telling? Anyhoo, when I get there, I want to see you and Misha. We need to discuss some stuff."

"Okay, no problem. Oh, great. You can see my new house. Misha was supposed to bring Jaylin over, anyway."

Carmen frowned. "See, this is why we need to move to Atlanta. You and Misha get to have girl time, and I'm stuck in Memphis."

Lena pulled her wet curls back into a ponytail. "I wouldn't call it girl time. It's more like playdates with our children."

"Well, I don't care. I want to do it too."

"Trust me, you don't." Lena and Carmen both laughed.

"Well, I'll be there around sevenish. I'm going to drop my stuff at Carla's, and then I'll be heading over." Carmen always called Cooley by her real name.

"Okay, no problem. But you know, I swear you, Brandon, and my parents and these meetings are driving me insane. I'm headed to meet with them now."

"Uh-oh. Is this good or bad?"

Lena pulled the jeans on. "I'm not sure, but nothing has been bad with them recently. Everything is always about Bria."

Lena couldn't believe her parents' transformation, especially her mother's. The plastic-surgery-loving, spa-going woman had turned into a straight grandmother. Bria had them wrapped around her little finger, just like she did everyone else who met her. Her daughter was not only beautiful, but also personable. You couldn't help but love her.

Lena and Carmen hung up, and Lena finished getting ready. Lena gave herself one final look before walking out of her bedroom. She smiled. The Lena she knew pre-baby was staring back at her. She grabbed her purse and walked out of the room.

Lena and Bria walked into her parents' large mansion. Bria yelled, "Yaya!" as she ran toward the living room area. The house was quiet. Lena walked into the grand room and called her mother's name. She heard her mother yell, "Outside." Lena opened the door to the backyard.

"Yaya, Papi!" Bria squealed as she ran up to Lena's father.

"There's my *bella* Bria." Lena's father's deep voice always went an octave higher when he talked to his grandbaby. He picked Bria up and hugged her. "I've missed you." He tickled Bria, causing her to erupt in laughter.

"Wow. A hello for your daughter would be nice," Lena joked as she sat in the oversize, plush patio chair. She looked around the grounds. She loved her parents' house in the spring. The flowers were in bloom. She could smell the fragrant jasmine and orange blossoms as the breeze blew.

"Well, hello to you too, baby girl." Her father, Derrick, smiled as Bria lay on his chest.

"Yes, hello, darling. You are looking nice today." Lena's mother, Karen, looked her daughter up and down. She had a small smirk on her face. Lena was suspicious.

"So what's going on, parental units?"

"One moment." Karen called for the maid to come out. "Take Bria into the kitchen and get her a big bowl of ice cream," she instructed the maid when she appeared.

"Yea!" Bria clapped as she jumped down in anticipation of the treat.

"Not too big." Lena knew her request would fall on deaf ears.

As soon as the coast was clear, her father pulled a yellow envelope out and slid it across the table to her.

"What's this?" Lena questioned.

"Well, Lena, in just a few months, do you know how old you will be?"

"Twenty-three. Why?" Lena was curious as she opened the envelope. She pulled out a contract. The word *trust* made her heart skip a beat.

"As you know, your trust fund matures when you turn twenty-five," her father said. "Well, what you didn't know is that we had a clause in place that it could be accessed as early as your twenty-third birthday if we felt you were ready for it."

Lena's hands began to shake as she looked through the papers. "So what are you saying, Dad?"

"We are saying that you have proved a lot to me and your mother in the last three years. You didn't let the divorce or your pregnancy stop you from finishing school."

"And you have become an amazing mother," Karen added.

"So we are releasing your trust to you on your twenty-third birthday."

Lena's mouth dropped open as she stared at all the zeros. She had always known her trust would be big but had never expected it to be as much as it was. Lena felt a warm sensation of freedom come over her body. She never had to rely on Brandon, who was her ex-husband, or her parents for anything ever again.

"Also, Bria's trust has been set up," her father continued.

Lena wanted to scream but maintained her composure. "I don't know what to say."

"There's one more thing." Karen's perfectly manicured finger flew in the air.

Lena's smile instantly faded. She knew there had to be a catch. "Oh God, what is it?" Lena braced herself for the impact.

"Well, as you know, your father has decided to retire finally. We've decided to take a few months and travel. We're going to take a cruise, go to Europe, and finish off by spending the summer at the Vineyard."

"Sounds amazing." Lena poured herself a glass of the amazing lemonade that their maid was famous for making.

"And we want to take Bria with us," Karen added.

"What?" Lena stopped in her tracks. "You want to take my child out of the country? Without me? For God knows how long?" Lena frowned.

"Hear us out first, Lena," her father interjected. "It is a win-win for all involved."

"How is that?"

"You haven't had a break since you had Bria," he noted. "You are still a young woman. You will have time to catch up with your friends and rest without worrying about Bria."

"Yes." Karen stood up. "Didn't you say Carmen was going to have that ceremony with that girl?"

"Nic." Lena still couldn't stand her mother's attitude toward her lesbian friends.

"Yes, well, now you can be a good friend and help her plan it. It will be only a few months."

Lena stood up. "I have to think about this. You're talking about a long time. I haven't even let Brandon take her to Memphis alone yet, and y'all are trying to take her out of the country."

"Well, think about it and let us know. The cruise would be a Disney cruise, and we know she would love it." Her father stood up and put his arm around Lena.

"But it's your vacation. You want a two-year-old running around the whole time?"

"We would have help, of course," Karen stated, as though Lena didn't know they would probably have nannies at every stop. "Plan your friend's wedding, and spend time really finding Lena."

Lena let her words sink in. "This is so much." Lena shook her head.

Lena's father put his hand on her shoulder. "Think about it, sweetie. You are young. You will have time to really enjoy life for a little while."

"But we need to know soon, as Bria doesn't have a passport." Karen took a sip from her lemonade, which, Lena was 100 percent sure, was spiked with some type of vodka or rum.

"Okay. Well, I have to go. Bria has a playdate today."

"Okay, well, let us know," her father urged.

"Soon." Karen smiled.

Lena nodded before she headed inside. She looked at Bria's face, covered in vanilla ice cream. Lena sighed.

The break was looking better by the minute.

Chapter 2

Lena watched as Brandon raided her refrigerator. Li'l Brandon and Bria were making a ridiculous amount of noise in Bria's room. Lena tried to ignore it. Jessica must have known Lena wasn't going to check up on them, as she walked out of the laundry room toward Bria's room.

"So you don't mind?" Lena asked as Brandon downed almost a whole gallon of apple juice.

Brandon wiped his mouth. "I mean, I do, but then again, I don't. I trust your parents, and I think Bria would love to see some new countries."

"Yeah, but without us?" Lena sat down on the tall bar stool. "And for so long."

"I guess for me it isn't that bad, because I'm not with her every day."

Lena knew his underlying message. Brandon was still living in Memphis and hated not having Bria closer to him. Lena moving back to Atlanta was something he'd been completely against in the beginning. Even being divorced, he hated being so far from his daughter. Lena had to admit he was making it work. Almost every weekend Brandon was in Atlanta, sleeping in her guest room, so that he could be with both of his children.

It had taken two years, but they had finally repaired their friendship for the sake of their child. Brandon was a wonderful father and a great friend. Lena was able to forgive him completely for fathering a child with another woman while they were together. Brandon had even come to terms with Lena's sexuality. It was still difficult to think of his ex-wife as bisexual, but he felt better knowing that she was not completely gay. The turning point for them had come when Brandon tore his PCL. Lena was there for him, taking care of Brandon Jr. and Bria while he recuperated in her guest room. Brandon had sat out the whole last basketball season. Now his contract was up for negotiation, and it wasn't looking good. For once Lena was taking care of Brandon, and the closeness had helped their friendship to mature.

"So you think I should consider it?" Lena leaned on the countertop.

"Yeah, I think it would be good for her, and for you."

Lena sighed. "I just can't shake the feeling that if I say no, they will keep my trust from me. I don't want to be forced into anything."

Brandon laughed. "Lena, please. No one is forcing you. Your mom may be a bit twisted at times, but I doubt she would even do something that low. But think about the flip side. They are right. You do deserve a break. You are twenty-three, and for the last couple of years you haven't done anything for yourself."

"God, what is this? You sound like them now. What am I? Some old spinster or something?"

"Not quite, but close to it."

Lena hit Brandon as he giggled.

"Lena, I'm just thinking about you. You take amazing care of our daughter, and you took care of my big ass when I was down and out. Maybe you do deserve this break."

Lena's and Brandon's eyes met. She smiled. This was the Brandon she wished she had married to begin with.

She couldn't help but think about how much he'd matured in the past few years.

Brandon sat on the stool next to Lena. He put his big hands on her leg. "But seriously, um, we need to talk about something."

Lena turned her head.

Brandon's face was serious as he tried not to look directly at her.

"What is going on?"

"Um, you know our rule, right?"

Lena nodded. They had one main rule: no partners around their kids unless it was serious. Lena didn't have a problem in that area, as she hadn't dated anyone since leaving her ex Terrin at the Westin.

"Well, it's time to talk about that." Brandon looked at Lena. "Symone is, um, moving in."

Lena's eyes widened. "Moving in where?"

"Come on, Lena, you know where."

Lena stood up. "So Symone is moving in. Interesting. So it's to that point now?"

"Well, we've been seeing each other for about a year. It's just time, I guess."

"You guess? You don't sound too sure about it." Lena poured herself a glass of water.

"I am sure. I care about her, Lena. And I think it's time she's able to be around Bria more than just in passing."

First, her parents wanted to take her child out of the country, and now Brandon wanted to have his girlfriend around her. Lena felt the room spinning. Things were changing around her, and she didn't know if she liked it. She knew she didn't want Brandon back, but she realized something. He truly had moved on.

"Well, I'd like to have dinner with her first. Just so we can really talk, get to know her." Lena forced a smile.

She had met Symone only a few times. She remembered when Brandon met Symone. She was in her last year of law school at the University of Memphis. Lena had always been suspicious of women trying to date Brandon due to his athlete status, but even during his injury, Symone was still around. She knew Brandon was more serious about her than about other women, but she didn't realize just how serious he was, especially since she knew he wasn't faithful. A few of his slipups had been with her, in fact. She might have turned her emotional side off, but the physical side still had needs, and Brandon had come to the rescue on a few occasions while living with her.

"That's cool. I understand." Brandon hugged Lena. "I'll set it up for next weekend, when I come back."

"All right."

The three women held their wineglasses in the air.

"Here's to Carmen and her upcoming nuptials to that fine-ass Nic." The three toasted as Misha gushed.

"Hey, you aren't allowed to talk about women like that anymore. You're a straight, remember?" Carmen joked.

Misha rolled her eyes. "Please! I'm married, not blind."

"Ugh. I don't see how y'all do it," Carmen squealed.

"Please, girl, you get dicked down too." Misha nudged Carmen.

"The only dick that goes in me is plastic and strapped on. And even that's on a rare occasion."

They laughed.

Carmen looked at Lena. "And what's been going in you lately?"

Lena's mouth dropped at Carmen's crude statement. She walked over to the counter and grabbed the bottle of wine. "None of your nasty-ass business."

Misha looked at Carmen, then shook her head, knowing Lena wasn't getting any.

Lena hit Misha's arm. "I've had some recently."

"Please! Getting a fix up from Brandon doesn't count. And you better hope that chick doesn't find out you're using her man as your personal maintenance man." Carmen finished off her glass, and then Lena poured her some more.

"Please. That was my man first. And Brandon and I haven't done anything since he moved back to Memphis."

"Okay, so if it isn't Brandon, who is it?" Carmen's big curly 'fro bounced with the smallest movement of her head.

"No one."

Both Misha's and Carmen's faces dropped.

"What? I have a child, remember? Bria is the only thing I've been focused on."

"All, Lena, but you know what they say." Carmen walked over to Lena. "All work and no play makes Lena . . ."

"A horny-ass bitch." Misha's statement caused them all to burst into laughter.

Lena couldn't get the conversation with Brandon out of her head. She turned the TV on, hoping some celebrity gossip would take her mind off the day. Her attention was quickly captured by a story on TV One about a hot new movie and a hot new star.

Denise's face flashed on the screen as the reporter talked about Denise Chambers, the hot new rising star of the new movie *Ball*. Lena had seen her share of stories in which critics praised Denise. Denise was becoming a star. Lena's stomach dropped when an image of Denise and her gorgeous long-term girlfriend, Farih, came on the screen. Lena felt her heart sink. Everyone around her was living amazing lives, especially Denise. Lena smiled. Her intense, determined roommate had completely changed in three years. Lena's smile faded. She wondered if Denise ever thought of her in the midst of living the Hollywood life. She wondered if she ever crossed Denise's mind when Denise was surrounded by gorgeous people, including her model girlfriend, Farih.

She thought about her dream. Lena felt pathetic. Denise was living a fabulous life, and she was still having crazy dreams about her. Lena didn't know what had happened to her life. It was as if they had switched places. When she met Denise, Lena was the "it" girl on campus. She was gorgeous and was dating the star of the basketball team. That life was a distant memory. Lena felt left behind. While others blossomed, she was nothing more than a basketball wife/baby mama. Lena realized the "it" factor she had had was gone. She couldn't help but wonder if she would ever get it back.

Chapter 3

Denise stared at the door to the SoHo apartment she shared with Farih. She sighed. She didn't want to go in. She missed the days when she was excited to come home after being in L.A., to crawl into their platform bed, and snuggle with her girlfriend. The light in their relationship seemed to dim as soon as her celebrity star began to glow brighter and brighter.

Denise could hear Farih's voice, with its strong Nigerian accent, coming through the door. Her accent always came out when she was angry. Denise rolled her eyes, knowing what she was about to walk into.

Farih paced the floor with the Bluetooth in her ear. Her face was stern, and she didn't notice Denise as she put her bag on the floor.

"And so there's nothing you can do?" Farih sounded desperate. Denise knew that meant bad news. "Well, then, I guess there's nothing else to say." Farih hung the phone up and sighed.

Denise's voice startled her when Denise called her name. She turned around and looked at Denise.

"Hi."

"What's going on?" Denise tried to sound as concerned as possible.

"Nothing . . . absolutely nothing." Farih poured a glass of rum and Coke. "That's the problem." She drank until the glass was empty. Even though the cocktail burned, it didn't burn as badly as her feelings at the moment. "I'm not going to be an Victoria Secret Angel this year."

Denise's face dropped. "I'm so sorry, babe." She walked closer and put her arm around Farih.

"Don't." Farih pulled away immediately. "Don't do it."

"Don't do what, Farih?"

"Don't put on the fake caring routine."

Denise wanted to scream. "Okay, whatever! I am not about to let you do this now." Denise grabbed her bag and headed to the bedroom.

Angry, Farih followed her. "Let me do what, Denise? I'm not doing anything. Isn't that obvious!"

"Farih, I'm not talking about this right now."

Denise's calm voice only infuriated Farih more. "I think we *are* talking about it! You aren't going to let me do what, Denise? What is it that I'm doing?"

Denise snapped. "This." She motioned with her hands. "All this! Every time I try to be there for you, I get my damn head chewed off."

"You don't understand what I'm going through, Denise."

"Farih, you aren't the first person to have a little downtime in their career."

Farih's head snapped around. "Downtime? Denise, I don't have a career. That call, that call was my last job, and it's *gone!*"

Denise sighed as she sat on the edge of the bed. Her glimmer of hope of having a stress-free break was gone. She rubbed her hands over her hair, as she always did when she was frustrated. "Farih, I understand your frustration. I really do. But I'm really not trying to fight with you right now. I'm just getting home, I wanted to relax, and I wanted to spend some time with you."

Farih held her tongue. Even though Denise's voice was calm, she knew she meant business. Farih knew she had been taking her anger out on Denise, something she had been doing ever since her jobs started to dry up, but she couldn't stop herself. "I'm sorry, Denise. I don't mean to act the way I do, I'm just so . . . scared."

Denise looked into Farih's brown eyes. She wanted to be mad, but she couldn't. She opened her arms.

Farih sat next to her, laying her head on Denise's chest.

"Farih, things are going to work out. But getting angry and stressing aren't helping the situation."

"I know." Farih said. "Did you talk to Cooley about me yet?"

"Not yet. I'm going to when I go to town. We barely talk about anything besides work. I'll have more time when we are face-to-face."

Denise could feel Farih's mood change immediately.

Farih smiled. "Thanks, baby. I really think having Cooley as a manager might be the move I need. I mean, look at what she's done for you and Sahara."

Denise was offended but decided not to mention it. She hated when Farih made statements like that. She knew Farih was envious of her success, but when she made it seem like it was all because of other people, Denise got upset. Denise knew she'd been fortunate to meet people who were able to help her get the career she had. Her old sports agent Mariah had helped her land her first modeling job after a run-in with her crazy ex-girlfriend, Rhonda, ruined her basketball career. From modeling she met Melanie, her mentor who introduced her to the director who casted her in her first movie. Denise was eternally grateful to them, but Farih's statement angered her. They might have given her a boost, but she had worked very hard and hated that her girlfriend made it seem that she was successful only because of others.

"Look, I'm really tired. I think I'm going to take a nap before we go to Mel's tonight." Denise pulled her shirt over her head, threw it on the floor.

Farih knew she was tired and upset, since Denise never threw her clothes on the floor.

Denise crawled into the bed and covered her face up. She didn't want to give Farih the chance to say anything else insulting.

"Okay, I'll wake you when we need to get ready." Farih turned the light off and closed the door. Farih knew she and Denise were on thin ice and it was all her fault. She needed to fix her attitude, and immediately, before she was really left with nothing or no one.

In the dark Denise couldn't sleep. She started to think about her relationship. She wanted the woman she'd fallen in love with to reappear, but she had a feeling that Farih was gone for good. Denise sighed. She was seeing the ugly side of fame, and she didn't want any part of it.

"So the piece on TV One was really good. They are predicting awards." Melanie raised her expensive glass of champagne as she, Denise, and Farih sat at her dining room table.

Melanie Guston had become like a mother to Denise. She was the closest thing she had to family. Denise couldn't help but laugh at how they had met a few years ago. Melanie had taken Denise under her wing, only for Denise to find out that Melanie's real reason for mentoring her was that she'd been friends with, and in love with, Denise's mother, Tammy, when they were teen-

agers. Denise had forgiven Melanie for hiding that secret from her and now looked up to her more than ever.

"I don't know about all of that." Denise found it hard
to talk about her accomplishments, especially when
her fragile girlfriend was present.

"I think she's going to take it all. Golden Globe and
Oscar too." Farih beamed with pride.

Melanie agreed. Denise looked over at her girlfriend.
Denise didn't know why Farih was having such a hard
time getting a movie role, because the girl could act.
She played the part of supportive girlfriend unlike any
other. On the outside they were still the perfect lesbian
couple. Denise knew it was all a lie.

"So, Farih, I heard about Victoria's Secret." Melanie's face was straight. She knew how to cut to the bottom line. "How are you feeling?"

Farih sucked up her feelings and smiled. "Hey, we
knew it couldn't last forever, right?"

"Well, you know you are on my runway for my new
collection."

"Thank you, Melanie." Farih hated the idea of being
a charity case, but she knew that might be her only way
to let others see she still was a force to be reckoned
with. She just wished Melanie would make her the face
of the collection.

"No problem. Oh, there is something that I heard
about that you might be very interested in." Melanie
walked over to her desk. They watched as she thumbed
through a Rolodex, then picked out a business card.
Melanie was approaching fifty, but you wouldn't be
able to tell by her looks. The little bit of gray in her
mini 'fro gave her a very mature look, but it was still appealing. "Have you seen that show *The Buzz?*" Melanie
walked back over and sat down. She handed the business card to Farih.

"I've heard of that. It's like *The View*, but younger and edgy," Farih responded as she looked at the business card.

"Well, I know the producer, and I heard they were looking for someone to replace one of the women."

"Really?" Denise looked at Farih. "Babe, you would be perfect for that."

"I would. I really would." Farih couldn't hide her excitement. She really wanted to do movies, but a successful talk show could get her the buzz she needed to get into movies.

"Well, I'll call Harrison in the morning. Have your agents submit you for it. I think it would be a great look."

"Me too." Farih wrapped her arms around Melanie. "Thank you so much."

"Anytime."

A few minutes later Denise and Melanie excused themselves from the table, giving some excuse to have some alone time. They went into Melanie's bedroom, and Denise plopped down on Melanie's plush bed.

"Uh-oh. What's that all about?" Melanie asked.

Denise smirked. Melanie reminded her so much of her grandmother. She always knew when something was on her mind. "Mel, I don't know what is happening with Farih and me, but all the fighting is driving me insane."

"Uh-huh . . ." Melanie sat down at her vanity. "I wasn't buying that happy couple act in there for one minute. What's going on?"

Denise frowned. "She's just not the woman I fell in love with anymore."

"Well, Dee, she's stressed. She's lost all her major contracts in the past year. You would be stressed too if you didn't know where your next paycheck was coming from."

"I don't know where my next paycheck is coming from."

"But you have options. I heard you have a few offers on the table right now."

"Yeah, but nothing's written in stone. She's so mean to me. She takes it all out on me, like I'm the reason she's not getting booked."

Melanie smiled. "Denise, just give it a little time. You two are going on what? Close to three years? The honeymoon is over."

"It for damn sure is."

"I think things will be okay. Just understand where she is coming from. Don't take her attitude to heart."

"I hope it's only temporary, 'cause I don't think I can take much more." Denise stood up. "You know, I used to hate having to leave so much when I was shooting. I swear, I can't wait to get to ATL next weekend."

Melanie laughed. "Young people, always quick to throw in the towel. It's just a rough patch, trust me."

The cab ride was quiet. Denise stared out the window at the city lights. She had grown to call New York City home. She loved the city, but although she thought she would never hear the words come out of her mouth, she missed Memphis.

"I'm sorry, Denise." Farih broke the silence.

"It's cool." Denise continued to look out at the passing lights and yellow taxis.

Farih put her hand on Denise's thigh. "No, really, I'm so sorry, baby."

Denise turned toward Farih and put her hand on Farih's thigh. "Okay, just you gotta work on it. I know things are hard, but I'm here for you. I'm not going anywhere—unless you push me away."

A tight smile appeared on Farih's face. Denise leaned in and kissed Farih's soft lips. That was the Farih she loved and missed. She wondered how long she would stay around.

Denise decided to take advantage of the sweet Farih. Before they could make it into their bedroom after arriving back at their SoHo apartment and paying the cabbie, Denise had Farih's dress off and on the floor. She explored Farih's body inch by inch, trying to fall in love with her chocolate skin all over again.

Farih arched her back in anticipation as Denise's tongue kissed its way up her inner thigh. Denise was the best lover she had ever had.

Denise's hands caressed Farih's smooth skin. The taste of her sweetness was familiar, but something was different. She tried to focus, tried to stay turned on. She eased her fingers inside Farih's walls. The wetness covered her fingers. Farih was ready, but Denise wasn't. There was no way out; she was going to have to perform or risk another argument.

Denise dove headfirst into Farih's pussy, sucking and licking, nibbling on her clit. Denise ground her pelvis against the mattress in hopes of turning herself on enough to enjoy the moment, one that she hadn't had in a long time. Farih moaned as she arched her body, pushing Denise's tongue deeper into her. Farih's pussy was still the sweetest, besides that of one other person. Denise thought about Lena.

Denise closed her eyes. Suddenly she was back in Memphis, in her small two-bedroom apartment she shared with Cooley. It was the wee hours of the morning of Lena's wedding. While Lena should have been in the hotel room, dreaming about walking down the aisle, she was at Denise's house, in her bedroom, moaning her name and not that of her soon-to-be husband, Brandon. Denise had Lena the day of her wedding.

Denise grabbed on to Farih's sides, pulling her closer to her. She ground harder against the mattress as she devoured Farih's sweetness, her entire womanhood now wet and throbbing. Farih exploded in Denise's mouth. Denise opened her eyes. She instantly felt bad. Farih's heavy breathing was a good sign of her blissful state, and she was completely oblivious to the fact that Denise wasn't in the moment with her.

Denise rolled over on her back. Farih wanted her chance at the action. Before Denise could object, Farih had her briefs down. Farih's lips kissed Denise's lips before she used her manicured fingers to open Denise. Denise wanted to tell her to stop, but she couldn't. She was horny and wanted the release. She closed her eyes as Farih licked her love over Denise's walls. Farih's fingers fucked Denise while she sucked on her swollen knob. Denise assisted, grinding against Farih's fingers and tongue.

Denise bit her lip as she came. Farih took extra moments to catch every sweet drop. It was a treat when Denise let her go down on her. She wanted to savor the moment. Denise didn't care who was doing it. She needed the release, and Farih was a pro at giving head.

It was wrong, but Denise didn't care. Lena was in the room with them tonight, something that had never happened before. Lena hadn't been on her mind in a very long time, and she didn't know why she had suddenly reappeared in her thoughts. Denise turned over on her side as cuddling was not an option for her tonight.

Farih didn't know what to think. She could tell from Denise's body that she had enjoyed the pleasurable act, but Denise was void of actual emotion. Farih turned over, away from Denise. They slept against each other, something that was becoming very frequent.

Chapter 4

Carmen packed her clothes into her duffel bag. She gave the apartment one final look over to make sure she didn't forget anything she wanted to take.

"You got everything?" Her fiancée, Nic, walked into the room. Her wavy hair hung down her back.

"Yeah. Are you sure you don't want to come, babe? I'd really like you to come."

Nic shrugged her shoulders. "Nah. I'll let you have your time with your friends. Just don't have too much fun." She smacked Carmen on her ass and walked out of the room.

Carmen closed her bag and headed into the living room. She was ready to get back to Atlanta even before she hit the Six Flags exit on her way back to Memphis the weekend before. She wanted to move back so badly, but Nic wasn't ready to leave her job at FedEx, and due to the sluggish job market, no jobs in Nic's field had come open at the company's branches in Atlanta.

"So what are you going to get into this weekend?" Nic asked as she flipped through the television channels.

"I don't know. I know that Denise is hosting a party with Traxx Girls, so I'm going to that, but besides that, I think we are going to just chill and do some wedding planning."

"Tell everyone I said hi."

"You could tell them yourself." Carmen attempted to get Nic to go along one more time.

"Good try, babe." Nic turned around toward Carmen. "Hey, if you use a card, use the AmEx. I'm almost finished paying off the Visa."

Carmen nodded. "I doubt I'll use any money. You know how they do it."

Nic frowned. She hated that Carmen let her friends give her so much. "Well, in case, just use it."

Carmen kissed Nic and walked out the door. She knew Nic didn't like that her friends spoiled her, but she didn't care. They weren't bad off, but they didn't have the money that Denise, Cooley, or Lena had.

Carmen felt like she lived in two different worlds. When she was with her friends, she was living the glamorous Hollywood life. She had met more celebrities in the last two years than she had ever imagined. But as soon as she was back in Memphis, she was back to watching TV on the forty-two-inch Vizio with Nic and babysitting the bad kids in her classes.

She couldn't help but want the life her friends lived, even though she loved her life with Nic. Nic was the love of her life and had been there for her in some of her darkest times. Nic had forgiven Carmen for cheating on her with Carmen's terrible ex, Tameka, and for being a brat. Nic had helped Carmen develop the love she had for herself as well. Carmen, who had been overweight, had suffered from horrible self-esteem issues most of her life. Even after she lost the weight, she couldn't seem to feel worthy of anything real. Nic had helped her realize how special she was. Nic was her soul mate, and she couldn't wait to marry her

The two had been saving for almost three years for their wedding. It was crunch time, as they planned to get married in July. Carmen had started watching all the TLC wedding shows the day after Nic proposed. Like the rest of the world she was obsessed with the royal weddings—both Kate Middleton's and Kim Kardashian's seventy-two-day fiasco. She wanted the fairy tale she had always dreamed of, but she knew their finances wouldn't allow for it. And Nic wouldn't allow her friends to foot the bill.

Carmen arrived at the airport. She felt bad but knew she couldn't tell Nic that Cooley had paid for a last-minute first-class seat for her. She didn't feel like making the six-hour drive. The forty-five-minute flight was much more appealing.

She settled into the oversized seat and ordered her first Coke from the flight attendant. She pulled her iPad out and shot a text to Cooley, letting her know she would be there soon.

The short flight flew by, thanks to Carmen's new addiction to Scrabble. She quickly grabbed her things and got off the plane. The Atlanta airport was busy, as usual. Carmen smiled when she saw a billboard ad for Denise's movie in the airport terminal. Carmen noticed a group of people gathered around one of the belts in the baggage claim area. She noticed the flight was from New York City. She walked over to see Denise signing a few autographs for some young girls.

Denise noticed Carmen as she smiled for a picture. Denise's long hair was hanging down under her fitted baseball cap. After another photo with the girl's mother, she excused herself from the group.

"Hey, you," Denise said as she wrapped her arms around Carmen.

"Hey, superstar. Did you see the billboard?"

"Unfortunately."

Denise and Carmen walked out of the building. Carmen watched as people turned their heads, some knowing who Denise was, and others wondering why she looked so familiar to them.

"Shut up, girl. You know you like it." Carmen looked at Denise's mortified face. Even after years of attention, she still was uneasy about being in the spotlight.

A limo pulled up in front of them as they looked for Cooley's car. The driver stepped out. "Denise Chambers?"

"Um, yeah," Denise answered. Denise and Carmen looked at each other, confused by the arrival of the driver, who was putting their bags in the trunk. All eyes were on them. "I'm going to kill Cooley."

Denise opened the back door of the limo, and they heard a pop. Cooley started laughing as she poured champagne into a glass. "What's up, bitches?"

"You are so dead," Denise said as they climbed into the black stretch.

"I figured since I was picking up my two superstars, I would do it in style." Cooley knew Denise was pissed. Carmen, on the other hand, was eating it up.

"Don't do this shit ever again," Denise snapped.

"Oh, enjoy it." Cooley handed Denise the glass. She poured and handed another glass to Carmen. Her look had evolved, just like Denise's had. The oversize designer clothes had been replaced with fitted jeans and a button-down. Her swag was still unlike any other, but more professional. Just like her look, her hair had changed as well. She sported a short, curly faux hawk.

"So to what do I owe this, anyway?" Denise sat back with her arms crossed.

"Because we have cause to celebrate!" Cooley sipped the bubbly. "Guess who is not only up for the new *Fast and Furious,* but has also been offered a small part in a new James Cameron movie."

"What!" Carmen and Denise yelled at the same time.

"You heard me right."

"Are you serious?" Denise stared at Cooley.

Cooley took another sip of the bubbly. "Now, don't get too excited. It's a super small role, Denise. But it's James Cameron."

"How small?" Carmen asked.

"It's very small. Just a few speaking lines, but you are in a few scenes. The point is that it's James Cameron. Any role in one of his films is the shit. And how about that isn't the best news of all? I have something even bigger than that."

"Bigger than James Cameron?" Even Denise was excited at this point. Cooley threw a book in Denise's lap.

"Aqua Team Adventures?" Denise and Carmen said in unison.

"What is this?" Denise flipped through the book.

"Only the hottest youth novel series out right now."

"I've never heard of it." Denise frowned.

"I have. A lot of my students are reading the books," Carmen said. "It's a bit juvenile, but they seem to like it."

"It's the new *The Hunger Games, Harry Potter, Twilight* phenomenon," Cooley boasted. "It's, like, five books already, and they are hot. It's about teens who fight crime or some shit. I really don't know. All I know is the books are hot, and movies based on books always blow up. They want you as Aqua!"

"What!" Denise and Carmen yelled in unison again.

"The lead character! That's awesome!" Carmen squealed. Denise didn't seem as enthusiastic.

"What the hell is wrong with you?" Cooley grumbled.

"What about *Fast and Furious* and the James Cameron movie?" Denise asked.

Cooley bit her lip. "You have to decide on one. They are all shooting around the same time, so you can't do them all. But, Dee, Aqua is a lead role. Neither of the other two will give you that."

"I know, but it seems like a lot to take on." Denise glanced at the book. "It's a big responsibility."

"It is, but it's also easy fucking money. You already know they are going to have at least four movies. That's guaranteed money, Dee."

"And it also means I'll be known as Aqua for the rest of my life. Look at her. She turns blue, for God's sakes." Denise held up the book.

Cooley threw her hands up. "So the fuck what? It's a series, and you will be the lead."

Denise put her hand on her head. "This is too much."

"Consult with Farih on it," Carmen advised.

"Yeah, right. That's the last thing I want to do. I'm not gonna let her chop my head off for getting some teen movie I don't even know if I want."

Carmen and Cooley looked concerned.

"Hey, Cooley, can I ask a favor?" Denise said.

Cooley nodded.

"Would you consider representing Farih? She can't seem to get anything and—"

"Let me stop you now. Sorry, Dee, but no. I have my hands full with you and Sahara."

"Come on, Cooley. She really needs to get something."

"Is it that bad?" Carmen finished her champagne and put the glass down.

"She got dropped from Victoria's Secret," Denise revealed.

"I wish I could help, but no, it's a conflict of interest. What happens if y'all break up? And I don't know anything about that industry," Cooley observed.

"You didn't know anything about movies, either, but somehow I might be playing some blue chick." Denise smiled.

Cooley shook her head. "That's not 'cause of me. That's 'cause of your agency and your amazing acting skills. I mean, who knew you would actually be a great actress?" Carmen and Cooley laughed as Denise threw her middle finger up. "But real talk . . . Farih is old news. Have you seen some of the new chicks in the game? Farih's best bet would be to land a reality show or something."

Denise knew she and Fariah had been approached for a reality show on Logo but had declined it. Denise had cringed at the thought of cameras following her every move.

"Well, Melanie is trying to hook her up with some talk show. I hope something comes through, 'cause if her attitude doesn't change soon, I don't know what I'm going to do."

"So the green-eyed monster is showing his ugly-ass face, huh?" Cooley asked.

"You have no idea."

"Well, Denise, when you two met, she was at the top of her game. Now your star is a hell of a lot brighter than hers," Carmen said.

"Is that my fault, though?" Denise snapped. "I didn't tell the jobs not to hire her."

"It's this lifestyle. You have to be a strong person to be able to go from being in the spotlight to being in the background to your mate's foreground. Maybe Farih isn't that strong."

All three sat in silence as they pondered Cooley's words.

Denise felt all the pressure of New York City drop the second she made it to Atlanta. She zoned out the back-and-forth between Carmen and Cooley as she settled into one of the guest rooms in Cooley's home. There was something about being in the South—and being away from Farih in her new state of mind—that was comforting to her.

"Hey." Denise turned to see Carmen standing in the doorway. "Food?"

Denise shook her head. "I ate already. I just want to rest before tonight."

Carmen knew Denise didn't want to discuss her troubles with Farih anymore, so she didn't bring it up again. She headed back into the living room to join Cooley.

Denise spread her long body out on the comfortable bed. She stared at the ceiling fan, which was rotating slowly. She knew she should call Farih and let her know she made it, but she didn't. She didn't feel like any attitude, even over the phone.

The sexual experience last weekend entered her mind. After almost two years Lena had entered her thoughts. Denise missed Lena. Before anything, they were friends, but Denise's work and Farih's comments about Lena and Denise's past had made her slowly pull away from Lena. The only thing she knew about Lena was the tidbits Carmen talked about. She wondered how she was doing.

She pulled out her phone and opened Facebook. She did a search for Lena Jamerson, but nothing came up. She shook her head, remembering that that wasn't Lena's name anymore. She searched for Lena Redding but got the same results. She couldn't believe in this day and age Lena didn't have a Facebook page. She wanted to ask Carmen about Lena, but that would open up a discussion she didn't want to have. Denise wondered what Lena's daughter was like. The only picture she had seen was of her as a newborn. She was gorgeous, so perfect she almost didn't look real. She looked more like a perfect little doll.

What did Lena look like now? Denise wondered if motherhood had changed her sexy physique. She knew Lena would never let her body go, so it probably was just as sexy as ever. Denise shook her head. She knew she shouldn't be thinking about Lena or her sexy body. She turned over on her side and closed her eyes, hoping to push the thoughts out of her mind, then fell asleep.

Chapter 5

Lena wanted not to like her, but she couldn't. She sat across from Symone at Dave & Buster's. Brandon was watching as the kids played in the little kids' section. Every now and then someone asked him for a photo or an autograph.

"So did you have any particular questions for me, Lena?" Symone smiled. She had very nice teeth, except for one that was a bit crooked.

Lena shook her head. She was trying to find something wrong with the girl.

Symone wasn't anything like her. She didn't come from wealth, and she had to struggle, working various jobs, to put herself through school. She had just passed the bar and was taking a job with a prestigious law firm, as a junior associate, in a few weeks. Symone was attractive but not stunning. Nothing really set her apart from any other attractive women. Lena didn't know what Brandon saw in her. She definitely wasn't on Lena's level when Lena was with Brandon.

"No, there's nothing I really want to ask. I know you have been around Junior for a while now."

"I know you are probably worried, me being the new woman and being around your daughter. I totally understand. But trust me, Lena, I love Junior, and even though I haven't had the chance to really get to know Bria, I already adore her." Symone looked over at Brandon, who was hugging Bria.

Lena smiled. She could almost see little hearts flying from Symone's eyes.

"I'm not worried about anything like that. I know you love Brandon. I do want to apologize for the hesitation. Brandon had a lot of women in the past that weren't real."

Symone nodded her head as she listened to Lena.

"I have to know my child is around someone who is in it for the long haul, and not just some groupie trying to sleep her way into the wife role."

Symone was a bit offended, but she knew where Lena was coming from. She had actually wondered the same thing about Lena when she first saw pictures of her. It wasn't until Brandon explained their relationship that she saw Lena as something more than a groupie who had come up in the world.

Symone nodded. "Trust me, I know what you are talking about. These women are scandalous. I've seen it already."

"And you think you are going to be okay with dealing with it? Honestly, I wasn't." Lena looked over at Brandon Jr. He was the product of an outside affair Brandon had had with another woman. Lena found out about the affair because the other woman dropped info in her lap while she was getting her hair done.

"I really don't know. All I know is that I love Brandon, and I think he loves me too." Symone's face was serious. "I trust him. I realized that while he was living with you when he got injured. Face it. A lot of women would have been totally freaked if their man moved in with his ex."

Lena took a sip of her cocktail. She hoped her face didn't give away the guilt she was feeling. Symone was trusting, but during that time Lena had had Brandon sexually on many occasions.

"I just have to hope that he has enough respect for our relationship not to ruin it for a piece of cheap tail." Symone sipped from her glass of Coke. Deep down she knew Brandon and Lena had probably fooled around a few times, but she had decided to ignore her women's intuition.

The two kids ran up to the women. Bria ran straight into Lena's arms; Brandon Jr. ran to Symone, as though she was his mother.

"So how are things over here?" Brandon asked as he sat down.

"Things are good, honey," Symone responded.

Lena nodded her head. She noticed a quick exchange between Symone and Brandon.

"So, Lena, is it all right if Bria comes back to the hotel with us? We are going to take Junior to see that new cartoon and wanted Bria to come along . . . and stay the night."

Lena instantly knew what that exchange had been about. They had planned this from the beginning, to butter her up so they could take her child away for the weekend. She wanted to call them out on it but thought about Carmen, who was in town. It would give her time to spend with her friends.

"Sure. I don't see the problem with that."

They all stood up, and Brandon hugged his beautiful ex-wife. They grabbed their belongings and headed out the door.

Lena sat in her house. It was quiet. She flipped through the TV channels. She stopped on *Basketball Wives Miami*. She remembered when they asked her to be on the new *Basketball Wives Atlanta*. She would never put her business out there on reality TV.

It was only eight, and Lena was bored out of her mind. She picked up the phone and called Misha.

"What's up, girl?" Misha paused. "Jaylin, if you don't stop running around . . ." Misha yelled at her son, who was running around in his Barney underpants. She looked at Patrick, who was in his man cave, with large headphones on and an Xbox joystick in his hand. Every now and then he would yell something to the players in his game of Call of Duty.

"I am lonely."

"Girl, tell me to come over there, and I'm there." Misha lowered her voice. "If I don't get away from these men, I am going to kill myself."

Lena laughed. "Come over. I'm sure we can get into something."

Misha heard a loud crash as she hung the phone up. She threw the phone on the couch and ran into Jaylin's room.

"Jaylin!" she screeched when she saw the massive mess. His toy chest was toppled over, and all his toys were spread over the room. Jaylin sat in the middle of the floor, with a worried look on his face. He immediately started to cry, knowing a spanking was on the way.

Misha was frozen. She couldn't think. She walked out of the room and into Patrick's room. She stood directly in front of the TV.

Patrick sat up and pulled the headphones off. "Mish, what are you doing?" he asked, trying to see past her.

"I'm out of here." Misha turned around and walked out of the room.

Confused, Patrick jumped up and followed her. "Mish?" Patrick was completely confused as he watched Misha grab her purse and her keys.

"I can't take it anymore. I need some time. I'm going to Lena's. Do *not* call me." Misha was fed up.

Patrick attempted to argue, but his words fell on deaf ears.

Misha walked out the door and to her car, completely ignoring her husband. She sped off without another word.

Misha breezed past Lena after she opened the door. "Thank you, Lord. I think I was about to lose my damn mind. So what do you want to do? Go get something to eat? See a movie? Anything?"

"Damn, was it that bad?"

Misha's facial expression said it all. "I have a three-year-old and a grown child living in the same house."

"And I'm sitting up here, sad that my baby is leaving me."

Misha fell down on Lena's couch. "Please, I wish someone would give me a break. You better take it and enjoy every moment of it."

Lena sat down next to Misha. They laid their heads on each other. Their lives were so different from their best friend's. Carmen had it easy. It was just her and Nic. They were free to go and do whatever they pleased. Lena thought about having a few months to live that life again. It was sounding better every moment.

"So what do you want to do?" Misha asked again.

"I don't know. I wanted to hook up with C, but you know she's headed to that party."

Misha sat up. "That's right. Traxx Girls, right? Hmmm."

Lena's right eyebrow rose like the Rock. "What is that 'hmmm' about?"

Misha stood up. "How about we go?"

"Misha?" Lena could almost hear the wheels turning in Misha's head.

"Girl, I haven't been to a club in ages. Why not go be with our homegirl?"

"Well, for one, our homegirl is going to a lesbian event. . . ."

Misha turned around. "So what? It's not like either of us is new to the gay club scene."

"Yes, but think about who else will be there." Lena's heart started to race. Her dreams about Denise were becoming frequent. Now the thought of being in the same place completely freaked Lena out.

Misha paused. She thought about Cooley—something she did on a regular basis. Whenever Patrick did something to piss her off, she thought about Cooley and the life she had left behind. She couldn't help but wonder what her life would be like if Patrick had never shown up at Lena's wedding.

"Again, so what?" Misha said. "I'm not trying to get at Carla, and you aren't trying to get at Denise. They were our friends, remember? It would be like the old gang is back together."

Lena hesitated. She didn't know what it would be like to see Denise again. She still got butterflies when she saw her on TV. What would it be like to see her live?

"We're going. I need to raid your closet real quick." Misha ignored Lena's hesitation and headed to Lena's bedroom.

Lena quickly followed. If she was going to see Denise, she wanted to at least look her absolute best.

Chapter 6

The club was packed as only Traxx Girls could do. Lena glanced down at the massive sea of bodies from the comforts of the plush VIP section. It was standing room only and was filled with lesbian women dressed in their sexiest outfits, all with the same purpose, to find someone if they were alone or to find a replacement for who they were with. Video clips and images from previous LGBT prides and other club events played on the giant big-screen TV on the stage. The regular VIP people stood down in their small section right in front of the stage, not realizing they were merely semi-VIP for paying more to get in. The real VIP section was above, and Lena and Misha were a part of it.

Carmen had already arrived at the club when they'd called and told her they were on their way. Denise, Cooley, and Sahara wouldn't arrive till later. At the request of Lena and Misha, Carmen didn't tell Denise and Cooley why she was leaving for the club so early. Carmen was happy to keep the secret. Immediately after Lena and Misha got to the club, Carmen and Misha were lost in the crowd. Lena had opted to chill in the V.I.P. section; she never was a big club person. Lena watched out of her peripheral vision as a taller stud walked right up to her. She knew what was coming. The stud looked her up and down. Lena continued to stare down at the crowd.

"Excuse me."

Lena turned her head. "Yes?"

She was pleasantly surprised. The masculine female was actually very attractive. She was tall and had dark brown smooth skin and long locks with traces of red on the ends. Lena quickly turned the rest of her body toward the cutie.

"Look, I couldn't continue to watch you from afar. You have to be the sexiest woman I've seen in here." The stud smiled, showing her deep right dimple.

Lena gave her sexy smirk.

The stud extended her hand. "My name is Danni."

"Lena." Lena extended her own hand. Danni's hands were soft and obviously manicured. She wasn't the typical stud. She was soft, and it was very attractive.

"Why are you standing here alone, Ms. Lena?" Danni's locks touched her shoulders. She stared directly at Lena.

"I might be standing here alone, but that doesn't mean I'm alone." Lena smirked.

The DJ made an announcement about the upcoming musical act. The crowd was in a frenzy, as most people were waiting until after the celebrity appearances to really get down and party.

Danni smiled, nodding her head. "I hear ya. So I guess the only other question is, do I need to slip my card in your pocket, or are you free to take it in public?"

Lena's eyes widened as Danni's accent hit her. "Where are you from?"

"NYC." Danni was still fixated on Lena's eyes.

"I figured as much. That's a long way from here," Lena said, flirting. She couldn't believe she was flirting with a woman so easily after so long.

Danni shrugged her shoulders. "It's just a plane ride away."

Lena could tell just by looking at Danni that she was serious with her statement. She reeked of money. Lena could spot the real money from the fake money from a mile away. One thing about her city was that everyone wanted the same thing: to be rich, powerful, or famous. Lena had grown up meeting people who tried to live outside their means just to erect a facade of wealth.

The DJ's muffled voice echoed with the loud bass backdrop. "It's time, y'all. Are y'all ready to see the hottest, sexiest woman in the game?"

Lena and Danni both turned their attention to the stage. The promoters walked out onstage. The women all watched in anticipation of the appearance of the secret celebrity guests that they had been promoting for several months.

A hand touched Lena's shoulder. She turned around to see Misha standing behind her with a drink in her hand. Lena smirked. She hadn't seen Misha look that good since college. Misha had raided Lena's closet and had found the hottest outfit to show off her baby-made curves. She had pulled her hair out of her usual ponytail and had flat ironed it till it was bone straight. Lena knew Misha was on a mission, namely, to show Cooley what she didn't have anymore. Misha couldn't stand Cooley's new girlfriend, although she had never met her. In Misha's mind she had trained Cooley, only for another girl to come and enjoy the benefits. Misha was the first person Cooley had ever settled down with, and she was Cooley's first love. In Misha's eyes, Sahara was the bitch who was enjoying all her hard work.

"Hey, Carmen wants us to come to the stage," Misha yelled over the voice of one of the promoters onstage. Misha looked over at Danni. "Oh, hello."

"Misha, this is Danni. She's from New York."

Misha smiled. "Well, hello, New York." She shook Danni's hand. "Don't worry. I'll return her to this same spot."

"Do that. . . ." Danni's facial expression was strong, and she gave no smile. Lena felt herself getting turned on.

The club was more like a large warehouse, but the large open space had been transformed to resemble a jungle setting. Go-go dancers decorated with animal-print body paint danced on platforms, with women standing around, watching in awe. Lena felt like her old self. Various women attempted to talk to them. Some tried to get their attention by grabbing at their arms, but with no luck. Others realized they were way out of their league and just watched from afar.

The spotlight hit the middle of the stage as they made it to the backstage entrance. Misha flashed her arm band to the security guard, who slowly moved so they could walk up the stage steps. The DJ's voice began to echo again. Suddenly Lena's stomach began to knot up. She felt goose bumps on her arms. As she stepped up on the first step, she looked up at the small portion of the backstage area that she could see. Lena gasped.

There stood the one who got away.

"We thought we'd have someone real special to bring out our entertainer. Y'all know we do it big. Bringing to the stage the star of *Ball* and the upcoming star of *The South*. Y'all give it up for Denise Chambers!"

The shrieks from the crowd pierced Lena's ears. The spotlight hit Denise's face perfectly. Her hair was flat ironed and hung on her shoulders. Lena couldn't believe her eyes. Camera flashes went off around the building. Lena smiled. She could tell Denise was nervous and a bit uncomfortable by all the attention.

Denise took the mic in her hand. "What's up, Atlanta!"

Denise's voice brought the tingly bumps back to Lena's arms. Denise wasn't sporting her half-feminine, half-boyish look. Tonight she was back in her comfort zone, rocking a pair of fitted jeans, a nice black tee, a pair of limited-edition sneakers, and a snap back. Although it was a familiar look to Lena, she could tell the difference Denise's new Hollywood money was making. Her shirt was no longer a poly/cotton blend. The way it hung on her body, clinging to the right spots, let Lena know it had to be 100 percent cotton, probably even Egyptian. She liked the Hollywood Denise.

Lena couldn't take her eyes off of Denise. Denise's smile lit up the room. She blushed as the promoter joked about Denise taking someone back to her room. Denise played it off, joking and blushing.

"These women don't want to come back to the room with me," Denise retorted.

The crowd went wild. Hands flew in the air, letting her know that her statement was dead wrong.

"She looks good, huh?" Carmen said in Lena's ear, causing her to jump.

"She does." Lena looked at Denise. They were pulling two girls onstage. "Amazing. I'm so proud of her."

"Tell me about it." Carmen was proud of both of her best friends.

Misha walked over. The three watched Denise as she hugged the two fans and the club photographer snapped photos of them hugging Denise.

The three were almost mesmerized by Denise's strong presence. She wasn't the serious ballplayer that roomed with Lena. Even though she looked a bit uncomfortable onstage, she still seemed to be having a good time. Lena hadn't seen Denise smile so much before. Lena realized that that was because Denise didn't have a lot to smile about back then. In the course of two years she'd lost her beloved grandmother and her mother. Denise had grown up working hard, and it was all she knew how to do. It warmed Lena's heart to see Denise finally getting all she deserved.

"Oh . . . my . . . God . . ." Misha grabbed Lena's and Carmen's arms with force. Lena and Carmen turned around to see Cooley talking to security guards farther behind the stage. "Shit." Misha's nails dug into their skin.

"Ouch, bitch!" Carmen yelled as she pulled away from Misha's grip. "You knew she was going to be here."

"I didn't know she was going to look like that." Misha's heart was racing. Cooley hadn't noticed them. She was in business mode, and it was turning Misha on. Misha didn't think it was possible for Cooley to look better than she had in college, but she was wrong. Cooley's jeans were fitted, and she wore a blue- and black-striped button-down. Her large-carat diamond studs flashed every time the spotlight hit her.

"Damn, she does look good," Lena agreed. She couldn't believe it herself. Cooley wasn't the hip-hop stud anymore. She looked like she had stepped out of an Armani ad.

Cooley went over the final details with the security guards who would be watching Sahara. She gave them daps as they headed to their positions. Something was telling her to turn around. She instantly thought she had seen a ghost. She looked back at the wall. It couldn't really be Misha. Cooley turned back to see her past staring at her with a grin on her face. Cooley took a deep breath and headed over.

"Surprise!" Carmen yelled. She hoped Cooley didn't kill her when they got home.

"This *is* a surprise." Cooley made a mental note to kill Carmen when they got home. Standing in front of her was her first love, and she looked good. "I almost couldn't believe it was you." Cooley extended her arms.

Misha hesitated for a second but then received Cooley's hug. Not only did Cooley look good, but she smelled good too. The scent was all too familiar. Although Cooley owned tons of expensive bottles of colognes, she had always been partial to Pleasures by Estée Lauder. Misha felt her knees buckle. The instant connection was present. They hugged until Misha couldn't take it anymore and pulled away.

Cooley could tell Misha was turned on. She could still read Misha like a book.

"Damn, Lena too? This is a surprise for real." Cooley gave Lena a much shorter but endearing embrace. "Carmen, why didn't you tell me they were coming?"

"Well, I didn't know till a little bit after I arrived here. I was just as shocked as you to find out they were coming," Carmen replied, playing it off.

"How are you, Mish?" Cooley focused her attention back on Misha.

"Fine . . . fine . . ." Misha felt like an idiot. She couldn't think of any other words to say.

Cooley grinned. She could tell Misha was struggling, so she turned back to Lena. "Lena, you see ya girl out there?" Cooley could still feel Misha's eyes burning into her.

"I know, right? I'm so proud of her." Lena smiled like a proud mother.

Cooley nodded. "Yeah, she's doing big things, up for some pretty big roles."

"That's amazing," Lena said. She couldn't take her eyes off of Denise. Denise had the mic in her hand again. The promoter asked her if she would bring out the next entertainer.

"All right, what y'all have been waiting for," Denise announced. "I am proud to bring my sister out to the stage. Make some noise for Sahara!"

The lights in the building went out as the crowd went wild. A montage of Sahara's videos played on the screen.

Misha grabbed Carmen's hand again. She was already having a hard time seeing Cooley, and so she definitely wasn't ready to meet her replacement.

Cooley suddenly realized her first love was in the same room with her new love. Her mind raced with how she would play this one off. She knew she would finally have to introduce the two. Sahara had never bit her tongue about the woman who broke Cooley's heart. Cooley didn't know how Sahara would react to meeting Misha, especially since she hadn't had a chance to prepare for the moment.

"I'll be back." Cooley quickly excused herself from the group. She made her way farther into the backstage area as the lights came up and Sahara walked out onstage.

Sahara's dancers danced as she strutted out onstage. Misha couldn't hate; the girl was bad. Sahara's body was incredible. She had curves like Beyoncé's, an ass like Nicki's, and a gorgeous face, and the leather shorts she had on looked more like they'd been painted on. Not only was she gorgeous, but she could actually sing. Misha wanted to throw herself off the side of the stage.

While Lena and Carmen danced to Sahara's number one hit, Misha couldn't take her eyes off of her. Misha decided that Sahara's butt had to be the product of injections, and her face couldn't be that pretty without some type of surgery.

Misha had done a good job the past few years of steering clear of Cooley and Sahara. Whenever she saw a magazine with Sahara's picture in a store, she would just walk away, and she'd change the channel whenever Sahara came on the TV screen. The only place she didn't encounter her was on the radio. Her son, Jaylin, would throw a fit if she tried to change the station when Sahara's upbeat song "Dance Diva" came on.

There was only one magazine she had bought. It was a copy of *Ebony* with Cooley, Sahara, Denise, and Farih on the cover. It contained interviews with them, along with other members of the black GLBT community. She had been in the store and couldn't help purchasing it. She'd sat in her car and read the whole magazine before disposing of it. If Patrick had found the magazine, it would have caused a big issue. There was only one subject they just didn't talk about, her past lesbian life.

Cooley walked into Denise and Sahara's dressing room. She stood against the wall, staring at Denise. Denise took a sip from her bottle of water. She looked at Cooley, who was still in shock.

"What?" Denise asked, bringing Cooley back to reality.

"You have to see it to believe it."

The two walked to the side of the stage. As soon as Denise turned the corner, she froze. She knew she had to be seeing things.

"Whoa! Is that?"

Cooley nodded. "Yep."

Denise couldn't believe her eyes. A few feet away from her stood Lena. She knew she was losing her mind. She hadn't seen Lena in years. Now, after fantasizing about her, Lena was suddenly a few feet away from her. She took a deep breath and followed Cooley.

"Lena Jamerson."

The voice paralyzed Lena. She wanted to turn around, but she couldn't. She took a deep breath. She could smell Denise's cologne; it was intoxicating.

"Denise Chambers," Lena said as she exhaled and turned around. It felt like slow motion as Denise reached in to hug Lena. They both could feel the energy between them. It was dynamic, like the connection had never gone away.

"It's *so* good to see you." Denise held on to Lena's small frame. She finally pulled away.

Lena didn't want her to.

Denise looked her up and down. "Damn, will you ever age? You look amazing. And Misha . . . Oh my God, what is going on tonight?" She hugged Misha.

"I think I've changed some." Lena looked down at herself.

Denise smiled. "You look as good as you did the first time I walked in our dorm room."

Lena blushed, and an uneasy feeling came over her. Had she really not changed in five years? All her friends looked different. Did she really still look like a freshman?

"I know. It's like senior year all over again," Carmen quipped. She could feel how uncomfortable everyone was, but she couldn't help but feel happy to have all her closest friends in the same room again. This hadn't happened since her birthday three years ago.

The five stood in silence for a moment. Cooley and Misha looked at each other. What could they say to each other after so long? Last time Cooley saw Misha, Misha was very pregnant by the man she had cheated on Cooley with. Lena looked at Denise. The last time she saw her, Denise once again walked out of her life, but this time with her model girlfriend. It was awkward. They weren't in college anymore. Lena and Misha were mothers now, and Denise and Cooley had moved on to brand-new lives with new women.

"Yeah, I feel like we should head to IHOP, like we used to after the club," Carmen joked, trying to lighten the mood in the air.

"I don't know." Lena smirked. "We have Denise Chambers in our midst. There might be a riot at IHOP." She grinned.

Denise blushed as she brushed it off. "Please, no one is checking for me like that."

They all laughed, and the tension lifted some.

Lena looked at Denise, then motioned with her head for Denise to follow. They walked to the backstage exit. Denise led Lena outside. The door closed, muting most of the sound from the club. They stopped and leaned against the wall. Lena patted Denise on her shoulder.

"I saw your movie. It was so good. You were really, really amazing in it." Lena's heart skipped a beat.

"Thank you." Denise's and Lena's eyes met. Denise wondered if Lena felt the attraction she felt. She caught herself staring again and looked away. "I still can't believe my life. Can you?"

Lena's eyes met Denise's again. "Denise, I always knew you were going to do amazing things." Lena reached out and grabbed Denise's hand. It was like a jolt of electricity coursed through her body. Her smile died a bit. Denise was a new person, and Lena suddenly felt out of place.

Denise noticed the mood change. "So what are you thinking right now?" She picked up Lena's other hand. They stood in front of each other.

Lena took a deep breath. "I don't know. This is all so unreal."

"Is it?" Denise's smile had turned into her familiar serious stare. Denise wasn't going to take her eyes off of Lena.

Lena squirmed. She wanted to tell Denise that it wasn't unreal and that they were right where they were supposed to be. She wanted to tell Denise to take her and never let her go. Suddenly, Bria's smiling face popped into her head. Lena let go of Denise's hands.

"Things are so different now. You're a movie star, Denise, and I'm a mom."

Denise's eyes widened. In the moment she had totally forgotten about Lena's child. "That's right. Tell me you have photos."

Lena smiled, pulled her phone out, and opened one of several galleries of Bria. She handed the phone to Denise.

Denise's eyes popped as she looked at the photos. "Oh my God, Lena, she is absolutely gorgeous. Such a mini you."

"Thank you. She's pretty much my world."

Suddenly there was a shift in the electric energy. It was no longer about romance. It was the friendship again.

Sahara was on her last song. The crowd was singing along with her. She was looking off to the side of the stage when Cooley caught her eye. She saw a girl standing with Carmen and Cooley. There was something oddly familiar about the girl, but she couldn't put her finger on it. As she dropped down in one of her dance steps, it hit her.

It can't be, Sahara thought to herself. She turned around toward that side, doing the booty bounce. She noticed the look on Cooley's face. She was smiling. Sahara knew instantly that it was Misha.

Cooley felt a sharp pain in her side. She looked at the stage, and her eyes met Sahara's. She could tell by the look on Sahara's face that she had put two and two together.

"Ya girl is really good," Misha told Cooley. The words tasted like vinegar coming out of her mouth.

"Thanks. I'm glad you think so."

"I really don't." Misha laughed. Cooley laughed it off with her, but they both knew she meant it.

"Yeah, she's pretty cool. I guess you'll finally be meeting her tonight."

"I guess so." Misha's stomach was in knots. She suddenly didn't feel good anymore. She realized that she didn't hold a candle to Sahara. Sahara was an international superstar, and she was the housewife who had cheated on Cooley with a man.

Sahara said her final good-byes to the crowd and walked off the stage. The club DJ began to play songs, and the crowd began to disperse to various areas of the club.

"Let me go take care of things with the promoter. Give us just a few, and we will be back," Cooley told Misha and turned around to see Denise and Lena headed back over to them. She walked past them, taking Denise with her.

Misha turned away from the girls. She fought back tears. Carmen and Lena quickly came to the rescue, placing their arms around her.

"Mish, sweetie." Lena rubbed Misha's back.

"I don't know what I was thinking." The tears rolled down her face. "I can't go meet that girl."

"Misha, it's not going to be that bad." Carmen held Misha's hand.

Misha pulled away. "No, Carmen, seriously, I have to get out of here. Now!" Misha's hands were shaking.

Lena and Carmen knew she wouldn't be able to regain her composure before Cooley came back.

"Let's go."

As soon as Lena said the words, Misha was headed down the steps.

"C . . ." Lena said.

Carmen just nodded her head. Lena headed down the steps after Misha.

As they made their way through the club, Lena looked up at the VIP section. Danni was talking to a group of women. As soon as she saw Lena, she smiled. Lena mouthed, "I'm sorry" as Misha pulled her out of the club, leaving Danni with a confused expression on her face.

Carmen walked back to the dressing room.

"Carmen, you little devil." Sahara smiled, but Carmen could tell she wasn't happy. Carmen liked Sahara, but she would never take the place of Misha in her heart.

"I'm sorry, girl, but I didn't know. I haven't kicked it tough with my girls in forever." Carmen sat down on the couch and watched Sahara's assistants help her change.

"Told you." Cooley shook her head. She had already had an earful.

"I guess. Well, how did it feel seeing her?" Sahara took her black wig off. Her regular curly hair fell down. Her hairstylist immediately started quick styling it.

"I mean, it was cool. You forget we were all friends, so it was just like seeing an old friend," Cooley replied.

Denise and Carmen smiled at each other. Denise put her head on Carmen's shoulder as she listened to Cooley talk her way out of the small disaster.

"Okay, so when do I finally get to meet the infamous Misha? Carmen, where are they?" Sahara asked.

All eyes were on Carmen. Denise gave her a curious look.

"Oh, they left," Carmen announced. From the looks, Carmen knew she had to think of a quick reason that Lena and Misha had fled. "They were only supposed to be out for a bit. You know, they had to get back to their kids."

"That's right. Misha *is* married, isn't she?" Sahara noted and looked at Cooley.

Cooley just shook her head at Sahara's jab. She loved her girlfriend, but her mouth sometimes made Cooley want to shake the shit out of her.

"Did Lena say anything?" Denise whispered in Carmen's ear as Cooley and Sahara continued their witty snaps at each other.

Carmen shook her head. She knew there wasn't time to say anything. She could see the disappointment on Denise's face.

Tee, Cooley's longtime assistant, walked into the room. "They're ready to move you all to the VIP section."

Everyone but Sahara and Cooley stood up and walked out.

Sahara looked at herself one last time in the mirror, then grabbed Cooley's hand before she headed out. "I just want you to know I'm cool. It was just a shock."

"I know." Cooley kissed her cherry-red lips.

"I love you," Sahara said as she wiped the leftovers off of Cooley's mouth.

"Love you more."

"I can't believe I melted down like that." Misha put her hand on her forehead. Lena held her friend as they lay in her large bed. They had arrived back at Lena's house after a long drive, during which Misha had ranted about how messed up her life was.

A gallon of cookies-and-cream ice cream sat between them as they watched *Love & Basketball* on Lena's fifty-inch LED TV. Misha was finally calm and back to her normal self.

"It's okay. I wasn't too far behind you. Neither of us knew what we were in for." Lena was staring at the TV screen but wasn't paying attention to the movie at all.

Misha sat up in the bed. "How are you feeling?"

Lena continued to stare into space. "Do I really look the same way I looked when you met me?"

"Yeah, lucky ass." Misha ate a big spoon of ice cream. "I wish I could look the same."

Lena turned to Misha. "Seriously? Nothing has changed?"

"Why?" Misha questioned as soon as she saw the worried look on Lena's face.

"I don't know. I just figured I would look somewhat different after five years and a baby, more mature or something."

"You better enjoy those girly features while you can." Misha put the container of ice cream on the side table and rolled over. "I need sleep. I can't believe I'm actually going to get some sleep tonight. I never want to go home again." Misha quickly drifted off into a peaceful slumber.

Lena quietly got out of her bed. She walked into her bathroom and turned on the light. Lena stared at herself in the mirror. They were right; she still looked the same. Her hair was still long and flowing against her baby face. While her life had changed drastically, her looks were the same, innocent, immature. It hit her that things in her life had changed but she hadn't. She was still the same girl she was years ago.

She hadn't found herself. She didn't know if she liked women more or men. She didn't know if she wanted a relationship or if it was just seeing Denise that had sparked her interest. She lived for her daughter but never had time to live for herself. She had broken the vow she made to herself three years ago to focus on Lena. She had focused on everything but herself.

She knew it was time to finally find Lena.

Chapter 7

Misha knew she couldn't put off the inevitable anymore. It was time to face the music and go home. Although her night didn't go as planned, she had still enjoyed the mini break. She loved her son and husband, but she couldn't help but think something was missing.

After leaving Lena's house, Misha decided to treat herself some more. She headed to one of the nearby full-service salons for a day of beauty. She got her hair done, had a facial and a mani-pedi, and finished her day off with an hour-long massage that was like heaven to her back. She used the time to relax and think about her life.

Patrick coming into her life had changed her whole life plan. Instead of attending law school and pursuing a future as a hotshot entertainment attorney, she was running after a baby boy who just wanted to get into everything. She loved her son, but she couldn't help that he got on her last nerve. She had never thought being a housewife was in her future, and now she was starting to rethink the whole thing.

Misha thought about Cooley. She wondered what would have happened if she had said no to Patrick and had worked on her relationship with Cooley. Cooley was living a life she had never even imagined Cooley having. After watching her sister ruin her life with all the children she had, Misha had made a decision that kids were not in her future. Somehow a chance encounter with her first love at Lena's wedding had altered her whole life plan.

Misha pulled up to her home. Patrick's car was in the driveway. She looked down at her phone. After countless angry text messages, Patrick had given up on calling her the night before once her voice mail was full. She knew it was wrong to ignore him, but she had needed the break. She was home with their son every day, all day, while he enjoyed life. She never got to experience the finer things in life that he always talked about. As a sports agent, he attended functions without her most of the time. She was tired of sitting at home while his job took him to exciting cities and introduced him to athletes and celebrities. She had an itch for more, and she needed to scratch it.

Misha finally talked herself into going into the house. She braced herself for the hell storm she knew was about to hit her. Misha walked into the kitchen. It was quiet, too quiet.

All the lights were off in the house. She walked into the living room and quietly placed her bag on the coffee table.

"Welcome home." Patrick's deep voice almost caused Misha to jump out of her skin. She regained her composure.

"Thanks." Misha turned the light on. She saw Patrick sitting in his favorite leather recliner. His face was still, stern. Worry lines had formed at the edges of both his eyes. She refused to feel bad about her decision to take the day off. "Where's Jaylin?"

"With my mother." Patrick didn't move.

Misha sat down on the couch and braced herself.

Patrick still didn't move. He just stared at her.

"Look, I know you are mad, but I needed a break."

"And you figured that was the way to take it? I was worried out of my mind."

"I told you where I was going to be."

Patrick's calm voice was starting to scare Misha. Over the years they had had their share of arguments. This was new to her. Patrick shifted his eyes away from her.

"Sorry if I worried you," Misha added.

Patrick looked back up. "What are you apologizing for? You know you aren't sorry."

"Yes, I am."

"No, you aren't." Patrick shook his head. "Because you don't have a reason to be." Patrick stood up. "You see, when you left, I was pissed, but then I started wondering what I did to make you feel you had to run out like that." Patrick continued to talk as he went into his office. "I realized that I have put too much on you."

Misha didn't know what to think. She stood up and walked toward his voice. The hallway was dark. He hadn't turned on any lights.

"No, you haven't," Misha's voice cracked as she ran her hand along the wall to find the light switch.

"Yes, I have."

Misha's hand reached the light switch. She flipped it up and gasped.

On the floor were what seemed like a million red and white rose petals leading to their bedroom. Shocked, Misha covered her mouth with her hand as she walked toward their bedroom. Suddenly Patrick's hands covered her eyes. He guided her into their bedroom.

Patrick removed his hands, instantly leaving Misha speechless. A trail of petals led to the bed, and in the middle of the bed were tons of gifts wrapped in different size boxes.

"What is all of this?" Misha's voice cracked again. She turned around to see Patrick holding a single red rose.

"I realized that I don't tell you or show you how much I love you. You gave up a lot to be with me, and you are the best mom to our son. I figured it was time I show you. Starting with today. Happy Misha's Day." An adoring smile appeared on Patrick's face.

Misha turned around and looked at the lavish display. Suddenly her thoughts of Cooley and what could have been disappeared. She remembered the important thing. She hadn't given up her goals; she had simply altered them. Patrick and Jaylin were her new future, and it was looking pretty bright.

Chapter 8

Carmen stood on the large platform in the middle of the famous Bridals by Lori wedding dress store. She felt as though all eyes were on her. The three-way mirror showed all her sides in the beautiful dress. She turned to the right and then to the left. She, like most of the world, had royal wedding fever, and the dress had just the right amount of Kate Middleton meets the beach.

"And how much is it again?" Carmen admired each side again. Everything about the dress was perfect; it was her vision for her wedding.

"It's normally ten thousand, but since this is our sample, we can give it to you for six as is," said the slender, chic wedding dress coordinator without skipping a beat.

Carmen sighed. She wanted to cry. She had a very tight budget of two thousand to spend on her dress, and there was no way to cut enough corners to pay for the dream dress.

Carmen knew she had no business walking into the upscale boutique, but she just couldn't help herself. Dress shopping was something she was supposed to do with Lena and Misha, but the elegant window display had her hooked. Not to mention that her obsession with wedding shows only heightened when she was standing in front of the store, where she watched women say yes to the dress over and over. She hadn't expected to walk in, see the dress of her dreams, and have it fit her perfectly.

She turned to her right side again. "I don't know. Something doesn't look right."

"I beg to differ. That dress looks outstanding on you, like it was meant for you." The coordinator knew exactly what to say to brides.

"Oh, my goodness."

Carmen turned around to see a young white bride-to-be and her friends and family standing behind her.

The young bride walked up closer to her. "You look absolutely amazing. Oh, Mother, I want a dress that can make me look as good as she does."

"Yes, dear," said her very professional and obviously rich mother, while typing away on her iPad.

"When is your big day?" The bride walked closer to Carmen.

"July tenth. My birthday." Carmen smiled.

"Really? I'm next May. I'm so excited. Aren't you just excited?" The bride was giddy with glee.

"I'm getting there. I just want everything to be perfect."

The bride nodded her head. "Oh, honey, if you wear that dress, nothing in the world could go wrong."

A different coordinator walked out of the back. "Ladies, we are ready for you."

Carmen knew they were headed to the VIP section of the store. She remembered from Lena's wedding. The large group of ladies giggled as they headed back to watch the young bride-to-be try on dresses. Sadness filled Carmen's body. She stepped off the platform, grabbed her phone, and sat on a white couch across the way.

***

Cooley was going through the large stack of photo proofs of Sahara on her home office when she heard her phone buzzing. She caught it right before the last ring. "C, what's going on?"

Carmen sighed. "I'm sitting here trying not to cry and ruin this amazing dress I have on right now."

Cooley looked up from the photos. She hated the way Carmen sounded lately whenever they talked. "What's going on?"

"Carla, I'm sitting here in this fabulous dress shop, with my dream wedding dress on, all because I walked into this store I knew I couldn't afford. Serves me right, I guess. This sucks." A tear rolled out of Carmen's right eye. She wiped it before it hit the dress.

Cooley rubbed the top of her head. "I thought you were waiting to go with Lena and Misha . . . and I thought you were doing it in Memphis."

"I know. I told you I was crazy. I just couldn't help myself. Damn Atlanta and its amazing stores."

"Maybe it's not perfect. I mean, it's what? The first dress you tried on?"

"Kate Middleton."

Cooley paused. "Oh." She knew Carmen had been obsessed with the wedding and the dress. "Well, if you think it's the one, why don't you call Lena and tell her to meet you there? You could just be in crazy bride mode right now, and it might not be perfect."

Carmen really wanted to die. "Nah, I'm just going to leave."

Cooley already knew the problem. She knew Carmen wanted a royal wedding on a ghetto budget. "How much is it?"

"I really don't want to talk about it. Let's just drop it. I'll just leave before I shoot myself. Hold on a second." Carmen stood up and walked back to her dressing room.

Her coordinator walked over to help her into the dressing room. "Have you decided on anything?"

"Yeah, I think I'm going to have to pass." Carmen fought to hold in her tears in front of the woman. The coordinator closed the door behind her. She put her phone back to her ear. "I knew better than to come into this store. Hell, this is where Lena's dress came from, so I should have known anything in here would be out of my budget." Carmen wanted to scream.

"Damn, Carmen, can you listen to me for one moment? Call Lena or Mish, and tell them to meet you there. Who knows? They might not agree. I gotta take this call. Can I call you right back?"

Carmen wanted to throw the phone. "Yeah, I need to take this dress off, anyway."

Carmen hung the phone up. While tears ran down her face, she took the beautiful dress off. She handed the dress to the coordinator and finished getting dressed.

"Are you sure you don't have anyone to come give you a second opinion?"

"That's what my friend was just telling me. I guess I'll call my friend." Carmen picked her phone up and called Lena, who, surprisingly, was in the area. Carmen forced herself to smile at the woman. She knew, no matter what, she couldn't leave with the dress, but at least she'd have a few more moments with it.

"Okay, here I come."

Lena sat in anticipation of the dress, which Carmen had claimed was the dress of all dresses. She watched as the door swung open.

"Well?" Carmen looked up at Lena, whose mouth was covered. Tears began to form in Lena's eyes. "Lena!" Carmen yelled as Lena began to cry like a little baby.

"I'm sorry, Carmen, but it's just . . . it's just so perfect."

The coordinator clapped. Carmen was doomed. She couldn't help it. Tears began to fall, and they weren't tears of joy.

"Carmen." Lena stood up. She asked the coordinator to excuse them. "What's wrong?"

Carmen held up the price tag. Lena knew Carmen couldn't afford that dress or any other dress in the store. She smiled.

"We're getting this dress." Lena turned to call the woman back into the room, but Carmen grabbed her arm.

"Nic will kill me. This is damn near the whole budget."

"Carmen, I'm buying you this dress." Lena grabbed her purse, but Carmen stopped her again.

"No, Lena, you don't understand. I can't come home with a ten-thousand-dollar dress, even if it's on sale for six. Nic already doesn't like that you guys are always doing stuff for us."

"What? Come on, Carmen, you are my best friend." Lena crossed her arms.

"It doesn't matter. She thinks I rely on you guys too much. It's a pride thing."

Lena could understand where Nic was coming from, but she didn't agree. She hated that Carmen felt she couldn't ask her for things, but she also understood that Nic wanted them to live within their means.

"Nic doesn't have to know. I'm sure they won't mind tacking on a different price tag or something."

"But I'll know."

"Carmen, your wedding is in two months. We don't have time for this silly pride crap."

Carmen's phone rang. Lena answered it.

"So?" Cooley's raspy voice came through the speaker.

"It's perfect." Lena hated saying the words as Carmen walked back into the dressing room. "But she's not going to get it, and she won't let me get it."

Lena hung up with Cooley as Carmen came out in her regular jeans and shirt. She tried to put on a happy face, but she couldn't. She was hurt. It had finally hit her that her dream wedding wouldn't happen without dream finances.

Carmen walked past all the beautiful dresses on the racks. She could hear the other bride's friends' oohs and aahs coming from the back. This was not how she had expected her wedding planning to go.

Carmen and Lena headed toward the front door. A case of sparkling tiaras caught Carmen's attention. She couldn't resist. She walked over to the beautiful diamond tiaras, admiring their beauty. She wanted the fairy-tale wedding she'd been dreaming about her whole life. She wanted to feel like a princess, but her situation was making her feel more like a servant. She forced herself away from the case of tiaras and headed to the door.

Carmen heard her name as she was walking out of the door. She and Lena turned around to see the coordinator rushing toward them with a big smile and a large white garment bag in her hand.

"You don't want to leave without this." The coordinator held her arm out. Carmen's confused face said it all. "It's been taken care of."

"What do you mean?" Carmen hesitated.

"Your friend Carla Wade called in and told me to charge the dress and whatever else you wanted. She must be an amazing friend."

Carmen's body felt like it was about to explode from happiness. Lena hugged her. She couldn't contain herself. Her phone began to ring. It was Cooley's personal ringtone.

"Carla, no."

Cooley was grinning from ear to ear. "Shut up and enjoy it."

"Carla, I can't."

"You didn't. *I* did. Now, can I please get back to my work?" Denise walked in the room just in time to hear Carmen's squeals coming through the speakerphone. Cooley motioned for her to come over. "Denise is here too."

"I can't believe you did this."

"You better chill before I undo it," Cooley said. Denise was now smiling too. "Carmen, you deserve the Disney princess fairy tale that you've always wanted."

"That's right, girlie. Whatever you want, we got ya," Denise chimed in.

"I agree," Lena squealed. Denise's heart skipped a beat when she heard Lena's voice.

Carmen couldn't contain herself anymore and broke down. "I love you guys." She hugged Lena. She had no idea how she would explain it to Nic, but she didn't care. In that moment it was about her, and she was happy.

"We love you too. Now, stop being so depressed and go plan away. I gotta talk to Dee."

"Wait!" Denise yelled. "Yo, let me speak to Lena."

Cooley grinned as she shook her head. Denise threw her middle finger at her friend. Carmen was grinning just as hard. Lena looked confused as Carmen handed her the phone. Denise took the phone off speaker and walked to the door.

"Um, hello?" Lena said, still looking puzzled.

"Hey, Lena." Denise lowered her voice. "It's Denise."

"Oh." Lena's stomach dropped. She turned away from Carmen and started to walk off. "Hey, what's up?"

"So yesterday we kinda got cut off. I was wondering if we could catch up a bit. How about dinner?"

Cooley made a noise like she was clearing her throat. Denise motioned for her to shut up, only adding to Cooley's amusement.

"Sure!" Lena instantly felt dumb for her excitement. "How about tonight? Wait. Shit, it's my last night with my daughter before Brandon takes her to Memphis for two weeks."

"Well, you can bring her. I'd really love to meet her." Denise leaned against the wall. She was smiling from ear to ear.

Lena couldn't stop smiling. "Well, how about instead of going out, you come over to my place?"

The statement made Denise stand straight. "Uh, yeah, that's cool. I'll get the address from Carmen. How's seven?"

Lena couldn't stop smiling. "Seven is perfect."

"Great. See you then."

Lena hung up, feeling like she was walking on cloud nine.

Denise hung the phone up and turned toward Cooley. Cooley's dimples were deep from her grin. "What?" Denise sat down in the chair across from Cooley.

"As much as I want to get in ya ass right now, *we* need to get back into professional mode. So even though the statement I'm about to make can go for all aspects of your fucked-up life, I'm dealing only with the professional part at this moment. . . . Dude, what the fuck are you doing?"

Denise sighed. "I know. . . .Wait, what?" Denise didn't know if Cooley was referring to Lena or to something else.

"Do you? You are making my life a living hell right now. You need to pick the damn project you want to do."

Denise's happiness quickly faded. "I just don't know. The teenybopper thing is big, but it just seems silly. Cameron would be cool, but it's only a few words. I like *Fast and Furious,* and I kinda wanna do it."

"Kinda wanna do . . ." Cooley dropped her head. "Look, Dee, I love you, bruh, but this holier-than-thou attitude you have has got to go. You made one hot movie, and we don't even know how the indie one is going to do yet. Two films don't make you irreplaceable. You don't know what the second movie is going to do. It could suck. You got these amazing directors wanting you for their movies, and you acting like you fuckin' Halle Berry or some shit."

"I'm not. . . ."

"Yeah, dude, you are. Hell, look at ya, girl. No offense, but no one is checking for her, and just two years ago she was one of the hottest in the game."

Denise thought about Farih. She knew that Cooley was right. "I know this is the opportunity of a lifetime. It's just . . . I don't know if I'm really meant for Hollywood."

Cooley's eyes widened. "Are you fucking serious? Dude, James Cameron. Denise, James fucking Cameron!"

"So you think I should do Cameron?"

"Fuck no. I think you should do the Aqua movie. Are you serious right now? What the fuck, Dee? What do you want to do? Go coach basketball somewhere? Give up all you've worked for to go live in a one-bedroom apartment in Memphis, 'cause if you keep on, that's what you will have."

Denise stood up and began pacing the floor. "That's not cool, C."

Cooley got up from behind her large mahogany desk. She walked up to her best friend and put her hands on her shoulders. Denise and Cooley met eye to eye.

"Bro, I know this whole Hollywood thing isn't what you thought your life would be. But now it is. God dealt you an amazing hand, and it's like you want to give up a hand of blackjack for a bust."

Denise knew Cooley was right. "But what if the only reason I was good in the movie was because of the content? I mean, a ballplayer with a junkie for a mom. Not so far-fetched, ya know."

"Dude, when you got it, you got it. Dee, you got it. Now, please make up your mind."

Denise lowered her head in defeat. She hated when Cooley was right about things. "I'll decide tonight."

Denise knew deep down there was nothing else she could do that would make her the amount of money that either film would make her in a few months. Just the idea of her being a star was hard to swallow. Since her film, things hadn't been the same. She couldn't go to the local park and play ball without being stalked for pictures. And ever since she went public with her relationship, the paparazzi had been trying to catch her in a compromising position to write crazy stories for MediaTakeOut and Sandra Rose, who seemed hell-bent on finding some dirt on her. She wished there was a way to have her film career without the extra craziness.

"I will give you my answer before the end of the night," Denise added.

"Before nine," Cooley said without hesitation.

"Fine. Before nine. Damn. What happened to my friend who wasn't so focused?"

Cooley turned back toward Denise. "I left that bitch at Freedom University for this life of money and power." She laughed.

Denise chuckled, but she knew Cooley was telling the truth. Cooley was driven now like Denise was in high school and college. It was like they had switched lives. Denise didn't know where her focus had gone, but she knew she needed to get it back.

Denise's phone began to ring as she walked into the living room. She hesitated. It was Farih, and she really didn't want to talk to her. A few moments later the phone began to ring again. She knew if she didn't answer, Farih would continue to call.

"Hey, babe." Denise rolled her eyes as she forced the words out of her mouth.

Farih frantically flipped through the clothes in her closet. "Denise, baby, you won't believe this." She pulled out a black dress and threw it on the bed.

"What's up?" Denise jumped over the side of the couch, falling down on the plush cushions and making a loud thud.

"I told ya ass about jumping on my furniture," Cooley yelled from the other room, causing Denise to grin.

"I'm packing," Farih announced.

Denise panicked. "To go where?"

"There, silly." Farih folded the clothes neatly into her small suitcase. "I got an interview for the show!" She squealed.

"Oh, wow. Really?" Denise's heart began to race. "When are you coming, and when is the interview?"

"Well . . ." Farih headed back to the closet. "I was so shocked that they got back to my agent so soon, but they said they think I would be a perfect fit. My interview is going to be as a guest host for one show, and if it goes well, who knows? I might start immediately."

Denise stood up. She wanted to be happy for Farih, but she had more pressing issues. There was no way she could see Lena with Farih in the same city.

"I'm so happy for you, baby. When are you getting here? Do you need someone to pick you up?"

"I'm not leaving till the morning." Farih threw her toiletry bag filled with travel-size bottles in her carry-on. If there was one thing she knew how to do, it was pack a carry-on.

Denise let out a sigh of relief. She could still see Lena. Suddenly a bad feeling came over her. She realized what she was doing was wrong, but for once in her life she didn't care, or at least she didn't want to care.

"I'm so excited, baby. This could be the big break I've been looking for," Farih remarked.

"I think it just might be." Denise smiled. A warm feeling came over here. She couldn't help it. She still loved Farih, and hearing her so happy made her happy.

"And who knows? We might just be making a move from New York back to your precious South." Farih's call-waiting chimed, and she looked at the phone. "Oh, baby, this is my agent. I'm going to talk to you later, okay?"

"Okay."

"I love you."

"Love you too."

A large lump became lodged in Denise's throat.

Chapter 9

The soft female navigation voice alerted Denise that her destination would be on the right. She looked at the neighborhood. The houses were all unique in their own way. Some were bigger than others, but all were modest. She smiled. She could tell the home looked like something Lena would like.

Denise pulled into the circular driveway. She stepped out of her car and admired the quaint house. The Spanish-style house was only one story and had light blue stucco that reminded her of Lena's favorite color, Tiffany blue. The front doors were large, and ivy grew on the walls. Denise walked up to the front door and rang the bell.

Denise couldn't help but smile when she saw a small figure run toward the door through the beveled-glass panes. A little hand moved the shade and peeked out the door. She heard the little girl call for her mommy. Denise could see Lena's frame walking toward the door. She looked out the little window and smiled while unlocking the door.

"Hey, sorry about that," Lena said as Denise walked into the house. "Someone doesn't listen when I tell her not to go to the door."

"Is that someone hiding behind your back?" Denise watched as Bria poked her head from behind her mother's back. Denise couldn't believe how beautiful Bria was. Denise kneeled down. "You must be Miss Bria."

"Yes." Bria smiled.

"Don't act shy." Lena gently pulled Bria's hand. Bria walked out from behind her mother. "This is Mommy's good friend Denise. Can you say hi to her?"

"Hello, Denise."

"Hello, Bria." Denise was impressed by how properly Bria spoke.

Bria giggled, then ran to her room. Lena and Denise laughed.

"Lena, she's gorgeous."

"Thank you. She's my everything."

They walked farther into the house. A colorful book caught Denise's eye. She walked over to the coffee table. She picked up the familiar novel.

"Are you really reading this?"

Lena smiled. "Guilty. I started reading it to Bria, but I find myself reading it alone more than anything. It's actually pretty good. I like it better than *The Hunger Games*."

Denise snickered.

"What?"

"Nothing. It's just . . . I've been offered the role of Aqua."

Lena's eyes widened. "Oh my God, that's so cool. You know when reading it, I could totally see you as her."

Denise frowned. "She turns blue."

"Yeah, when she's about to kick some major ass. Aqua is real badass, Denise. In real life you wouldn't think she's as awesome as she is, but when she transforms, she's the shit."

"Well, since you explain it like that."

"I think you would make an excellent Aqua." Lena nodded her head. "Consider it."

"I will."

Denise and Lena talked for hours, catching up on the last two and a half years. Denise told Lena about her experiences in Hollywood while working on the two films she'd made. Lena listened, completely fascinated by all the things Denise had done and the people she'd seen.

Night arrived before they realized it. Denise looked at a large wall of photos while Lena prepared Bria for bed. She noticed photos of Lena while she was pregnant. Even at nine months, Lena was beautiful to her. She couldn't help but smile at photos of Brandon holding Bria for the first time. Denise felt a pain in her gut.

"Oh, please don't look at those. I was huge," Lena said as she walked into the living room.

"You still looked beautiful." Denise looked at Lena and smiled.

Lena blushed.

"Man, so much has happened. I mean, I thought my life was different, but damn, Lena, you are a mother. That is just so unreal." Denise sat down next to Lena.

"Trust me, I have a hard time believing it sometimes too. But in the end I think that Bria is the best thing that ever happened to me." Lena ran her hands through her hair. "When I think about how I was back then . . . I was so screwed up."

"What are you talking about?"

Lena looked at Denise. "Come on, you know I was . . . I was, so . . . confused. No wonder you sent me packing in New York." Lena smirked at the comment.

Denise's face was serious. She picked up Lena's hand. "Lena . . ." Denise's eyes stared directly at Lena. Lena could feel tears starting to swell. She couldn't look at Denise. Denise took her right hand and slowly turned Lena's head until their eyes met. "About New York—"

"Denise, please, you don't have to—"

"No. This needs to be said."

Lena could see the seriousness in Denise's expression.

"I was so messed up, Lena. I didn't know if I was coming or going. But I really need you to know that it was one of the biggest regrets I've ever had. I never wanted to hurt you . . . ever."

A tear rolled from one of Lena's eyes. Denise's soft hand wiped the salty water from Lena's cheek.

Lena took a deep breath. "After all the things that happened after I came home from coming to New York, I really thought I was being punished for all the things I'd done."

Images flashed through Lena's mind. She had left Brandon to follow Denise to New York, only to be turned down by Denise. She'd returned home, only to be met with a furious husband. The stress of her whole situation, including the arguing she endured when she arrived home, caused her to miscarry.

"I was so messed up. I knew what I wanted, but my mind and heart just wouldn't let me do right." Lena lowered her head.

"Lena—"

"No, I should be the one apologizing to you. You gave me so many chances to come to you, and I just couldn't let go of Brandon. I was scared. Scared of what my family would say, but more important, I was scared of what I was feeling." Lena let out a loud sigh as tears streamed down her face.

"What were you feeling, Lena?" Denise couldn't take her eyes off of Lena.

Lena knew it was the moment of truth. There was no turning back. She had to finally let the words come out of her mouth. She had to tell Denise that she loved her, and that she was still in love with her.

In the heat of the moment Lena couldn't take it. She grabbed Denise's head and pulled it close to hers. Their lips met. Lena didn't know if Denise would kiss her back, but she had to take the chance. Suddenly she felt Denise's mouth part. Denise wrapped her arms around Lena, pulling her close to her. Their tongues were reintroduced to each other as though it was the first time.

They stopped for air. Lena stood up. Denise watched as Lena's arm reached out. Hand in hand, they walked back to Lena's bedroom. Lena locked the door as Denise stood in the middle of her large master bedroom. There were no words. Lena walked closer and wrapped her arms around Denise's athletic physique. Denise leaned down, planting her lips back on Lena's soft lips. They stood in the same spot, embracing, kissing passion into each other.

Suddenly Denise's phone began to ring "Love of My Life" by Common. Her head fell. Lena took a few steps back. She knew that ringtone could be for only one person. Lena wanted to scream, take Denise's phone, and throw it out the window. Denise didn't know what to do. She silenced the ringer.

"Just too unreal, all this," Lena said, quoting a line from the musical *Spring Awakening*. She paced the floor to calm her hormones.

"I . . ." Denise silenced the her phone that started to ring again.

"Don't say anything." Lena snapped. She sighed as the phone began to ring again. "I'm going to get some wine. Take your call." Lena left Denise standing in her bedroom, dumbfounded.

Lena walked into her kitchen. She threw a quiet mini fit in the middle of the floor, jumping up and down and punching the air. She grabbed a bottle of Relax Riesling and popped the cork. She grabbed a glass but paused before pouring. Lena took the bottle to her mouth and downed some of the wine like it was a soda.

Lena walked back into the bedroom as Denise was ending her conversation. Lena leaned against the door with the wine bottle and glass in hand.

"Okay, I'll be there. . . . Bye. Love you too." Denise tried to whisper the last three words, but she knew Lena heard her loud and clear. "What? No glass for me?"

Lena's eyebrows rose. "Oh, you drink now?"

"When the moment calls for it." Denise shook her head, still in disbelief over what had gone down.

Lena sat on the side of the bed. She poured some of the wine into the glass and handed it to Denise.

"What about your glass?"

Lena lifted the bottle up to her mouth. Denise and Lena both laughed. Denise took the bottle from her and downed the wine the same way.

"Okay, look at you," Lena murmured.

They both erupted in laughter. Neither knew what they were laughing at, but suddenly the moment was the most hilarious thing ever. After a few minutes they finally stopped.

"See, this is what I love." Denise fell back on Lena's bed. "No matter how screwed up we are, we can still laugh and be friends."

"That's because we were friends first." Lena lay back next to her. "So how about two friends watching a movie?"

"Whatcha got?"

"How about *Love Jones?*" Lena smiled. Denise smiled. They both knew the last time they watched the movie, a heavy make-out session happened as soon as Darius and Nina got it on for the first time.

Denise and Lena lay in her California King and watched their favorite movie. By the time Darius and Nina had their first date, they were asleep in each other's arms.

Chapter 10

Denise thought she was dreaming when she heard Common rapping in her ear. She jumped up when she realized it was her phone. She picked the phone up off the side table. She had five missed calls. She looked at the time. It was 7:19 A.M. She was late.

Farih was pissed as she sat on the plane, waiting on people to get off. "What the hell?" she said when she answered Denise's call.

"Man, I'm so sorry, babe. I completely overslept."

"Are you kidding me, Denise? I have to be at the studio at eighty thirty this morning."

Denise quietly got out of the bed. "I know. I'm so sorry. I'll make it up to you. Just take a car. I'll pay for it and meet you at the studio."

"I can't believe on my big day you oversleep." Farih was fuming. Denise was irritating her more than ever. Their relationship had been in a downward spiral for months. In her mind this was the final straw. "You know what? Go back to sleep. Don't fucking worry about meeting me. I don't want to see your face." Farih hung the phone up and threw it in her bag.

Denise sat in shock on the side of the bed. She knew she was wrong, but it didn't warrant Farih's attitude. She knew she was at her wit's end with Farih and her mood swings.

"Someone is in trouble." Denise turned around to see Lena lying there with her eyes open. "You better go."

Denise stood up. She could feel the aftereffects of the wine they'd consumed last night. Denise looked down, saw that she was fully clothed, and breathed a sigh of relief, realizing she didn't cheat completely.

"Yeah, I need to run."

"I'll let you out."

"No, you stay. I can see myself out. I'll call you later, okay?" Denise hoped Lena didn't tell her to get lost forever.

Lena smiled. "Sure. Now go."

Denise hugged Lena and walked out the door.

Suddenly Lena felt sadness take over, and she wondered if she would actually hear from Denise soon or if another three years would pass before they connected again.

Farih put her anger toward Denise behind her as she sat in the makeup chair, getting primped for her day. She had met the other three hosts, all of whom were nice. Cassi was a twenty-seven-year-old DJ for a popular hip-hop station in Atlanta. Adrianne Disher was a popular child actress when she was younger and was using the show to try to rebuild her career. The most credible of the group was Relonda Frazier, a thirty-five-year-old lawyer turned newscaster.

The producer went over various key points of the day. He handed the script of hot topics they were going to discuss during the show, before a chef came out and cooked barbecue for the cooking segment. The show consisted mostly of talking about various celebrities and news headlines.

"So your segment will be the hot-or-not category," the producer informed Farih. "We will let you lead that, considering you are a specialist in fashion."

"Great. I can do that." Farih flashed her amazing smile.

"Good, good," the producer responded without looking up from his iPad. "Now, besides that, just jump into the conversations, give your thoughts, keep it real, and everything should be great."

The assistant attached the mic and pack to her back.

"I am really excited," Farih said.

The producer finally took a break from his iPad to look at Farih, who was all smiles. The producer smiled back. He turned to walk away but stopped. "Hey, um, Farih, how comfortable are you talking about you and Denise?"

Farih wanted to roll her eyes. "What do you mean?"

The producer walked closer to her. He leaned in. "Well, one thing people love is that our hosts do talk about everyday life, which includes their relationships. We would like, if it comes up, for you to throw something in there about you and Denise. You know just everyday things. Show why they call you two the Ellen and Portia of the black community."

Farih's smile faded. "Well, I mean, Denise is a very private person." Farih didn't know what to think.

"Oh, we totally understand. We aren't expecting major details of your relationship, just mention here every now and then."

Farih nodded as the producer gave her a quick handshake before he was rushed off, with three assistants following him. Farih quickly grabbed her phone and called her agent.

"I don't see the problem. Ellen brings Portia up all the time on her show," her agent said after listening to Farih's complaint.

Farih stood in the corner as she heard the audience warm-up happening. "But you know Denise. She will be furious."

Farih's agent, Janet, turned around in her chair. "Look, Farih, this is go time. Do you think they want you just because you are a model? Do you know how many other people were up for this job? You had that something extra. Use the gay thing to your advantage."

"So I'm just supposed to put our business out there?" Farih frowned. Not only did she not want to bring Denise up, but she also didn't know how long there would be a Denise and Farih.

"You are supposed to do what you have to do to get the job. Being gay is the way nowadays, and not only that you are showing it in a positive light."

"Farih, we're ready for you," one of the production assistants called.

Farih was stuck. "I have to go. Wish me luck."

"Knock 'em dead."

Farih closed the phone and walked out of the room.

Farih saw the other three hosts getting their final primping before walking out onstage.

Cassi smiled. "Hey, girl. You ready for this?"

"I hope so." Farih was nervous.

Cassi held her hand. "Don't worry. You will be great. I saw your girl out there. So cute."

The music began to play.

"My girl?"

"Yeah." Cassi looked confused. "Denise, sitting in the audience." Cassi pointed at Denise, who was sitting on the second row, clapping with the audience.

Suddenly Farih felt like a weight had been lifted off of her. Even after another one of her blowups, Denise was still there for her.

"Yeah, she wouldn't have missed it."

Adrianne made the announcement. Farih took a deep breath and walked out onstage with a big smile, ready to take the job at any cost.

"And today we have a special guest host. You've seen her as the face of Victoria's Secret, in *Sports Illustrated,* and on the covers of such major magazines as *Vogue* and *Elle*. Please give a warm welcome to Farih Okoro."

Farih smiled as Adrianne introduced her. The crowd clapped on cue. Farih knew she looked amazing. She flashed her smile and nodded.

"Thank you so much. I'm so excited to be here."

"So you watch the show?" Adrianne smiled.

Farih smiled. "Do *I* watch the show?" Farih looked at the producer. "*We* watch all the time."

Cassi smiled. "And when you say *we,* I'm guessing you're talking about your longtime girlfriend, Denise Chambers?"

"Who is also in the audience," Relonda added.

Denise forced a smile as a camera was immediately pushed into her face. She blushed, embarrassed by the scene. The three hosts and the audience aahed and clapped. Farih smiled with her eyes, hoping they gave off love and not the anger that she had toward Denise.

"You guys are embarrassing her. She's real shy," Farih gushed.

"Aw, are we embarrassing you, Denise?" Cassi said.

A production assistant handed Denise a microphone. "Um, just a little," Denise admitted.

Farih smiled. She knew Denise had no idea what to think in that moment, but she played it off. They might have been having problems, but to the world they were madly in love.

The rest of the show was amazing. Farih was brutal but honest during her hot-or-not segment. The audience agreed with her and the other hosts about various outfits a few stars had been seen in recently. The crowd got a kick out of her judging an outfit Denise wore to a movie premiere. Farih boasted that Denise looked amazing because she hadn't picked the outfit out. Farih had. Denise even laughed when the camera showed her agreeing with Farih's statement.

Afterward, Farih sat in her dressing room while various people came in and out, congratulating her on a great show. She simply smiled, hugged them, and thanked everyone, making sure every person knew she really loved the show and the other hosts. When the room cleared out, she took a moment to jump for joy, doing a silly dance.

"I know that dance." Farih jumped when she heard the familiar voice behind her. Denise stood in the doorway with a smile on her face. Then she walked in and closed the door behind her.

Farih wrapped her arms around Denise. The anger she'd felt earlier was gone. Denise had played her part perfectly, and she didn't even know it.

"Oh, baby, I just feel so good. What did you think of the show?"

"You did a great job." Denise pulled away from Farih's embrace. The smile had faded. "But you pick my clothes out for me?" Denise sat on one side of the small couch in the room.

Farih shrugged it off. "Oh, honey, it was just for TV."

"Yeah, I figured as much." Denise knew her irritation wouldn't help the situation. She chose to suck it up. "But, really, you were amazing. I bet the job is yours."

Farih could feel the shift in the energy. Their relationship was far from the perfect image she had cast on the show. They were treading on really thin ice, and she had to do something to fix it before she lost not only her girl but also the only job prospect she had.

Farih walked up to Denise. She got down on her knees in front of Denise. Denise looked down at Farih's eyes, which were glistening with tears.

"Denise, I know these past few months have been difficult. I know I've been hard to deal with, and, well, baby, I just really want to thank you for sticking by me." Farih held Denise's hand.

"Farih, we don't need to talk about this right now." Denise knew it wasn't the time or the place. She didn't know who might be listening on the other side of the door.

"I just want you to know that the darkness that was growing in me, it's gone. I promise I will never take my frustrations out on you again." Farih poured it on thick. "Do you forgive me?" Farih could see Denise's hard exterior softening from her words. She stared into Denise's eyes.

Denise looked away. "We can talk about this later. Get dressed. I'll be waiting outside." Denise stood up.

Farih was stunned.

Denise walked past her, not looking back, then closed the door behind her. She didn't know what to think. She was tired of the mood swings and the attitude. She wondered how long the nice Farih would last before something caused her to lash out again. She had grown tired and didn't know if she wanted to continue. Denise thought about Lena. She knew she couldn't let her feelings for Lena alter her judgment. Denise thought about it. Was she really tired of Farih, or was the reappearance of Lena causing her to have second thoughts about her relationship?

Farih paced the floor. She didn't know what to do. Denise's response had her nervous. Denise not forgiving her was something she wasn't used to. She wondered if she had finally ruined her relationship completely.

Farih heard a faint ringing coming from the couch. She noticed Denise's phone between a pillow and the couch's arm. She picked it up. Farih's whole body froze when she saw Lena's name appear on the screen. Her blood began to boil. Things were making sense. She didn't know Denise was even in touch with Lena. Now Lena was calling, and all of a sudden Denise didn't know if she could forgive Farih or not. Farih wanted to throw the phone.

Denise knocked on the door.

"Hold on one moment." Farih quickly put the phone deep between the couch cushions. She sat down in the chair in front of the large vanity mirror. "Come in."

"Hey, are you almost ready?" Denise asked. She noticed the hurt expression on Farih's face. Denise suddenly felt horrible. "Farih . . ."

"No, there's no need to say anything. I'm ready. Let me grab my bag." Farih stood up. She made her lip quiver. She could see Denise was concerned.

Denise quickly grabbed the bag before Farih could pick it up. Farih paused. She put her large croc purse on the table and began searching through it.

"Where in the heck is my phone? Can you call it?"

Denise patted her jeans pocket. "Whoa. Where is my phone?" She looked around on the floor.

"Oh, wait, here it is." Farih held her phone up. "You need me to call yours?"

Denise nodded. Farih quickly dialed Denise's number. The ringtone was just loud enough to lead Denise directly to her lost phone. Farih watched as she looked at the screen. She could tell by the shift in Denise's facial expression that she saw the missed call from Lena. She tried to play it off, putting the phone back in her pocket.

They walked out of the building. Lena was now at the top of Farih's hit list. Farih knew this bitch was not only messing with her girl but, more importantly, jeopardizing her career, and no jump-off was going to ruin all she had worked hard for.

Chapter 11

Carmen walked into her apartment, exhausted from her trip. What should have been a forty-five-minute flight had turned into a three-hour wait due to bad weather. She knew Nic would be home from work soon. She threw her clothes into the washer and started dinner.

Carmen had gone over the scenarios in her head a million times. She would tell Nic the truth, that her friends had bought her a dress as a wedding present. If Nic got angry, there would be nothing she could do about it. Carmen figured the best way was to start with an amazing meal.

The smell hit Nic as soon as she walked in the door. She smiled when she saw Carmen's fried chicken sitting on the table. Nic loved Carmen's fried chicken more than anything. It was only reason she didn't go vegetarian.

Carmen walked out of the bedroom, wearing a form-fitting pink and white pencil dress.

"All right, what did you do?" Nic asked as she sat down at the table.

Carmen's jaw dropped. "Seriously? I slave in the kitchen to make you a good meal, and that's the way you greet me?" Carmen dramatically threw her hand on her forehead.

Nic ignored her as she picked up a wing. "So what did you do?" Nic asked with a mouth full of chicken.

Carmen sat down in the chair next to Nic. "You have to promise not to get mad at me." Nic looked at her. Carmen knew Nic would never agree to that.

"I found my wedding dress."

"How much?"

"Ugh."

"How much?"

"More than two thousand." Carmen folded her hands.

"No, we can't afford it," Nic said as she continued to eat.

"That's the other thing. Actually, we can afford more than you think, because we have two thousand left in our budget."

Nic looked up at Carmen. Her expression said it all.

"It wasn't my fault. I put the dress back, and then I got back to Cooley's place, and it was there. They bought it for me without telling me. As a wedding present."

"Carmen."

"Nic, please, before you go off, understand that I *love* this dress. There is *no* other dress for me. It is the *one!*"

"Well, let me see it."

"No!" Carmen stood up. "It's bad luck, which is why it's safely hanging up at Cooley's place."

Nic swallowed the last piece of the wing. She put her hand on top of Carmen's. "Babe, look. I don't want you thinking that I don't want you to have whatever you want. But we have to live within *our* means, not your friends'."

"They're your friends too." Carmen hated when Nic referred to them that way.

"If we broke up today, do you really think I would hear from Denise or Cool?"

Carmen knew Nic was right. "Nic, you do realize that we could have more means if you took Carla up on her job offer."

"Not interested." Nic immediately lost her appetite. She got up from the table and headed to their bedroom.

Ever since Cooley left Jam Zone to manage Denise and Sahara, she had asked Nic to come work for her as an accountant. Carmen wanted it more than anything. They would be making amazing money as they worked to build an empire. Nic was completely against the idea. She didn't want to give up a job where she was financially stable for a start-up, even if the clients brought in millions. Carmen believed in taking chances; Nic believed in being secure.

"Nic, listen, things have changed since then," Carmen said as she followed Nic into their bedroom. "They are bringing in so much money between them that Cooley would prefer having someone she completely trusts, and not some money-hungry company taking them for more than they deserved."

Nic unbuttoned her button-down shirt. "Carmen, this isn't up for discussion." She slid out of her loafers. She wiggled her aching feet.

"Nic, you come home every day feeling like crap. You're wearing these semi-feminine clothes that you hate just to work at a corporate job that isn't paying you what you are truly worth." Carmen took the shirt from Nic's hands. "Don't you want to just work somewhere where you can be you and make the amount of money that you truly deserve?"

"And when you or I get sick, that's gonna pay the doctor bills, Cooley's nonexistent insurance plan?"

"Baby, with the money we will be making, we can afford to pay our own damn doctor bills." Carmen wanted to pull her hair out. Nic was so stuck on being secure that she didn't see the amazing opportunity in front of her.

Nic sat on the side of the bed. She loved Carmen, but at times like these she wanted to throw the towel in. Carmen was draining her, and even Carmen knew it.

"Carmen, drop it. I'm tired, and I want to go to sleep. You've already ruined my meal. Can you not fuck up my nap too?"

The words stung Carmen. She could tell Nic meant every word. She wanted to go off but knew it wasn't the time. She had learned when to push Nic, and when she was sleepy and cranky wasn't the time. Carmen threw her hands up in defeat and stomped out of the room.

A while later Carmen felt a warm sensation come over her body. She opened her eyes to see Nic covering her up with her favorite fleece blanket. Carmen yawned.

"What time is it?" She yawned again. It was dark outside.

Nic picked Carmen's feet up and sat down. She placed her feet in her lap. "Eleven." Carmen didn't realize she had fallen asleep on the couch while watching a *Harry Potter* marathon on ABC Family.

Nic stared at the television screen. "What is this? *The Deathly Hallows?*"

Carmen chuckled. She knew Nic knew nothing about her love of the wizard movies and books. "No, it's *The Order of the Phoenix*."

Nic cracked a smile that quickly faded. She stared at the screen. "Carmen, are you happy here with me?"

Carmen sat up. "Yes, Nic. Why would you ask me that?"

Nic turned to Carmen. "You hate your job, you hate this city, and every other weekend you are flying to Atlanta."

"Nic . . ." Carmen felt terrible.

"If that's what you really want, then I'm not going to stop you. I want you to be happy, and if being with your friends is what's going to make you the happiest, then I'm cool with it."

Nic couldn't look at Carmen. She continued to stare straight ahead. Carmen knew it was killing Nic. Carmen wanted to cry, but she held it together. Carmen moved in close to Nic. She put her hands on Nic's face. She could feel the tears on Nic's cheeks.

"Nicole Marie Santiago, you listen to me. I love you more than anything. The only reason I even enjoy going to visit my friends is that I know I am coming home to you."

Suddenly the beautiful dress, the fairy-tale wedding, and the lavish decor didn't matter anymore. Carmen knew she had her priorities mixed up. Seeing Nic that way put everything into perspective.

"I can't work for Cooley, babe," Nic stated. "I am a firm believer that you don't mix business and pleasure. That would be too close for comfort."

Carmen nodded. She knew Nic was right. Everything made sense. If she and Nic ever broke up, it would be a major conflict of interest. Nic put her arm around Carmen.

Carmen rested her head on Nic's chest. She looked out the window. They could see the lights on the Memphis-Arkansas Memorial Bridge from their window. She might not have the money that her friends had, but she had something better. She had found her soul mate. She didn't need the royal wedding anymore. She just needed Nic.

***

Farih was confused. Denise acted like everything was fine in the car. She didn't bring up their fights or the plea Farih had issued at the studio. They listened to music and discussed Farih's new job opportunity and the opportunities Denise had. Farih kept it quiet about Lena. She didn't know how she wanted to move with that yet. She figured she would enjoy the moment and hold that information in her back pocket for now.

Denise and Farih heard the loud music coming from Cooley's house. They opened the front door to discover that Sahara's assistants, Cooley's assistant, and some of Sahara's dancers and musicians were having a get-together. Denise noticed a tattoo artist setting up a station on the kitchen table.

Sahara noticed Farih. She jumped up and ran over to hug her friend. They had become good friends over the years due to the closeness of Cooley and Denise. Cooley walked out from her office, wearing a pair of jeans and a tank top.

"What's up, y'all?" Cooley said as she took a seat next to the dining room table.

"What's going on here?" Farih said as Sahara poured her a glass of wine.

"Tattoo party!" Sahara held her glass up. All the others followed suit, holding their glasses up, as if they were toasting.

Denise made her way through the sea of people. "Seriously?" She picked up one of the tattoo books on the table. "What's the occasion?"

"Well . . ." Sahara walked over to the table and sat in Cooley's lap. "Baby, you wanna tell them?"

The expression on Cooley's face indicated that she wasn't as enthusiastic. "I told Sahara that if her new album went platinum, I would get a tattoo."

"So?" Farih's face lit up.

"Tee!" Cooley yelled.

Denise and Farih turned around. Cooley's longtime assistant, Tee, picked up a large picture frame. She turned it around to show a platinum album and a copy of Sahara's album cover. The room erupted in cheers.

"Oh my God, that's so awesome!" Farih said and hugged Sahara.

Denise gave Cooley daps. "So what are you getting?" she asked Cooley, who still looked apprehensive.

Cooley looked at Denise with a defeated expression.

Denise's jaw dropped. "Ah, hell naw!" Denise erupted in laughter.

"What?" Farih asked, completely oblivious.

"You have got to be kidding me!" Denise couldn't stop laughing. Cooley punched her hard on her arm, which just made Denise laugh more.

Sahara playfully hit Denise. "Stop laughing at my baby. I don't see the big deal."

"This is so messed up." Cooley pouted.

Sahara kissed her on her forehead. "It's nothing I wouldn't do for you."

"I don't see you doing it," Cooley retorted.

"Oh, really?" Sahara stood up. "Where do you want it?" Sahara pulled her shirt over her head. The gang made goo-goo noises at the sight of her sexy red and black bra.

Farih walked over to Denise. "Can someone let me in on the joke?"

Denise put her arm around Farih's back. "There is only one thing we always said we would never do. And Cooley is about to break the rule."

"Not by choice," Cooley grumbled. Farih was still confused.

"Cooley is going to get branded." Denise laughed.

"Branded?" Farih questioned.

"She's going to get Sahara's name tatted on her," Denise explained.

Even Farih's mouth dropped when she realized what was happening. Sahara sat down in the chair next to Cooley. Cooley was not happy, she could tell.

"You don't have to do it if you don't want to, babe. I didn't expect you to go this far," Sahara told her.

Cooley looked at Sahara. She could tell Sahara was disappointed but wouldn't show it. Cooley couldn't take her eyes off of Sahara. She wasn't made up like she usually was. Cooley loved her even more without the makeup and extensions. Sahara had stuck by her even when she didn't deserve it. She had changed all her ways for Misha, but Sahara was the one who had deserved it from day one.

Cooley stood up in the chair. "Hey, yo, turn the music down. I have something to say." One of the dancers hit the music. The room was instantly quiet. "Dee, you know me better than anyone. You know I'm a muthafucka with myself."

"Who you tellin'?" Denise remarked, and the crowd laughed.

"But . . ." Cooley got off the chair. "There is one person who has been able to deal with me and my crazy ass for all these years." Cooley stood in front of Sahara. "And that is my sexy, talented, amazing . . ." Cooley took Sahara by her hand. Sahara's eyes were filled with tears. "Baby girl, Faith Sahara Stanton."

Farih held tight to Denise's hand. Sahara jumped up and embraced Cooley. Cooley joked that gay marriage was illegal but that she did not need a certificate to show how she felt. They had matching tribal bands with a heart in the middle around their ring fingers.

"You know I would do it." Farih handed Denise a bottle of water.

"Do what?" Denise asked.

"Get your name tattooed on me." Farih smiled. Denise's expression was stern.

"Don't." Denise gave Farih a serious look. She walked off to join a spades game in progress. Farih kept her composure but wanted to die on the inside.

To try to calm down, Farih poured herself a concoction of various liquors and sat down next to Sahara and some of her dancers. They were laughing about various bloopers during practice. Sahara noticed that Farih was staring into space. She nudged her. Farih smiled.

"So how did you react to finding out about the little reunion last week?" Sahara asked.

"What?" Farih took a sip of her drink, hoping to numb her emotions.

Sahara looked at Farih. "You know. The exes showing up." As soon as Sahara saw Farih's face, she knew she had let the cat out of the bag. "You didn't know?"

"No, I didn't." Farih knew that was the perfect moment to bust Denise on her deceit. She stood up and walked calmly behind Denise's chair and placed her hands on each of Denise's shoulders. Sahara knew Cooley was going to kill her. She quickly followed Farih.

"So, you saw Lena?" Farih said as she stood behind Denise's chair. She was completely calm.

Denise looked at Cooley, who instantly looked at Sahara, knowing she was the culprit. Denise didn't turn around; she played her next card.

"Yeah. She was at the club." Denise tried to keep her cool.

"When were you going to tell me, babe?" Farih smiled.

"I forgot about it, actually." Denise stared at her cards.

Cooley lowered her head into her cards. She knew Farih would never believe that line.

"It wasn't anything. They weren't there but a quick minute. I didn't even get to actually meet the infamous Misha," Sahara said, hoping to diffuse the situation, which she had mistakenly started.

Farih leaned down to Denise's level. "So you forgot that you saw Lena after almost three years?"

Denise turned her head to face Farih. "Yeah, it wasn't that big of a deal. She was there to kick it with Carmen. We said hey, caught up a bit, and then they rolled out."

"So she's in Atlanta now. Damn, is this the spot. Maybe we do need to leave New York." Farih laughed. Sahara laughed along with her. Farih stood back up. "I think it's cool she came out to see you."

"She didn't come to see me. She came to see Carmen." Denise felt herself getting defensive.

"Can we talk about something else please?" Cooley asked, breaking in, also in hopes of diffusing the situation before her name came up.

"Why is everyone so tense?" Farih took another gulp of her drink. "I couldn't care less that you saw her. Actually, I think it's good. You guys were really close at one time. You should be in contact. I mean, she was your roommate."

Denise's head jerked toward Farih. She couldn't tell if Farih meant her words or if she was just being sarcastic. She decided to play along.

"I agree. She is a friend. I should have remembered to tell you. I honestly felt bad knowing it's been so long since we've communicated. Cool. Did I tell you she had a little girl?"

"Damn, I bet that child is spoiled as shit." Cooley recognized the game Denise was playing. She played along.

Sahara stood there with her arms folded, shaking her head.

"She has a little girl. I bet she is just too precious. You should give her a call. Let's set up a lunch or something, catch up." Farih smiled.

Cooley and Denise looked at each other, communicating nonverbally. Denise wasn't sure what to do next. She eyed Cooley so she would take over.

"Yo, that's a good idea. We should all do it. You know, have a good ole sit-down," Cooley said. "Babe, you can finally meet Misha."

"Oh, hell to the naw. I'm good." Sahara was done. She couldn't believe Farih wanted to sit down with Lena. Cooley couldn't help but laugh. "I mean, what the fuck? Want me to call up my ex too?"

"Gotta love my girl. Hell naw. If I ever see that bitch, it's gonna be a new world war." Cooley winked. She couldn't help but remember Sahara's abusive ex, with whom they had had a threesome when they first met.

"Well, I guess it is a bit different for you two, being that Misha and Cool were actually in a relationship. But, Dee, you and Lena never actually dated," Farih noted.

"Yeah, but they messed around," Sahara said.

Cooley shot Sahara an evil glance for butting in again.

"So what? Who didn't mess around with their roommate in college?" Farih said casually. "I say, set it up." Farih glanced at the clock. "Man, it's getting late. I have to get up at six. I need to get to the room."

Denise got ready to stand up, but Farih stopped her.

"No, babe, you can stay. I have to get up early, not you. I'll catch a cab."

Tee spoke up. "I can drop you off if you like. I'm about to head out, anyway."

"Great." Farih kissed Denise on her lips. "I'll see you guys later. Sahara, have a great tour, honey, and call me." Farih picked up her bag and headed to the door, saying her good-byes.

Denise was speechless. Other people took Farih's departure as a cue and started to disperse. As soon as everyone had left, Denise and Cooley looked at each other and started laughing.

"Oh, hell no, nigga. What were you thinking?" Cooley giggled.

"I don't know what just happened." Denise snickered.

"I know what happened. You just got caught the fuck up." Cooley stood up and picked up a few cups on the table.

Denise leaned back in her chair. "I didn't expect her to go there." She smirked. "Oh, I got caught up. Nigga, you beyond caught up. You like *Deadliest Catch* caught up."

Cooley threw her middle finger up. "Whatever. This isn't about me. It's about you and this upcoming dinner you got with your girl and . . ." Cooley leaned in to Denise's ear. "The girl you want."

"Shut the fuck up." Denise started helping Cooley clean up. "I am surprised that she was so calm. The girl has been a ticking time bomb lately. I never know what I'm going to get."

"Well, you know what she's been going through."

Sahara emerged from the back room. Denise and Cooley both looked at each other, wondering how much she had heard.

"Denise, I talk to Farih all the time, and she has been hella stressed lately," Sahara said.

"I know, but am I supposed to let her just talk crazy to me? Like today, yeah, I overslept and didn't pick her up. But she tore my damn head off. But when I got to the studio, she's all sweet and loving. I can't take this shit."

"Denise, come on. She was jealous. She didn't mean it. And all day long you've been being pretty asshole-ish to her." Sahara popped Denise on the top of her head.

"I have not."

"Yes, you have. That poor girl looked like she was about to cry." Sahara shook her finger like a school-teacher.

"Yeah, but damn, is it my fault her career had some bumps? As my girl, she is supposed to support me, not treat me like shit 'cause I have a job and she doesn't." Denise sat down on the couch.

Cooley sat down in her oversized chair. Sahara joined her, sitting in her lap.

"All right, well, the career thing seems to be okay now," Cooley observed. "Word on the streets is she killed it on the show today. She's going back to host again tomorrow, right?"

Denise nodded her head.

"So now what?" Cooley asked. "You gon' let a few bad months fuck up all y'all have, or are you gonna be the Denise I know you to be and forgive her and move on?"

Denise thought about Cooley's statements. She knew Cooley and Sahara were right. She and Farih had four years invested, and to give it all up over a few bad months wouldn't make sense. Lena's face entered her mind.

"It's not that simple." Denise fidgeted with her fin-gers.

Cooley's eyes widened. "Oh, I get it."

"Get what?" Sahara was confused.

"It's not worth it, man." Cooley knew the look. Denise was thinking about Lena. "Not worth it."

Sahara looked at Denise. "What the hell did you do?"

"Nothing," Denise said quickly. The last thing she needed was Sahara thinking she was cheating on Farih.

"Keep it that way," Cooley added. "Well, Big Ron wants me to check this new group out he wants me to manage that is new to Jam Zone. I need to get ready. You wanna come?" Cooley asked Denise.

Denise thought about Farih. She had a beautiful, intelligent woman who loved her waiting in a hotel room, and she couldn't get the one who got away off of her mind. She thought about Lena and her daughter. Pandora's box was open, and she wanted to close it and fast.

"Nah, I'm gonna go be with Farih." Denise stood up. She gave Cooley daps. "We need to fix this."

Cooley nodded. "Yeah, go home to your *woman*." They did a bro hug.

"Oh, by the way, congratulations," Denise said to Sahara. "I never in a million years would have thought I'd see the day come when Carla Wade branded herself in any form." Denise hugged Sahara.

"Hey, when you find the right one, why not? Maybe you should think about it." Cooley kissed Sahara.

Denise didn't know when she and Cooley had switched bodies, but she knew she had to get back to the old Denise before she messed up something special.

Farih heard the door open. She sat up in the bed as Denise walked in. Denise looked at Farih. She looked so beautiful. Denise knew there was only one thing to do. She dropped her jacket on the floor, rushed up to the bed, pulled Farih close, and planted a sensual kiss on her.

It took only a minute to get Farih's T-shirt off. Her chocolate skin was calling Denise's name. It wasn't like the last time. Denise was ready, and the only person she wanted was Farih. They kissed passionately as Denise ran her fingers down the nape of Farih's neck, sending chills through her body and causing her brown nipples to instantly become erect.

"I don't want us to ever again be like we were these last few months." Denise looked into Farih's big brown eyes.

Farih nodded in agreement. "Never again. Never, baby." Farih's lips met Denise's again.

Farih didn't know what had come over Denise, but she was ecstatic. She quickly remembered why she fell in love with Denise. She was back in love, and she didn't want to lose her.

Tears rolled down Farih's face as Denise sexed her like it was the first time all over again. She had her Denise back. They fell asleep in each other's arms.

Chapter 12

Carmen normally couldn't wait for the day to end, but today she could hardly contain her excitement. She watched as her unsuspecting students conversed with their peers. It was the last day of school, and doing schoolwork was completely out of the question.

"Ms. Carmen." Julia, the epitome of a teacher's pet, waved her hand in the air. Carmen acknowledged her swinging hand. "Well, it's the last day of school, and you said if we all passed, you would give us a surprise." Julia smiled. Suddenly the whole room was focused on Carmen.

"Okay, fine." Carmen looked at the clock. She smiled. She knew it was almost time. "So as you guys know, I am very good friends with Denise Chambers from the movie *Ball,* and I am also friends with the singer Sahara."

"Man, she is so fine. That's gon' be my wifey, watch." The class clown, Jason, walked to the front of the room to get a better view of a photo of Carmen with Denise, Cooley, Sahara, and Farih that Carmen had pulled out.

"That's Cool Wade. She dates Sahara, right? They are always on the blogs, along with Denise and Farih," said Toni, one of the popular cheerleaders. Her followers all nodded their heads. Carmen wanted to laugh. The first time Nic saw Toni, she was shocked that she was in high school.

"We are all friends." Carmen knew she couldn't answer Toni's question. If it was one thing she hated about teaching, it was the censorship placed on her. She knew she couldn't teach any grade below eighth due to a bill passed in Tennessee making it illegal to discuss homosexuality in school with students who have not yet reached eighth grade. Even though she taught tenth, she knew she had to watch everything.

"Well, so here is my surprise." Carmen walked to the closet and pulled out a big brown box. Jason and two of the other students rushed to help her. She pulled out copies of Sahara's CD and Denise's movie from the box. "Now, you have to get permission from your parents to watch the movie, as it has an R rating, but Sahara and Denise wanted me to give these out to you guys."

The class cheered as Jason and the other two guys passed out the gifts.

"Wait a minute. I wanted to give those out." The door opened, and the kids went wild as Sahara walked in with her arms folded. Denise and Cooley walked into the classroom next, with the principal and the vice principal behind them.

"All right, students, settle down, or we will have to ask them to leave." Principal Mitchell's baritone voice rumbled. The kids eagerly walked back to their desks.

It had taken a lot of convincing, but Carmen was allowed to let Sahara and Denise visit the school on the last day as long as sexuality was not discussed. The smiles on her students' faces made Carmen almost not hate teaching for the moment.

"All right, students, so I made a promise that if you all passed the English board test, I would bring a surprise, so here is that surprise. Meet Sahara and Denise."

"Hey, everyone." Sahara was in her character. Her pink wig had blue tips, and her dress had vibrant colors. She looked more like a cartoon character than a real person. Carmen noticed the cheerleaders all crying from joy.

"So they are here to answer any questions you might have," Carmen announced. "Any questions?" Hands shot in the air. She knew Jason would have something funny to say. "Jason."

Jason stood up. "Sahara, would you please marry me?"

The class laughed. Denise looked at Cooley, who was also amused by the statement.

"Aww, come see me in seven years," Sahara told him.

"I will! I will!" Jason sat back down, instantly getting daps from the other guys in his crew.

"Ursula." Carmen almost didn't call on the tall girl. She already knew that Ursula was gay and so were her friends. They all walked around like mini Cooleys, rocking the hottest male fashions, braids, Locs, and short haircuts.

"Yeah, I have a question for Denise. I play ball too, and I was wondering if you ever miss basketball since you are making movies now."

Carmen let out a sigh of relief that nothing gay had been brought up. She could tell the principal felt the same way. He nodded his head and walked out of the classroom, feeling comfortable that Carmen had everything under control. The vice principal followed him.

Denise swallowed the knot forming in her throat. It had been years, but it still stung whenever her failed basketball career came up.

"I do miss playing for the crowds and fans, but I love what I am doing now. It's just a different type of excitement now. I still play ball to stay in shape."

"I think I could take you," Ursula boasted.

"Oh, really? We might have to see." Denise smiled. She glanced at Carmen, who already knew what she was thinking. It was funny to see how out kids were now in comparison to when they were in high school.

"Where is Farih?" one of Ursula's friends blurted out. Carmen's body tensed. She was glad no administrators where in the room.

"She's working right now but sends her love to everyone," Denise answered quickly and professionally. "Carmen." She threw it back to Carmen before any other relationship-type questions came up.

"Kelly." Carmen called on one of the loners in the room. Out of all the students, she truly cared about Kelly. Kelly was an attractive plus-sized girl who struggled to find friends due to her weight and her inability to afford the expensive clothes at Lane Bryant and other stores for larger sizes. She was stuck wearing Wal-Mart's best, which had at least improved from when Carmen was a young overweight girl.

The young girl struggled to get out from behind the small desk. Carmen cringed. She remembered those days and still hated desks like that.

"My question is for Cooley, actually. I was wondering what you look for when you are looking for an artist to represent."

A few snickers came from various students, but most waited in silence to hear the answer.

Cooley put her phone in her pocket and stood up. She hadn't expected any questions for herself. "Well, I look for the whole package, but talent is the most important thing. Why? Do you do something?"

"I sing." More snickers came from the room. Carmen shot the class a stern glare. She looked at Kelly.

"Really? Let me hear something." Cooley leaned back on Carmen's desk.

Kelly looked at Carmen, who reluctantly gave the okay. Carmen knew this could end in disaster. Kelly closed her eyes and began to belt out the chorus of Christina Aguilera's "Reflection" from *Mulan*.

The class was in awe, as Kelly owned the song. Carmen's mouth dropped open. She was completely in shock. Kelly's voice didn't tremble or falter. Everyone could feel her emotions pouring through the song. As soon as she finished, the classroom erupted in applause.

"Goodness, girl, that was amazing." Cooley felt her arm. "You definitely have talent, sweetie."

"So you think I could make it?" Kelly's eyes were brighter than Carmen had ever seen.

"Tell you what. Stay in school, graduate with honors, and when you get out, come and see me."

Everyone in the room listened as the principal made the announcement for all classes to come to the auditorium. It was a part of the deal that if celebrities visited, something would have to be done for the whole school. Sahara had agreed to perform a song and answer a few questions. Carmen's students headed to the auditorium as Sahara's security prepared to usher Sahara, Denise, and Cooley out of the room.

Carmen hugged Sahara. "Thank you so much."

"Girl, anytime. This is actually fun. I need to do more of this."

"Yes, this is a PR gold mine. We have interviews set up afterward. This is going to be great for the image of our little engine that could." Cooley tapped away on her iPhone.

"And some of us care because it's actually a good thing to give back to the community," Denise remarked and shook her head. She loved her friend but hated how money hungry she had become.

Carmen knew she would be voted teacher of the year for her gift to the school. Sahara's performance was amazing. For once, the students didn't want to leave the school. Carmen walked back to her empty classroom after the majority of the students had left for the summer.

"Feels different, doesn't it?"

Carmen turned around to see the French teacher, Michael, standing in the doorway. His bright white smile lit up the room. Michael was from the Ivory Coast, and French was his native language.

"What feels different?" Carmen put her last items in her bag.

"Come on, Carmen. You are a first-year teacher. You know you feel it. We always do. We hate the school year, but then, in the end, we miss the little monsters."

Carmen laughed. "I guess you are a little right. But I don't get to miss them for too long. I'm teaching summer school."

"Really?" Michael sat on the edge of her desk. "Why?"

"Only the first term. I wanted to earn a little more money for my wedding this summer."

"Oh, that's right. You are committing to a woman."

"Nicole." Carmen turned her head.

"So do I get an invitation to this wedding of yours?" Michael resembled Blair Underwood to Carmen. She had to admit for a man, he was very attractive, which was why so many of the teachers—single and married—threw their pussy at him. It made Carmen laugh knowing he took pleasure in flirting with the one adult lesbian in the school.

"It's a destination wedding, but you will be invited to the reception when we get back."

"Nice. Well, I'll see you in two weeks. I'm teaching the full summer." Michael stood up. He walked closer to Carmen. *"Adieu, très belle fleur. Si seulement j'ai eu une chance avec vous, je ne serai jamais vous laisser aller."* He smiled and walked to the door.

"Okay, what did you just say?" Carmen smirked.

"Nothing much. See you later, Carmen." Michael winked and walked out of the classroom.

"Well, my Bobby is lactose intolerant, so we have to have something other than milk."

Misha rolled her eyes. She hated the sound of the cackling housewives she was forced to socialize with every week at Jaylin's day care. Patrick had to put him in a fancy day care that required mothers to actually participate in fund-raisers and activities for the children on what seemed to be a weekly basis.

"We could do punch," one of the mother's interjected.

Vivian, the leader of the pack, frowned. "So we can take home sugar-crazed children afterward that won't be able to sleep?"

"Ugh." Misha sighed before realizing she was loud.

"Misha, have something to add?" Vivian asked. She hated Misha, and the feeling was definitely mutual.

"Oh no. I'm good."

"No." Vivian held her hand out. "Tell us what's on your mind." She smiled the fakest smile in history.

"I just think that we are putting too much thought into beverages," Misha said. "Seriously, we go through this for every event, and in the end we always end up bringing both juice and milk. Why are we even discussing this?"

"Well, because maybe we want to change things up for a change." Vivian scowled.

Misha nodded. "Okay, well, do a sorbet punch and call it a day. I just know that my time and all our time could be better served discussing more important aspects of this event."

"I do love sorbet," another mother added. The others all nodded and made approving sounds, infuriating Vivian. She took a deep breath and flashed her wicked smile.

"Well, I guess it's sorbet, then. Seriously, Misha, you really should add your input more often, instead of just showing up and doing nothing."

Just as Misha was about to rip Vivian a new one, the children came running into the room. The two women exchanged evil glances, followed by their normal fake smiles, before grabbing their children.

Misha headed out the door. She wanted to grab all of Jaylin's things and un-enroll him immediately. They were headed to their car when she heard her name being called. Misha turned around to see Lisa Murell, one of her Chi Theta Sorority sisters, headed in her direction.

"Fuck me."

"Ohh, Mommy, you said a bad word," Jaylin said, shocked.

"Sorry, baby. Get in your seat." Misha sighed and turned back around. "Oh my God, Lisa, is that you?"

Lisa looked good in her black pin-striped suit. She had put on weight, but it was in the right places. The two hugged.

"Girl, I saw you walking out of the day care and couldn't believe it. I'm trying to get my little Tamar in here."

"It's a great school." Misha nodded.

"I know, right, and so close to my job." Lisa pointed at a large glass building. "I'm with Wheeler & Moss now."

Misha's eyes widened. "So you did go to law school?"

Lisa nodded. "Girl, yes, I'm just an associate, but you know I have my eyes on the prize. Give me a few years, and it will be Wheeler, Moss and Murell." Lisa and Misha gave each other a high five. "What firm are you with?"

Misha's heart skipped a beat. "Oh, actually, I changed my mind about law school."

"Oh, so what did you decide to do?"

"Actually, I'm raising this little one here. I didn't want to be a working mom, at least not in the first years."

Misha could see the disappointment on Lisa's face. Both of them had talked about going to law school more than anything in school. Misha had been accepted to a few prestigious law schools, but all her dreams of the courtroom faded when she chose marriage and children.

"Well . . ." Lisa forced a smile. "Good for you. If I had a good man, I would probably do the same thing. Are you considering going back?"

"Yes, I've even been looking into reapplying after he's four."

Lisa's smile reappeared. "Well, good for you. Look, we need to keep in touch. I heard about Carmen marrying that beautiful girl. I swear, if I was gay, that would be the way to go." Lisa and Misha laughed. Misha knew that was closer to reality than Lisa would ever let on.

The two exchanged numbers, and Misha got into her car. She couldn't shake the feeling she got when she was with Lisa. She hated how Lisa seemed to perk up only when Misha mentioned the possibility of going back to school. Misha felt like a complete failure.

Jaylin ran into the house as soon as Misha opened the front door. She could hear the video game coming from Patrick's study. Misha wanted to kill him. She stormed back to the room.

"Why are you here?" Misha snapped.

Patrick pulled off his headphones. "Had an early day. What's up, boo?"

Misha picked a Transformer action figure up off the floor and threw it at Patrick, hitting him in the back of his head. Patrick jumped.

"What the fuck, Misha?"

"This, all of this is what the fuck!" Misha paced in the room.

"Misha, I'm not in the mood for this shit right now. I had a long day."

"*You* had a long day? *You* had a long day? Did you wake up at five to get your son breakfast and get him ready for school? Did you spend the day in a room of screaming toddlers? Did you have to endure the most irritating woman on the planet and then come home and find me chilling, playing a stupid video game? You could have at least picked some of this shit up!"

"Misha."

"I'm tired of this, Patrick. I don't want to be a house-wife anymore."

Patrick turned his head. "What is that supposed to mean?"

"Just what I said." Misha sighed. "I am tired of this. This isn't me. I want to go back to school or get a job, just do something besides cook and clean every fucking day for the rest of my life."

"Misha . . ." Annoyed, Patrick sat down on his love seat. "We've gone through this. I am not making the money I was making when we got married. We can't afford for Jaylin to be in preschool full-time."

"Well, let's find a cheaper preschool."

"Out of the question." Patrick folded his arms.

"Patrick, neither one of us came from some fancy preschool. Why is—"

"I said no!" Patrick's voice echoed throughout the room, sending chills through Misha's body. "Look, I don't know what has gotten into you lately—maybe it's because you're spending more time with Lena and them—but this shit is getting out of hand."

Misha knew exactly where Patrick was going. No matter what he said, she knew the idea of her continuing her friendship with Carmen was a problem. Although he liked Carmen, the idea of Misha being so close to someone who was close to Cooley was always going to be a problem.

Misha knew she was talking to a brick wall. She walked out of the room without saying another word. She headed to their large master bathroom. Misha started the shower, pulled all her clothes off, and stepped into the steam. The hot water hit her face and her soul at the same time.

It was evident, she was unhappy.

Chapter 13

"So you got everything you need, right?"

Cooley was finding it difficult to focus with Sahara's half-naked body lying on top of her. The only time she found her new managing job hard was when she wanted to talk business and Sahara wanted only to talk sex. Sahara's soft lips kissed Cooley's abs slowly. Completely ignoring Cooley's question, Sahara used the tip of her tongue to lick around Cooley's navel and then down, until reaching her boxer briefs.

"Sa. Come on, girl." Cooley felt herself aflame. Her girlfriend still turned her on like it was the first time. Sahara knew what to do to get Cooley going. Within an instant, Cooley's professionalism was out the window. With a quick push, Sahara found herself back down on the bed, with Cooley on top. She bit her lip.

"Now . . ." Cooley held Sahara's arms down. Sahara's black lace bra was barely holding her breasts; her areolae were already showing. "Do you have everything for your trip?"

"Not everything." Sahara bent her knee so she could press it against Cooley's crotch. Sahara smiled.

Cooley shook her head. "You are a mess." With one hand Cooley moved the small piece of lace in front of Sahara's vagina. Cooley rammed two fingers into Sahara, causing her to gasp. "Wanna keep talking shit?"

Sahara nodded yes. Cooley finger fucked Sahara roughly. One of the things Cooley loved about her girlfriend was that she could take it and love it many different ways. Sometimes they made love, but right now they were fucking.

Sahara wasn't going to let Cooley stay in control. She pushed Cooley's head down. Cooley didn't need any coaching and buried her head between Sahara's thick thighs. Sahara didn't moan; she talked shit.

"Yeah, Daddy, eat this pussy. Shit, nigga, damn." Sahara's dirty comments only enticed Cooley more. "Nigga, fuck me, fuck me."

Cooley loved when they made love, but fucking was her specialty. She bit Sahara's clit with just enough force to make her scream. Sahara's sweetness shot into Cooley's mouth. She loved when she squirted.

Before Cooley could catch her breath, Sahara threw her man to her. Cooley quickly strapped up. Sahara turned over on all fours. Her round ass was calling Cooley's name. Cooley used some of Sahara's own sweetness to lubricate the tip as she entered Sahara from behind. Sahara's ass bounced as Cooley pumped, causing vibratory waves in her soft ass.

"Oh, shit, Daddy."

"Whose pussy is this?"

"Yours!" Sahara moaned.

"What was that?" Cooley slapped Sahara's ass.

"It's yours, baby." Suddenly the potty mouth was gone. "It's always yours."

Cooley stopped pounding and started stroking slow and long. She ran her fingers from the nape of Sahara's neck to her lower back, stopping only to kiss her on the Chinese symbol for love in the middle of her lower back. They came together.

Afterward, Sahara lay in Cooley's arms in the dark room. Their naked bodies were intertwined. Cooley gave Sahara a sensual forehead kiss. Sahara smiled.

"I do," Sahara whispered.

"What?" Cooley looked down. Sahara looked up, and their eyes met.

"I have everything for the tour. I just wish you were coming with me."

"I wish I could, but I gotta get stuff together here. It's only three weeks. We've done longer."

"But I don't want to do a day, let alone three weeks." Sahara poked out her bottom lip. Cooley touched it with her index finger.

"You will be good. I'll try to make it out to L.A. for the last show."

"Promise?"

"Of course."

They lay there in silence for a few moments. The only sound was their hearts beating. Sahara put her hand on Cooley's chest.

"Do you hear that?" She smiled.

Cooley looked at her beautiful girl.

"Our hearts are beating in perfect sync," Sahara said. She and Cooley both smiled.

They fell asleep in each other's arms.

Carmen poured a cup of coffee from the teacher's coffeemaker. She tasted it and immediately spat it out. She turned around when she heard a loud, deep laugh come from behind her.

"I know you didn't just try to drink that coffee." Michael grinned. He was holding a cup holder with three cups of Starbucks coffee. He held it out to Carmen, offering her a cup.

"Oh my God, you are a lifesaver." Carmen took one of the cups out of the holder. The overpriced coffee woke her senses, helping her to fully gain consciousness.

"Rule number one of summer school, never drink or touch that coffee. Mrs. Mildred makes it for herself, and she likes her coffee bitter and disgusting. Bring your own. Come."

Carmen followed Michael toward their classrooms.

"So is summer school as bad as everyone makes it out to be?"

"Nah, it's actually worse." Michael snickered. "Think about it like this. You have our school and the neighboring schools worst students here in an attempt to help these idiots pass to the next grade so they can get the hell up out of our classes. Most of them are the troublemakers, the ones that love to skip school or get suspended. You have a few who are honestly just dumb, and every now and then you get a smarty-pants who is using summer school to graduate early, but most of those somehow always end up in Mrs. Mildred's class."

Carmen frowned. "That doesn't seem very fair."

"She's two hundred years old, Carmen. These other kids would kill her in an instant." They both laughed.

The noise coming from Carmen's classroom hit them as soon as they reached their hall. Carmen rolled her eyes. Michael's smile faded. He opened her door to find the class in hysterics. The desks had been moved into clusters, and various groups of friends were loudly discussing their weekend and their plans for the rest of the day. One group of guys was watching an arm wrestling competition between two guys, all of them yelling for the one they wanted to win.

Carmen turned, determined to walk out of the school building, hoping never to return. Michael grabbed her arm. He put his finger up to his mouth. He walked in the room and slammed his briefcase on the desk.

"This will not be going on in this classroom." His baritone voice echoed throughout the room. The students instantly stopped everything. All eyes were on him. "Fix these desks the way they were, and settle down immediately." The students did exactly what he said. Carmen was impressed. She walked in and placed her bag on her desk.

"They're all yours." Michael winked as he walked out of the room.

Carmen silently thanked him as he closed the door. She made a mental note to buy him lunch. She turned around to find thirty pairs of eyes on her, all staring at her like she was the enemy.

"All right, so welcome to summer school. I am Ms.—"

"Um, you the one who know Sahara, ain't you?" A girl wearing the worst lace front Carmen had ever seen stood up.

"Um, I do. Now, like I was saying—"

"You gon' get ha' to come hur this summer too?" The girl smacked the gum in her mouth.

Carmen instantly wished she'd never opened that door. The kids stared at her, all wanting to meet a celebrity, like her students had during the year. The difference was she actually liked some of those students.

"Sorry, but that was a onetime thing."

"So we can't meet ha'?"

"Not by her coming to this school. Now, if you can take your seat, we can get started."

"This is some bullshit," the girl huffed as she sat down, while her friends nodded.

"Excuse me, but what did you just say?" Carmen rolled her neck.

"I said that's messed up. We wanted to meet ha' too."

"Maybe you should have done what you needed to do during the school year and you could have. This is summer school, and for most of you, it's your final chance to pass. This is not a gift. This is work. So if meeting celebrities is what you are here to do, there is the door. But if going to the next grade is what you are here to do, then I suggest you open up the book to page five so we can get started. After all, you have only four weeks to learn what you should have learned during a full year."

Embarrassed by Carmen, the girl stood up. "I don't need this shit." She grabbed her fake Louis Vuitton bag and walked out of the class.

"Anyone wish to follow?" Carmen was now the one staring. She didn't know what to expect. Half of the students looked like they were her age, while the others looked like they wouldn't hesitate to kill her at any moment.

No one moved.

"Great. Well, let's get started."

The kids all opened their books. She knew it was going to be the longest four weeks of her life.

The one thing Carmen loved about summer school was that it wasn't a full day. The four hours breezed by once the students took to her and her laid-back approach to teaching. She had a brief moment where she felt like she actually was teaching them something. Carmen packed her items into her bag. She looked up when there was a knock at her door.

"You survived the first day." Michael walked in.

"I did. Had one bad apple, but so far not so bad."

"So you think you might sign up for next semester too?"

The look on Carmen's face answered his question. The two walked out of the classroom together.

"Thank you again for earlier. I think it really made all the difference," Carmen said.

"No problem at all."

"How about a drink on me? We can go down to Side Street Grill."

"I would love that." Their eyes met. Carmen felt a twinge on her right side.

The popular cigar bar was already crowded with the after-work set. They grabbed a table, and Michael motioned for a waitress. Carmen pulled her hair down out of the tight ponytail she had. Her curly hair fell to her shoulders. Michael watched as she ran her fingers through her hair.

"Can I ask you a question, Carmen, without you turning me in for sexual harassment?"

Carmen smiled. "It depends on the question." She winked.

"Why are you gay? I mean, damn it, woman, you are gorgeous. Any man would love to be with you."

Carmen shook her head. It never ceased to amaze her how straight men could compliment and offend in the same sentence.

"Michael, I'm not gay because I couldn't get a man. I am gay because I just am. I love my fiancée. She is the most amazing person in the world."

"Have you never considered trying to be with a man?" he asked, completely baffled by Carmen's response.

"Why should I? I have what I want."

"But how can you know if you have never had the other option?"

"I have never eaten shit, but I know I don't want it." Carmen took a sip of her lemon drop martini.

"Touché." Michael nodded his head. "I think you are an awesome chick, Carmen."

"And you are pretty cool yourself, for a guy." Carmen laughed. She focused on Michael's face. She had to admit he was a beautiful man. His dark skin was smooth, altered only by his manicured beard. He obviously worked out, since his shirts always fit snugly around his biceps. And his almond eyes could have a mesmerizing effect even on the gayest female. Carmen felt the twinge in her side again.

"Michael, let me ask *you* a question now. Why are you single? I mean, I know for a fact Adrianne and Danielle both would give you children, not to mention the students who are determined to make you their man."

"Ha!" Michael laughed. "Let's just say I have a tendency to want a challenge or, in my case right now, the one thing that I can't have." His eyes focused on Carmen's face.

Carmen could feel that twinge turn into a piercing sensation. "You are silly." She took another sip of her drink, glancing down at the table. In that moment all she wanted was for him to take his eyes off of her.

Michael could tell the effect he was having on Carmen. Even though she was gay, she was still a woman, and the signs of her being affected were all over her body. He didn't know what it was, but he was taken by her. Since she started at the school, he'd known he had to have her. She was one of the more attractive teachers, but there was more. She was down to earth, something the teachers who threw themselves at him were severely lacking in. He was smitten, and Carmen's lesbianism wasn't enough to deter him.

Two hours passed, and their one drink turned into three cocktails and three shots. They couldn't stop giggling like the kids they taught. They swapped funny war stories about kids and coworkers.

Carmen jumped when her phone vibrated in her pocket. She pulled it out. It was Nic.

"Hey, baby. I'm at Side Street, a little tipsy. With my coworker Michael. Okay, babe."

Michael hung on every word, trying to decipher what was being said.

She hung the phone up. "Nic's pulling up."

"I guess that's my cue."

"Why?"

"You think the girlfriend will be happy to see you with the likes of me?"

"Boy, if you don't sit down . . ." Carmen pulled Michael's shirt.

Michael felt nervous. It was one thing to be around Carmen, but the thought of sharing time with Nic didn't sit well with him. He didn't know if what bothered him was the guilt from knowing he wanted to take Nic's girl from her or the fact that she was almost as masculine as he was.

All eyes were on Nic as she walked into the bar, oblivious to the lustful stares of women and the angry eyes of men. Michael felt jealousy rearing its ugly head when Nic gave Carmen a peck on her lips. She held her hand out to him.

"So you are the infamous Michael. It's nice to finally meet you."

"Likewise." Michael knew he couldn't hate. The girl was nice, and he could tell she truly loved Carmen.

The three continued their conversation until Carmen excused herself to go freshen up. Michael noticed two men staring at Nic. He suddenly felt protective. No matter what, Nic was still a woman, and his male instincts were kicking in. Nic put her hand on top of his.

"Don't worry about it," she said.

"So you see that too?"

"It's normal. We just ignore it."

Michael noticed the snickering of the two men. "I don't know if I could do it."

"It's life." Nic finished off Carmen's shot. "Hey, so I wanted to thank you for being so open to Carmen. I know some of the teachers have been a little bitchy, especially after that stunt with Denise and Sahara."

"Oh, those women are just crabs in a barrel. Carmen is one of a kind."

Nic noticed the starry look in Michael's eyes. She knew he was smitten. Nic smiled.

Michael sighed. "Man, I better get home before I don't make it to work tomorrow. Can you tell Carmen I'll see her tomorrow?"

"Will do." Nic gave Michael daps. Carmen returned to the table a few moments later. Nic grabbed her girlfriend. Carmen smiled as she stood between Nic's legs.

"You know he's crazy about you, right?"

"Shut up." Carmen blushed. Nic pulled her head to hers, planting a long erotic kiss on her lips. The mouths of the men who were watching dropped. "What was that for?"

"Just because." Nic stood up. She placed two twenty-dollar bills on the table. There was no better compliment than knowing someone else wanted what she had. "Let's go home."

Michael watched from his car as Nic and Carmen walked out of the bar, holding each other. He couldn't help but feel envious. Although he liked Nic, he couldn't shake the urges he had toward Carmen. He had to have her, and although Nic was cool, he knew Carmen was batting for the wrong team, and he had to at least try to get her on the right team.

Chapter 14

It had been weeks and no word from Denise. Unanswered questions clouded Lena's mind. She busied herself with preparing Bria for her long trip. She didn't know what she was going to do. Without Bria and with no romantic interest anymore, she would be so lonely.

Lena realized she didn't have enough friends. Misha was focusing on fixing her marriage, and Carmen was trying to keep Nic happy by staying in Memphis, instead of running to Atlanta every weekend. Lena didn't have anyone to turn to.

Her house was now haunted with the memory of Denise. Everywhere she turned, she could see Denise standing there. She wanted to move just to lose the brief but unforgettable memories they had created in just one night.

Adele's *21* CD became Lena's best friend. The songs seemed to speak directly to her. She couldn't listen to "Turning Tables" or "Don't You Remember" without tearing up. Lena knew she needed to get over Denise before she was a wreck again.

Lena heard Bria's little feet running toward her. Bria looked at her with her big doe eyes and put her hand on Lena's face. The softest touch melted Lena's heart. She was regretting her decision to let Bria go with her parents. She knew without Bria, she would be forced to face her own skeletons, which were toppling out of her closet.

Lena looked at her daughter. She knew she had to be strong for her. She couldn't let one person break her down the way Denise did a few years back.

To make matters worse, Farih was now a host on one of her favorite talk shows. Every afternoon she tortured herself by watching the other woman flash her amazing smile. Lena felt like Farih was throwing her happiness with Denise in her face. She hated having to hear about Denise and Farih's amazing relationship on the show, but for some reason she couldn't turn the station.

Lena kept up with what was going on with Denise via Carmen and gossip blogs. Denise and Farih were hot topics again. Denise was going to be a guest star on *Law & Order: SVU,* another one of Lena's favorite shows. Every time they showed Denise on TV, Lena watched like a little girl waiting to see her favorite celebrity come on.

Lena knew she had to get out of the house. She forced herself to go to the mall for some retail therapy. Phipps Plaza was relatively empty, unlike on the weekends. It wasn't a hangout spot like Lenox Square, due mainly to the quality of the stores it had. Lena walked out of Janie and Jack with some new clothes for Bria's upcoming trip. She knew she was going to overpack, but she wanted to make sure Bria had clothes for every occasion. Bria twirled in her new pink skirt, which she just had to have while in the store.

"Well, isn't this a surprise?"

Lena looked up to see Danni, the cute girl from the club, standing in front of her. Danni removed her shades and walked closer. Bria took her mother's hand, not taking her eyes off the stranger.

"It is." Lena smiled. She instantly noticed Danni's suave appearance. Her locks were braided into a ponytail. She didn't think she had seen locks so perfectly manicured before. Her jeans fit impeccably, Lena almost thought they were tailored. "Long way from New York, aren't you?"

Danni smiled. "Well, I figured I would scour the streets of Atlanta until I found Cinderella."

"You know Cinderella?" Bria's eyes lit up, and she was immediately fascinated by Danni.

Danni looked down, then looked back up at Lena. She realized that the girl had to be Lena's daughter. Danni bent down to Bria's height. "Actually I do. She's very beautiful, just like you." Bria smiled hard and giggled when Danni poked her stomach like it was the Pillsbury Doughboy's.

"Bria, say hello to Mommy's friend Danni."

Bria shyly said hello.

"So she remembers my name." Danni winked at Lena. Lena felt her insides burning, a sensation she hadn't felt in a while. "Well, hello, Ms. Bria. Have you been shopping?"

"Yes, my mommy bought me this." Bria turned in her new skirt.

"Oh, it's very pretty on you. But that couldn't have been all she bought you. A beautiful girl like you needs a lot more bags."

"Mommy only has two hands," Lena protested.

"With my two, that makes four." Danni took the two big bags from Lena's hands. Lena was instantly impressed.

"Danni, we don't want to stop you from whatever you were doing."

Danni shook her head. "I was just walking around, wasting time until a meeting, about to spend some unnecessary money. Shopping for this beautiful princess seems a lot more productive."

Bria giggled.

The trio headed to Saks Fifth Avenue. Bria ran straight to the toy department. Then she begged to have her face made up in a little girls' beauty salon in the store. Danni insisted and told the attendants to give Bria whatever she wanted. Lena protested, but Danni insisted again. Lena gave in, realizing it would give her some time to talk to Danni.

"So if you think spoiling my daughter is going to win points with me, you are very wrong." Lena smiled seductively as she smelled one of the many Paris Hilton fragrances. Even though it smelled great, she knew she would never be caught dead wearing a Paris Hilton fragrance.

"Well, I have no problem spoiling the daughter or the mother, if she would let me." Danni winked. Lena felt butterflies in her stomach. "So why don't you tell me why you left me high and dry in the club?"

"I'm so sorry about that. My friend had a mini meltdown when she saw someone she used to be involved with. I really didn't mean to."

Danni leaned against the display counter. "You really hurt my feelings when you left like that."

"Yeah, right. I saw that group of girls you were talking to. I'm sure one of them took your mind off of me pretty quickly." The collection of Bond No. 9 fragrances caught Lena's eye.

"No, actually, you are very wrong about that. I can't tell you who those girls were or are. Maybe you can't tell this about me yet, but I am very selective. It takes someone special to catch my eye."

Lena asked the sales associate for a bottle of Bryant Park. She knew the second she smelled the top, it was for her. "What makes you think I'm so special?"

Danni squinted her eyes. "Well, for one, you were standing in the VIP and you weren't attempting to hook up with any of the basketball players or celebrities that were in there."

"Oh." Lena shrugged her shoulders. She hadn't realized there were other celebrities in the building. She'd been focused on only one.

"Also, I could tell you had real class. You just reeked of it."

"Well, thank you, I guess." The associate rang up the two-hundred-thirty-dollar bottle of perfume. Lena opened her purse, but Danni put her hand over Lena's hand.

"I got it." Danni pulled out her platinum American Express.

Lena put her hand over Danni's. "No, I got it." Lena pulled out her equally impressive platinum card.

"Touché." Danni let Lena pay.

The two walked back over to the kiddie salon. Bria smiled as she showed off her made-up face, especially her pink lip gloss and her eye shadow, and her hair, which was up in a ponytail with a long pink feather hanging out of it.

"Well, don't you look beautiful!" Danni smiled at Bria as she handed the associate her credit card.

"What do you say, Bri-Bri?"

"Thank you, ma'am." Bria gave Danni a hug.

"Anytime, sweetie pie. I want you to do me a really big favor, okay?" Bria was fixated on Danni. Danni handed a card to Bria. "I want you to hold on to this right now, and give it to your mommy when I leave. Tell her that the only way Cinderella can get her glass slipper back is to call me."

Bria grinned as she ran over to Lena. Lena smiled. The fact that Danni was okay with her daughter gave

her major points. Danni and Lena nonverbally exchanged their good-byes, and then Danni walked off.
Lena watched her for a moment, then took the card
from Bria. She looked at the card. She would definitely
be calling Danielle Campbell.

Chapter 15

Denise admired her beautiful SoHo loft. She didn't realize how much she was going to miss living in New York. Due to the housing market, they had decided to rent their loft to two of their model friends instead of attempting to sell it. Now that Farih was officially a host on *The Buzz*, Atlanta was their new permanent home.

They decided to rent an apartment in Atlanta's trendy midtown area. The last thing Denise wanted was to take on another mortgage with Farih. Although she was once again happy with Farih, she couldn't shake the feeling that the angry Farih would show her face again.

Farih was back in bliss. She had an amazing job, and other offers were appearing. She was a hit on *The Buzz*. Her agent was right: gay was in. Her relationship with Denise was good, but they still hadn't gotten to the place they were in when they first got together. The honeymoon was over, and she was happy Denise was willing to stick with her and attempt to make all they had accomplished last.

The only regret they both had about moving was Lena. Farih wondered when the past would reappear in their lives. For weeks Farih was Inspector Gadget. She would check Denise's phone while she was asleep just to see if she had been in communication with Lena. After she realized there was no more communication, she began to trust Denise again, but Denise was also still stationed in New York. Farih wondered how things would change when they were both living in the same city as Lena on a full-time basis.

"We totally have to hang this in the new place." Farih held a giant picture frame with the first photo spread they did together for Jocku Fashions, Denise's first major fashion campaign.

Denise couldn't see anything but Farih's feet as she held the large portrait. Denise smiled. "Yeah, we do." Denise couldn't believe how much she missed the simple life of modeling. It was a lot easier than dealing with the movie business. Cooley and her agent were held up in contract negotiations with the *Fast and Furious* movie, which was in turn holding up the Aqua movie. Denise loved making movies, but the business aspect made her want to quit and just be a basketball coach at a high school.

Denise stood up and walked over to Farih. She put her hands on both sides of the frame. "Let me help you before the photo takes you down." Denise walked it over to the wall. She turned around and saw Farih standing completely naked in the middle of the floor. She smiled.

"I figured since it's our last night, we should go out with a bang," Farih whispered.

Farih's body called to Denise. She nodded her head as she walked closer to Farih. The physical thing she loved most about Farih was her dark chocolate skin. Denise ran her hands down Farih's arms, and they intertwined their fingers. Their lips met. Denise wrapped her long arms around Farih. Her fingertips traced the arch in Farih's back. When Denise's hands cupped Farih's bare bottom, Farih jumped, wrapping her long limbs around Denise's torso.

Denise carried Farih to their long tan chaise. Farih shivered when her backside hit the cold leather. Her nipples instantly perked up when the tips of Denise's fingers touched them.

Denise sucked on Farih, while her long index and middle finger stroked in and out of Farih's wetness. Farih moaned, closing her eyes tight. Her lips quivered each time Denise hit the spot that made her whole body jump.

Farih's hips moved in unison with Denise's fingers and pelvis. Farih wanted to tear all of Denise's clothes off. Denise's body was still ripped due to her continuous workout plan. Farih wanted to feel Denise's skin against her mouth. She pulled at Denise's shirt until Denise finally pulled out for the quick second it took for Farih to remove her shirt and sports bra.

Farih wanted Denise. She pulled her body close to Denise and began to suck on her breasts. Denise watched as Farih's mouth sucked and her tongue licked Denise's small but ample breasts. Denise unbuttoned her pants. She was soaking wet and wanted more.

Farih's long fingers made their way to Denise's womanhood. She rubbed Denise's swollen clit, and Denise's sweetness covered her hand instantly.

"I want it," Farih moaned.

"No." Denise pushed Farih back and lifted her legs onto her shoulders. "It's mine." Denise's tongue entered the familiarity of Farih's walls with force. Farih's legs shivered as she climaxed once, then twice, and then her body reached full convulsions from the third straight climax in a row. Each explosion in Denise's mouth made her want more and more.

Denise's hair was entangled in Farih's hands as she struggled to maintain a bit of composure. She finally couldn't take it anymore. The fifth orgasm came hard, causing Farih to grab Denise's hair so tightly, Denise had to let out a scream. Farih looked up. Small strands of Denise's hair were in her hands. Denise rubbed her head.

"What you trying to do? Make me bald?" Denise looked at her girlfriend. They both began to laugh.

"Don't think you are getting away that easy," Farih said as she yanked on Denise's pants.

"No, I don't want it today." Denise moved back. She had to be in the mood to receive head. She got the majority of her pleasure from pleasing Farih. Every orgasm Denise gave Farih only excited Denise more, until she reached her ultimate point of pleasure.

Farih pouted but was okay with the hurting Denise had just put on her. She stood up, her wetness on the edge of the chaise. Denise and Farih headed to the bathroom. They got in their large double shower and turned on the hot water. Steam quickly covered the glass door.

Farih wasn't going to be outdone. While Denise adjusted the water pressure, Farih got down on her knees, pulled Denise close, and sucked Denise's clit from behind. Denise's mouth dropped as she held on to the wet wall. Farih had quickly turned her into her little bitch, and she didn't mind one bit. Farih rimmed Denise's ass, wanting to taste all of Denise, from her ass to her pussy, and all the sweetness that came along with it. Until Farih, Denise was not one for ass play. But after one night when Farih took it without asking, Denise couldn't deny the feeling was amazing, and Farih was once again taking it—and she loved it.

Denise was also not one to be outdone. After her final climax she left Farih in the shower, only so she could break out the finale. She strapped up with their large black dildo. Farih's body twitched from anticipation as Denise hopped back in the shower.

"Assume the position," Denise joked, but Farih quickly obeyed. She bent over, with her hands holding on to both sides of the shower wall. Denise entered Farih's pussy as Farih began to grind her hips in sync with Denise. Denise held on to Farih's sides as she stroked in and out. The intensity against her own pussy caused her knees to buckle a few times, but she held on like the pro she was.

Denise wasn't going to let Farih have the final laugh. She fingered Farih's asshole with her thumb, then rubbed the tip of the dildo up and down Farih's crack. Farih took a deep breath as the thick dildo entered the small hole. Her body jumped. Denise held on, entering her slowly. Denise kissed Farih's back as she slowly stroked the head of the dildo in and out of Farih's ass. Moans wouldn't leave Farih's mouth, only small sounds, as the dildo rendered her nearly speechless. Farih took it like a champ. She leaned her body up, wrapping her right arm around Denise's neck. Farih turned her head as Denise fucked her from behind. They kissed passion into each other's mouths.

They both came, causing them to fall down slowly into each other's arms in the shower. Denise didn't want to leave Farih's arms, and the feeling was mutual. Sitting on the bottom of their large shower for the last time, they made out like teenagers. Their final shower in New York would be remembered forever.

The couple finally pulled away from their amazing shower. It was like old times. Farih brushed Denise's hair back into a ponytail, while Denise massaged lotion into Farih's long legs. They laughed and giggled like schoolgirls while they listened to music and continued to pack their belongings for their move.

"I am gonna miss it here," Farih said as they stood on their balcony. They could hear the sounds from local nightclubs. New York had always been Farih's home. Denise had fallen in love with the magical city over the past four years of being there.

"You act like you won't ever be back." Denise stood behind Farih. She placed her hands on top of Farih's on the rail.

"Visiting isn't the same as living here." Farih sighed. "At least I'm going with you."

The words warmed Denise's heart. She kissed Farih on the nape of her neck. She could feel herself falling in love with Farih again. Suddenly there was a sinking feeling in Denise's gut. Denise pulled away and headed into the apartment. Farih turned around.

"Everything okay?" Farih asked. She could feel the shift in their perfect mood.

"Everything is fine. We just need to finish packing." Denise's eyes shifted. Lena's face had entered her mind again. Every time she thought she was free, Lena appeared. She just couldn't shake her.

Farih couldn't shake the feeling that Denise's mood change was due to Lena. She knew Denise was happy with her, and she couldn't understand why Denise couldn't let go of the past. She knew Denise was faithful in deed, but knowing she wasn't the only one in Denise's heart stung worse than anything. Farih tried to shake it off, as she wanted to continue packing, but her gut wouldn't let her. She then decided it was best not to press the issue and ruin their day, but she could feel in her soul that soon this would be a major topic of discussion.

Chapter 16

Lena tried on another one of her many little black dresses. She didn't like the way any of them made her look. She had never been so nervous about a date before. There was something about Danni that had her on edge. She didn't know if it was the idea of actually liking someone or the fact that Danni was a woman. She hadn't been with a woman since Terrin and hadn't loved a woman besides Denise.

She noticed a navy blue dress in the corner of her closet. It was one of the post-baby dresses she bought. She had purchased a few sexy dresses for the day that she was back to her pre-baby weight. Hiring an amazing trainer and having an athlete for an ex-husband had helped her achieve that goal rather quickly, but she hadn't had a need for one of the dresses.

The navy dress draped artfully on her body. A sparkling canary rhinestone pendant gave it a little extra flare. She pulled out a pair of her red bottom shoes and admired them. She hadn't had much need for stilettos since having Bria.

Lena heard the front door close. She placed a pair of earrings to her ears, modeling them to see if the diamonds went with the outfit.

"I'm in my bedroom," Lena yelled as she held up a pair of Tiffany teardrop earrings.

"My, my, what's this all about?" Brandon stood in the doorway. Lena turned around.

"What?" A sly smile crossed her face.

"Got a hot date?" Brandon sat on the edge of her bed.

"Something like that."

Lena quickly realized something. Brandon was too comfortable coming in and out of her house. Even though they were just friends, she didn't want to experience an awkward moment of him walking in when she was entertaining guests.

"How do I look? And why are you here?" Lena decided on the teardrops and attached them to her earlobes.

"Just wanted to stop by before I left town. Is that a problem?" Brandon couldn't take his eyes off of Lena's ass.

"Not really, but I'm going to need you to start calling first. What if I had company?"

"Company?" Brandon frowned. As much as he wanted Lena to have a life, the idea of her actually having one didn't sit well with him.

"You didn't tell me how I look." Lena turned around, changing the subject.

"Like the shorty I fell in love with back in the day." Brandon could feel the stiffness growing in his pants. Even with all the women he'd been with, no one compared to Lena. He was her first, and in his mind his manhood would always be the perfect fit for her.

"You're so silly." Lena stepped out of her shoes and walked into the bathroom. She rummaged through the ridiculous number of M•A•C containers, trying to find the right combination. "What are you doing here, sir? I thought you were leaving the other day."

Brandon watched as Lena put her makeup on. His man was telling him to run in, grab her, and tear the sexy dress off. He knew he didn't have that right anymore.

"Damn, Lena, you got a little date, so now you trying to get rid of my black ass. Shit. I am about to head
back to Memphis. Just wanted to stop by since I guess
I won't be seeing you for a while, but obviously that was
a bad idea."

Lena turned around. She realized that with Bria
leaving, he wouldn't have a reason to come to Atlanta
every weekend. She walked to the bathroom door. She
could see the lust on his face. She tried not to smile as
he undressed her with his eyes.

"Don't act like that. I mean, you should be happy.
Now you can concentrate on your new roommate."
Lena walked back into the bathroom. She heard Brandon huff. She knew his girlfriend was the last thing on
his mind at that moment.

"Let me get out of here before your *date* shows up."
Brandon stood up. He shifted his weight, hoping his
growing limb wasn't exposed.

"Call me and let me know you made it."

Brandon walked to the bathroom door. "You really
look amazing. Whoever it is will love it. I know I do."
Brandon sounded like a lovesick puppy.

Lena smiled. She walked over and gave him a hug.
She could feel the stiffness as his body grazed hers. She
knew he wanted her to notice, but pleasing Brandon
was the last thing on her mind. She couldn't get the
sexual chocolate she was about to meet up with out
of her mind, a major departure from thinking about
Denise.

Lena was without a doubt on the best date she had
been on in ages. Not only was Danni attractive, wealthy,
and intelligent, but she was down-to-earth and funny
too.

Lena pulled up to the downtown W Hotel. Danni had already gained cool points for staying at one of Lena's favorite chains. The artfully chic hotel was classy and hip. She walked through the whimsical front entrance and headed to the Drinkshop lounge, which was already buzzing with people socializing. Lena looked around but couldn't spot Danni in the sea of adults. She felt her clutch moving as she sat down at the bar. She opened it and heard her phone buzzing.

I see you.

Lena smiled as she read the cryptic text message. The phone buzzed again.

You look good as hell.

Lena stood up, but with her short frame, she couldn't see past a group of men, all of whom were eyeing her. She wondered which one would have the nerve to come up and talk to her. Her phone buzzed again.

Keep looking.

Lena decided it was time to respond.

Wouldn't you prefer a closer look? Men are swarming.

One of the fellas decided he would be the first up to bat. He adjusted his suit jacket and tie. Lena sat back down in the chair and braced herself for the kill. The light-skinned guy walked up to the bar and stared directly at her. Lena couldn't ignore his stare. She looked back at him.

"Hello." The forty-something man extended his hand. "My name is Darrius, and I need to buy you a drink."

"Is that right?" Lena reluctantly shook Darrius's hand.

"Oh yes, that is right. Let me guess. A martini?" Darrius motioned to the bartender, who was showing off his mixology skills by mixing and pouring three drinks at one time.

"Actually, I'm more of a cognac woman myself," Lena said with a straight face.

"Cognac?" Darrius couldn't believe his ears.

"Yes, some Hen straight." Lena kept her straight face.

Darrius smiled. "Well, that's different, but whatever you say. . . ." He motioned to the bartender, who just continued to ignore him.

"Sorry I'm late. I was stuck staring at how good you looked at the door, and couldn't move."

Lena and Darrius both turned to see Danni standing behind them. Darrius's smile quickly faded at the sight of Danni's attire.

Lena quickly had to regain her composure. Even in a simple pair of jeans and a black button-down Danni looked good enough to eat. Her locks hung down to her shoulders. Lena couldn't help but wonder how Danni's dark skin would feel next to hers. In a room full of successful black men, Lena realized she was in heat and Danni was the alpha male over all of them.

"Oh, so this is you?" Darrius interrupted the fantasy happening in Lena's head.

"Yeah, son, thanks for watching my boo for me." Danni's New York accent was thick. She watched as Darrius stood amazed by the situation in front of him.

He walked off, but not before making sure they heard his parting comment.

"Man, they're everywhere."

Danni and Lena looked at each other and laughed at his comment. Danni extended her hand. Lena put her hand in Danni's hand and stood up. A breeze came through the lounge, sending a bit of Danni's cologne into Lena's nose.

Lena smirked. "What are you wearing?"

Danni smiled. "Let's just say we have something else in common."

"Bond? Ugh, you just have to be like me. Which one is that?" Lena said, realizing she hadn't smelled that scent before.

"What else? Brooklyn, baby." Danni winked. Lena felt heat rising.

They headed to the second floor for a little music and drinks. The local band played a hot mix of neo soul and jazz. Lena swayed her hips to the beat. Danni couldn't resist touching her whenever possible. Each touch felt like electricity shooting through Lena's skin. She didn't know what spell Danni was casting, but it was working.

The two then headed out of the busy lounge and up to Danni's spot. Danni's points continued to add up as they got off the elevator on her floor. Lena was impressed. Danni wasn't merely a guest in this building, but a resident. Danni opened the door to her lavish condominium, and Lena instantly took in the breathtaking view. Downtown Atlanta was lit up and gorgeous. Lena glanced around the rest of the place as Danni grabbed a bottle of wine.

The condo made her downtown Memphis loft look like a shabby apartment. The architecture mixed with the contemporary furnishings was out of Lena's dream-home book.

"I'm guessing you like blue." Lena walked on a plush navy area rug before sitting on the edge of the chaise end of the black contemporary sectional. The accent wall was stunning with its various shades of black and blue and its soft swirl effect. Lena could see herself staring at the wall for hours.

"Yeah, it's my favorite color. You like it?"

"I love blue." Lena sat back. For some reason she felt at home in the new environment.

Danni joined her on the couch after pouring two glasses of wine and handing one to Lena. "So Miss Lena Jamerson, or should I say Redding?"

Lena's body froze. "How do you—"

"Come on, girl, I do my research. You didn't think I would just let some stranger come up in my crib, did you?" Danni laughed as Lena playfully shoved her.

"Well, so now you know. Any questions?" Lena braced herself. She didn't know how Danni would take being with the ex-wife and baby mama of a star athlete.

Danni shrugged her shoulders. "Not really. Why? Is there something I should know?"

"I guess not."

Lena wanted to jump for joy while she added more points to Danni's list. She wasn't intimidated by Brandon, which was a major plus.

"Why don't you tell me a little about you?"

"What do you want to know?" Danni took a sip of wine.

Lena looked around the lavish pad. "Okay, for starters, what the hell do you really do? Don't tell me being an agent has you balling like this?" Lena threw her hands up.

Danni laughed. "What is that supposed to mean? I might just be hot shit. And technically I'm not an agent."

"I'm not saying you aren't, but come on now. You are living large in New York and Atlanta and who knows where else. I bet you have property in L.A. too."

"Among other places."

"So what are you?"

"What are you?" Danni stared into Lena's eyes. Lena felt the heat rising like the sun under her dress.

"I am Lena."

"Lena, huh? So what are you? I mean, come on. Keep it real with me. You aren't some baller wife living the high life. You are a different kind of wealthy. You are that old money wealthy, aren't you?"

Lena just took a sip of wine. Danni had hit the nail on the head. Lena's family's money went way back. She smiled and nodded her head.

Danni chuckled. "So are you going to answer my question or evade it?"

Lena gave Danni a seductive look.

Danni took notice immediately. "I'm not too different from you, actually. My family comes from wealth. But I dabble in real estate with my pops's company, and I own an entertainment firm out of New York."

Lena nodded her head. She was impressed by Danni's résumé. She wondered if Danni knew Denise. Lena quickly shook her head. She refused to let thoughts of Denise ruin this moment.

Danni's eyes shifted to Lena's thigh. She licked her lips. Danni returned Lena's seductive glare with a sexy piercing look of her own. "So, Lena, why did you decide to come up here with me?"

"Why did you invite me?"

"Because I want to have sex with you."

Lena's mouth dropped. She hit Danni. "Oh, really? Bold, aren't we?"

Danni laughed. "What? Come on, you knew what you were doing when you put that dress on. I'm just being honest with you."

"So that's all you want? All of this showing off has just been to get in my panties?"

Danni shook her head. "No, honestly, if that was all I wanted, we wouldn't be here right now. I told you, girl, I don't just get with anyone. If you were just a piece of ass, I would have taken you down the street to Gladys Knight and Ron Winans' Chicken and Waffles and to the Marriott or something."

Lena couldn't help but laugh. Danni's eyes were fixated on her. Lena's body was on fire. She tried to keep her cool. No matter how many seductive looks Danni gave her, she didn't want to give it up that easy. Lena shifted her body in an attempt to cool off some.

"So, Lena, why did you come up here with me?" Danni didn't take her eyes off Lena. Her eyes were burning into Lena's skin. Her looks, along with the full flame coming from Lena's panties, was setting Lena ablaze.

"I wanted to get to know you better. I don't know. . . . There is something about you that is . . . different."

"Is that a good thing?"

"Great thing."

"Good to know." Danni inched closer to Lena.

Their eyes connected. Lena's palms were sweating. She knew what was next. Danni's hand caressed the back of Lena's head. She pulled Lena into her. Their lips met. Their tongues became instant friends. Danni's plump lips were soft. Her cologne inflamed Lena's nostrils, only adding to the attraction.

Danni's fingertips traced the nape of Lena's neck. Lena's body shivered from the soft touch, causing the hairs on her neck to stand and her nipples to ache from hardness. Lena's panties were soaked from her wetness. Danni was easily going to get her wish.

Danni pulled her lips away only far enough to speak. "Maybe we should call it a night."

Lena knew she couldn't be coherent, because Danni's words weren't making sense to her at that moment. The much-needed break helped Lena regain her composure. Although Danni seemed to be the perfect woman, Lena still didn't know much about her, and giving it up on the first date wasn't a good way to start whatever it was they were starting.

"Maybe you are right." Lena slowly pulled away. "I probably should go."

"Who said anything about going?" Danni's hand rested on Lena's thigh. "I want you to stay."

Lena shook her head. She thought about her daughter. She had only a few more days with her and wanted to get as much time in as possible. She also knew if she stayed, sleeping would be the one thing they would not do. Lena remembered who she was. No matter how bad she wanted it, she had to remember she wasn't the type of chick to give it up on the first date.

"I have a daughter to tuck in." Lena hoped her knees didn't give out when she tried to stand up.

"That's right. My bad, boo. Yeah, you get on home to that beautiful child of yours."

Danni stood up, holding her hands up to help Lena off the couch. Danni walked Lena to the elevator. Lena walked into the elevator after the doors opened. Suddenly she felt someone grab her arm. Before she could blink, she was in Danni's arms. Danni held her tight, running her hands through Lena's hair as she pulled Lena's face close.

That was the final straw for Lena. They kissed passionately, and Lena wrapped her arms around Danni's neck. She felt like Scarlett O'Hara, and Danni was Rhett Butler in the infamous fire scene in *Gone with the Wind*. Danni's strong hands roamed up and down her back before settling on her ass. Danni reached under Lena's dress, cupping her plump ass with her hands. Lena's feet barely touched the floor as Danni consumed her. She wanted Danni to rip her dress off in the hallway and claim her pussy as her own. Instead, she felt her feet meet the floor. They stood face-to-face, and she could feel Danni's breath on her lips.

"Tell Bria I said hello."

"I will."

"Kick it tomorrow, before I leave?"

Lena couldn't speak; she nodded her head. Danni placed another sensual kiss on Lena's lips. Lena wasn't sure how she managed to pull herself away from Danni long enough to get into the elevator. It was the longest ride home ever.

Lena sat in her bed. Her MacBook Pro was covered with Danni's face. Danni had given her the idea. As soon as she'd kissed the sleeping Bria on her forehead, she'd grabbed her MacBook and headed to her bedroom. She sat in her bed, Googling the enchanting stranger. She stared at pictures of Danielle "Danni" Campbell with various celebrities and socialites. According to a Wikipedia bio, the money in her family came from her father's side, which had amassed wealth by doing everything from owning crazy amounts of land and property to dabbling in movie producing. Her heart skipped a beat when she read that Danni was not only sexual chocolate but was half West Indian, from Trinidad. She made a mental note to learn more about that.

Lena couldn't stop staring at the screen. She searched for some imperfection in Danni but came up with nothing. Although Danni was a ladies' woman, Lena couldn't find any scandals involving her new interest. Lena clicked on Danni's Facebook profile. She rolled her eyes at the private status blocking access to her photo albums. She thought about sending a friend request but opted against it. After all, she didn't want to let on how much she was digging her.

Danni had taken more interest in the entertainment side of the family business than the property side. She had opted to graduate with a law degree and open up a small entertainment agency. Lena looked at the few Google images of Danni, mostly of her standing in front of backdrops from premieres and award shows. She could picture herself on Danni's arm at the various events.

Lena's daydream faded when a particular photo popped up. Danni was standing in front of the backdrop from Denise's first movie. Lena's mind raced. Did Danni know Denise? They were both black and lesbian in the same community, and therefore, they had to have crossed paths at some time. Had Danni been at the club that night because of Denise? Lena's heart was now racing as fast as the questions in her mind.

Lena closed her laptop, hoping to stifle the thoughts consuming her mind. Even with an amazing woman like Danni staring her in her face, she couldn't completely shake Denise. A strange feeling started to consume Lena's body. Her toes began to tingle. The tingling crept through her body. She closed her eyes. The kiss. The last kiss Danni had planted on her was electrifying her body, as though it was happening in that moment. Lena licked her lips. She could taste her. Danni was on her skin. The Brooklyn Bond girl had given her a fever she hadn't experienced since . . . Denise. It was wrong, but she knew Danni had to be the answer to her prayers. If this sexy specimen of a woman couldn't rid her mind of Denise, no one would.

Chapter 17

Carmen watched her class of juvenile delinquents disperse. She pulled her cell phone out to text Denise. She missed her friends, and although the days were passing quickly, she couldn't wait to get out of the classroom for the rest of the summer. Like clockwork, Michael appeared at her door to walk her to her car for the day. Carmen didn't know why she looked forward to that so much each day.

"So what does the rest of the day hold for you, Ms. Carmen?"

"I am wedding planning via Skype with my best friend."

A knot formed in Michael's throat. "Oh, I guess that is coming up pretty soon."

"Two months."

"I guess it must be nice. I don't think marriage is in my cards." They walked out the large door to the teacher's parking lot.

"Oh, don't be like that. Again, there are at least three teachers inside that would marry you tomorrow." Carmen playfully hit his arm. His hard bicep stung her fingers as she hit him. "God, what are you? A man of steel or something?"

"Just a little working out, that's all." Michael noticed the stares of two of the teachers who flirted with him daily. They didn't understand why he spent so much time with the lesbian.

"I need to work out with you, get in shape for this wedding."

"You don't need to get in shape. You look amazing." Michael realized what he had said too late. Carmen was giving him an awkward look. "What? Do you work out, like, two times a week?"

Carmen didn't know how to respond to his statement. Ever since Side Street, Michael's flirting had intensified. It made her feel uneasy and excited at the same time. Carmen wasn't used to the attention. Even though she didn't share his feelings, it was nice to know someone else wanted her besides Nic.

"I don't really work out like I should. Just a little walking."

"Well, I work out every morning at six if you ever want to join me."

Carmen frowned. "As in six A.M.? Yeah, no, I think I'll pass on that." They laughed.

"Well, keep it in mind. I'd love to work you out. . . . . I mean work out with you." Michael knew exactly what he was saying that time. His statement caused Carmen to blush. He watched as she got on her car and drove off. He could tell she was starting to warm up to him.

Misha felt refreshed as she walked the Clark Atlanta University campus. Watching the students brought back memories of her time at Freedom. She missed it all. She could picture sitting outside with Carmen, Nic, and Cooley. It felt like it was yesterday when Cooley would flirt with her and she would ignore her advances.

Misha couldn't shake the thoughts of Cooley she had. She had flashbacks at random times during the day. A flashback of the first time they had sex almost made her burn dinner the night before. The thoughts were maddening and were taking a toll on her marriage. She didn't want to be touched by Patrick. Even the slightest touch made her feel ill. She forced herself to endure sex with him after he made a comment about the lack of sex in their relationship.

She knew the problem was more than Cooley. Patrick wanted another child, and he wanted it now. She knew there would be no way to explain to Patrick that she wanted him to wear condoms, so getting the birth control shot was her only option. The last thing she wanted was another child.

Misha stood in front of the admissions office. Patrick had made it very clear that school was not a financial option for them, but Misha knew there had to be a way. She knew she didn't want another student loan. They had just finished paying off the loans they both had, and didn't want that headache again. She was going to need grants and scholarships to go back to school.

Misha suddenly didn't want to go back to school. A sense of loneliness came over her. She felt lost. There was a hole, something was missing in her life, but she didn't know what it was. Cooley entered her mind.

A sexy young group of studs walked past her. She felt her stomach knot up. One was too cute. She was tall, with enough meat on her bones to notice she had hips and an ass, even though she tried to hide them. Her hair hung back in a ponytail, and she had a fitted cap on her head. Misha smiled as the girl looked at her. The girl nodded and winked her right eye. Misha felt butterflies.

Misha knew she loved Patrick, but there was something missing. She had an itch he just couldn't scratch, no matter what he did. As much as she tried to deny it, she knew the problem. She missed the touch and the taste of women, and as the days passed, the feelings grew stronger.

Misha took a deep breath. The stud glanced at her again. She knew all it would take was a nod of her head to get the stud to come over. She contemplated the idea. A quick sex session with a nameless undergrad might just satisfy the itch, or it could make the urge worse. She knew the stud was waiting on her cue. Misha turned around and walked away from the building. She knew if she stayed, something bad would happen that she wouldn't be able to turn back from. She had too much to lose if she had one night of pleasure. In the end she didn't know if it was worth it.

Misha climbed in her car and drove home. When she arrived at her house, she couldn't pull herself from the car. Going inside meant she was back to reality. Her son and husband were on the other side of the door, waiting on her return to them. She felt guilty for feeling the way she did. Her son was her world, and she loved Patrick with all her heart. The thoughts of the past were haunting her and making her despise everything he had given her. It wasn't right, and he didn't deserve it, but she didn't know what to do to stop it.

"Hey, you." Patrick was usually pleasant when she walked in the house.

"Hey, baby." She forced herself to use a pet name.

Patrick walked over to her. He pressed his lips against hers. His prickly hairs from his recently cut beard repulsed Misha. She missed the smooth touch of a woman's lips. She pulled away.

"What have you two been doing?"

Patrick's demeanor changed. "Jaylin isn't here. He's with my mother."

"Oh . . ."

"Where have you been, Misha?" Patrick demanded.

"Just out."

"Humph." Patrick paced the floor.

"What?" Misha snapped.

"You tell me." Patrick stopped. "Misha, do you think I'm a fool? You have been acting different. You think I didn't notice you weren't into it the other night? And now that kiss . . . It's like you don't like me to touch you anymore."

Misha's heart was racing. She was busted. She hadn't realized how obvious her feelings were. Sweat began to form on her brow. "Patrick . . ."

"Are you seeing someone else?"

"No! How can you even think that?"

"You know exactly why I can think it. You think I didn't notice after you spent your little time away that you changed? It would be after you go kick it with Carmen that you start acting brand new." Patrick was fuming.

Misha's head jerked around. "Are you serious right now, Patrick? I thought you were past that. . . ."

"I was. You are the one who is acting different. Were you around *her*, Misha?"

Misha couldn't believe her ears. Four years and Patrick still was stuck on Cooley. She couldn't help but feel a twinge of guilt. She'd been affected by seeing Cooley, and she was having feelings she hadn't had in years, but thinking wasn't the same as cheating.

You could hear a pin drop in the room. Patrick wouldn't take his eyes off of her. He wanted answers and knew that she couldn't lie to him. Misha lowered her head.

"I haven't cheated on you. I wouldn't do that. I love you. . . ." Her heart was breaking. She could see the fear in his eyes.

"Misha, I love you, but I'm not going to try to make you stay somewhere you don't want to be. If you want . . . that . . . then by all means, there's the door. I'm not going to compete with . . . with no one, especially not a fucking dyke."

Misha felt her world crashing down around her. As much as she wanted to punch him for his homophobic attitude, she also wanted to hold him and make him see that she was committed to him. Misha knew she had to get her feelings in check before she lost her family over feelings that she couldn't completely explain.

"Patrick, I chose you. But I'd be lying if I didn't admit that there is something missing in my life. Patrick, I don't want anyone else, but I can't continue to just be a housewife. I feel myself dying each day that I'm not doing something productive."

"And raising our son isn't productive for you? That's the most important job in the world, Misha."

Misha wanted to scream. She again felt like she was talking to a brick wall. His statement rang true, since raising their son should be the number one priority. But Misha didn't see why she couldn't do more than one thing.

"Patrick, listen to me. I am unhappy just cooking and cleaning. I want more."

"So leaving our son with some strange people so you can go out and pull in a check we don't need is that damn important to you?"

"Why do you have to say it like that?"

"Because, Misha, admit it. You didn't want this. You didn't want a family. You still don't want one!" His voice carried throughout the house.

Misha was offended. "So me wanting to do more with my life besides cook, clean, and wash your fucking dirty drawers means I don't want a family? Fuck you, Patrick! I love you and I love our son, but that doesn't mean I can't love and want more for myself as well, you insensitive asshole!" Misha pushed him with all of her might, but he didn't move.

"Misha, we both gave up *I* for a *we* when we got married. You think I don't miss my old life? I used to travel all over. Now I'm stuck behind a desk because I can't be the agent I used to be due to my love for my family. We could be bringing in so much more money, but I took the promotion so I could be home instead of on the road. But you don't fucking get that. All you think about is you!"

Misha felt horrible. Patrick was right. He had taken a management job, which meant an end to the high commissions he was making as an agent, just so he could come home to them every night. Although he was right, she still couldn't shake the emptiness that was in her heart.

"Patrick, I knew what I was getting into when we got married, but I never knew I would have to give up everything that I wanted in life. You've known me my whole life, and you've always known how badly I wanted to be a lawyer. You know how hard I worked to get into college. You, of all people, should understand why I'm not completely fulfilled."

Patrick sat on the couch. He sighed. "I know. But we don't have the money to put you through law school right now."

"Can I at least try? Let me try to get some financial aid, maybe even a scholarship. I won't know until I at least try." Misha sat down next to him. "I'm feeling empty inside, Patrick. I need this. Please."

Patrick sat so still, Misha wondered if he was breathing. "Misha, look me in my eyes and tell me that this feeling of emptiness has nothing at all to do with your past lifestyle."

Misha knew this was it. She inched her body closer to her husband. Misha put her hands on Patrick's waist. She stared directly into his pain-stricken eyes.

"It has absolutely nothing to do with my past. I gave that up, Patrick, and I don't want it. I just want to be happy with you and our son."

Patrick stared into his wife's eyes. He searched for any sign that she was lying, but saw nothing. He let out a sigh of relief. Patrick couldn't take seeing Misha in so much pain. He put his arm around her.

"Fine. I don't want to see you unhappy. See what you can do, and we will work on it from there."

Misha felt a warm sensation come over her body. She threw her arms around him. She kissed his lips. His beard no longer bothered her, and she found herself aroused. Patrick pulled Misha close. She pulled his shirt over his head. Her name and Jaylin's name were tattooed over his right bicep. She kissed her name.

Patrick entered her. Her wetness covered his shaft. She was wetter than she had been in a very long time. She moaned for more as he made love to her. It wasn't the touch of a woman that excited her. It was the strong touch of a man. His massive arms made her feel safe in every way. The hardness of his body was something no woman could match. He let out a loud groan when he came. She could feel his seeds rushing through her body.

He sat up. "I think I just made you pregnant with that one, baby." He smiled.

Misha turned her head. She knew it was one secret she couldn't tell, or it would mark the end of their relationship, and losing him—or having another child—

was something she wasn't willing to do. She locked it away in the vault of secrets, which was growing. She could never tell him that she didn't want another child or that she still craved women.

Chapter 18

"So, superstar, how does it feel to be home?" Carmen said as she plopped down on her plush couch next to Denise.

"Believe it or not, it feels great." Denise smiled as Nic joined them, sitting down in her recliner chair.

Denise wanted to enjoy her two last months. In two months she would be leaving to spend the next six months of her life on a remote island in the Caribbean to shoot the next installment in the *Fast and Furious* series. Although in interviews most actors said it was amazing to shoot films in gorgeous places, Denise had heard the behind-the-scenes talk of long hours, the hot sun, bugs, and dirt. Even though the stories put her on edge, she was still excited. *If* she was going to be an actress, at least she got to be a gun-toting, fast-car-driving actress.

"So you are okay about Cameron?" Nic took a sip from her favorite mug.

"Yeah, it's cool. I mean, sure I would have loved to do it, but in the end *Fast* just was a better fit for now. And the Aqua movie is a great opportunity."

"I'm just glad you came to visit." Carmen hugged Denise. Denise put her arm around her best friend. She felt bad that missing Carmen was not the entire motivation for her visit.

Denise couldn't take it anymore. She felt as though the amazing feeling she had had with Farih must have been left behind in their apartment in New York. As soon as they made it to Atlanta, the super-short honeymoon was over.

Farih without a job was almost as bad as Farih with a job. As soon as they landed in Atlanta, it was the Farih and Denise show. Farih felt the need to be on the scene at all times. Denise knew the reason why. Farih finally had fame again, and she was doing everything in her power not to let it go. Once again the Farih she loved was gone, now replaced with an attention-seeking. always-on-the-scene Farih. She didn't have an attitude, unless Denise didn't want to go to some swanky nightclub where they could be seen and photographed. Denise missed the days of chilling in the house and calling for late-night takeout.

What made matters worse was that Farih seemed to want to go out only with Denise. Denise didn't know when the dependency had started, but since making it to Atlanta, it had only gotten worse. Farih used to go out with her model friends all the time in New York without Denise. Now she didn't want to go anywhere without her. Denise needed a break before she did something she might regret in the end.

"So this wedding . . . Canada, aye?"

Carmen's face lit up at Denise's words. Nic had managed to talk Carmen out of a royal wedding, but she had only talked her into something else, a destination wedding. Carmen and Nic knew that in Tennessee the only thing they could do was exchange vows that would mean absolutely nothing. They decided they wanted to go somewhere they could legally be married, even if when they returned to Tennessee, it wouldn't mean a thing.

"Well, Canada is on the list," Carmen replied. "It's that or just going to Lena's house in the Hamptons since gay marriage is legal in New York too. Those are two of the best options. Canada is awesome, but Lena's house is free."

"And I mean, who wants to get married in Iowa?" Nic frowned.

"What about Mass? You could go to P-Town." Denise offered her little bit of knowledge. She had hosted an event in the small town on the extreme tip of Cape Cod, which was a lesbian and gay paradise. Denise had fallen in love with the friendly locals and the old beauty. "I mean, it kinda reminds me of the Hamptons but super gay."

"We thought about that, but again, we can have Hamptons luxury for free." Nic nodded.

"But Canada is Canada," Carmen added.

"Well, whatever you choose, I'm sure it will be perfect." Denise gave Carmen a peck on her cheek, causing Carmen to blush. Denise hated that her friend's main issue was financial. Nic wanted to be responsible, whereas the free spirit Carmen didn't want to look at numbers when it came to her life. Denise understood Nic's concerns. Even though she had money now, it was only a few years ago that she didn't have much at all. The three sat in silence. Denise closed her eyes. "Man, this is the life."

"What? Hollywood's not all it's cracked up to be?" Nic asked and glanced at Carmen, giving her a look that said "I told you so." Carmen rolled her eyes.

"Oh, it's everything you think, and then some. But this, this is living."

"Is something wrong?" Carmen instantly picked up on Denise's emotions.

"Nah. It's just . . . I miss this. Just being able to kick it without any fame shit, ya know. If I was in Atlanta right now, I wouldn't have homemade fried chicken and be chilling with my friends."

"What about Cooley?" Nic asked.

"What *about* Cooley? She's so busy, I hardly ever see her. That girl is focused. She hasn't even been able to go catch up with Sahara on tour yet."

"Damn." Nic shook her head.

"How are things with Farih?" Carmen asked. She could feel that Denise was leaving out important information.

"They're okay," Denise lied. She didn't want Carmen to worry. "I guess I'm just homesick."

Carmen let out a loud chuckle. "Not Miss I Can't Wait to Get the Fuck Out of Memphis."

Denise smiled. "Yeah, I know. But there were some good things about Memphis. My grandma Mema, you guys, school." Denise thought about Lena. "Those years at Freedom, even with the drama, were great."

They all thought about Denise's statement. Their lives had changed drastically since college. Denise was right: Their college years were full of ups and downs. Cooley and her share of crazy girlfriends, Carmen and her horrible taste in an ex-girlfriend, and Denise and her Lena love issues. Denise didn't realize then how many good times they had had because of the craziness. She missed playing basketball and kicking it in their dorm rooms. She missed going to the club, where she would turn down every girl who even attempted to get with her. She had been so focused on graduating that she had let the good times pass by without pausing to reflect. She didn't think about them then, but they were always on her mind now.

"Why don't we go on campus?" Carmen sat up. "Don't you know what weekend it is?" Carmen could tell by the lost look on their faces that she was the only one who actually had school spirit. "It's alumni weekend, jerks."

"Wow, it is the end of the year, isn't it?" Denise could not help but think about Lena. It was during alumni weekend that Lena revealed that she wanted to sleep with Denise, though moments before Brandon had asked her to marry him. "I'm down."

"Yea, and the Chi Thetas are coming out tonight, so that makes this even better. I'm sure they aren't expecting a real live Hollywood star to be at their probate."

"Hell, do I need to wear black and act like security?" Nic asked, joking with Denise about her fame.

Carmen jumped up to get dressed. She wouldn't miss a chance to wear her sorority letters.

"Hey, I need to stop by my school real quick. I left my iPod in my desk, and if I don't get it, I bet it won't be there tomorrow," Carmen said as she, Nic, and Denise drove to Freedom.

"It's probably gone by now," Nic joked.

The trio pulled into the teachers' parking lot at Carmen's school. They noticed Michael walking out of the building, wearing basketball shorts and a tee, covered in sweat. He waved as they got out of the car.

"Who is that?" Denise asked, wondering if she needed to stay in the car.

"That's Carmen's boyfriend." Nic smiled.

"Shut up. Hey, Mike," Carmen said as they walked up to each other. "What have you been doing?"

"Just decided to get a quick workout in at the gym before I left. What brings you back?"

"Left something in my desk. I'll be right back." Carmen skipped off, leaving the three together.

Michael looked at Denise. "Hey, aren't you . . ."

"This is Denise." Nic introduced the two.

"I remember you from the end of the year. I saw your movie. Very good."

"Thank you, man." Denise shook Michael's hand. "So you are the reason I have to wake up and work out tomorrow morning?"

"Guilty." Michael smiled. The new highlight of his morning was working out with Carmen. She had finally agreed to his 6:00 A.M. schedule. Seeing her in her spandex stiffened his manhood on a regular basis. "So you are joining us?"

"I haven't decided yet, but she wants me to."

The thought didn't sit well with Michael. He didn't want to share the little time he got with Carmen with the likes of anyone, not even a movie star.

"Well, I need to get going. Nic, Denise." Michael quickly disappeared.

Denise looked at Nic. Nic laughed. "I told you."

"Man, he does know she's gay, right?"

"When has that ever stopped a man?" Nic quipped. She and Denise leaned against their car as Carmen came running back to the vehicle.

"Carmen, what's with your dude? You know he's trying to fuck, right?" Denise joked.

"He's harmless. Just a friend."

Denise shook her head. "Friend, my ass. That man is in love with you."

"Told you." Nic patted Carmen on her ass.

"Come on, so a guy can't be friends with a lesbian without wanting to screw her?"

"Sure, but not that dude," Denise said as they got back in the car. "You better check that before it gets out of hand. Most men aren't going to spend this much time on a woman if they aren't getting anything in return. One day he might expect you to pay up."

"Like hell he will," Nic interjected.

"Okay, my two protectors. I'm good. Trust me. He's just a friend. I actually think he's dating someone." Carmen knew she was lying. Michael's flirtation gave her something to get her through the days with the kids, and she didn't want to give it up yet.

A warm feeling came over Denise as they drove past memorable campus spots. She saw the route she took on her morning runs. She couldn't help but feel a sense of pride when they passed the women's gym, where she broke school records as a ballplayer. They passed the University Center where Cooley was confronted by a scorned lover named Cynthia their junior year and where Carmen finally stood up for herself after her ex Tameka had broken her heart for the last time. Mixed emotions came over Denise when they passed the hall where her ex Rhonda changed her life.

As much as she wanted to hate Rhonda, she couldn't. Her ex was the reason for the complete change in her life. Their senior year, before Denise left for her new career on the New York Liberty, her ex went crazy. In a dorm room standoff Denise was stabbed while Rhonda attempted to attack Cooley. The injury and the bad press caused the Liberty to change their minds and drop Denise. With the help of her agent, Denise was able to book her first modeling job. Although the small scar would always be there, Rhonda's attack gave her a new career and a new outlook on life. But sometimes she couldn't help but wonder, *What if . . .*

"You okay?" Carmen had noticed the blank expression on Denise's face.

"Yeah, I'm cool. I was just thinking about our old crazy days."

"They were crazy." Carmen smiled.

Denise nodded and continued to look out the window.

They pulled in front of Jamerson Hall, the dormitory named after Lena's mother and where the Chi Theta coming-out would happen. Denise's whole body tensed. She saw the parking spot where Lena had parked the first time she'd ever laid eyes on her. She remembered walking with Cooley, staring at the beautiful stranger. Denise thought about walking in to their room for the first time to see Lena standing on a chair. She could see Lena's eyes when she caught her when she lost her balance on the chair.

A few years felt like a lifetime. Carmen and Denise snapped photos outside of their old dormitory. The three laughed about past times as they walked to the University Center. When Denise was in school, the only thing on her mind was getting out. Now that she was out, she missed the old walls and the safety inside them.

Carmen yelled her Chi Theta call and greeted tons of her sorority sisters as they arrived in front of the University Center. It took only a few moments for people to realize who Denise was. Soon she was smiling for flashing cameras and signing autographs. Nic made a joke about being security. Denise had to admit it felt good to be shown so much love in Memphis.

"I'd like a photo too."

Denise felt a tap on her shoulder and heard an oddly familiar voice. Denise's face lit up like a light bulb when she saw the familiar face. She couldn't believe her eyes as she stood in front of her was her old teammate Stephanie.

"Oh my God!" Denise didn't know if seeing Stephanie or seeing her standing up was the bigger surprise.

Denise threw her arms around Stephanie, holding her in a tight embrace. "I can't believe you are here!"

Stephanie wanted to burst when she saw Denise. The flame that was growing between them had died after she was injured in a hit-and-run. Stephanie never thought she would see Denise again.

"You can't believe I'm here, and I can't believe you are here."

"Denise Chambers!"

Denise's and Stephanie's heads turned. Michelle strolled toward them with her arms open. Together they had made Freedom's women's basketball dream team. The school hadn't gone to a championship since their departure.

Elated, Denise gave Michelle their typical guy dap before wrapping her arms around her. They play fought for a moment. Stephanie laughed, not taking her eyes off of Denise.

"I can't believe both of you are here." Denise was over the moon. It felt like college all over again, except for a few noticeable differences.

Stephanie, the girl who went from stud to femme their senior year, was now sporting a very tomboy pair of loose-fitting jeans and a Hollister fitted tee. Her hair was pulled back in a demure ponytail, with a pair of silver hoop earrings adding a bit of femininity. Stephanie had always reminded Denise of the late Aaliyah, on whom, like most lesbians, Denise had had a huge crush as a teenager.

Denise noticed that Michelle's look had evolved as well. She wasn't in sweats and a shirt two sizes too big anymore. Her jeans were loose but didn't hang off of her butt anymore. Her polo shirt had a Central High School crest engraved on it. She had also traded her usual short boy cut for locks, which, Denise could tell, she had just begun to grow.

Denise noticed how the two looked at her. She knew what they were thinking. Denise had long changed her look. The last time they were on campus, she had mostly rocked Freedom sweats and shirts, and had had her hair pulled back into a ponytail so it didn't get in her face. Ever since her first modeling gig, she had been sporting a tomboy look. Her jeans were fitted, and her button-down didn't hang off of her body, but clung to her in just the right places to show off the fact that she still had an amazing athletic body. Her hair hung down to her shoulders. She suddenly wished she had a ponytail holder.

"Yeah, right. You the one off making movies and shit," Michelle joked. "We never in a million years would have thought *you* would be here."

"Oh, whatever." Denise blushed in embarrassment. She wondered what her friends thought of the drastic career change.

"Only Denise would go off to New York to play ball and end up a damn movie star. Lucky muthafucka." Stephanie's smile still warmed Denise's heart.

"Trust me, it's not all it's made out to be." Denise thought about her looming relationship issues in Atlanta.

Michelle scanned the area around them. "Yo, tell me that fine-ass girlfriend of yours is here."

"No, she's in Atlanta." Denise noticed the shift in Stephanie's eyes.

"Oh, you should have brought her." Stephanie rubbed her hands together. "A Victoria's Secret model, Denise? Seriously? How the hell did you pull that off?"

Denise smiled. "I'm not really sure myself." Denise knew from the outside looking in that Farih was beyond a great catch. Denise snuck another peek at Stephanie. Even with her model girlfriend, Denise couldn't take her eyes off of Stephanie's natural beauty.

"Man, that sucks. I really, *really* wanted to meet her," Michelle whined.

"Yeah, hell no! So you can taint my image? So glad she didn't come now," Denise said. Michelle hit Denise on her arm, causing Denise to giggle.

Stephanie could feel Denise's eyes on her each time she gazed at her. "Whatever. You never did anything that we could use against you."

"I know, right?" Michelle interjected. "If you did, it would have been sold to the papers by now."

The three giggled like schoolkids. Their attention wasn't on the step show happening just like when they were in college. Denise could remember attending only one step show, and that was Carmen's, Lena's, and Misha's probate when they all crossed into Chi Theta Sorority.

"You know what we would be doing when this type of stuff was going on?" Denise watched the Kappas throwing their canes to each other, to the crowd's delight.

"In the damn gym." Michelle had a goofy grin on her face.

All three looked at each other with the same thought on their minds. Before the Kappas could finish, Denise had shot Carmen a text to let her know where she was going and they were running off in the opposite direction.

The ladies' gym was dark. They quickly fell back into the same motions. Denise headed to turn on the court lights, while Stephanie and Michelle headed to the equipment room. It didn't take them any time to pop the lock and grab two basketballs.

"Yo, Chambers. When was the last time you held one of these?" Michelle called, then tossed the ball in a hard chest pass. Denise caught the ball with both hands and tried to remember the last time she'd played ball. She thought about the days when she and Farih would play. Basketball was another thing they shared that had disappeared from their life over time.

Denise gripped the orange Spalding. She closed her eyes. It felt so natural in her hands. She opened her eyes and tossed the ball at the basket. The ball flew through the air like it was in a slow-motion segment in a TV commercial, and landed in the basket with a clean swoosh. Denise smiled. Michelle and Stephanie laughed and cheered.

"Maybe it hasn't been that long," Michelle joked as she picked the ball up. She looked at Stephanie, who was sitting on the bleachers. "How about you, ma'am?"

Even with a smile on her face, Denise could see right through Stephanie. Stephanie rubbed her bum leg. "I'll leave it up to you two."

"Nah." Denise walked over to Stephanie. She held her hand out as she looked into Stephanie's eyes. "Can't be the dream team without you."

Stephanie hesitated. A warm feeling consumed her body. She placed her right hand in Denise's hand. With Denise's help she stood up. Denise handed her the ball.

"I haven't played in almost five years," Stephanie confessed.

"No time like the present." Denise pointed at the basket. Stephanie threw the ball. The shot wasn't as clean as Denise's, as the ball circled the rim before going in. Stephanie yelled in excitement as Denise picked her up, spinning her around in the hug.

The three took turns taking shots. Michelle and Denise ragged on each other, trying to show off the various facial expressions they used to make during games. They took a much-needed break after Michelle's phone began to ring. She ran across the gym to take the private phone call from one of her girlfriends. Denise and Stephanie sat on the bleachers, laughing at Michelle's expense. Denise's and Stephanie's eyes met. Stephanie quickly shifted her glance, unable to stare into the eyes of the one that got away.

"So how are you, Steph, for real?" Denise glanced at her bum leg.

"Much better. You know, I really thought I would never walk again. But as you can see, that's not the case."

"I'm really happy to see it." Denise's guilty conscience started to bother her. She and Stephanie had been on their way to dating when the accident happened. She felt bad she hadn't kept in touch with her friends, especially Steph.

"Steph—"

Stephanie grabbed Denise's upper arm. "Don't do it." Stephanie looked right into Denise's eyes. "I know what you are going to say, and it's not needed."

"But I really should have kept in touch. I don't want you to think—"

"I didn't, Dee. Look at your life. I know you have been busy. By the way, I saw your movie. It was amazing." Stephanie smiled. "And besides, things aren't terrible for me. I have a job I love, writing about women's sports in Houston." Stephanie looked into Denise's brown eyes. "And I have a girlfriend."

Denise's eyes instantly widened. "That's wonderful, Steph. I'm really happy for you." She put her hand on top of Stephanie's hand. "Really happy."

Denise hoped she was a good actress, because she was putting on the performance of a century. She could tell by Stephanie's face that as much as she might be interested in Denise, she was actually happy with the Houston mystery person. Denise realized the two women she had feelings for didn't feel the same about her anymore.

Denise leaned back, resting on the bleachers. She wasn't a star with Stephanie and Michelle. She was back to what made her who she was and was surrounded by people who didn't care if she ever made another movie. It was calming, and she missed it.

"I really need for us to keep in touch. Seriously, I hate that we haven't been in touch in this long. I never want to lose this."

"Then don't, nigga." Michelle joined them with her usual humor. It quickly brought the room back to a light level.

"I'm in Atlanta now. You two have to come visit. For real," Denise urged.

"Shit, I'm there. Just tell me when." Michelle said and sat next to Stephanie.

"Me too." Stephanie squeezed Denise's hand. "Besides, you have to meet Lauren."

"And I have *got* to meet Farih and all her model friends." Michelle rubbed her hands together.

"So let's make a date. Atlanta soon." Denise extended her arm, with her fist balled. Stephanie smiled, placing her hand on top. It was their tradition before games. Michelle stood up. She shook her head as she smiled, placing her hand on top.

"Freedom on three." Denise led with her captain's call. The three did their old Freedom chant, ending with their hands in the air. They laughed at the nostalgic chant as they headed out of the gym.

Denise couldn't help but feel thankful for her life. Stephanie and Michelle had as much talent as she did, but they hadn't had the career outcome she'd had. Michelle had played overseas but had never made it to the WNBA, and now she was a high school math teacher and a coach. Stephanie had been headed to the pros when the accident ruined her chances. Now the closest she got to the game was writing about it. Denise knew her life was completely different. She wasn't playing ball, but she was doing something she enjoyed, which was all she wished for her friends as well. Her visit to Memphis had been long overdue.

Chapter 19

Lena walked into the lobby of the W. She had never been so excited for a date before. She headed to the familiar elevators. Her stomach jumped when she pressed the button. A flashback of the last time she was in the elevator hit her. She closed her eyes and took another long, deep breath. When she exhaled, a calming sensation spread through her body.

Danni opened the door while talking on the phone. She put her finger up to her mouth, alerting Lena to be quiet. It wasn't the greeting Lena had expected, but she followed the instructions, walking in quietly. Danni headed back to her office. Lena could hear her deep voice sternly telling someone that the price she'd given would be her final offer. Everything about Danni seemed to excite Lena. The idea that she wasn't some rich snob, but a serious businesswoman, gave her even more points in Lena's mind.

Lena wanted to make herself comfortable but opted to stand against the bar top. She poked her ass out, wanting her body to be the first thing Danni saw when she walked out of the office. She opened *Angry Birds* on her phone; she had become addicted to the silly game.

Danni ended her phone call, happy with the results. She walked out of her office and stopped dead in her tracks. Lena's tight pants were putting on a show for Danni. Her perky ass and thighs were calling Danni's name. Danni shook her head as she walked up behind Lena. Lena felt Danni's hands on her waist.

"*Angry Birds,* really?" Danni joked.

"It's so addictive." Lena turned around, finding herself face-to-face with Danni.

"Yeah, tell me about it. I play the *Angry Birds Seasons* one on every flight, when I should be reading." Danni planted her lips on Lena's forehead. "Sorry about that a minute ago. I had to finish up that call."

"I understand." Danni's cologne was making Lena's body heat up. She needed Danni to move before she became an inferno. Lena turned away.

"Is something wrong?" Danni noticed Lena's movement.

"No! I mean, no. I just . . . um . . . So what would you like to do today?" Lena didn't want to let Danni know what she was doing to her. She tried to keep a poker face.

"Well, since I'm leaving tomorrow, I was thinking, how about we just chill? Watch some movies, order some takeout or something?" Danni looked at Lena's amazing figure. "Or if you want to go out . . ."

"I think staying in sounds nice." Lena smiled.

"Good." Danni walked into the kitchen. She grabbed a bottle of wine from her wine chiller. "'Cause I'm not trying to go anywhere with you wearing those pants."

Lena looked down at her pants. "What's wrong with them?"

"Are you trying to have me fighting off every man in Atlanta?" Danni winked. Her phone rang. Danni pulled the iPhone out of her pocket. She rolled her eyes. "Yes, Mother?"

Suddenly Danni surprised Lena again. Out of nowhere a deep island accent emerged as Danni went back and forth with her mother. Lena could make out only certain words. She heard something about visiting and a promise.

Danni hung the phone up and looked at Lena, whose shocked face was priceless. "What?" Danni tried not to laugh.

"You tell me what." Lena couldn't stop grinning.

"Sorry. When I talk to my mother or grandmother, it just kind of comes out."

"Okay, what are you?" Lena questioned, causing Danni to laugh.

Danni held Lena's hand. "My dad is from New York, and my mother is Trinidadian."

"So you are from Trinidad?"

"Well . . ." Danni led Lena to the couch. They both sat down. "So that old money I was talking about is from my father's side. He is mixed, black and white. His mother is white, and his father was black. He met my mother at carnival while he was in college. To make a long story short, they hooked up in Trinidad, got busy, and she got pregnant. So I lived in Trinidad until I was ten, then moved to New York to live with my father and his family."

"Wow. Every day is a surprise with you." Lena loved it.

"And you haven't seen anything yet." Danni winked.

They spent the remainder of the day watching movies and enjoying each other's company. Lena felt at ease with Danni. She told her about Carmen and her upcoming marriage. She talked about her relationship with Brandon and how they were still good friends.

"So are you out, Lena?"

The question put Lena on the spot. "Well . . ." She sat up on the plush couch. "Not really." Lena knew the answer was no. Her mother had caught her with her ex Terrin, but Lena had assured her it as an experiment. When faced with the question again in front of her mother and father, Lena had opted to say no, she wasn't gay.

"It's cool. I just like to know what I'm dealing with." Danni rubbed Lena's leg, sensing how uncomfortable the question had made Lena.

Danni's touch soothed Lena.

"I don't want you to think I'm some type of closeted weirdo. I just honestly don't know what I am yet, so I didn't want to label myself as anything." The words even made Lena not want to date herself.

Danni smiled. "You're a newbie, aren't you?"

"Newbie?" Lena smiled. "I wouldn't say that. I've had experiences."

"Experiences." Danni laughed. "You make it sound like a science project. So how many *experiences* are we talking about?"

"Well, two. I fell for my college roommate, and that was the first girl I ever did anything with. But it didn't go far, as I was with Brandon. When I finally realized I wanted to be with her, she had moved on." Lena's voice trembled.

She hated thinking about the way she had treated Denise. She could understand why Denise would pick Farih over her. Lena cringed at the idea of all the missed opportunities she had had with Denise. Danni's eyes were burning a hole into the side of Lena's face. Lena fought to keep all her emotions inside. The last thing she wanted Danni to think was that she was still stuck on someone from her past.

"I dated one other girl after her. She was cool, but she wanted more than I wanted. Then I found out I was pregnant, so I moved back to Atlanta, and that was it."

"So at this moment, right now, do you like being with men more or women?" Danni said, never taking her eyes off of Lena.

"Honestly, I'm really not sure. I haven't dated since Bria, so I haven't really had to figure that out."

Danni nodded her head, taking in everything Lena was saying. "So what made you want to try now? I mean, you are sitting here in my living room, wearing jeans that are making it very hard for me to control myself. You had to do that for some reason."

Lena turned toward Danni. She studied every inch of her face. Danni's chocolate skin was flawless. "You." She gazed into Danni's eyes. "I don't really know what you are doing to me, but I find myself oddly attracted to you."

"Oddly?" Danni's eyes tilted.

"Not in a bad way. It's just I haven't felt anything like this since . . ." Denise's face entered Lena's mind. "Let's just say it's been a while."

A wicked smirk appeared on Danni's face. "Well, I'm glad that you are *oddly* attracted to me, because I'm very attracted to you." Danni's eyes were fixated on Lena.

Lena felt the sun rising between her legs. "Is that right?" Lena narrowed her eyes, giving Danni a sexy look.

"That is very right. I told you those jeans are making it very hard for me to behave myself." Danni inched closer to Lena. Her hand grazed the back of Lena's neck, causing every tiny hair to stand on end.

Danni took the cue. She slowly pulled Lena's head toward hers. Their lips instantly became familiar again. Danni sucked Lena's lips, the tip of her tongue dancing on Lena's. The sun was up, bright and hot.

With one hand Danni unbuttoned Lena's tight jeans. With ease her hand made its way down Lena's flat stomach to the heat coming from Lena's legs. Not wanting to tease, Lena waited as long as she could, then slowly parted her legs for Danni's hand.

"Mmmm." Danni's small moan let Lena know she was happy with the wetness she was greeted with in Lena's pants. Danni's index finger parted Lena's other lips. Lena's poker face was exposed for the fraud it was, as she wanted Danni, and there was no way to hide it anymore. Danni softly thumbed over Lena's swollen knob. Lena had never wanted sex so badly before. The drought was definitely over. Lena's wetness covered Danni's hand as she entered her, applying pressure to the floor of Lena's cave. Lena's body jerked from the sensation. Danni couldn't help but smile.

"Lena," Danni whispered in her ear. "Before we do anything, I think we need to talk about a few things."

Lena nodded her head, unable to speak. Whatever Danni wanted, she could have at that moment. She was willing to sign over her trust, just as long as Danni didn't stop doing whatever she was doing to her in that moment.

"I like you. I really like you. But I just want to make sure you know that I'm not looking for a relationship."

The statement caught Lena off guard. She opened her eyes to see Danni staring at her with a very serious look on her face.

"Um . . . okay." Lena didn't know what to say.

"I don't want you to think I'm just a fuck, because I'm not. But you know how busy my life is, and it wouldn't be fair to you if I didn't keep it a hundred with you."

Lena could feel the pressure slackening as Danni's hand began to retreat. Lena had to stop her: she didn't want that hand to leave her pussy for one moment. Lena wrapped her hand around Danni's wrist, causing Danni's hand to stay on her heat.

"Danni, I understand what you are saying. I'm cool with that. It's refreshing, actually. Most people try to wife me. Something strings-free sounds like music to my ears."

Danni bit her lip as her fingers continued to explore Lena. The erotic look was the sexiest thing Lena had ever seen. Lena's hand met the back of Danni's head. She pulled Danni's face to hers, taking control in the moment. Danni was pleasantly surprised. Their tongues made love as Danni's fingers worked their mojo on Lena's heat. Lena felt her body betraying her in the most pleasurable way. She began to tremble. She held her lips tightly together, biting her bottom lip, afraid of what might come out if she opened her mouth.

"No." Danni's index finger touched Lena's bottom lip. "I wanna hear you."

Danni kissed Lena as a falsetto moan came from Lena's mouth as her orgasm erupted on Danni's hand. Danni pulled her hand slowly out as Lena struggled to catch her breath. Danni licked the wetness from her index finger. She had expected Lena to taste good, but it was sensational. She had to have more.

Danni stood up. She pulled her black shirt over her head. Lena admired Danni's amazing physique. Her stomach was chiseled, with a sexy tribal band reaching from her belly button around her right side.

Danni didn't take her eyes off of Lena's while she pulled Lena's shirt over her head. Lena's black and silver push-up bra was a work of art in itself. The lace, with hints of Swarovski, made Lena's breasts look like she was fresh off the Victoria's Secret runway. Lena knew what she was doing when she purchased the Very

Sexy set at Victoria's Secret. Danni traced the lace with her fingertips, stopping only when she felt Lena's hard nipples protruding.

Danni released Lena's hair from the clamp holding it back. Her waves fell to each side of her face. Danni admired the beauty in front of her. She loved beautiful things, and she had come across a rare work of natural beauty, unaltered by injections or surgeries. She wanted to savor every moment.

Lena suddenly felt uneasy as Danni stared at her. "Is something wrong?" Insecurity set in.

Danni shook her head. "Chill, girl. Don't fuck up my moment." Danni stared like she was trying to remember every inch of Lena's body.

Lena's whole body felt like it was on fire. Danni held her hand out. Lena put her hand in Danni's. She stood up, and Danni led her to the bedroom.

Lena was more impressed by the bedroom than the living room. Two large brown platforms stacked on top of each other created steps to the massive platform bed. The two walked up the steps, light panels illuminating each step they took like they were in Michael Jackson's "Billie Jean" video.

Even with the amazing decor, Lena's mind was on one thing. She stood still as Danni walked around her, stopping at her backside. Lena waited, anticipating what would be next. Danni continued to admire Lena's body. She loved the way Lena's back curved. She traced the little ankh tattoo at the small of Lena's back.

"Nice." Danni was commenting on the ink. Lena couldn't help but think about Denise and the matching tattoos they shared. But even thoughts of Denise weren't stopping this moment. Lena's body needed sexual healing, and Danni was the doctor on call.

Lena could feel Danni's breath on the nape of her neck. Her touch sent chills through Lena's body. Danni's hands moved down Lena's sides until making it to her jeans. She slowly pulled the jeans down, and then Lena stepped out of them. Her lace panties matched the bra.

"Are you sure you want to go further?"

Lena answered by planting her lips on Danni's. Then Lena stretched out on the California king. Danni stood over her, looking like a female Adonis. Danni's hands picked up one of Lena's feet, and she kissed, sucked, and licked her way from the top of Lena's foot to her inner thigh.

Danni pulled the thin piece of lace down and off. The heat coming from Lena called her, and she was ready to answer. Danni's fingers circled Lena's clit. Out of all the sexy parts of Lena, Danni knew her favorite had to be her womanhood. Lena's Brazilian wax job left her soft and bare. Danni lowered herself between Lena's thighs.

Lena's mouth dropped as Danni's tongue forcefully took her by storm. Danni's figure eights were perfect on her throbbing clit. Lena felt a tingling growing in her toes. Danni lightly growled as her tongue sought refuge in Lena's cave.

Lena ground against Danni's tongue, hoping for it to go deeper. She got her wish. Danni's tongue fucked her, causing Lena's nectar to splash on her tongue. Danni moaned, tasting the sweetness. Out of all the women she had been with, she had never tasted anything so sweet. It made sense to her now why everyone wanted to wife Lena. Lena was holding magic between her thighs.

Lena felt the tingling intensifying from her toes through her legs. Her legs tensed up, causing her toes to curl. Her hands became entangled in Danni's locks, causing the ponytail holder holding them to break, letting them free.

Lena's body was being invaded by an unknown sensation. She was dying the most pleasurable death imaginable. She couldn't scream; no moans were left in her mouth. Danni's tongue was a beast. Lena's fists balled up, then relaxed, and her ass lifted as she shifted her position.

"No," said Danni. "Don't run." Danni's arms gripped Lena's ass, and she pulled Lena in closer, her tongue hitting the deepest depth.

Lena's body no longer belonged to her. Danni had claimed it, staking her property with every lick. Danni's fingers found their way into her, causing the tingling to turn into a sharp electric current.

"Danni! Shit." Obscenities flooded from Lena's mouth, only arousing Danni more, intensifying the moment. Lena's fists hit the bed. Over and over she hit the bed, as if she were in a wrestling match. She didn't think she could take any more.

Danni's growl let her know that it wasn't going to end. Danni was Lena's grim reaper, bringing the sweetest, most sensational death.

Lena died: her orgasm caused her body to jerk uncontrollably. A flood of Lena's sweetness filled Danni's mouth. Danni's senses became numb from the amazing taste. She had never tasted a woman like Lena before. She could live inside Lena. She knew nothing that amazing could be good for you. Lena's pussy was the type to render a man deaf, dumb, and blind. Danni stood up.

"Shit," Danni mumbled as she walked down off the platform, leaving Lena in her blissful state. Lena turned over, watching as the bathroom light illuminated the room. Lena could hear water running and was confused, as she was gearing up for the after-sex cuddle, but instead was alone in the large bed.

Danni made her way back into bed. She wrapped her arms around Lena and rubbed the goose bumps on Lena's arms until they disappeared.

"Um, is everything okay?" Lena's voice trembled.

Danni kissed her lips, soothing any uneasy feelings Lena had.

Danni sealed the night with a kiss on Lena's forehead, the ultimate closer.

Chapter 20

Cooley pulled her headphones off as the plane coasted into LAX. It had been over a month and a half, and Cooley's responsibilities had halted every planned trip to meet up with Sahara. She was in desperate need of some sexual healing, and she really was missing her woman.

Sahara's last two shows were in L.A., so Cooley figured that would be the perfect time to meet up. She decided the best way was to surprise Sahara. Cooley retrieved her rolling bag from the overhead bin and headed off the plane.

As soon as she turned her phone on, it began to blare. The demands of being the manager of two of the hottest new celebrities were starting to take their toll on Cooley. Her phone never stopped ringing. Her days consisted of nonstop meetings, phone calls, e-mails and outings. An opportunity to join forces with a firm out of New York was starting to sound better by the day.

Cooley took a limo to the venue where Sahara was performing and flashed her all-access pass at the back door. Cooley could hear Sahara's voice echoing through the halls. Cooley greeted various celebrities and their entourages, along with the men and women who worked hard to make the show a reality. Cooley quickly nodded, gave daps, and made phone gestures to those she planned on calling. She was in a rush to make it to Sahara's dressing room before Sahara got off the stage.

Cooley laughed and chatted with Linda, Sahara's on-the-road vocal coach and some of her staff. They watched on the television as Sahara finished her last song and took her final bow. They all dispersed to get into their places when Sahara came off the stage. Cooley had sworn them to secrecy about her arrival.

Cooley sat on the couch, facing the door. She heard Sahara's entourage making its way to the dressing room. She was excited to see her woman. The door opened, and Sahara walked in, talking to Tamera, one of her principal dancers. Then Tamera's face dropped when she saw Cooley. Confused by the look, Sahara turned to see Cooley grinning on the couch.

"Carla!"

Cooley found it funny that Sahara was in shock. Sahara couldn't move. She looked back at Tamera. Tamera forced a smile.

Sahara looked back at Cooley. "Oh my God, what are you doing here? I thought you weren't going to be able to make it." The expression on Sahara's face was price-less.

"It's called a surprise." Cooley stood up. She paused. Something didn't feel right.

"Well, I'll see you two later," Tamera called. Cooley looked at Tamera, who quickly averted her eyes. She walked out of the room.

Cooley and Sahara stood in silence for a moment before the door swung open. Sahara's hair and makeup artist quickly began to remove her stage clothes and makeup. Cooley sat back down on the couch.

The room was soon filled with Sahara's team. They all laughed and joked with Cooley and Sahara, filling Cooley's ears with stories from the road.

"NYC had to be the best," said Jahil, one of Sahara's dancers.

"Are you serious? Did you not hear the crowd in Orlando?" argued Jasmine, Sahara's background singer. "I could hardly hear myself sing."

"What we need is a Nicki and Sahara tour. Now, those tickets would sell like Justin Bieber's," Harrison, Sahara's main agent, said to Cooley. "I think we can make it happen."

"If anyone can, my baby can." Sahara beamed as she looked at Cooley.

Cooley smiled back.

The last of the crowd began to disperse as the tour buses filled. Cooley watched as the team packed up the last of Sahara's clothes. The whole tour was a finely tuned machine that worked like clockwork every night. Soon it was just Cooley and Sahara in the room.

"I don't care what any of them say. Tonight was the best. I love the last night of tours. That's when the crowd just seems to be the most hyped." Sahara checked her makeup in the mirror. She noticed Cooley staring at her. "Babe, I'm so happy you finally made it—"

"How many times?" Cooley asked with her eyes still fixated on her beautiful fiancée.

"I don't know. I think I did two encores, but they wanted more—"

"Sahara," Cooley said, cutting her off. "How many times?"

Sahara turned toward Cooley. "How many times what?"

"How many times have you slept with her?"

You could hear a pin drop in the room. Sahara's heart began to race. Cooley continued to stare, not taking her eyes off of Sahara's face.

"Cooley . . ." Sahara's hands began to tremble.

"I knew it, you know." Cooley sat back on the couch. Her calmness scared Sahara. "I knew it the moment she looked at me when she was leaving the room. So just tell me. How many times?"

If Cooley didn't know for sure, she knew now. Sahara's eyes filled with tears. She knew if she blinked, they would pour down her freshly powdered face.

"One time." Sahara lowered her head.

"When?" Cooley didn't move.

"A few nights ago." Sahara rushed over to Cooley. She fell to her knees and grabbed Cooley's hand. "Baby, it just happened. We were drunk, and I was missing you. One thing led to another, and it just happened. I told her it could never happen again."

Cooley turned her face away. She couldn't look at Sahara anymore. She felt like someone had taken a knife and cut her. Cooley wiggled her hand, trying to break free from Sahara's grip. "Let me go."

"No, Cooley, please!" Sahara cried. She held on to Cooley's hand with all her might.

"Let. Me. Go!" Cooley yanked her hand away from Sahara, causing Sahara to lose her balance and fall on her butt. Cooley stood up and walked out of the room without saying another word.

Cooley could hear Sahara crying her name, but she didn't care. She continued to walk until she made it to her car. She drove with no destination in mind.

The sun woke Lena up. She turned to find herself sleeping alone in Danni's bed. She sat up. It was noon. She had slept all morning. She tried to stand but almost lost her balance. She could feel the aftereffects of the night of sex.

The first round was amazing, but the late-night surprise session was an unexpected delight. Lena was awakened in the wee hours of the morning by Danni's tongue parting her lips. Before Lena could speak, she was back in ecstasy, Danni's figure eights fucking her into an erotic frenzy.

Danni's normal routine was already in motion. She had got out of bed slowly, not to wake Sleeping Beauty. She had made the mistake at looking back at Lena. Her naked body had looked enchanted with the amazing mood lighting in the room. Lena's hair had covered the goose-feather pillows. Even while she slept, Lena's pussy had called Danni's name. Lena's taste still lingered on her taste buds. Danni would be leaving in a few hours and wouldn't be able to taste it again. Work suddenly meant nothing to her. She knew she had to shake that feeling immediately.

Lena knew Jessica was going to kill her. She had let Danni sex her into a dumb stupor. She hadn't called to check on her daughter. Lena suddenly felt sad. She was losing two people today: her daughter was leaving with her parents, and Danni was going back to New York.

Lena walked into the living room to find Danni completely dressed in a pair of Jordan running pants and a matching shirt. To finish the look, she had on a pair of Jordan shoes that looked like they were fresh out of the box. Lena could hear music coming from Danni's headphones, which also seemed to match her outfit. Lena noticed the luggage sitting next to the couch.

Danni looked up to see Lena standing half dressed in front of her. She smiled, pulling the headphones off. Lena walked farther into the living room, picking her shirt up off the floor where Danni had removed it.

"So you're leaving?" Lena tried to hide her emotions.

"Yeah, in a few. I was wondering how long you were going to sleep." Danni chuckled.

"I'm sorry. I'm usually up at the crack of dawn. Blame yourself for my oversleeping."

"I'll take that." Danni stood up. She helped Lena put her shirt on.

"So when will you be back this way?" Lena ran her hands through her hair.

"Not sure, actually. I have a few deals to finish up in Miami, and then I am going to Trini to visit my mom."

"Oh." Lena couldn't hide her disappointment. "Well, just hit me up." Lena tried to turn, but Danni's hand pulled her close.

"Don't act like that."

"Act like what?" Lena pouted.

"Like that."

"Sorry. I'm not used to anyone doing what you did to me last night, then not knowing when I will be able to have it happen again." Lena smiled.

"Oh, so you are only using me for my body."

"And your lips and your mouth and your tongue . . ." Before Lena could finish her playful line, Danni's lips were against hers. The passionate kiss told Lena all she needed to know.

"Trust me. I won't be able to stay away from you for too long," Danni whispered in Lena's ear.

"I'm going to hold you to that." Lena finally forced herself to pull away. "Ugh, this is going to suck. You are leaving, and so is my daughter. Talk about boredom," Lena said as she put her shoes on.

Danni closed her computer. "Well, if you get too bored, give me a call. Maybe you can meet me somewhere."

Lena wanted to jump for joy, but she just smiled and nodded her head. "I might do that."

They said their final good-byes before Lena walked out the door. Lena pressed the button for the elevator. She turned when she heard Danni yell her name. She saw Danni rushing toward her. Lena dropped her bag as Danni wrapped her arms around Lena. They kissed passion into each other.

"I needed one more." Danni held Lena. Lena's lace panties were instantly soaked.

They parted once more, and as Lena made her way down to the lobby, she hoped that when the elevator doors opened, she'd find Danni standing there for more, but she didn't. Lena skipped out of the W, fully sexed, but craving more.

Chapter 21

Denise walked into her new Atlanta condo. The walls were still bare. Farih and Denise were still practically living out of boxes. Denise could hear Farih's stilettos clicking on their hardwood floor.

"Hey, baby." Farih smiled. Denise had to admit that Farih looked stunning. Her high-waisted, black, pin-striped pants hung off her slender frame. Her hair was pulled back into a perfect bun, which was the way most models wore their hair. "What do you think? With or without the hat?" Farih put a black floppy hat on her head. The whole ensemble gave her a classic, elegant look that was guaranteed to turn heads.

"You look stunning." Denise felt uneasy when Farih kissed her cheek.

Farih felt Denise tug at her arm when she tried to walk away. She turned to see a worried expression on Denise's face. "What's wrong, honey?"

"We need to talk." Denise sighed.

She knew the moment she saw her old teammates that she didn't want to be with Farih anymore. There was no denying it. She was no longer in love. She didn't know when they fell out of sync, but no matter how well they worked together, or how amazing the sex was, there was no denying it. Denise wasn't happy in her relationship.

Farih sat across from Denise at their new dining room table. She knew what was coming. Denise struggled to find the words. Farih's mind raced. How she could talk Denise out of it this time?

"You know we have been having some issues for a while."

"Denise, I know we *had* issues, but things have been amazing lately."

"Have they?" Denise looked at Farih. "Farih, it's like we're on two different paths. We haven't been on the same page for a long time."

"But we can get back." Farih was prepared to do anything necessary to stop the train wreck happening in front of them.

"I don't think we can."

"No!" Farih stood up. She was pissed. Denise was about to ruin not only their relationship but also everything she had been working so hard for. "I'm not going to let you do this."

"*Let* me?" Denise couldn't believe Farih's words.

"Four years, Denise. We are coming up on four years. You don't just throw that away because we've had some issues."

"Farih—"

"No, listen to me. I know we haven't been in sync. You think that doesn't happen in relationships?"

Denise sat and listened as Farih's stilettos clicked as she paced the floor.

Farih's African accent was pronounced. "You don't just do that. You don't get to do that."

"Farih, we've been trying for how long now?" Denise stood up.

"Where is this coming from?" Farih threw her hands up. "We haven't argued in God knows how long. And might I say, our sex has been outstanding."

"It's not always about sex."

"I'm not saying it is!" Farih had to catch herself before she exploded. She sighed. Farih walked closer to Denise. She held her hands. "Denise, this is me. You can't do this to me, to us."

The tears forming in Farih's eyes were breaking Denise down. She had expected Farih to scream, yell, and possibly throw things, but this was unexpected. Farih stood in front of her, begging her not to give up on them.

Denise stared into Farih's oval-shaped eyes. She was stunning, but was beauty enough to stay in a relationship? Denise's mind raced as she thought about all the things she would be giving up. She had a woman standing in front of her that loved her enough to beg her not to leave. Who would she have if she left? Denise thought about Lena.

Lena was always there, looming in the background. Denise still couldn't shake the feelings she had for Lena. But even though Brandon wasn't a factor, there were other things that could keep them apart. Lena was young and still didn't know if she preferred women or men. Not to mention that she had a baby now, which could be a recipe for disaster. Lena had turned away from Denise on more than one occasion, so who was to say it wouldn't happen again?

"Is it someone else?" Farih's voice lowered.

The question caused Denise's heart to skip a beat. "No. I just . . . Farih, I'm just not happy."

Denise's statement broke Farih's heart. It would have been easy to process Denise leaving her because of another woman, but to know she wanted to leave just because Farih wasn't making her happy hurt more than she could imagine. "Denise, please, whatever I'm doing wrong, just tell me."

"You aren't doing anything wrong. You just want things I'm not interested in." Denise sat on the couch arm.

"Like what?"

"This." Denise threw her hands up, waving them at the lavish condo. "You want to be Hollywood. I don't."

Farih sighed. "Denise, whether you want to believe this or not, you *are* Hollywood. Hell, you're more Hollywood than me. You are an actress, for goodness' sakes."

"Yeah, but I don't want to live the Hollywood life. Farih, I would have been happy in a small crib. You had to have this oversize place."

"So it's because I want us to have nice things? This place is just as nice as our place in SoHo."

"It's not just the apartment, Farih." Denise walked into the kitchen.

Farih followed, kicking her shoes off.

Denise turned toward Farih. "Remember when we first were dating and we used to go play ball at the community center? I was so impressed by you and your basketball skills. That was fun."

"I loved it too, but we both have busy schedules."

"And remember how we used to just order in and spend the night watching movies?" Denise held Farih's hands. "I miss that about us. Now it's all about going out and being seen."

Farih wanted to hit herself. She realized it was all her fault. She had forgotten the type of person she was with. Denise wasn't the type who liked publicity, which posed a problem. Farih loved the fame she was gaining, and being seen was only helping her to grow.

Farih dropped her head. "Denise, please. I'm begging you. Don't give up on us so easily." She raised her head.

Tears ran down her cheeks, creating streaks in her perfect makeup. "I love you, and I'm so sorry. I realize now that while I was just trying to make us both become the superstars we deserve to be, the way I was going about it wasn't the right way. I can change. I will change. Just don't give up on what we have built together."

Denise could feel Farih's hands trembling as she held on to Denise. Denise's plan unraveled in front of her. She knew Farih was right. Denise thought about her grandmother Mema, who had always told her that relationships took understanding, communication, and hard work. Denise realized she wasn't following her grandmother's advice, which was not like her.

Tears continued to flow down Farih's face. Denise couldn't take it anymore. She inhaled. "Come here." Denise pulled Farih close.

Farih wrapped her arms around Denise and held on for dear life. She knew she had won the battle, but she had a feeling the real war was still to come.

Carmen walked into her guest bedroom. She wanted to turn the light on but didn't want Cooley to rip her a new one for doing so. The only light in the room came from the sides of the bamboo window blinds, which Cooley had closed as tight as she could. Cooley sat with her headphones on, staring at her computer screen. Carmen put her hand on Cooley's shoulder. Cooley looked at her worried friend and took off one of the earpieces of the headphones.

"Are you hungry, Carla?" Carmen asked as she placed a bottle of Simply Orange on the nightstand.

"Nah."

"Are you sure? You haven't eaten anything since you got here."

"I said no," Cooley snapped. She sighed. "I'm sorry, C, but no, I'm not hungry."

Carmen took the cue and headed out of the room.

Cooley had left the theater in L.A., driven straight to the airport, and taken the first flight back to Atlanta. She didn't sleep on the flight. She couldn't seem to close her eyes and not think of what had just happened. She had turned her cell phone on when the flight attendant made the announcement that it was okay to do so, and had been met by the instant ringing of missed calls and text messages. She'd looked down to see Sahara's face and cut her phone back off.

Walking through the Atlanta airport, she'd realized she would have to face Sahara. She knew Sahara had probably caught a flight back since the tour was over. She probably would be at their place within a few hours. Anger set in; Cooley wasn't ready to see her. She had to get out of Atlanta, and there was only one place she could think of.

Carmen thought she was dreaming when she received the phone call from Cooley asking her to pick her up from the Memphis airport. Before she could question why, Cooley said, "Can you pick me up or not? And don't tell anyone." Worry had set in when Carmen saw Cooley sitting on the concrete bench outside the airport terminal. Carmen had never seen Cooley look the way she did. She stared at the ground like she was in her own world. Her face was pale, and she looked like she hadn't slept in days. Carmen did the best friend thing: she honked her horn and smiled. Cooley looked up at Carmen, walked to the car, and threw her bag in the backseat. Before Carmen could say anything, Cooley had her headphones on and had closed her eyes.

Cooley hadn't turned her phone on in two days. Carmen and Nic both worried as she made their guest room her own little dungeon. Cooley didn't talk about what was going on. Carmen was beyond worried. Cooley gave strict instructions not to tell Sahara where she was. Carmen could tell after first frantic call from Sahara that it obviously had something to do with their relationship, but she knew better than to pry. Cooley would open up when she was ready to.

Denise and Farih arrived three hours later. Carmen loved that Denise was in Atlanta now because there was always a seat available from Atlanta to Memphis on AirTran flights. Farih had decided to come with Denise. She wanted to show her support for her girlfriend and wondered what was bringing her back to Memphis just a few days after she made it back to Atlanta.

"What's going on?" Denise whispered.

"I have no idea," Carmen said as she and Nic walked outside with Denise and Farih. Carmen closed the front door. "She won't talk to me or Nic. She hasn't left her room. Sahara has called a few times. I could tell by her voice something has happened with them."

"Man, Dee, she looks bad. She just does work and listens to music. She hasn't eaten since she got here, and that was two days ago." Nic added.

"All right." Denise opened the front door and headed to the guest bedroom.

Denise turned the light on, causing Cooley to yell. Cooley took off her headphones and turned to see her best friend standing in the doorway.

"I swear, Carmen can't listen for shit." Cooley put her headphones back on. Denise quickly snatched them off her ears, causing Cooley to growl.

"Look, I'm not going to ask you anything. I'm just gonna tell you to get ya ass up. We're going for a walk." Denise's straight-faced expression let Cooley know she wasn't taking no for an answer.

Cooley and Denise walked in silence. The Mississippi River was calming. Denise followed as Cooley walked down the large white rocks on the bank of the Mississippi. Cooley picked up a small rock.

"Sahara cheated on me." Cooley chucked the rock into the muddy water.

Denise was shocked. She watched Cooley's face; it was devoid of emotion. Cooley stood staring at the water.

"When did this happen?"

"On tour. She said it was one time, by mistake. Right." Cooley threw another rock into the water.

Denise walked closer to her friend. She had never seen Cooley this way and was at a loss as to what to do or say. She stood next to her. Various phrases ran through her head, but they all sounded corny for this situation.

"Okay, so what are you going to do about it?" Denise felt the direct approach was best.

Cooley shrugged her shoulders. "I haven't figured that much out yet."

"Well, the torture approach you're taking right now can't go on for forever. You have to face it sometime."

"I know." Cooley turned around. "I just needed some time to figure out my feelings right now." She began to walk back up the rocks, and Denise followed.

"I remember that time when Lena was all pissed about Brandon, and I told her fucking isn't the same thing as cheating." Cooley stopped. She turned back around toward Denise. "It's like a piece of me feels that way now, but another piece is telling me she was dead wrong. This emotional shit is for the birds." Cooley started to walk again.

"Yeah, but at the same time it feels so good to have someone that loves you in your corner." Denise put her hand on Cooley's shoulder. "I know what she did was fucked up, but think about it. Sahara has accepted you from day one for who you are. It's not like you haven't had your share of indiscretions. Even when you tried to push her away, she was still there." Denise thought about her situation with Farih.

Cooley couldn't argue with Denise. She knew that she was right. No matter what the situation, Sahara had been there for her. Sahara had accepted Cooley with all her flaws, and so maybe she did deserve a pass.

"You know, the only completely functional and long-lasting relationship in my life has been with yo' ass." Cooley laughed. It was the first time she'd felt like laughing in two days.

Denise smiled. "Talk about opposites attracting." They both laughed.

Carmen jumped off of her couch when she heard the front door open. Denise and Cooley walked in, still laughing about their bromance.

"Carla?"

"I'm cool, C." Cooley hugged her worried friend. "I'm gonna get my shit together and head out."

"Why the rush? I mean, how often do I get my two favorite people in my apartment at the same time? Let's go out and get something to eat or something." Carmen bounced around in anticipation. Cooley knew she wouldn't take no for an answer.

Cooley walked back into Carmen's guest room. Her phone was buzzing. She picked it up.

Please don't do this.

Cooley stared at the text message. She pressed DE-LETE. She knew she had to deal with it, but now wasn't the time.

***

Lena tried to hold back her tears, but the river began to flow. She hugged her daughter for dear life as they stood in front of the airport security. She knew it was going to be hard, but she didn't expect it to be this hard. Bria's grip loosened.

"Why are you crying, Mommy?" Bria's eyes watered.

Lena knew she didn't need to make Bria panic. "Mommy's just really happy that you are going to get to spend time with Yaya and Papi in some really beautiful places."

"I get to go on an airplane!" Bria's excitement helped Lena relax.

She knew her daughter was in excellent hands. Jessica had jumped at the opportunity to go on a two-month paid vacation to some places she had only dreamed about.

"Don't worry, honey. We will check in daily." Karen hugged her worried daughter. "If you want to join us at any time, feel free."

Lena hugged her mother and father. She gave her daughter another long hug and kiss. She stood frozen as they walked through security. She knew she couldn't break down until she made it back to her car.

Lena couldn't crank the car. She sat in the parking lot of the airport, watching as the flights took off. She knew it was too early to be one of their flights, but she couldn't help but think about her daughter being on a plane without her.

Lena's blaring phone snapped her back into the real world. She pressed her Bluetooth button.

"Are you a blubbering mess yet?"

The sound of Danni's deep voice was soothing to Lena.

"Not completely, but close."

Danni stood on her terrace. "Well, I just wanted to call and check on you. Where are you now?"

"Sitting in the airport parking lot, trying not to run inside and buy a ticket to go with her." Lena fixed her makeup in her mirror.

Danni stared out at the ocean. "Well, I think the 'buying a ticket' thing sounds pretty good." She smiled.

"No, I promised I wouldn't visit for at least a few weeks." Lena cranked her car.

"I was thinking more about a flight to Miami." Danni walked back into her room.

Lena smiled. "Miami? Why on earth would I want to go to Miami?"

Danni sat on the red chair in the lavish hotel room. "You want the PC answer or the truth?"

"Both . . ."

"Well . . ." Danni leaned back. "PC. I want to see you on this beach with me."

Butterflies flapped their wings in Lena's stomach. "And the truth?"

Danni smiled. "I want to eat your pussy."

Lena felt the flood coming. "Crude, aren't we?"

"I didn't say the truth would be pretty. But it's the truth."

"I'll check flights."

"There's one in an hour and a half. Go get your ticket. See you soon." Danni hung the phone up without giving Lena the chance to answer.

Lena couldn't stop grinning. The snappy crab in her wanted to drive off and show Danni she didn't have it like that, but the hopelessly romantic Cancer was eating it up. The dominance of Danni was driving Lena's hormones crazy. She put the car in drive.

It's just a little crush. Nothing more.

Lena repeated that over and over in her head as she parked in long-term parking and headed back into the airport. It was time for her vacation to begin, and being in Miami, with Danni's head in between her legs, was a great way to start.

Chapter 22

Cooley placed the key into the door lock. She couldn't hear anything coming from inside. She wondered if Sahara had been back to their home. Her stomach turned as she noticed the tattoo on her hand. She felt anger boiling inside of her.

Cooley knew Denise was right. After all, even though they had been together four years, only about a year and a half was Cooley and Sahara only. Sahara knew the woman she was dealing with. Sahara didn't trip when she caught groupies trying to get the best of Cooley. Cooley recalled a day when she came home to find a groupie lying naked in their bed.

"If new pussy is what you need, then there ya go. Just don't do the shit behind my back," Sahara had said and had handed Cooley her strap-on. Sahara had watched Cooley fuck the girl with her strap. The groupie's pussy did nothing for Cooley. She couldn't take her eyes off of Sahara, who was staring directly at her with an expressionless face. Cooley left the girl mid-orgasm and walked over to her girlfriend. She took her strap off, led Sahara to their guest room, and made love to her all night long.

After that experience Cooley's need for various women seemed to disappear. Cooley had completely given up her player ways for Sahara, the woman of her dreams. Now her dream was shattered.

Cooley walked into the house. All the lights were out. She let out a sigh of relief. She didn't have to deal with the situation right away.

"You're back."

Cooley turned to see Sahara standing in the bedroom doorway. She was a wreck. Her normally polished hair was pulled back into a messy ponytail that looked like it hadn't been combed in days. Her sexy attire had been replaced with a pair of Cooley's sweatpants and a baggy shirt.

"I didn't think you would be here." Cooley dropped her keys on the coffee table and walked past Sahara. Sahara followed her into the kitchen.

"Where else would I be?" Sahara's voice trembled. "I've been worried sick."

"Have you?" Cooley's nonchalant tone cut Sahara.

Sahara knew she was defeated. "I know I deserve that. Baby, please, can we talk about it?"

Cooley opened an individual bottle of Simply Orange juice. She drank until the bottle was empty. She wiped her mouth, taking as much time as she wanted.

"Nah, I really don't feel like talking." Cooley brushed past Sahara, leaving her hurt and confused. Cooley grabbed her laptop, headed to her home office, and closed the door. Sahara sat on the couch and sobbed.

Misha gave a sigh of relief. It had taken two hours, but she'd finally got all her financial aid and scholarship applications completed and turned in at the school. Instead of law school she had opted for an easier course of study. She'd decided to take the same route as Carmen and get certified to teach. She had no ambition of being a teacher, but she knew it was a step toward a better position in administration.

"Admissions lady."

Misha turned to see the cute stud from the other week. She smiled as the cutie walked closer.

"I thought that was you."

Misha nodded. "Yes, it's me."

The stud smiled. "I was hoping I would run into you again, since you ran off so fast last time."

"Were you, now?" Misha noticed the girl's attire. From her appearance, Misha knew the girl couldn't be more than nineteen. You didn't see very many older lesbians still rocking oversize clothes to show off their masculine side, even if they were studs.

"Yeah, I was. I mean, why wouldn't I? Look at you."

Misha couldn't believe the younger woman was really flirting with her. "How old are you, honey?"

"Eighteen."

"Lord." Misha shook her head. "You are too cute, but, baby, you are way too young for me."

The stud took two steps back. "Age ain't nothing but a number. I like older women."

Misha paused. She had never considered herself an older woman. She suddenly felt silly for even talking to the girl. Even with her urges to dabble with women again, she didn't want it to be with a baby gay.

"I'm flattered, but I really have to go. I have to pick up my son."

"Oh, for real? I love kids."

"Yeah, my husband and I are pretty fond of him also." Misha watched the stud's demeanor completely change. She walked off, leaving the girl baffled.

Cooley had never been so productive. Punishing Sahara helped her get caught up on her work. Even though she was pissed at Sahara, she was able to book her for a few appearances, along with getting Denise completely squared away with the *Fast and Furious* movie. She heard the television on in the living room. It was now or never. Cooley walked out of the office in complete manager mode.

"So I got you booked on Jimmy Fallon finally. It's next week, and Diddy wants you to be on some song, so you can do that while you are up there."

Sahara stared at her. She wanted to scream, but she knew it wouldn't help the situation.

Cooley sat down on her favorite recliner chair. She glanced at Sahara, whose glazed look told her she couldn't care less about any bookings.

Cooley inhaled and exhaled. "Look, I don't really want to talk about it, but I guess we need to."

"Baby, I'm sorr—" Sahara's cries were quickly cut off.

"Don't give me the 'I'm sorry' shit. We are supposed to be better than that." Cooley's straight face caused Sahara to sit up.

"All right. Well then, what is the deal?" Sahara's tone changed. "Do you want me to leave or something?"

"Chill out, girl." Cooley could feel her blood boiling. She held her emotions together. "You fucked a bitch. Okay . . . shit happens."

"What?" Sahara was confused.

"You think I give a fuck about you fucking some broad?"

"Then what is it, Carla? What made you stay gone for three damn days, not returning any of my calls?" Tears rolled down Sahara's face.

"You lied about the shit." Cooley's words ripped through her teeth. "I talked to you every fucking day, and at no time did you feel the need to tell me you fucked another bitch!"

"I'm sorry, Carla! Please, God, you don't know how bad I wanted to tell you. I was scared. I had fucked up, and I didn't know what to do, or how to tell you." Tears rolled like the Nile down Sahara's face.

"Well, you should have tried." Cooley couldn't take it. She grabbed her keys.

"Where are you going now?" Sahara cried.

"Out!" Cooley slammed the door.

Cooley sat on a bench, watching tons of children and tourists run through the shooting water fountains in Centennial Olympic Park. She watched their happy faces, heard their laughter while they played in the water. She wished her life could be that simple and happy.

She didn't have her phone, so she didn't know if Sahara was blowing her up. She was conflicted. Half of her wanted to hold Sahara and tell her everything would be all right, while the other half wanted to tell her to go fuck herself. All logic seemed to fly out the window as soon as she was standing in front of Sahara.

"Cooley?"

Cooley wanted to scream. She hadn't expected Sahara to follow her. The last thing they needed was a stampede of fans.

"You shouldn't be out here. . . ." Cooley turned around and froze. A familiar face stood in front of her, but it was not Sahara.

"I thought that was you." Misha smiled. "I almost thought I was dreaming. I mean, what in the world would Carla Wade be doing at Centennial Olympic Park?" Misha walked closer.

Cooley scooted over so Misha could sit next to her.

Misha's body had frozen when she saw Cooley sitting on the bench. Out of all the people to run into, it would be the one woman who could completely derail her plans for steering clear of temptation. Even in plain clothes Cooley oozed sex appeal. It was like the snake was dangling the ultimate apple in front of her face, and she really wanted to take a bite. Misha looked at her attire. She was in Mommy mode, jeans, and had no idea how to make jeans and a tee look sexy.

"What are you doing here?" Cooley watched as Misha put down a large brown bag. Her hair fell to her shoulders, a headband pulling it off of her face. Cooley loved when Misha dressed up, but she had always admired her natural beauty.

Misha pointed at Jaylin, who was running through the water.

"Wow, is that . . ."

"That's my boy, Jaylin. He's been exceptionally good lately, so I decided to bring him to the aquarium." Misha smiled.

"He's beautiful."

"Thank you."

Misha's and Cooley's eyes met briefly. Misha hadn't known what to expect when she saw Cooley. She'd thought about grabbing Jaylin and running to the car, but she knew this could be the test she needed. If she could control her feelings around Cooley, she could control her urges for women altogether. She noticed the puffiness of Cooley's eyes.

"Umm, is everything okay?"

Cooley looked at Misha. "Yeah, of course."

"Yeah, right. Come on, Carla. Who are you talking to? What's going on?"

Cooley turned her head. In that instant Misha wasn't just the ex; she was the friend she used to confide in.

"Sahara did something that . . . Well, she fucked up." Cooley could feel her hard wall building.

"Was it that bad?"

"She cheated."

"Oh." Misha surprised herself. She didn't want to jump up and down or call Sahara names. She noticed Cooley's pained expression. She was hurting, and hurting bad. It would be in bad taste to take advantage of the moment. And regardless of anything, she loved Cooley as a friend and didn't want to see her hurting. She put her hand on Cooley's knee. "I'm sorry to hear that."

The single touch was calming to Cooley. She turned her body toward Misha.

"It's like I'm starting to really think I should have followed my original mind. Relationships are for the fucking birds."

"Oh God, are you really going there?" Misha rolled her eyes. "Let me guess. When you leave here, you are gonna find some random piece of ass to fuck."

Cooley was speechless. She knew the thought had passed through her mind. What better way to get back at Sahara than with an indiscretion of her own? She hated that Misha had read her on it. She knew why: after their first breakup Cooley retaliated by having a threesome with two coeds. Suddenly the idea didn't seem so good anymore.

"It's not like that."

"Really?" Misha didn't take her eyes off Cooley.

Cooley averted her eyes. She knew she had to be crazy, but she felt some heat coming from Misha.

Misha shifted her body. She couldn't help but be attracted to Cooley. A flashback entered her mind of Cooley's tongue pleasing her. Misha shook her head, trying to get the flashback to cease.

"Look, I can't speak about you and Sahara, because I don't know anything about your relationship. What I can speak about is what I know about you. When things don't go your way, you have a tendency to make some really bad decisions, vindictive ass."

Cooley huffed. "Well, I am who I am."

"No, you are who you want to be. Look at you right now. You are sitting on this bench because you know deep down you don't want to go screw some random broad. You have grown out of that stage in your life."

Cooley sighed. She put her arm on the back of the bench, grazing Misha's back in the process. The slight touch sent chills through Misha's body. Cooley noticed the reaction. "Are you okay, Mish?"

Misha sat up. "Yeah, I'm good. I'm just more worried about you." She shifted again; she could feel the moisture forming between her legs.

They sat quietly and watched Jaylin play in the water. Cooley thought about the day that she found out about Patrick.

"You know what, Mish? I just feel like I'm losing myself. Here I am, working my ass off for her. I gave it all up, everything about myself, to be with her, and she cheats on me. I don't know how I can forgive that."

"Carla, you didn't give up anything for her. You just changed. We all have to make changes for love." Misha thought about all she had given up for her relationship.

"And you know what the crazy thing is? I don't really give a damn that she fucked the bitch. I'm more pissed that she didn't tell me first."

"So would you have been okay with it if she had told you?"

Cooley thought about the question. Early in their relationship she knew the answer would have been yes. But now she was committed, and the thought of any other person touching Sahara made her blood boil. "I don't know."

"I think you do. Goodness, Carla, what happened to the chick who believed that fuckin' isn't cheating? You know, I used to think you were crazy for some of the things you thought, but nowadays, I think you were on to something."

Cooley's eyes shifted. "Oh, wait a minute. Is Mrs. Whatever the Fuck His Last Name Is cheating on her little husband?"

"Let's just say that lately I've been thinking about the things I've given up to be Susie Homemaker, and I'm starting to wonder if it was worth it." Misha stared out at Jaylin, who was having a ball in the water. Cooley could see the concern in her eyes.

"Misha, I think you make an excellent mother."

"Yeah, but what about all the things I wanted? I wanted to be a hotshot entertainment lawyer. Now my life consists of playdates and coupons."

"So why don't you go back to school? If you want to be a lawyer, go be a lawyer." Cooley nudged Misha.

"I actually put in my application to go back to get certified as a teacher today." Misha beamed with pride. "But regardless of how much I do in school, I'll never be able to do the things I dreamed of. I dreamed of industry parties and private planes whisking me off to exotic destinations. That can't happen with my son and husband. Hell, you're living the life I dreamed of, that we dreamed of."

Cooley placed her hand on Misha's knee. "Misha, for real, it's not all that it's cracked up to be. You are doing the biggest job of all. Raising a child is hard shit. I know I couldn't do it."

"But look at what all you get to do. You, Dee, y'all are living the dream."

"The dream that ends with your girlfriend cheating on you with a background dancer. . . . That's some dream."

The two sat in silence. Cooley put her arm on the back of the bench. The past flooded through her mind. She remembered the life they used to have. Misha was her first love, but Sahara held her heart more than Misha ever had.

"I am starting to wonder if I'm cursed." The statement made Misha looked back at Cooley. Cooley stared at the dancing water. "I have fucked over so many women in my past that the only two that I've ever cared about have both cheated on me. Maybe it's karma's way of dealing with me."

Guilt overcame Misha. "Carla, I know what happened between us was, well, fucked up on my part. I never expected my life to take the turn it did, but in the end I think that all things happen for a reason. Maybe Patrick coming back into my life happened to help you in the end. After all, before there was ever a Misha and Cooley, there was a Sahara and Cooley."

It pained Misha to admit it, but Sahara was the one for Cooley. Suddenly she didn't feel the urge to jump on top of Cooley anymore. She missed the times they had spent together, the whole crew. Even spending time with Carmen and Lena wasn't the same. It always felt like something was missing.

Cooley thought back to the day that she met Sahara. It was the night she spent with Sahara years ago that had opened her closed heart to the possibility of a relationship. Misha just so happened to gain the rewards of the seeds planted by Sahara.

"I really do miss you, Mish. I miss having you in my life. Even with the bullshit, you always kept it real with me. Well, except for the whole 'falling for the dude' shit." Cooley laughed.

"Yeah, well . . . *que sera, sera*." Misha nudged Cooley with her shoulder. "Cooley, forgive her. It was a mistake, and I'm sure she regrets it. How could she not?" Misha smiled.

Cooley suddenly felt better about the whole situation. "I hear ya. And you consider doing something you want to do. You gotta be happy in your life, Mish. You deserve that, even if it is with a *man*." Cooley kissed Misha on her cheek and stood up. Before she walked away, a thought caused her to turn around. "Yo, Mish. Can I ask you one more thing?"

Misha nodded her head.

"Last month at the club, why did you skip out like you did?"

Misha thought about the last time she saw Cooley. "Temporary moment of insanity."

Cooley tipped her head at Misha's vague answer. She knew exactly what it meant. Misha's heart was with her husband, and if she did slip up with a girl, it would be just a physical thing—no love, just sex. Cooley knew in that moment that Misha was right. Sahara's heart belonged to Cooley, and it was time for Cooley to claim it as her own.

Cooley's could sense the uneasy feeling brewing as she opened the door to their home. She walked in to see Sahara sleeping on the couch. Cooley hovered over Sahara's sleeping face. She didn't look peaceful and beautiful, like she usually looked when she slept. Instead, Sahara looked like she had been through hell and back. Cooley knew that was her fault.

Thoughts of Sahara sleeping with another woman entered her mind again. She shook her head, hoping to shake the thoughts out as well. She knew she had to forgive Sahara, even if her heart hadn't caught up to her brain. She kissed Sahara on her forehead, causing her to jump.

"Carla . . ." A single tear fell from Sahara's eye. Cooley wiped the tear and put her arms around Sahara as Sahara's arms wrapped around Cooley's neck. Cooley picked her crying girlfriend up and carried her to the bedroom. She slowly sat her on the unmade bed.

"Don't cry. We will be all right." Cooley pulled the comforter over Sahara's body.

"Promise?"

"Always." Cooley kissed Sahara on her forehead, giving Sahara the first piece of relief since L.A. "Get some sleep." Cooley turned the light off. Cooley knew she had to keep remembering that it was just sex, nothing more. Now, only if her heart would understand as well.

Chapter 23

Sweat dripped down Carmen's arms. She was sweating from everywhere. Her body felt like it was about to completely give up on her. She couldn't take another step. She sat down on the bleachers. Michael turned around when he didn't hear Carmen's grunts and groans behind him.

"No! Up!" Michael ran back down the steps. He pushed her back. "Come on, only a few more to go."

"I can't." Carmen fought to catch her breath. "I quit."

"No quitting. Get up, Carmen."

Carmen lay down on the bleachers. "You keep going. I'll be right here when you finish." Carmen pulled her shirt up to wipe the sweat from her face. Michael admired her stomach and her jeweled belly button ring. He felt his manhood rising. He sat down next to her.

"Fine. I'll let you give up this one time. It is really hot out here."

"See, you're trying to kill me. I need water, but I can't move down the steps."

"Awww, let me help." Michael picked up one of Carmen's legs. He began to massage her thigh. "This should loosen you up a bit, make it a bit easier to walk."

Carmen felt his strong hands deep massaging her leg. She felt the familiar twinge in her stomach. She sat up, pulling her leg away from him.

"Thanks, but I think I'll be okay in a minute."

Michael smiled. He knew again he was having an effect on her. They sat silently for a moment, neither wanting to make the first sound. Michael couldn't help it. He was crazy about her. It took everything in him not to confess his feelings every time they spent time together. He knew time was running out: he needed either to make his move or let it go.

Carmen stood up. "As much as I hate you for making my body ache, I have to admit my clothes are fitting a lot better even in this short amount of time. I might just keep this up after the wedding—"

Before she could finish, Michael grabbed her, pressing his lips against hers.

Carmen didn't know what to do. She was frozen. She wanted her body to respond, but she couldn't move. She was screaming inside, but she couldn't get the words out due to the fact that his lips were against hers. She mustered up all her strength and pulled away.

"Michael!"

"I'm sorry, Carmen, but I couldn't hide it anymore. I know you got your situation, but damn it, I'm crazy about you. Can't you see that?"

"Oh my God." Carmen didn't say anything else. She began to walk down the bleachers. She wished she could run, but her body hurt so bad, she might have fallen to her death if she tried. She could hear him calling her name. She wanted to move faster, but he quickly caught up to her. He grabbed her arm. Carmen pulled away.

"Carmen, tell me you don't feel anything for me."

"Michael, it's not like that between us." Carmen knew she had evaded the issue. Truth was, she had developed a man crush, but it was nothing she actually wanted to act on.

"That's not true. Tell me you don't feel anything."

"Sure I do. I have a crush. The same type of crush I have on Bruno Mars, Ginuwine, and Robert Pattinson. Michael, I'm sorry, but I don't see you in a romantic way like that. We are friends. I want to stay that way, but I can't if you are going to do things like this."

"Carmen, you can't be serious. I know this is more than just a little harmless crush. I'm crazy about you, and I think if you would get past your gayness, you would realize you are crazy about me too."

"Oh my God, Michael, listen to yourself. I am gay, honey, and I am very much in love with my fiancée. I don't want you like that. Please don't ruin what we have."

"What do we have, Carmen?" Michael threw his hands up. "This, us working out and chillin' in the teachers' lounge. There's more there. I know it."

"They were right." Carmen continued to walk down the bleachers. She knew it was all her fault. She turned around. "Michael, I am so sorry if you feel like I led you on. I care about you, but not in the way you want me to. You are my friend, and I thank you for all you have done for me. But this will never happen."

Michael took off running down the steps, leaving Carmen on the bleachers. She slowly walked down. She knew she was at fault. All the signs had been there, but she'd loved the attention. Now she had hurt her only ally at the school and a person she genuinely cared about. By the time she made it to her car, Michael was leaning on the side of it.

"I am so sorry if you felt I led you on in any way." Carmen stood in front of Michael. He wouldn't look at her.

"It's all good. Hey, I tried. I gotta go. See you later, Carmen." Michael got in his car, leaving her alone in the parking lot.

A while later Carmen opened the door to her apartment. Nic sat with her large headphones on, talking to the TV. She knew when Nic was in Black Ops mode on Xbox, there was no talking to her. She sat next to Nic and picked up a controller. Carmen wondered if she should tell Nic. She didn't want Nic to blow up or forbid her from talking to Michael. She joined the session in progress. Nic smiled. She loved it when Carmen played video games with her. Carmen decided to let the kiss die like the players she killed in the game.

Chapter 24

Lena felt the sun soaking into her pores. Two days of sex and sun had her in an ultimate blissful state. Danni had cast a spell on her more powerful than anything she had ever felt before. It wasn't love. It was pure lust, and she was loving every minute of it.

Lena was accustomed to the finer things in life, but Danni did extravagant to the next level. It wasn't enough for them to stay in a nice hotel. She had to borrow a luxury beach house from a client, one equipped with a staff and a private beach.

Lena draped the Egyptian cotton towel around her body, even though she knew she looked all right in the sexy cutout swimsuit Danni had waiting on her when she arrived. The swimsuit left little to the imagination, and she woke up every morning and went for a run just in an attempt to tone up more.

Lena had been spoiled by her parents and Brandon, but this was a different level. It wasn't regular spoiled; Danni was spoiling her rotten. Even when Lena attempted to pay for something, Danni would one-up her by buying her a pair of shoes, a purse, or jewelry. Lena couldn't help but wonder, if Danni was doing all of this for her now, what would she do if they were in a real relationship?

The cold floor sent chills through her body when she walked inside, overhearing Danni on another business call. That was the one thing she wasn't used to. Danni might spend money, but she worked hard to make it. She wondered when Danni slept. It seemed like no matter what time she woke up, Danni was off in the office or the living room, on her computer or on the phone. Most of the trip Lena had spent on the beach due to Danni's business calls.

Even with how amazing Danni was, Lena's mind had drifted to Denise on numerous occasions. She found herself comparing the two. Danni was amazing in bed, but so was Denise. Their skills were different. Danni aimed to please sexually, and Denise aimed to please and connect on a romantic level. Danni threw lavish gifts at her, while Denise gave her the ultimate gift— her heart. Danni had her body, but Denise still owned her heart.

"Where was your mind just now?"

Danni's voice startled Lena out of her Denise day-dream. She smiled as Danni walked up to her. She'd traded her usual look in for Miami khaki shorts and a blue and white button-down shirt. Her locks were pulled back in a ponytail. Danni tugged on the towel, pulling Lena close to her. Their lips met. Lena's pussy jumped, and she wondered if kissing Danni would ever not soak every pair of panties she owned.

"I was just thinking about how nice it would be if you were lying on that beach with me now," Lena told her.

Danni pulled the towel off Lena. She admired Lena's physique in the green swimsuit. "Now, see if I was out there, this sexy-ass swimsuit would be in the ocean and you would be naked on top of me." Danni's hands roamed until finding their way under Lena's swimsuit. She rubbed Lena's hard nipples with her fingers.

"Is that all I am to you? A piece of ass?" Lena smiled, hoping her comment came off as a joke. Secretly, she was starting to wonder if she wasn't anything more than a jump-off with perks.

"Come on, now. Don't do that." Danni knew Lena wasn't joking. "We are having fun, right? And the way you be pushing on my head, I'm starting to think I'm nothing but your headpiece." Danni winked and walked toward the kitchen.

"What can I say? Stop telling me how much you want to taste me, and I won't push on your head." Lena picked up a bottle of Moscato. She squealed when Danni scooped her up and sat her on the counter.

"You will never hear me say that. This right here"— Danni pulled the little piece of fabric covering Lena's womanhood to the side, then ran her finger over Lena's lips—"is my drug." Before Lena could respond, her legs were draped on Danni's shoulders. She bit her lip as Danni licked and sucked her walls, devouring her like she was the juiciest piece of fruit ever.

Danni didn't know what had come over her. Lena's sweetness called to her unlike anything she'd ever experienced. Lena never disappointed. She wasn't excellent in bed, and Danni could tell it was a lack of experience that was hindering her. But the sweetness in her pussy was unreal. It didn't matter if it was morning, noon, or evening, or if she surprised her, like she was doing at that very moment. It was always sweet, leaving her with a toothache only Lena's body could fix.

Danni's phone began to blare. They ignored it as she tongue fucked Lena. Her ponytail was gone, another holder lost to Lena's fingers gripping her locks. Lena's sweet moans only intensified the experience. Danni's heat was at full blaze, and with every tug and moan, she felt her own body combust.

Her phone began to blare again. She fidgeted in her pocket, pulled the phone out, and pressed the speaker button without leaving Lena's thighs.

"What?" she yelled, pissed at whoever was interrupting her meal. Lena couldn't help but giggle.

"Danielle." A deep, stern voice blasted through, causing Lena to jump. Danni immediately jumped up. She grabbed the phone and walked off, as though she hadn't just been deep-sea diving in Lena's ocean.

"Yes, sir?" Danni closed the door to the office.

"Am I interrupting something?"

"No, Father, I couldn't find my phone." Her heart raced.

"Tell me, Danielle, are you getting any work done or spending all your time screwing your whore of the week?" Danni's father turned around in his chair.

Danni lowered her head. "I'm getting a lot accomplished, and she's far from a whore."

"Is that right?" Danni's father stood up in his lavish office, which was bigger than some apartments. "Why is it that I got a call from the partners saying you didn't sign three of the agreements?"

Danni's mouth dropped. She had noticed the three documents, which were supposed to be sent off the day before. "I . . . I . . ."

"You packed some random piece of ass away on business, and you're doing more than fucking her. You are fucking up." Danni cringed at her father's harsh tone. She knew that Lena was more than just a random piece of ass but she also knew her father would never believe her.

"Sir, I do apologize, I will—"

"Just get them sent in." Her father calmed down. "Danielle, I don't mean to be hard on you. But you wanted these apartments, and I'd hate to see all of your hard work go down the drain because your mind is on other things."

"It won't, Dad. I promise you I am focused. I will have these off in thirty minutes."

"Good."

Danni hung the phone up, drained. She pulled her hair back and used one of her locks to hold it together. She quickly prepared the documents for FedEx.

Lena didn't know what to think about Danni's abrupt departure. She pulled on one of the colorful maxi dresses that she had bought. She sat on the couch and wondered when Danni would reappear.

Lena grabbed her phone when it started to ring.

"Hey, Carmen."

Carmen stood at the bakery, going through the book of cakes. "I just want you to know you are a sucky best friend."

"What did I do this time?" Lena stretched out on the couch.

"Nothing. That's the damn problem. I thought you were coming here to help me get things prepared for my wedding. *Sucky* friend!" Carmen closed the book.

Lena hit herself on her forehead. In her blissful state she had completely forgotten about her trip to Memphis to see Carmen.

"I'm sorry, honey. Something came up."

"Really? What could that be? You don't have a child to worry about."

Lena glanced at the office door. She hadn't told anyone about her time with Danni. She secretly wondered why.

"I kind of met someone and—"

"So you are blowing me off for some nigga!" Carmen's tone startled the little white bakers. She smiled, excusing herself and heading to her car.

"Not exactly."

Carmen paused. "Wait, what? It's a girl?"

Lena remained quiet.

Carmen's high-pitched squeal caused Lena to pull the phone from her ear. "Who the hell did you meet? OMG. Spill it."

"I can't right now. But I will come to Memphis first thing tomorrow if I can get a flight."

The door to the office opened, and Danni walked out with a very serious look on her face. She walked right past Lena.

"I'll call you back," Lena told Carmen.

"Wait."

"C, I will call you back." Lena hung up before Carmen could get another word in. Lena stood up. She walked over to Danni, who was deep in thought, looking at her iPad. "Is everything okay?"

"Yeah, it's cool." Her dry tone let Lena know she was lying, but she didn't want to press the issue.

"Well, that was my best friend, the one I told you is getting married. She's pissed at me 'cause of you," Lena joked.

Danni looked at Lena with an irritated expression on her face.

"I was supposed to help her with her wedding plans this weekend, but I got this amazing offer," Lena said and attempted to wrap her arms around Danni, who quickly pulled away.

"You didn't tell me you had something to do."

Lena didn't know what to think. "I'm just kidding. I told her I would fly in tomorrow."

"So you need to roll?" Danni's quick response angered Lena.

"Um, I guess so." Lena walked into the bedroom she had claimed as her own during her stay.

Danni realized her tone was harsh. She sighed and followed Lena. "I didn't mean it like that." Danni watched as Lena threw her items in the large Gucci bag Danni had bought her.

"I think you did."

"Lena." Danni grabbed Lena's arm. Lena turned and looked at Danni's face. She looked stressed. "I'm sorry. It's just that I forgot to do something, and my dad just handed my ass to me." She sat on the edge of the bed.

"I'm sorry. I didn't—"

"It's not you. It's me. I broke my own rule. Never mix business with pleasure. I'm here for business, but I asked you to come, so I haven't been on my A game. You and that damn sweet ass of yours." Danni pulled Lena close to her. "My bad. Excuse my attitude."

"I do. I guess we are both a little oversexed." Lena cracked a smile, causing a small smile to appear on Danni's face. "I do need to let you go before you get tired of me."

Lena turned but instantly found herself tightly gripped by Danni's arms. Her heart raced. Danni's lips were hypnotic. She could smell traces of her sex still lingering on Danni's skin. Danni planted her lips against Lena's.

"I'm not getting tired of you anytime soon. Trust," Danni assured her.

Lena felt like she was floating on cloud nine. In that moment Danni could have her any way she wanted her. Her high feeling quickly began to fade. If Danni cared so much, why didn't she want to keep Lena for herself? Insecurity took over, and Lena pulled away. Danni noticed the shift in energy.

"What's wrong, boo?"

Lena took a deep breath. "Look, I want to ask you something without you flipping out." Lena watched as Danni sat on the bed, bracing herself for whatever was about to happen. "I am sitting here, living on this cloud. I'm completely into you, but I'm a bit torn. Honestly, I'm not used to this."

"Not used to what?" Danni asked.

"This . . ." Lena waved her hands. "The fact that you say and do all the things you are saying and doing with no strings attached."

Danni smirked, lowering her head.

"Seriously, I'm used to people wanting to tie me down. What is your deal?"

"Lena, we haven't known each other a month yet."

"I know. I'm just wondering, when you say you don't do relationships, is it something that is a never thing or a 'possibility in the future' thing?"

Danni motioned for Lena to come over to her. With her bottom lip poked out, Lena walked over and sat next to Danni. Danni locked her fingers with Lena's. Their eyes met.

"Lena, I'm diggin' you, boo. Like I said before, I'm not the type of person to just do all the shit I'm doing for a chick. I'm about business. But, baby, today is a good example of why I don't lock chicks down."

Lena continued to listen.

"There's something my father taught me at an early age. Never let anything come in the way of your business, and, Lena, locking you down spells disaster for business. I let it happen once before, and I won't make that mistake again, not for anyone."

"So I am a distraction?"

"No . . . well, honestly, yes. But you are a welcomed distraction, in moderation." Lena could tell that Danni was serious by her expression. "I'm in grind mode, baby, and I am not in a place to lock anyone down, no matter how amazing the person might be."

Lena didn't know what to think. A guilty feeling came over her. She thought about Denise and the night she turned her away in New York. Denise had blamed Lena for her career loss. She had let her feelings for Lena interfere with the goal she had set for herself, and in the end she lost her basketball contract. Lena hated to admit it, but she knew Danni was right.

"Lena, I'm gonna keep it a hundred with you right now." Danni stood up. "You aren't ready for a real relationship, either."

"Okay, what is that supposed to mean?" Lena was offended.

Danni sighed. "Okay, Lena, real talk. You aren't girlfriend material . . . yet."

Lena's face dropped. She had always been girlfriend and wife material. Danni could see the irritation forming in Lena's face.

"I know you don't want to hear this, but it's the truth. Lena, it's more than being a good housewife when you are dealing with a person like me. I'm not trying to just have an arm piece. I want a partner in crime. Ya feel me?"

"No, honestly, I don't feel you. I'm not a damn trophy."

"Really? Tell me, Lena, what have you done with yourself besides being a stay-at-home basketball wife and mother? Have you ever even had a job?"

Lena's face cracked. She had never had a real job. Danni didn't take her eyes off Lena. Lena felt like Danni was staring right into her soul.

"Yeah you got married, but, baby, that wasn't a childish relationship from the jump. You were his high school and college sweetheart, but once in the actual trenches you didn't last."

"Okay, now you are overstepping." Lena was fuming. "I worked my ass off for that relationship. I gave up a hell of a lot." Denise entered Lena's mind.

Danni shook her head. "No, you didn't. Babe, when you got to college, from what you've told me, you fell for your roommate but never had an actual relationship with her. You never explored the real possibilities. You only got married because it was the right thing to do."

"Are you saying I didn't love Brandon?"

"No, I'm not saying that. But, Lena, Brandon was your first and only guy, and you've messed with only two chicks, and neither one of them was a real girlfriend."

Danni's words stung. Lena didn't want to admit it, but she knew Danni was right. She was reading Lena like a book. She couldn't believe she was so transparent.

"And I know you probably want to slap me by now, but there's more. Lena, what the hell are you doing with yourself besides taking care of Bria and shopping? Are you seriously content just being a stay-at-home mom? I know it's more to you than becoming a damn ex-ball wife. You gotta be deeper than that."

"Um, okay." Lena stood up. "So I'm not deep, now?"

"Honestly, no. You are an excellent mom, but what else can you say about yourself? I mean, what did you go to school for? To sit at home and go shopping? To me, sexy is more than a look. It's an attitude and a way of life. Wearing hot clothes and having a banging body aren't sexy. An independent woman about her grind is what's truly sexy."

Lena didn't know what to think. No one had read her like that before. She felt like shit. She had never thought past being Brandon's wife and Bria's mother. Now that she was single and rich, she had never thought about doing anything productive.

Danni could tell she had hurt Lena's feelings. She massaged Lena's shoulder. "I'm not trying to make you feel bad. But if you can't handle what I have said to you, then that's just another reason why we could never be more than we are right now. It's a dog-eat-dog world. You gotta have tough skin. I just want you to live up to the potential I see in you."

"I know. And yeah, it stung a bit, but I can take it." Lena held her head up. Although Danni was rough, she knew she had her best interest in mind.

"Right now you are in a position to do whatever the hell you want to do. Get out there and do it." Danni's phone rang. "I gotta take this and go drop this package off. Check flights to Memphis. You need to be there for your friend."

Lena shook her head. No one had ever been so direct with her. Danni's forceful words sank in deep. Danni kissed her on her forehead, leaving Lena to her thoughts.

Chapter 25

Cooley walked into the dance studio. Tamera's face was the first one she saw. She kept her shades on as she watched Sahara's backup dancers practicing for their upcoming Jimmy Fallon performance.

Tamera tried to hold her cool. Even though Cooley had shades on, Tamera could feel her eyes on her. She continued to do the routine. She watched as the choreographer greeted Cooley. Cooley and the choreographer watched. Cooley kept a straight face, with her arms folded.

Cooley wanted to beat the hell out of the traitor. She had trusted the girl with her woman, and they both had betrayed her. She could understand Sahara's need for a little side piece while she was away, but she knew Tamera's reason for bedding her woman was that she was hoping for the ultimate come-up.

Cooley whispered in the choreographer's ear. Tamera knew it was about her when she saw the disappointed look on his face. Everyone knew what had happened between Sahara and her. It was obvious after Sahara's meltdown in Los Angeles. When she'd tried to console Sahara, she'd quickly pushed her off and told her to stay away from her. Later Sahara apologized, but the damage had been done. Cooley knew what had happened.

Cooley left the studio, pulling her phone out of her pocket. Less than a minute later she heard the door to the studio fly open.

"Cooley!"

Cooley stopped. She turned to see Tamera storming up to her. Cooley kept her cool. She didn't flinch.

"You had me fired!" Tamera yelled. She quickly remembered Cooley had every right to. After all, Tamera had slept with her girl. She took a deep breath and tried to calm down. "Look, can we please be adults and just talk about this?"

"What the hell do we have to talk about? You fucked up, Tamera. Did you really think you were going to keep eating off of us after what you did?"

"Oh, come on. Yes, I . . . *we* made a mistake. If I could take it back, trust me, I would. But come on. This is my job, my career, and my livelihood. I have a daughter. I need this job."

Cooley took two steps toward Tamera and removed her shades. "Maybe you should have thought about that before you fucked where you eat."

Tamera wanted to scream, but she kept her cool. "Cooley, please, I need this job. I am sorry. Hell, if you want to kick my ass, do it. But don't take my job from me. It was one night, one mistake. I swear to you, it will never happen again."

"Oh, I know it won't happen again. But do you really think I'm gonna let you go on tour with her again? Please."

Tamera knew it was too late. She had nothing to lose. "Wow." She took a step back. "You do know it takes two to tango, right?"

Cooley's head snapped around. "What the fuck did you just say to me?"

"You heard me. I wasn't the only one in that bed, Cooley. It's not like I drugged her, seduced her, or anything else. We were both drinking, and some shit went down. But I wasn't alone, and I for damn sure didn't force her to do anything."

Cooley couldn't speak. She knew Tamera was telling the truth. Sahara never did anything she didn't want to do. Anger spilled from Cooley's pores. She wanted to kill them both—Tamera for fucking her girl, and Sahara for being stupid enough to let her.

"We made a mistake. She regretted it, and so did I. The girl was a mess when she woke up and realized what had happened. I understand you might not want me around, but come on. You are much too smart to think that I'd be dumb enough to do it again, or that Sahara would. What are you gonna do? Make her dance one dancer short for Fallon? And even if you let me go, do you really think, if she wants to do it again, she won't find someone else?"

Cooley's hands began to tremble. Tamera was winning the fight. Firing her didn't mean there wouldn't be another slipup at some point. Cooley wondered if she would ever be able to trust Sahara again. Cooley thought about her reputation. Firing Tamera would only make her look like the scorned lover. The one thing people knew about her was that she was cool and confident. She wanted to kill Sahara for messing with her confidence. Tamera stood as still as a statue. Cooley walked back to the studio door. She tapped on the window. A moment later the choreographer joined them.

"She's good. She can stay. I'm a professional, and I temporarily mixed business and personal. I shouldn't have done that."

Before Tamera could say thank you, she felt Cooley's fist connecting her face. She fell on the floor from the blow. The gay choreographer's face dropped. He covered his mouth, trying not to laugh. Cooley stood over Tamera, who was holding the side of her face, in shock from the blow.

"That's what I should have done." Cooley turned around and walked away, leaving Tamera sitting there, her face throbbing.

Cooley was baffled. The punch did nothing to help her feel better. She felt empty inside. Sahara had her open in ways she didn't want or like. Cooley could feel herself losing control of who she was, and it was scaring her more than anything. She looked up to see Sahara walking into the building. Her blood began to boil again.

"Baby?" As Sahara walked closer, she could tell Cooley was not in a good mood. "What are you doing here?"

"What the fuck are you doing here?" Cooley snapped. "You know what? Don't even worry about it. Just go see your fucking girlfriend." Cooley brushed past Sahara.

"Wait, please!" Sahara followed Cooley outside. "Carla, please!" Her voice carried, causing people sitting out on the patio at the restaurant next door to look.

Cooley grabbed Sahara by her arm and took her back in the building. "What are you doing? Are you trying to end up plastered all over the Internet?"

"You think I care about a fucking gossip blog? The only thing I care about right now is you and me." Sahara folded her arms.

"I'm not doing this here."

"Carla, I came here to get rid of Tamera."

"Why? You already did the dirt. What's firing her gonna do?"

Sahara sighed. "I'm just trying to do anything I can to make this right. Just tell me what to do. I'll do anything. Don't you see that?"

"Right now the only thing you can do is get the fuck out of my face." Cooley placed her shades back on and walked out of the building, leaving Sahara in tears.

***

Denise sat on the couch, reading through film treatments and scripts that had been sent to her by her agent. She frowned at the number of gay roles she'd been offered. Cooley and Denise agreed, she didn't need to play any gay roles unless they were Oscar worthy. She didn't want the stereotype of being the gay actress.

Denise was restless. She didn't realize how anxious she was for the shooting to start. She was back playing the role of the loving girlfriend. Farih had made a vast improvement in a few days. They spent nights watching movies and talking, and were laughing like they used to. Farih didn't ask to go out to eat, and she had actually cooked a few nights after getting off of work. Although she was trying, something was different. They hadn't had sex since their argument. Things were nice, but it felt more like a friendship than a relationship.

The one thing that still bothered her about Farih was the fact that she was helping to solidify Denise as a gay brand. Farih talked about their relationship all the time on her show. Even though she kept it very brief and didn't go into details, every show she found a way to bring up Denise. Denise wished Farih would take a hint from Ellen, who mentioned her wife, Portia, only on rare occasions on her show. It bothered Denise that the show was using Farih's gayness as a marketing tool. Anything that happened in the gay and lesbian community was immediately thrown to Farih for her thoughts. Farih would just smile and give her opinion on any and all things gay.

Denise knew she was overreacting. It wasn't her career. If Farih needed to use her life to work, then who was Denise to question it? The only thing was, it wasn't just Farih's life. It was Denise's too. If Farih had her way, they would be starring in *The Farih and Denise Reality Show* on Bravo. The idea of having cameras following her every move repulsed Denise. She loved her celebrity, but she didn't want to become a Kardashian or a Real Housewife.

Adele's "Don't You Remember" began to play on Denise's iPod. She thought about Lena. Lena consumed her thoughts more and more each day. Denise wanted to call her, but she was fighting to get over her addiction to Mrs. Jamerson-Redding. Denise couldn't shake the feeling that Lena was who she was supposed to be with, even though the years told a different story.

Denise knew Lena was in Memphis with Carmen. She wanted to get on a plane and act like it was a surprise, but something was holding her back. She knew it was her feelings for Farih. Denise had never been so torn in her life. She loved Farih but had a feeling their season was ending. She also loved Lena but knew Lena was too complicated.

Denise shook her head, trying to focus on the film treatment in her hand. She knew work was the one thing that needed to be on her mind. She wanted her old focus back. She was having an internal battle with herself. She wished she could go back to her college days, when she didn't let women interfere with her goals.

The log line caught Denise's attention. She read the film treatment. The story, about a woman trying to rebuild her life after losing her family in a fire, touched her. She found herself absorbed in the treatment from page one.

The loud ring of the doorbell startled Denise. The doorbell rang over and over. She went to the door and peeked through the peephole.

Cooley stood there with a straight face. "Nigga, open the damn door," Cooley snapped.

"Okay. Damn." Cooley walked past Denise before she could get the door fully open. "Okay, what happened now?"

Cooley paused. She looked at her best friend's judgmental face. She felt her blood boiling. She hated when Denise automatically assumed it was something bad, even though she knew in this situation it was.

"Nothing." Cooley turned away. She knew her face would give her away.

Denise walked closer to her. "Cool, what is going on?"

"Nothing, man. Look, I just came by to tell you I need you to come to a meeting with me next Friday, so put it on your calendar."

Denise sat on the edge of her couch. She knew Cooley was trying not to look directly at her. Something was wrong, but she knew Cooley well enough to know not to press the subject.

Cooley wanted to talk to Denise about Sahara, but she already knew what Denise would say. She knew Denise would tell her to let it go and forgive Sahara. She knew that Denise would fill her with guilt for all the things she did to Sahara in the past that Sahara put up with. She knew Denise was right about all these things, but Cooley didn't want that right now. She wanted to vent and have someone have her side.

"So I was reading this film treatment." Denise picked up the thick booklet and handed it to Cooley. Cooley looked at the top sheet. "It really seems good."

"An MOW? Are you kidding me right now?" Cooley's mind was back in business mode. Another thing that irritated her about her bestie was her inability to look at things from the point of view of dollars instead of passion.

"Yes, a Movie of the Week, but it's a really good one. I was really into the story until your excessive doorbell ringing interrupted me."

Cooley sat down on the leather couch. Stressed, she rubbed her hands thorough her hair. "Denise, you can't go from a blockbuster to a Movie of the Week. Are you serious right now?"

"C, I don't care if it's a blockbuster or an MOW. If I'm going to do this, I want to do things I'm actually passionate about."

"You obviously aren't getting me right now. That's why you have to come to this meeting. Maybe someone else can talk some sense into you." Cooley stood up, tossing the film treatment on the couch. "I gotta go."

"Where are you about to go?" Something wasn't sitting right with Denise. She knew her friend was troubled, but didn't know what to do about it. Cooley had never had women issues, so this was new territory for her. "How about we go get something to eat or—"

"Nah, I just want to be alone. I'll see you later." Cooley walked out the door, leaving Denise dumbfounded.

Misha watched her son playing in the bathtub. She couldn't help but laugh at some of his antics. She heard the front door slam shut. She knew that meant Patrick was not in a good mood. She dried Jaylin off and took him to his bedroom.

She walked into Patrick's home office to find him setting up his video game. He didn't say anything to her. "What's going on?"

"Nothing." His dry tone frightened her. She scanned her mind, trying to think if there was anything she could have done wrong. Lately, things had been good between them. She knew it must be a work thing.

"Patrick, talk to me."

"I just had a bad day at work."

Misha put her arms around him. "I thought we were going to go out to eat tonight."

Patrick sighed. "I'm sorry, baby, but I totally forgot all about that. I'll be good. We can still go."

"Thank you, baby."

They walked to their bedroom.

"So, Mish, what's up with Lena? Is she dating yet, 'cause I have a friend that is perfect for her."

"She's actually talking to someone now."

"Oh, really? Is it another ballplayer like Brandon?" Patrick rummaged through his closet.

Misha froze. She had to tell him that Lena's new friend was a woman. "Actually, it's a girl."

Patrick didn't move. He stared into his closet. "A girl?"

"Yes. Some hotshot chick in real estate." Misha tried to sound as nonchalant about it as possible.

Patrick turned around. His smile was gone. "So now Lena's messing with women?"

"Patrick, you know she used to. Remember Denise?"

"Yeah, but all the times we kicked it at her house, Brandon was always there. When did this happen?"

"I don't know. I mean, Brandon and her haven't been together in God knows how long. She is just now getting back into the dating scene."

"With a girl . . ."

"It just so happens to be a woman. What is the problem?"

Patrick stared at Misha. "So all this time you have been hanging with her, it's been around a bunch of lesbians?"

"What?" Misha knew exactly where he was going with this. Patrick's number one fear was that she would want to mess with women again. "Patrick, you have nothing to worry about."

"Why would you say that, Mish?" Patrick snapped. "Why would you think I even thought I had something to worry about?"

"Because I'm not stupid. I know you will always wonder. . . ."

"I wasn't wondering anything, but now that you say it, should I be? I mean, all your damn friends are fucking gay. Why can't you hang with some straight women?"

Misha threw her hands up. "What my friends do and what I do are completely separate things."

"Is it wrong for a man to want his ex-lesbian wife to find new people to hang with that won't have her around that type of shit?"

"That *type of shit?*" Misha shook her head. "So because you find out Lena dates women *and* men, now you have a problem with her? You want me to cut back on her, like you made me cut back on Carmen?" Misha wanted to run out of the room. She wasn't allowed to go to Memphis without him, just because of his fear that Carmen would have her around Cooley.

"Do you want to be gay again, Misha? 'Cause everything you fucking do is in that damn lifestyle. You won't even consider regular friends. God forbid you meet some straight women to hang out with. All you want to hang out with is fucking dykes!"

"I'm done." Misha grabbed her purse.

"Where do you think you're going?" Patrick followed her into the living room. "Misha!"

"I don't know. Maybe I'll go hang with my gay-ass dyking friends. Maybe I'll go back to dykin' myself, since my husband seems to think that's what I'm doing, anyway."

"Don't fucking leave this house, Misha!" Patrick's voice rumbled. She knew he meant business. "Call your friend and tell her we can't make it. We have shit we need to deal with here."

"Fuck you, Patrick." Misha picked up her cell phone and walked to the front door.

"If you walk out that door, the locks will be changed and you won't be getting back in."

Misha froze. She knew he was serious. If she walked out, her marriage would be over. Tears ran down her face. She dropped her purse on the floor.

"Fine, master. As you fucking wish." She ran past him and slammed their bedroom door.

Cooley walked into her house. Sahara stood up.

"Cooley."

"Not now." Cooley shrugged Sahara off.

"No, right now!" Sahara yelled.

Cooley stopped. She turned to see Sahara's stern face. Cooley knew what was coming. She sighed and sat down in her oversize chair.

"I thought you said we were going to be okay? If this is *okay,* I don't want to know what bad is."

"Sahara, I don't want to talk about this shit right now."

"I fucked up. Okay, it's obvious I fucked up. But all this shit you are doing to me . . . not cool at all." Sahara didn't move from her spot.

Cooley sat in silence, looking off into the distance. She didn't want to look at Sahara.

Sahara held her arms out. "So here. Do whatever you want to do to me. Do you want to hit me, yell at me, call me names? Just fucking do it. Get it all out, because I'm not about to continue to go on like this."

"So you really trying to stand in front of me, going off like *I've* done something wrong?" Cooley finally looked at Sahara. Her blood was boiling. "You are right. *You* fucked up. You fucked us up!" Cooley jumped up. Her hands were shaking.

Sahara huffed. "Are you fucking serious right now? Yes, I made a mistake, as in *one* fucking mistake. Do we need to go over your past indiscretions?"

Cooley looked away. "We aren't talking about the past."

"Maybe we need to. I took ya sorry ass back after you dogged me. I turned a blind eye to you fuckin' those bitches. I let it go because I knew you loved me."

"But you knew about all of that, Sahara!" Cooley yelled. "You knew who you were with when you got with me. And I stopped all that shit for you. But even then I still never lied to you. I kept it a hundred, something you obviously don't know how to do."

"I was going to tell you—"

"When!" Cooley's high-pitched voice reached a new octave. "When were you going to tell me? Why the fuck did it take me figuring the shit out for you to come clean?"

That silenced Sahara. She didn't have a comeback. "I—I . . ."

"Don't stutter now." Cooley pushed over the coffee table between them, causing Sahara to jump. She flinched, thinking Cooley really was about to hit her. Cooley paused. She didn't like that reaction. She didn't want Sahara thinking she would ever lay a hand on her, but in that moment the thoughts of another person's hands on what she thought belonged to her were consuming her.

Cooley grabbed Sahara by her jeans and pulled her close. Then she grabbed the hair on the back of Sahara's head, pulling her head back.

"What did she do to you, Sha? Did she fuck you rough like you like it, or was she gentle? I bet that bitch was a little pussy in bed. Probably had no idea you like this type of shit." Cooley pulled Sahara's hair some more, causing Sahara to let out a painful moan. With one hand Cooley unbuttoned Sahara's pants.

Sahara couldn't speak. She was in shock, scared but anxious at the same time. Cooley hadn't touched her since she found out about the other woman. With force two of Cooley's fingers entered Sahara, causing her to jump.

Cooley stared directly into Sahara's frightened but aroused eyes. She fingered her roughly. Sahara's body jerked with every stroke. Cooley's grip on her hair didn't loosen. She wanted it to hurt. She wanted Sahara to feel the pain she was feeling in that moment.

"Cooley . . ." Sahara tried to say more but couldn't.

"Shut up!" Cooley's voice rumbled.

Sahara didn't speak. Her mouth hung open, and only breath escaped.

Tears formed in Cooley's eyes. "Did you like it, Sahara? Did she make you cum?"

"Yes." Sahara gritted her teeth. She was pissed. Emotions flooded through Sahara. Even seeing the anger and pain in Cooley's eyes didn't make it okay. There was no love in what Cooley was doing to her.

Cooley's grip loosened, and her jaw dropped as she let go of Sahara. Cooley had fooled around on her more than once, but Sahara had never got upset.

"Are you happy now?" Sahara pushed Cooley with all her might. "Now, Carla, why don't you tell me how many bitches you made cum? How many of those hoes did you give orgasms to when you weren't thinking of me and what you had waiting at home for you?" She pushed Cooley again. "Tell me, Cooley. You tell me!"

"Fuck you!" Cooley turned, but Sahara grabbed her by her shirt. Without thinking, Cooley jerked away, mistakenly hitting Sahara with elbow, causing her to hit the floor. Cooley froze instantly at the sight of Sahara on the floor.

"Sha." Cooley fell to her knees. She put her arm on Sahara's back as Sahara sobbed. Sahara looked up. Blood ran from her lip. The sight sent chills to Cooley's core. "Baby."

Sahara slapped Cooley. She stood up and ran to the bathroom. Cooley couldn't move. She knew things had gone too far. Cooley ran to the bathroom. She knocked on the door.

Sahara listened to Cooley begging outside the bathroom door. She stared at her face. Her lip was beginning to swell. She ran cold water on one of their white washcloths. She put the cold towel against her lip.

"Sahara, please. Oh my God!" Cooley could feel the room spinning. She had lost a grip on everything. Things were out of control.

Sahara didn't respond.

Cooley didn't know if she was okay or if she was searching through the bathroom for something to use to kill her. "Baby . . ."

Cooley took two steps back when she heard the lock. She watched as the doorknob turned. Sahara walked out. Cooley wanted to die when she saw Sahara's protruding lip. She gasped. There was no coming back from this.

They stood staring at each other. No words between them. Sahara couldn't speak. Cooley was afraid to speak. Cooley had never feared a woman before, but in that moment she did.

Sahara broke the silence. "So I hope you got it all out now."

"What?"

"I said, I hope you have it all out now."

Cooley was speechless. Sahara stood there. She was not angry but was just hoping for a resolution to their problems. Cooley knew she deserved to be hit back, but Sahara just wanted peace restored in their home. Cooley nodded her head. She couldn't speak. She was speechless.

"Good." Sahara lowered her head. Without notice, Sahara slapped Cooley. The sound echoed throughout the apartment. "Now, if you ever do that shit again, I'm going to do more than slap yo' ass."

Sahara walked past, leaving Cooley standing in her spot, holding her face.

Chapter 26

Lena was growing restless. She hadn't talked to Danni since she left her in Miami. Spending time with Carmen wasn't helping as much as she'd hoped. Planning a wedding again was bittersweet. She couldn't help but think about her failed nuptials.

Lena tried to enjoy some of the TV shows that Carmen raved about. She couldn't watch *True Blood* or *Spartacus*. The vampire and gladiator sex just made her want Danni even more. She didn't know if it was Danni or her amazing sex that she missed more.

Lena thought about retail therapy, but that just made her think of the last thing she and Danni had talked about. She didn't want to come off as a spoiled rich girl who was only good for shopping and having kids. Lena's mind raced. She didn't know if she wanted her own business or wanted to work for someone. She thought about buying some investment properties, but she knew she didn't know that much about real estate.

Lena sat at Carmen's small computer desk in her living room. She was always amazed at how well Carmen and Nic were able to decorate their living spaces even with such limited space. Above the computer desk were mahogany square shelves with photos of all of them during their college years. Lena missed the University. She went to the Freedom University Web site. Her jaw dropped when she saw a photo of Denise with the new women's basketball team. She couldn't believe Denise went to Alumni Weekend and she didn't know about it.

Lena shook her head. *You are seriously screwed up,* Lena thought. One minute she was consumed with thoughts of Danni, and the next moment she couldn't stop thinking about Denise. Lena closed her eyes. Denise's face appeared. She didn't want to face the truth. No matter how amazing Danni and her lovemaking skills were, Denise still held a piece of her heart. That infuriated Lena. She wanted to shake the feeling. Denise was off living her lavish life with her girlfriend, and Lena was still stuck on her. She felt like an idiot.

She couldn't take it anymore. Lena picked up her phone and pressed Danni's name. The phone rang two times before Danni's sultry voice answered.

"Miss Lena." Danni smiled when she saw Lena's face appear on her phone. "To what do I owe this pleasure?"

"Are you fucking with me?" Lena paced the floor.

Danni sat up at her desk. "What do you mean?"

"I haven't heard from you since Miami, and you have the nerve to say that to me. What is your deal, Danni?"

Lena paced the floor some more, trying to remain calm. She was restless and anxious. She bit her bottom lip, waiting on a shocked Danni's response.

Danni was surprised by Lena's forcefulness. "I am sorry. I didn't know I was supposed to check in," Danni said, guarded. She liked that Lena was thinking of her, but didn't like being questioned.

"You don't have to do anything you don't want to do, but with the way things were, I expected you to at least call once or twice." Lena knew she sounded like a nagging girlfriend, but she didn't care.

"You know, the phone works both ways." Danni leaned back in her chair. "I've been busy, but I haven't forgotten you. Who could forget Lena Jamerson?" Danni smirked.

"Whatever." Lena tried not to blush at Danni's statement. "Well, I just wanted to say that, and now that I did, have a nice day."

"Whoa." Danni sat up in her swivel chair. "Don't think you are getting away that easy. Have you missed me?"

Danni's seductive, low tone made Lena's legs tremble. Her womanhood was awake and wanting to play.

"Hello?" Danni said when Lena did not respond.

"Maybe." Lena bit her lip again. "Not that I should have."

"Whatever, shorty. You know you missed me." Danni stood up.

"It would have been nice to know the feeling was mutual."

"Trust me, it is." Danni's all-work-and-no-play rule was taking its toll on her. Her New York jump-offs had nothing on Lena. She wanted to feel her, but work had to come first. "Actually, work is bringing me back to Atlanta next week."

"Is it now?"

"It is, and I need you at my house Friday." Danni sat back down.

"Um, is that a demand, or are you asking me?" Lena responded with attitude.

"I'm not asking, if that's what you mean. Be there. Seven o'clock."

Lena let out a grunt in protest.

Danni ignored her.

Lena tried to hide it, but she loved Danni's aggressive nature and her comment. She didn't notice Carmen standing against the wall with a large grin on her face. Lena hung up the phone, knowing she would be there with bells on.

Lena knew the best way to get over one was to get under another, and she was going to be under Danni as long as she could.

"What is that smile about?" Carmen noticed the expression on Lena's face.

"Nothing." Lena blushed.

"I'm guessing nothing is this mysterious Danni." Carmen laughed. Lena's flushed face gave her all the answers she needed. "Well, I can't wait to meet her."

Lena noticed a photo of the whole crew sitting on one of the square shelves. Her happiness over Danni faded.

"Damn, I really do still look the same, don't I?" Lena asked Carmen.

Carmen shrugged her shoulders. "So what? That's a good thing. I want to still look like I'm a freshman in college."

"See"—Lena stood up—"I don't want to look like a child anymore. Everyone around me has changed. Hell, you, Denise, Cooley. I can barely recognize Denise anymore. I'm tired of looking the same." Lena paced the floor. She paused. "In fact . . ." Lena rushed off to the guest room, leaving Carmen baffled. She came back out, holding her purse. "Are you coming?"

Carmen stood up. "Coming where?"

Lena smirked. She grabbed her keys and walked to the front door.

"Coming where?" Carmen yelled as she rushed to grab her purse and follow Lena, who was obviously on a mission.

Sahara walked into the kitchen to find Cooley sitting at the kitchen table. There weren't any words; neither knew what to say after the night before.

Sahara poured a glass of orange juice. Cooley cringed when she instantly noticed Sahara's puffy lip.

"Don't worry. It will be fine," Sahara said, not looking up from her copy of *Ebony*.

"Will it? Or better yet, will we?" Cooley asked.

She couldn't sleep the night before. Cooley wanted to go into the bedroom and hold her injured girlfriend, but she couldn't. She was so angry at herself.

"We will be fine, if you want us to be." Sahara finally focused on Cooley. She could see the hurt in Cooley's eyes. "It's okay, Carla. I know it was an accident."

"Sha, baby, I never—"

"No need for all of that." Sahara didn't want to talk about the night before. She wanted to move on. She wanted her relationship back, and if a small injury was what it took to get her woman back, she didn't care.

"Yeah, there is, Sahara. You can't just brush that off. I mean, yes, it was a mistake, but the whole thing, the way I've been acting in general has been . . ." Cooley swallowed a big knot in her throat. "I just really am sorry for the way I've been acting."

Cooley lowered her head. Sahara walked over and sat in the chair next to Cooley. Cooley couldn't look at her. Every time she tried to focus on Sahara, she noticed the lip. Sahara put her hand on Cooley's trembling hand.

"Carla, it was an accident. I know you would never hit me." Sahara smiled. "I remember back when we first met, you know, that fateful night?"

Cooley remembered the first night they spent together. It was during a threesome with Sahara and her then girlfriend, Michelle. Although Michelle wanted to be the center of attention, Cooley couldn't take her eyes off of the shy Sahara. Cooley broke not only her personal rule, but also the rules set by Michelle by not only seeing Sahara again a few nights later, but also embracing and kissing her—something Cooley never did with women.

"Remember that next morning, when we were in the bathroom and Michelle came in? She grabbed my arm, and you instantly got in her ass about the way she handled me. I knew then what type of woman you were. I know you would never put your hands on me."

Cooley forced herself to look at Sahara. The lip was bothering her more than she could ever imagine. Cooley didn't like what she was becoming. She was so angry that it led to Sahara getting hurt.

"Sha, it's something more than that. I don't know who I am anymore. I've never done anything like what happened yesterday, and I don't want that shit to happen ever again. It's like my feelings for you are turning me into something I don't want to be."

Sahara's smile faded. "Are you saying you don't want to be with me?"

"No."

Sahara's body was trembling.

Cooley put her hand on Sahara's knees. "I'm saying I am in a territory that I don't know anything about. Look how I've been acting lately. That's not me. Hell, regular me wouldn't have cared nearly as much about you sleeping with that bitch."

"Cooley, we are in a relationship, and we are in love. It's understandable that you would care about—"

"But you didn't." Cooley stood up. "You've said it yourself. I've fooled around with other girls, and you always knew that they meant nothing to me. I know you love me, but you just getting it on with someone else . . . nah, I can't accept that. Just thinking about it now still is pissing me the fuck off."

Sahara couldn't take her eyes off of her hurting girlfriend. "Cooley, I hate myself for making you feel this way."

"It's not your fault. It's something with me. I can't expect for you to be okay with me fooling around if I can't deal with you doing the same thing."

Sahara stood up. "So what are you saying?"

"I'm saying that from today on there will be no more slipups, no more being cool with me messing with other girls."

"Cooley, I don't expect—"

"But you should." Cooley's voice squeaked. "You should care, Sahara. You should be ready to knock my ass out if I mess with another chick. Why don't you care? How can you be so cool with it?"

"You think I don't care?" Sahara grabbed Cooley by her arm. "Carla, I cared. I cared every time you told me about your slipups. I never wanted to share you. I never wanted any of those threesomes. I never wanted to know you were sleeping with other women."

"Why didn't you say so?"

"Because I made a promise to accept you for who you were. I didn't want to drive you away, because I was becoming too possessive. It was killing me, but I wanted to make you happy."

Cooley couldn't believe what she was hearing. Tears flowed from Sahara's eyes. Cooley felt horrible. In front of her stood a woman who millions of people looked at as strong and independent, but the truth was she was damaged. Sahara wasn't strong. She was weak for Cooley, willing to take whatever Cooley gave her just as long as she had her. And Cooley had been taking advantage of her woman's love for years.

Cooley pulled Sahara into her arms. She held her sobbing girlfriend. "It's okay."

"I don't want you with other women," Sahara cried. "I don't want to be with other women, and I don't want to share you."

"You don't have to ever again. But you gotta tell me everything. Don't hide anything. We won't last that way." Cooley kissed Sahara for the first time since finding out about the other woman. Sahara's slipup no longer mattered to Cooley. Denise was right. She had put Sahara through a lot, and Sahara had never left her side. Cooley no longer cared about the other woman. She only cared only about fixing her relationship with the only woman she had ever truly loved. Cooley knew she did love Misha once, but the love she had for Sahara was on another level. Sahara was her soul mate. She had found the one.

They made love like it was the first time. Cooley wanted to rediscover Sahara's whole body. She kissed her with passion, from Sahara's toes to her forehead. There was no need for a strap. It was just them, and their skin intertwined, becoming one.

Chapter 27

Lena stood in the lobby of the busy W. She was nervous. She had never told Danni about her new haircut. Carmen had thrown a fit the entire time in the salon. Lena didn't have to react: Carmen's moans with every cut were enough. She couldn't believe how much a haircut could change her style. She looked different. Even with Carmen saying that she loved it, Lena was worried. Her hair was one of her prized possessions.

If men were her deciding factor, then she was good to go. The looks of the males seemed a bit more primal with her new style, possibly because they no longer had to wonder if she was sexy jailbait. The pixie haircut gave her a more mature look. The maroon dress hugging her curves only enhanced the image.

Danni got off the busy elevator. She loved her condo, but the popularity of the hotel was starting to cramp her style. She searched around but couldn't find Lena in the crowd.

Lena was having way too much fun watching Danni's worried expressions as she attempted to find her. Finally, Lena walked up behind Danni and tapped her on her shoulder. Danni turned around, paused, frozen by the new look. Lena's big smile began to fade as Danni stared at her new look. Lena couldn't tell if she was just shocked or disgusted.

"Oookkk . . ." Lena broke the awkward silence.

Danni finally blinked. "Damn."

Lena frowned. "You hate it." Lena wanted to run out of the hotel and hide.

Danni finally snapped back to reality. She shook her head. "Boo, damn, I'm sorry. No, I love it. I was just shocked. Why didn't you tell me?"

Lena wasn't convinced. "I wanted it to be a surprise." She frowned.

Danni could feel Lena's hesitation. She held the sides of Lena's face. "Boo, I love it."

"You're just so . . . silent."

"'Cause I was trying to decide if I want to skip dinner and just take you upstairs. You have no idea how fucking sexy you look right now. Shit, short hair suits you."

Lena blushed.

Two men walked past the pair. They looked at Lena and then at Danni. One frowned, while the other shook his head.

"See, now you gon' get me in trouble. I'm really gonna have to fight these niggas off."

They laughed as they headed out of the building.

The upscale restaurant was busy, as were most Atlanta restaurants on a Friday night. The valet opened Lena's door. Danni held her hand as she handed the keys to the valet.

They walked into the busy restaurant. Lena sighed. The aroma of Italian food was making her stomach rumble, and the endless line of people holding table pagers let her know food wasn't coming anytime soon.

"Do you want to go somewhere else?" Danni whispered in her ear.

"D. Campbell?"

Lena and Danni looked up before she could answer. Lena's mouth dropped. She turned her head quickly as Cooley and Sahara walked into the restaurant.

"Danni Campbell."

"Cool Wade," Danni said. She and Cooley gave each other daps.

Lena's hands were trembling. She wanted to scream. She should have known the possibility of running into people she knew would be high at the hot new establishment. She continued to stare at the large aquarium, hoping she wouldn't be noticed.

"What in the hell are y'all doing eating with the regular folks?" Danni said.

"Well, Sahara loves this place, but you know how we do it. We have a private room in the back," Cooley explained.

"Man, I didn't even think to do that." Danni shook her head.

"You should join us. We have been trying to get together for a while, anyway," Cooley said.

"Yes," Sahara added to make her presence known. "Join us. Room two." Sahara and Cooley followed the hostess to the back of the main dining room.

Danni walked over to Lena, who had made her way right in front of the aquarium. "Good news. We are going to a private room with some people I know."

"Oh, um . . . really?" Lena wanted to scream. She didn't know how she was going to get out of this one. Danni noticed her hesitation.

"Is something wrong?"

Lena smiled. "I just thought we would have time to be alone."

Danni smiled. "Oh, there will be plenty of time for that. Plus, in this place we wouldn't be able to hear each other, anyway." Danni grabbed her hand and pulled her toward the asile. "Come on. Plus, you get to meet a celebrity."

Lena followed, unable to object.

Cooley and Sahara walked into a room decorated like an Italian villa. Denise and Farih looked up.

"Late as usual." Denise shook her head.

"Sorry. I ran into this dude I've been trying to get up with for a long time. We invited them to join us," Cooley announced.

"Them?" As Denise spoke, the door opened.

Danni walked in. Lena couldn't seem to stop staring at the floor.

"Oh, here they are," Cooley said. "Danni Campbell, this is—"

"Farih . . ." The drop in Danni's voice caused Lena to look up. Her heart dropped.

"You two know each other?" Lena asked. She couldn't take her eyes off of Danni's blank expression.

Danni shook her head, pulling herself out of the daze. "Oh, yeah, Farih and I go way back."

Denise couldn't help but notice the stern look on Farih's face. She knew there was more to the story, but she couldn't focus on it. She couldn't take her eyes off of Lena.

Then a bright smile covered Farih's face. "Yes." Farih stood up and walked over to Danni. She wrapped her arms around her, placing a single kiss on both of Danni's cheeks. "It's been such a long time."

Lena watched. Danni's face didn't change.

Farih turned to Lena. "Lena, it's so wonderful to see you too." Farih hugged Lena.

Cooley glanced at Sahara. The tension in the room could be cut with a knife. She couldn't help but breathe a sigh of relief that the awkwardness wasn't caused by her or Sahara for a change.

"Well, it's obviously a small world. Now that we are all acquainted, let's eat." Cooley held her water glass up.

"I agree, baby," Sahara said, and she and Cooley tapped their glasses together as they all took their seats.

"Lena, I'm loving the new hair." Farih's smile lit up the room. "So chic, mature."

Denise couldn't believe how nice Farih was being.

Lena wanted to scream. She smiled. "Thank you. I just wanted to try something new."

"I can't believe you cut your hair," Denise mumbled, causing everyone to look at her.

Lena's smile faded. "Why not? Don't like it?"

Denise shook her head. "No, it looks fine. You just always seemed to love your hair."

"People change. But you, of all people, should know that," Lena snapped. Denise's eyes were burning a hole in her, and she didn't know how much more she could take. "I mean, look at you. Just a few years ago you were a determined basketball player who wouldn't touch liquor. Now you're famous and sipping bubbly."

Denise smirked. "Yeah, well, you're right. People do change—"

Cooley quickly interrupted before World War III broke out. "Okay, so, Danni, what projects are you working on right now?"

Danni didn't know what to think about Lena and Denise, and at that moment she didn't care. She couldn't take her eyes off of Farih, who was doing everything in her power not to look in her direction.

"Well, just the same ole real estate and the agency."

"And have you had any time to think about my offer?" Cooley sat up.

Danni tilted her head. "Um, I've been thinking about it. . . ."

"Just thinking, or really thinking?" Cooley's eyes didn't leave Danni's face. She'd learned to read people in the industry, because you never knew if they were serious or just putting on.

"It's a good idea, but a lot to consider. But I do know you need to get some real estate and stop working like a hobo out of your apartment." Danni smiled.

"Ah, that's a low blow."

"Hey, my baby works her ass off and is the best manager I've ever had." Sahara kissed Cooley on her cheek.

"You are right, Sahara." Danni sipped her wine. "Wade is amazing at what she does, and if I do expand, it will definitely be with her."

"Expand?" Denise looked at Cooley.

"Yeah, so I've been talking to Danni here about bringing her agency here and expanding to management and representation." Cooley took a sip of her drink. She could tell by the looks on Farih's and Denise's faces that the news wasn't sitting well with them.

There was a moment of silence. Denise quickly snuck a peek at Lena, who was concentrating on staring at her plate of salad.

The room suddenly felt like a sauna. Lena didn't know if it was Danni's hand massaging her leg or Denise's deeply intense stare that was causing a mixture of love, lust, and anger to take over her body.

"Let's face it. I started the agency for only one reason, and since that is done, I really haven't had the time to put into it," Danni remarked. "I pretty much let the other agents do all the work and collect the checks." Danni's eyes shifted quickly to Farih, then back to Cooley.

Lena noticed the quick exchange.

"So why have the entertainment thing at all?" Farih finally broke her silence. "Since you don't seem to really want it at all."

Danni's eyes focused back on Farih. "Because I don't give up on things that I commit myself to, and I committed myself to the agents and the clients that are with my agency."

Another silence hit the room.

Danni looked down at her salad. "I have a phone call I need to make. I'll be right back." She kissed Lena on her forehead.

Lena could feel the steam coming from Denise's direction.

Farih couldn't take it anymore. She stood up. "Excuse me. I need to visit the ladies' room."

"Want me to come with?" Sahara asked. She knew something was wrong with her friend.

Farih smiled. "No, girl, I'm okay. Stay and enjoy this food." She excused herself from the room.

Lena could feel Denise's eyes on her the second Farih walked out the door. Lena gazed at Sahara. "I love your new song, Sahara. So does my daughter. She really thinks she's you when she dances to it."

"That's—"

"So, Lena, what's up?" Denise cut Sahara off.

"What do you mean?"

"I mean, what's up?" Denise motioned with her hands toward Danni's seat. "Didn't know you were dating around."

Lena was fuming. "How would you? I haven't seen or heard from you in how long?"

Denise looked away. She knew Lena was right, but couldn't shake the rage she felt by seeing her with Danni. Denise shook her head and smiled. "Well, I think it's great. Good for you."

"Thanks. So glad to know I have your approval." Lena rolled her eyes and took another sip of wine.

"Whatever," Denise huffed as she finished off her glass.

Cooley and Sahara sat in silence, watching the scene unfold.

"Don't 'whatever' me. You stopped contacting me, remember?"

"I said whatever. Damn, drop it." Denise was furious. Not only was Lena dating someone else, but she also had the nerve to go off on her.

Lena wanted to jump across the table and smack the smug expression off of Denise's face.

Danni felt a tap on her shoulder as she closed her phone. She turned around to see Farih standing there with her arms folded and her usual smile missing.

"Yes, ma'am?" Danni put her phone in her pocket and braced herself for Farih's wrath.

"What are you trying to pull, Danni? Coming here, going into business with Cooley. It's not going to work."

Danni's head jerked. She noticed people looking in their direction, at the famous Farih. She motioned with her head for Farih to follow her. Farih quickly followed Danni to the closed patio.

"First off, who the fuck do you think you are talking to?" Danni's deep New York accent appeared.

"Danni, this isn't cool."

"Look, shawty, the days of Danni pining over Farih are over. I'm not doing shit because of you."

"Oh, and so you just so happened to pick the one manager who just so happens to be best friends with my girlfriend to go into business with. Ugh. And of all the girls for you to bring up in here, you bring her."

"What's wrong with Lena?"

"Like you don't already know." Farih crossed her arms.

"I don't know what the hell you are talking about. And obviously, you weren't listening. Cooley wants to go into business with me. I haven't said yes or no. Cooley sought *me* out, not the other way around, and sorry, boo, but I'm not fucking up business for anyone, not even you, never again." Danni fixed her shirt collar. "Now, if you will excuse me, I have a date to get back to." Danni walked back in, leaving Farih fuming.

"Look, as entertaining as this is, y'all need to both calm the hell down before your dates walk back in," Cooley advised Denise and Lena. Sahara and Cooley didn't know if they were minutes away from fighting or ripping each other's clothes off. They heard the doorknob turn. Danni walked back in and sat down.

"Sorry about that. One thing I hate about business calls, they can pull me away from beautiful things."

Lena blushed as Danni kissed her on her cheek.

Denise shifted in her seat.

Danni noticed Denise's movement. "So, Denise, tell me, what was Lena like in school? I bet all the girls wanted her."

Denise wanted to slap the smirk off of Danni's face. "Nah, Lena played for the other team back then."

The comment made Lena roll her eyes.

Danni went on. "I don't know how you did it . . . sleeping in the room with her every night. I think I would have had to try to get that at some point."

"You know, I used to say the same thing," Cooley joked, causing Sahara to jab her in her ribs.

Denise looked at Lena. She shook her head.

Farih walked back in the room.

"I'm not the type to mess around with straight girls. Too complicated, too much drama. They never know what they want," said Denise.

Danni nodded her head in agreement. She glanced over at Lena, who was as still as stone. "So, boo, you know what you want now?"

Lena didn't move for a moment. She pulled her eyes from Denise to Danni. Lena smiled. "I definitely do." She looked back at the table. "But again, you have very strong powers of persuasion." Lena bit her lip. She and Danni stared at each other like they wanted to jump on the table right then and there.

"Well, damn," Sahara interjected. "I know that look." She looked at Cooley. Cooley smirked.

Sex was in the air, but all Farih and Denise could do was stare at their former friends.

Danni looked down at her cell phone. "Man, it's getting late. I think we might just call this a night and head home. So much work to do."

"Work . . . Yeah, I bet," Sahara added. She glanced at Farih, who hadn't flashed her smile in a while.

"Ah, not leaving so soon, are you?"

Denise's sarcastic tone irritated Lena, causing her to roll her eyes.

"Yeah, well, I just got back into town, and I've missed this one over here something awful." Danni's words caused Lena to blush. "You guys know how it is." Danni smiled. Her eyes shifted to Denise, who quickly looked down at the wine she was guzzling.

Farih couldn't take her eyes off of Danni. She finally snapped back to reality. Farih smiled. "That's so cute." Farih's voice cracked. "How long have you been dating?"

"Just a few months." Lena smiled.

"And have you met her cute little child?" Farih asked, making Lena want to slap her even more.

Danni nodded. "Oh yes, that little girl has me wrapped around her finger."

"Like mother, like daughter, I see," Denise muttered. Lena looked at her.

Denise smirked. "I mean, Lena has always had the ability to wrap people around her fingers."

Farih and Lena were both fuming. Farih couldn't believe how blatantly disrespectful Denise was being around her. Even Sahara shot Farih a look, wondering why she was putting up with Denise's antics.

Cooley knew she had to break it up before things got out of control. "Look, man, we will get up later. Just continue to think about it."

Danni was heated too. She had noticed Denise's attitude toward Lena, and it was unsettling. She had to keep her cool. She wasn't in New York and couldn't act a fool, like she normally would.

Denise knew she was wrong, but she didn't care. The wine in her system was the added fuel to her feelings toward Lena.

"Most def." Danni threw three hundred-dollar bills on the table. She knew it was way more than what was needed. "This should cover tonight."

"You don't have to do that." Cooley put her hand up.

"Nah, it's nothing. It was nice seeing all of you." Danni's eyes focused on Farih, who looked like she was ready to kill someone. "Let's do this again." Danni took Lena by her hand as they walked out of the private room.

Lena watched Danni tip the valet. Thoughts ran through her head. She was furious at Denise and wasn't a fan of Farih at all.

Danni got in the car and started it up. Lena could tell Danni wasn't happy as she didn't hold the door for her. Lena closed her own door and Danni began to drive out of the lot.

Lena broke the silence. "So that was interesting."

"Very. So Denise Chambers is the infamous roommate?" Danni asked without taking her focus off of the road.

"What?" Lena knew the question was coming but still wasn't prepared to face the inquisition.

"Come on, Lena, keep it real. That girl was actin' thirsty as hell. She had to be the one." Danni quickly glanced at Lena before focusing back on the road.

Lena sighed. "Yeah."

"And you're telling me y'all never hooked up?"

"I mean, not really."

"Okay, so the whole 'I fell for her, but we never really did anything' was complete bullshit?"

"It's complicated."

"And you're trying my patience right now."

Even with her mellow tone, Lena could tell Danni meant business. Lena sighed. "At the time I was with Brandon. She tried to keep it platonic, but I didn't make it easy. We messed around a few times but never were able to get serious."

In that moment Lena realized the truth. She never was Denise's girlfriend. They had shared a few intimate nights but nothing more. The thought infuriated her. Why was she so stuck on Denise when they were never official?

"It's kind of hard to believe it wasn't anything more than a few nights."

"That's all it was. When I finally realized I was ready, she no longer was interested. It is what it is." The truth was sinking in. Lena couldn't help but realize that what she and Denise had was really just a fantasy and a figment of her imagination. They were never official, never had anything real.

"Interesting." Danni turned her Sirius radio on.

Lena looked at Danni, who didn't seem bothered at all. "Any more questions?"

Danni shook her head. "Should there be?" She glanced at Lena as they sat in traffic.

Lena shook her head. "Oh, but wait, I have a question for you." Lena turned her body toward Danni. "How long did you and Farih date?"

Danni's face was stern, emotionless. "A while."

"Really? That's all I get?"

"I really don't want to talk about it."

"She's the girl, the one you were talking about in Miami, isn't she?"

Danni sighed. "Look, Lena, I really don't want to talk about it, at least not right now. And I'm not trippin' off Denise and what you guys had. That's the past, and I make it my goal never to live in the past. I'm about what's going on right here and right now." Danni put her hand on Lena's bare thigh.

"What *is* going on here, Danni? Don't think I didn't notice the way you were acting in there. Were you being genuine or just trying to mess with Denise . . . or should I say Farih?"

"Well . . ." Danni glanced at Lena. "Don't get me wrong. It was fun fucking with yo' girl like that, but nah, boo, I'm too grown for games."

Lena smiled. "So all that stuff was legit about how you feel about me?"

"Lena, I've told you I'm feeling you, girl. I don't just take women around places, ya know. But like I've said before, I'm not try—"

"To be serious. I know. I know." Lena smirked. "But it's nice to know I'm more than just a random chick."

Danni massaged Lena's thigh. "Boo, there is nothing random about you." Danni leaned over and kissed Lena on her cheek.

Lena moaned. She bit her bottom lip. She wanted Danni; she wanted her right there. Lena placed her hand on top of Danni's and began to move it under her skirt. Danni giggled.

"Oh, really now?" Danni licked her lips. "In the middle of Peachtree traffic?"

"What's wrong with a little exhibitionism?"

"What have I turned you into?" Danni playfully shook her head as her finger massaged Lena's swollen clit through her moist panties.

"I don't know. But I like it." Lena's mischievous grin woke up Danni's inner sexual predator. Lena slowly pulled her panties off and threw them in Danni's lap. Danni took no time finding Lena's softest place. Her hand absorbed Lena's wetness as Lena ground her hips on the leather seat. She moaned for more. A loud car horn honked as a group of white partygoers rooted for the private show they were witnessing.

"Lena, we have an audience."

"I don't care." Lena moaned. She closed her eyes and let the seat slowly go back. Danni continued to fuck her in the expensive car until Lena's body exploded on her hand. Danni massaged her swollen clit as Lena struggled to catch her breath.

Lena opened her eyes. The people in the car next to them hollered for more. She realized what she had just done. Lena blushed. She was exploring new sexual territory, and Danni was the ultimate tour guide. She didn't want the ride to end.

Chapter 28

They arrived back at the hotel. Danni handed her keys to the valet. Lena hopped out of the passenger seat. She looked out at the busy street. She felt sexually free, but something was bothering her.

"Lena." Danni called Lena, who was staring into space. Lena turned and looked at her. She motioned for Lena to follow.

"Um, I think that I'm going to call it a night."

Danni frowned. "What do you mean?"

"I think I'm going to go home."

Danni laughed. "You're kidding, right? Come on." She put her arms around Lena's waist. "I've been waiting on this for weeks."

"And you can wait another day." Lena smirked. She had realized in the car that she was falling back into her old patterns. Danni held the cards, and Lena had almost forgotten she held the ace. Lena handed the valet her card.

Danni took a step back. "It's like that? You gon' leave me like this when I've already taken care of you?"

"Awww." Lena put her hand on Danni's cheek. "That was just a preview of what's to come. Tomorrow, my house. Eight o'clock."

Danni nodded her head. "Touché."

"Good night, Danielle."

"Good night, Ms. Jamerson."

Danni headed into the hotel.

***

Denise pulled her shirt over her head. She couldn't stop thinking about Lena and the attitude she displayed toward her. She wanted answers. She knew the way they ended things before wasn't perfect, but what about the times that Lena had left her because of her love of Brandon?

"So do we need to talk about this?"

Farih's voice brought Denise back to reality. She knew she was busted. There was no way Farih didn't notice the exchanges she had with Lena.

"Not really." Denise shrugged her shoulders.

"So we are going to ignore what happened tonight?"

"I guess so," Denise snapped. The last thing she wanted to think about was Lena and Danni, or Danni and Farih's past. Denise rolled her eyes.

Farih couldn't take it anymore. She threw her hands up and stormed out of the room. Denise knew she needed to follow her, but didn't want to. She forced herself off of the bed.

"What is wrong now?" Denise muttered when she caught up with Farih.

Denise's attitude angered Farih even more. Farih's head snapped around. "Are you fucking kidding me?"

"What?"

"Seriously, you fucking disrespected the hell out of me tonight. Fuck, Denise, you think I'm a fucking fool? Lena? Really? After all this time you are still stuck on her bony ass!" All of Farih's planned moves had fallen out the window. She couldn't take it anymore. No matter how much she loved Denise or what a breakup might do to her career, she couldn't continue to be disrespected.

Denise was busted but wasn't going to take it sitting down. "Oh, and you and Danni making googly eyes all night was a figment of my imagination?" Farih's face dropped. "Yeah, Farih, so how is it we've been together all this time, yet you never mentioned her before?"

"I . . ."

"I . . . I . . . whatever, Farih. While you want to point fingers at me, you aren't fucking innocent. You know all about Lena. You know about our past. But I got to be slapped in the face with your past tonight!"

"At least I didn't disrespect you! All those catty comments, the expressions on your face . . . You acted like I wasn't even there. At least I was respectful tonight. Besides a look here and there, I didn't broadcast my unrequited feelings for anyone in front of you!"

Denise knew there was nothing she could say. She listened, letting Farih get all her feelings about Lena out on the table. There were no tears. Farih wasn't going to cry. She was too mature for that.

"So do you want her back or what? Because if it's Lena you want, there is the door. Go get her. But before you do, you just take a moment and remember what all you will be giving up by taking the same chance you've taken time and time again."

Farih stared at Denise's face for a moment. Denise couldn't look at her; she was too ashamed. Farih had been there for her and had loved her for years, whereas Lena had always been a fantasy, someone that she had never truly had as her own.

Farih began to walk away but then paused. She turned back to Denise. "When you said I changed, I listened and I took everything in. I realized you were right and that I needed to work on myself. Well, Denise, *you* are not the woman that I fell in love with. What happened to the sincere, genuine, and loving Denise I met in New York? I miss her." Unable to hold back the tears, Farih headed to the bedroom.

Her words replayed in Denise's head.

Lena hated the mix of emotions flooding her body. Not only was she angry at Denise, but she was also sexually frustrated due to her declaration to Danni. She knew no toy was going to help her. She needed something more.

Lena's dress fell to the ground. She stared at the blue water illuminating her backyard. She dove into the cold pool. The water was like a reality check. She held her breath. The pressure began to grow in her lungs. She stayed under until her body couldn't take it anymore. Lena came up and took a deep breath, the oxygen alleviating the pressure in her lungs. She took another breath.

"I thought I was going to have to come in after you."

The voice startled Lena. She turned to see a dark figure walking toward her. She froze. She knew she was about to die.

"Who are you?" Lena's voice trembled. She had no way out. She was naked in her pool, and there was no way to get away. "I will scream!"

The person laughed. "You know, you really should lock your gate." Danni's smiling face came into the light.

"Oh my God, you scared the shit out of me!" Lena swam toward the edge of her pool. Danni picked up a towel off of a shelf. "What the hell are you doing here?"

"Well . . ." Danni handed the towel to Lena, who quickly wrapped it around her wet body. "It took me only a moment to realize that I didn't want to sleep in my bed alone tonight. I was in my car before you pulled away from the hotel. What was taking you so long to pull off, anyway?"

Lena smirked. "I was deciding."

"Deciding what?"

"If I really wanted to leave."

Danni nodded her head. "I didn't like your choice."

"Obviously . . ."

Danni placed her hands on Lena's thighs. "I didn't want you to leave." She didn't take her eyes off of Lena's.

"Danni . . ." Lena felt her body betraying her. She tried to stay strong, but her body was giving in quickly. "I'm not trying to be your fuck buddy. I can't. . . ."

"I don't want to sleep alone tonight," Danni said as she put her finger over Lena's lips. "Sleep with me."

There were no words. Danni led Lena into her house like she lived there. She walked through the house until she found the master bedroom. Lena was curious, so she let Danni lead. Danni walked into the bathroom. Lena could hear the water running in the bathtub. Danni walked out.

"Take a bath, and get the chlorine off your body. I'm going to make us a nightcap." Before she could respond, Danni was gone. Lena followed instructions.

Lena put her robe on after her warm bath. She walked out of the bathroom to find Danni sitting on the edge of her bed. The room was illuminated by Lena's candles. A bowl of strawberries sat on a tray with a bottle of Dom. Danni motioned for Lena to come closer. Lena walked closer. Danni slowly took Lena's robe off. Lena braced herself for what was about to come. She could almost feel Danni's tongue inside of her.

"Sit," Danni said, then walked into the bathroom. She walked out, holding the container of Lena's body butter. Danni's iPad music echoed through Lena's stereo system. The songs weren't sexual, just romantic.

Danni placed Lena's right leg on her knee. She began to massage the body butter into Lena's leg. Lena's pussy throbbed as Danni's hands worked like those of a highly trained masseuse. Lena sipped on champagne while Danni rubbed lotion on Lena's entire body, not missing a single inch.

Danni stood up. Lena watched as she pulled her pants and shirt off. Standing in just her bra and boxers, Danni pulled the covers back on the bed. Lena didn't know what to think.

"Are you getting in?" Danni asked her.

"Are you serious?" Lena's body was on fire.

"I said I didn't want to sleep alone." The straight-faced look let Lena know Danni was serious. Lena crawled into her large bed. Danni got in. She pulled Lena's body next to hers. They spooned, Lena's ass resting against Danni's pelvis.

"Farih and I met years ago, when she first moved here from Nigeria. I fell for her hard. We both fell."

Lena listened attentively. She could tell Danni was struggling to open up. Lena rubbed Danni's thigh while she continued.

"She wanted to make it as a model, so I dedicated myself to helping her. I started managing her, and soon she booked her first major campaign."

"So what happened?"

"Farih came from almost nothing. She got her first taste of fortune and fame and was hooked. She wanted something I wasn't willing to be a part of, so she left for her career. I gave up so much for her, put so much of my life on hold."

"That's why you are so about business now?" Lena realized Danni was just as damaged by a woman as she was.

"I can't let that shit happen to me again. I can't let myself lose focus over love. In the end that shit just isn't worth it."

Lena turned and put her hand on Danni's cheek. "I understand." Lena officially hated Farih. Not only did the chick have the first woman Lena had ever loved, but she still held the strings to the woman Lena was falling in love with.

Danni kissed Lena on the nape of her neck. "You aren't a jump-off or a fuck buddy. I need you to know that," Danni whispered as she held Lena close.

"I do." Lena smiled as she closed her eyes. The inferno was dying down at a rapid pace. A different warmth took over her body, and that scared her. Her emotions were in control, and not her brain. There was no denying it. Lena knew she wasn't falling for Danni; she had already fallen.

Denise woke up in a sweat. She looked around her living room. She had fallen asleep on their leather chaise. Denise peeled her arm off the leather. She couldn't stop thinking about Farih and her comment about how Denise had changed.

Denise spent the rest of the night soul searching. Had she changed into someone new? She thought about her relationship with Farih and her feelings for Lena, which instantly made her uneasy. She was doing it again. Her unhealthy feelings for Lena were affecting her relationship and her life. Lena was like a drug to her, and although she hadn't partaken of the drug, she was on the verge of a relapse. Denise knew she had to get a grip before she lost her woman.

Denise knew she owed Farih an apology. She tiptoed into their bedroom. Farih was sound asleep. Denise eased her way onto the bed. She could smell Farih's body from the edge. She had on one of Denise's favorite citrus scents.

Denise's cold hands woke Farih up as they roamed their way from her ankles to her thighs. She rolled her eyes.

"No." Farih moved her leg. She had no interest in letting Denise please her. She was too angry. Denise didn't cease; her hands found Farih's legs again. "No." Farih sat up in the bed. She hit Denise's arm with force.

Denise's head jerked around, and she caught sight of Farih's angry face. "What the fuck was that for?"

"Fuck you, Denise! You think you're about to come in here and just get some after tonight?" Farih's African accent basted Denise. "Fuck you!"

"Why are you cursing at me?" Denise felt herself getting angry. "I'm sorry, shit."

Farih folded her arms. "That's not good enough."

"What the fuck do you want from me, Farih? I said I was sorry. I am." Denise didn't even believe herself.

"Oh, whatever, Denise! You think your mediocre head is going to make me forget about you and that gold-digging bitch! Fuck you." Farih hit Denise again with more force.

Denise was pissed. With one forceful tug she ripped the expensive comforter and top sheet off the bed, startling Farih. Denise grabbed Farih's ankles and pulled her down toward her. Before she could object, Denise had ripped the pair of Victoria's Secret panties that Farih had helped to make famous off her brown skin.

Farih rapidly hit Denise. "No! Fuck you, Denise. No!"

Denise fought to take hold of Farih's hands, while at the same time trying to break through. Tears began to flow from Farih's eyes. Denise held her down. She kissed her perfectly flat stomach.

"I'm sorry, Farih."

"Fuck you!" Farih cried.

"I'm sorry." Denise's tongue danced down to Farih's belly button. She released Farih's hands as she moved farther south.

"Fuck . . . you. . . ." Farih's cries became whimpers as Denise's tongue parted her swollen lips. Her mouth fell open. Tears streamed down her face as Denise apologized with the most dynamic pressure she'd seen in a long time.

Denise tasted her woman. Farih's body responded, even though Farih was still hitting her back. Farih's curses turned into moans. Denise had a point to make. There was nothing mediocre about her, and the notion of Farih thinking that there was didn't cut it with her.

Farih's body trembled. Denise was apologizing, and she was taking it all in. Denise hadn't made love to her like this since their last night in New York. Her hands massaged Denise's thick hair as her legs tensed up. This felt like her Denise, the Denise she fell in love with.

Farih moaned and wrapped her long legs around Denise's torso. Denise's lips wrapped around Farih's throbbing clit. She sucked it while her fingers entered Farih's tight cave. Farih's toes curled as her orgasm flooded Denise's mouth. Denise didn't let go; she wanted every drop of Farih's sweetness.

"Denise," Farih whispered as she pulled Denise's shirt toward her. Denise moved up. Farih planted her lips against Denise. Their tongues danced, and Farih could smell and taste herself on Denise. "I love you." Their mouths met again.

"I love you too." Denise's strong arms pulled Farih as close as she could get her. She knew it was true. She did love Farih, and their love was real. The love she had for

Lena was a fantasy built on years of lust parading as a friendship. Farih's love was pure. There was no drama of ex-husbands and no closets to come out of.

Farih's love was what she needed, and what she desperately wanted to want.

Chapter 29

Lena stared at her bridesmaid's dress. Carmen's wedding was a few weeks away, and the thought of being in the same house with Denise and Farih was bothering her. The dinner days before still haunted her. She couldn't shake the way Denise had acted toward her. Denise had seemed so angry. Lena didn't understand why. If anyone should be angry, it should be her.

The doorbell woke her out of her trance. She hurried through the hallway toward the front door. Out of breath, she opened the door before looking through the peephole.

"Denise." Lena's heart skipped a beat.

"We need to talk." Denise stood there, with her familiar focused expression. Lena didn't know what to think. She left the door open, then walked back down her hallway. Denise followed.

"What do we need to talk about?"

"Look, the other night . . ."

"Yeah, Denise." Lena turned around. "What the hell was that about?"

Denise dropped her head. "I just wanted to apologize."

"I'm more interested in the reason for your actions, instead of the apology." Lena folded her arms. "You act like I've done something to you."

Denise's head jerked up. "You haven't? Really?"

"No, I haven't. Last time I checked, you made the decision to leave me alone and stop calling me. I didn't make that call."

"You know why I had to do that."

"No, actually, I don't. You just came over here, we almost hooked up, and then you never called again." Lena felt her body trembling.

"Lena . . ." Denise tried to think of the right words, but she didn't know what to say.

"I know I'm not innocent. I know I'm the cause for why we . . . well, why we never became anything. But I always thought that through it all, we were friends first. What happened to that? What happened to my fucking friend—"

Before she could finish, Denise grabbed Lena, pulling her body into hers. Their lips met, quickly becoming familiar again.

Denise didn't let go. Lena held on to the sides of her button-down shirt. After a minute or so, their lips finally parted.

"I don't know why, but no matter what, I can't seem to let go of you," Denise whispered.

"Then don't." Lena held on to Denise. She didn't want to leave her arms. She cared about Danni, but what she had with Denise was so much more. After this kiss, there was no denying that.

"But I can't do this." Denise pulled away. "You, this, it's not good for me. It never was."

The words smacked Lena in her face. "I'm not good?"

"Lena, I've loved you since I first saw you getting out of your car on move-in day at school. But when I needed you to love me, you couldn't. And you still can't."

"People change Denise. I'm not the same girl who you caught falling off the chair my freshman year. I came to you. I wanted you. Damn it, how can you not see how I feel?"

"Yeah, Lena, you've always felt like you wanted to be with me, until Brandon comes along or your family has something to say. Tell me, Lena, does your mother know about lesbian ways and ole girl?" Denise stared at Lena.

Lena couldn't speak. She looked away from Denise, causing Denise to let out a sigh.

"I can't live on a hope. I won't give up what I have for the chance that Lena knows for sure what she wants this time."

Lena's body was shaking. She couldn't stop shaking her head. "Then why are you here? Why the fuck did you just walk in my house, bringing all these emotions back up?"

"I didn't mean to kiss you." Denise felt horrible. She took a few steps backward. "I . . . I just wanted to apologize."

"You know what? Fuck you and your apology!" Lena's voice trembled. "Why you talk about how bad I am for you, guess what? You are just as bad for me. Because of you, my whole life and world was turned upside down. I gave up everything for you, and you left me hanging."

Denise's head snapped. "*You* gave up everything? Lena, if it wasn't for my fucking love for yo' ass, I never would have fucked with Rhonda's crazy ass to begin with. I lost everything because of you."

"And look what you've gained. You have the career and the fucking model girlfriend. You have it all, and all I have is a fucking confused mind and fucking feelings for a girl who doesn't want me in return!"

They stood in silence for a moment. Lena couldn't stop shaking her head. Denise knew she was in too deep.

"I'm sorry for coming here. I shouldn't have." Denise turned toward the front door.

"Why did you do this to me?" Lena yelled. "Why did you have to do this shit, Denise! Go back to your fucking glamorous life."

Denise walked out the door without turning around. Tears poured from her eyes as soon as she closed the door. She loved Lena but knew she couldn't be with her.

Lena's tears stopped as soon as the door closed. Lena couldn't cry over Denise anymore. She wasn't sad; she was mad as hell. She let out a loud grunt as she stormed to her bedroom. Despite everything that had happened between them, Denise had never made her so angry before.

Lena stared at herself in her full-length mirror. She knew she had done some messed-up things, but did she deserve what was happening in that moment? The reflection of the TV caught her attention. Lena rolled her eyes as Farih's perfect image walked out onstage with her other cohosts. Lena wanted to throw the TV. Instead, she picked up the remote and turned the sound on.

The camera focused on the main host of the show.

"So today we are celebrating all things wedding. In our audience are all brides to be." The audience clapped. "We have celebrity wedding planner Minka Objer here to give us tips on how to make a stunning wedding on a small budget. Also stylist Kellie Larsley will show us how to get that beautiful celebrity wedding dress look for less."

Lena sat on the side of her bed. She couldn't help but think about her wedding. Nothing about her wedding was budget. It was perfect, except for a small interruption by Brandon's baby mama—whose identity Lena discovered after the wedding—and the fact that she had cheated on Brandon for the first time with Denise just hours before their wedding.

Farih's face appeared on-screen. "Actually, Denise and I are attending a wedding for one of her best friends in three weeks."

"Is this a same-sex wedding?" another cohost asked.

Farih nodded her head. "Yes, it is. Carmen and Nic have been together for about five or six years and are the cutest couple. They are going to New York so that it will be legal." Farih smiled as the audience clapped.

"So when will we hear wedding bells for you and Denise?" the same cohost asked.

Farih's white smile appeared as she attempted to act shy. "Well, right now in Georgia it isn't legal, but the moment that it is, we will have the wedding of both of our dreams. But for right now we don't need a piece of paper to show that we love and are committed to each other one hundred percent."

Farih's speech made the crowd go wild. Lena couldn't take it anymore. She let out a loud growl and threw the remote at the television screen. She wanted Denise off of her mind. She had never wanted Danni to be in Atlanta more than she did at that moment. She had to get out of the house before her thoughts made her crazy.

Cooley couldn't take her eyes off the computer screen. The image of Sahara, her body naked, lying asleep in the bed with another woman's hands on her ass had rendered Cooley numb.

The headline read: SAHARA BUSTED FOR CHEATING ON COOLEY WITH BACKGROUND DANCER, AND WE HAVE THE PHOTOS AND VIDEO TO PROVE IT.

Things in lesbo land aren't as peachy as they appear. Seems Sahara was getting it on with her background dancer Tamera Hull during her last tour. No need for a snitch, since the info came directly from Tamera,who decided to snitch after an altercation between her and Cooley. Keep in mind the images and video are very explicit and not for the eyes of children.

Cooley stared at the black square with the PLAY button in the middle. The white walls of a bathroom appeared in the background. Tamera's face appeared on-screen.

"I can't believe what has happened to me, and just because I have a feeling I'm dreaming, I'm going to record this."

Tamera opened the bathroom door. The only light in the room beyond was from a lamp. The camera made it to a bed, where it panned up Sahara's legs to her naked butt and then continued until reaching her sleeping face. Tamera turned the video camera around to focus it on herself and smiled. She placed her hand on Sahara's butt, slowly caressing it, before she leaned in and placed a kiss on Sahara's right butt cheek. Sahara didn't move.

"My wildest dream has come true. I fucked Sahara, and I can't wait to eat that pussy again." Tamera smiled before the camera went black.

Sahara's managers and lawyers walked out from the Cooley's home office. No one said a word. Although plans were already in place to sue Tamera, they knew the worst was yet to come. Sahara closed the door behind them. She couldn't stop staring at the front door. She didn't know what was going to happen when she turned around, but she didn't want to face it yet.

Rage filled Cooley. She slammed the MacBook closed, stood up, and chucked it against the wall. The computer instantly broke into two pieces. The loud crash caused Sahara to almost jump out of her skin.

"Baby, please." Sahara turned around. Her tears had been flowing since she got the news early that morning about the leak. Cooley just stared at Sahara. Sahara had never been scared of Cooley, but the look in Cooley's eyes truly frightened her.

"You let her fucking record you!"

"I didn't know, Cooley. I had no idea she did that."

"She fucking recorded you. Now we both look like fucking idiots!"

"Baby, please."

"No, don't say shit to me."

"I was drunk, passed out asleep. You saw it. I didn't know."

"All I see is a dumb bitch who can't hold her fucking liquor." Cooley's words stung like venom.

The door opened. Denise walked in, with a look of anger and concern on her face.

"Now isn't a good time, Dee."

"No, Cool, I think it is." Denise stood her ground. She had heard everything from outside the door. "You two are loud as hell, and I could hear you all the way down the hall."

"Does it look like I fucking care who hears me? Fuck, why should it matter? Everyone knows my girlfriend is a cheating slut right about now."

Sahara couldn't take it anymore. She ran to the bedroom, crying, and slammed the door. Cooley paced in her little area. She knew she had taken it too far but didn't care.

"Denise, now is not a good time," Cooley repeated.

"Bruh, you need to calm the hell down." Denise walked closer to her friend.

Cooley stopped, looking at Denise like she had lost her mind.

"I heard the news on the radio, which is why I came right over here. I know it's a lot, but you really need—"

"Oh, so the shit is all over the radio now too. Fucking bitch, how could she do this to me?"

"Cool, even the DJs said it looked like Sahara was completely oblivious to what was happening. She was sleeping, and it's not like you didn't know about—"

"Now I'm the laughing stock of the fucking world. My bitch cheated on me and was dumb enough to get recorded in the process." Cooley began to pace again.

"Carla." Denise sat on the edge of the couch. "Listen to yourself. When have you ever cared about what someone thought of you? And put yourself in her shoes when all those various cheating rumors hit the Net when you were out doing your thing."

"I never got put on videotape!" Cooley rage caused her to hit a chair, knocking it across the floor.

Denise stood up. "Man, I know are angry, but you need to chill the fuck out. Yeah, a damn tape hit, but who the fuck cares? You knew about this. You knew she made a mistake, one damn mistake in your relationship. You had gotten over it. Yes, it's fucked up, but this shit you're doing is childish. The shit you said to her, you are dead wrong."

"What the fuck!" Cooley rushed up on Denise, but Denise didn't move. "Who's fucking friend are you, bruh? You can't see why the fuck I'm angry right now? What if Farih did this shit to you? What if she aired your dirty fucking laundry for the fucking world to see? How the fuck you gon' stand in my house and tell me I'm wrong?" Cooley turned around. "You know what? You can get the fuck out with all that."

"Cooley—"

"Nah, bruh, fuck that. You know what? How about you stay here with her ass since you so fucking concerned about her? I'm out."

Cooley ignored Denise's pleas, grabbed her keys, and stormed out of her home.

Misha beamed with pride over the meal she'd created. She didn't know what had come over her, but she had suddenly wanted to cook and cook a lot. She had let Jaylin spend the weekend with Patrick's parents. Tonight she was going to cater to her man.

Misha spared no expense making her deep-dish lasagna, which Patrick loved, along with salad and fresh garlic bread. She sat at the table in her new black mini-dress, waiting on Patrick to walk through the door.

Misha stood up when she heard the doorknob turn. She pressed PLAY on her stereo. Smooth jazz began to play. Patrick walked in the house, stopping in the doorway when he got the first whiff of the Italian cuisine.

"I've been waiting on you, Daddy," Misha said, doing her Marilyn Monroe impression. Her stilettos clicked on the linoleum floor. Patrick didn't move as Misha helped him out of his suit jacket.

"Mish . . ."

"Shhh. Just come over here and sit down. I made your favorite, so I want you to enjoy your meal before we spend the whole weekend together with no interruptions."

"Mish . . ." Patrick's voice cracked.

"Yes, baby?"

"I'm so sorry."

Misha turned toward Patrick. She couldn't help but notice his frightened expression.

"Baby, what is wrong?" Her heart began to race. "Is it Jaylin?"

Tears began to flow down Patrick's face. "I am so sorry. I fucked up. I fucked up bad."

Misha grabbed Patrick's face. "What is wrong?" Her hands were trembling. She knew something terrible had happened. Silent prayers started running through her head.

"I . . ."

"Patrick, what!"

"I cheated. . . ."

Chapter 30

Lena stared at the busy parking lot of the club across the street. She was already tipsy and knew she wasn't going to be able to drive home right now. She had started drinking as soon as she left the house. She'd left home with the intention of spoiling herself. She had got a massage and a mani-pedi and had got her hair done. She'd then headed to the mall and proceeded to waste a large sum of money on dresses she knew she would probably never wear.

She could see the club from the window of the restaurant she had stopped at to eat and drink her life away. Five *mojitos* later and she was still pissed at Denise. Carmen and Misha had been blowing her phone up nonstop, until she finally decided to turn the phone off. She knew Denise had probably told Carmen what happened. The last thing she wanted was to get questioned by her friends.

Lena headed to her car. She stumbled as she tried to pull the keys out of her clutch. She was in no position to drive and honestly didn't want the night to end. She pulled out one of the sexy dresses she bought and slipped into it in the car, along with a new pair of heels. It was a quick wardrobe change, but she knew she looked good. Lena walked across the street toward the VIP entrance of the club.

***

Cooley's eyes were blurry. She had already downed two bottles of complimentary champagne from the club owner and was halfway done with the bottle of Patrón she'd ordered. Random girls approached her, all knowing about the Sahara incident due to the Internet and the radio. Cooley couldn't help but snap at each of the whores, who were quite ready to take Sahara's place.

"Cooley?"

Cooley looked up. Her eyes finally focused in the dim club lighting, and she saw Lena standing in front of her with an inquisitive look on her face.

"Lena? What the hell are you doing here?" Cooley snapped. Out of all the people to call, she couldn't believe they'd sent Lena to get her.

"Trying to get away from life." Lena sighed as she looked around the club.

"Oh, well, that makes two of us." Cooley motioned for Lena to sit down. She poured Lena a shot, which Lena quickly took to her head. "Damn, you weren't kidding," Cooley said as she poured another shot for Lena. "Trouble in paradise?"

"Paradise? Yeah, right." Lena noticed the morose expression on Cooley's face. "Are you okay?"

"Fucking A-OK. I mean, I'm always supposed to be okay, cool as a fucking fan." Cooley poured herself another shot.

"Do you want to talk about it?"

"Not really."

"Good, 'cause I can't lie. The last thing I want to do is talk about anything." Lena forced a tiny smile. Cooley couldn't help but chuckle at drunk Lena.

"So where is Danni?" Cooley turned to Lena. "What is up with you and chicks with *D* names? You got a thing for the letter or something?"

"I guess, like you and your thing for *a*'s. I mean, Misha and Sahara." They both chuckled uncontrollably.

"Lena, you are drunk, boo." Cooley snickered.

"I know. Another shot please." Lena held the shot glass up. Cooley's hand trembled as she poured the shot, most of it landing on Lena's hand. They couldn't stop laughing when Lena licked the liquor off of her hand.

The laughter quickly stopped when Lena thought about Denise. "Your best friend isn't going to pop up here soon, is she?" Lena asked.

Cooley shook her head. "We aren't seeing eye to eye right now."

"Again, that makes two of us." Lena stared into the almost empty bottle until her eyes blurred, causing three Patrón bottles to appear on the table. There was silence as Usher's "Climax" played in the background. The words were haunting to both of them.

Cooley broke the silence. "I gave up everything for Sahara. I broke the rules. I fell for her, and this is what happens. I never should have fallen in love. Love is for the birds."

"Hear! Hear!" Lena's body slouched, and her shoulder rested against Cooley's. "Fucking love made me for real change everything about me. Before her, I knew what I wanted. Brandon. Now I'm . . . I don't know what the hell I am now."

"Girl, please." Cooley sat up and poured another shot. "You were *always* gay. I knew that shit the second we saw you on campus."

"What?" Lena turned her head.

"When we saw you get out of your ride on the first day. I could tell yo' ass was going." Cooley chuckled. "I told Denise that I was gon' get you. But that was before . . . well, before y'all met."

"You thought I was gay just from seeing me in a parking lot? What are you? Some type of gay whisperer?"

"Nah, I just know women. And you, Lena, had the tendencies, whether you want to admit it or not."

Lena thought about Cooley's statement. Had she ever thought about being with a girl before meeting Denise? Her mind raced. She had found women attractive, but that was normal, she thought. She shook her head.

"Well, I thought you were a man when I first met you, until you opened your mouth and that soft-ass voice came out," Lena said. She and Cooley both laughed. "You know, I bet that's why all those straight girls like you. They always think you are some sexy dude."

Cooley smirked. "Nah, I let them know up top what I am and what I can do to them. I had my shit right back then. No love, just pussy and money." Cooley stared at the table again.

"I can't lie. I've always wondered how you made all those girls go so crazy over you. I mean, that shit was unreal. All those women . . . I think you probably slept with half of the school."

"Not that many." Cooley thought about it. She smiled. "Well, maybe." She turned to Lena. "You are not so different from me. You had the folks falling for you left and right too."

"No, I didn't." Lena fell back, leaning on Cooley's side.

"Man, you made my best friend fall for you, and she doesn't fall for people, not back then. Not to mention Brandon, who probably is still sprung. And that funny-looking chick that you brought to my house for Carmen's party. I have no idea what you saw in her."

"Terrin. She was nice."

"She was funny looking. And was mean muggin' Dee all night." Cooley laughed. "That shit was hilarious."

"Shut up." Lena playfully hit Cooley.

"For real, Lena, like I told you before, you hold all the power. Hell, even I said to Dee when we first saw you that you could be wifey material. You weren't like those other chicks. I could tell that from looking at you." Cooley looked at Lena. "No wonder Denise can't let you go."

Lena looked into Cooley's eyes. "Can't let me go?"

"Man, Lena, don't play dumb. You know she still loves you. Denise. Oh, so perfect Denise. For someone so controlled, she never could just lose control and lock you down like she should have." Cooley shook her head. "All those years of pining for nothing. Couldn't have been me."

"Oh, so you think you could have made my confused ass move any faster than Denise?"

"Hell, yeah. It wouldn't have been all that Brandon shit with me. I would have shown you from day one who the boss was."

Cooley turned, and her eyes instantly met Lena's. They moved in, their lips meeting. Cooley's hand pulled Lena's head in closer. Their tongues danced. Lena pulled at Cooley's shirt.

A crash caused them to stop. They looked over to see that a girl had dropped her glass on the floor. They looked at each other but then quickly looked away.

"Um, I think we've both had too much to drink." Cooley shifted away from Lena in the booth.

"I think you're right." Lena tried to stand up, but the liquor quickly caught up with her, almost causing her to fall. Cooley caught her by her waist. They looked at each other; guilt covered both of their faces.

"Um, we need to call you a taxi," Cooley declared and helped Lena walk toward the door.

The hot Atlanta air didn't help at all in sobering either of them up. They stood next to each other as two taxis pulled up behind them. There were no words as they each got in their separate cabs.

Lena hit herself on the head over and over. "What the fuck did you do?" she repeated over and over. She knew there was no coming back from that. She wondered if Cooley would tell Denise. It was a secret she wanted to take to her grave, but she had a feeling she wouldn't be able to.

Chapter 31

Misha sat in her car with no place to go. She couldn't cry: tears wouldn't fall no matter how badly she wished for them. The whole conversation played over and over in her head.

"You what?"

"Baby . . ." Patrick attempted to hold Misha's hand, but she jerked away.

"You what?" Misha's head wouldn't stop shaking. She knew she couldn't have heard him correctly.

"I just . . . I was just fucked up, and I made a mistake."

"A mistake?" Misha's hands continued to tremble.

The rest of the words were a blur. Patrick explained how he ran into an ex, who was more than willing to give him time during the time that Misha wasn't. He had been holding it in but couldn't hold it anymore when he walked in and saw the lavish spread Misha created for them to enjoy.

"I just knew something was off with you, and I couldn't shake the feeling that you were cheating on me. I just wanted revenge," Patrick confessed.

"So you fucked some bitch because you thought *I* was cheating on *you?*"

With his back against the wall, Patrick couldn't think of anything to do but fight back.

"Well, you don't know how you were treating me. You weren't giving me any time, no sex, no nothing."

"Fuck you!" Misha snapped. She lost control of herself and began beating Patrick on his chest. He attempted to block the blows. "Fuck you! Fuck you! Fuck you!"

"Misha, please!" Patrick grabbed Misha's wrists. "Please, baby, don't—"

"Fuck you!" Misha broke down. "I sat up here, willing to give up everything for you, and this is how you fucking repay me. Fuck you, asshole. I hate you!" Misha attacked Patrick verbally like a rattlesnake attacking prey.

Misha couldn't stay. She ran to her bedroom and threw all the things she could grab into a bag. Patrick pleaded with her and attempted to pull the clothes out of the suitcase. Not willing to fight anymore, Misha grabbed her keys and purse, leaving all her other things in the house. She felt Patrick's hand grab her arm and jerk her around.

"No, Misha, I'm not letting you leave. You can't leave me." Patrick's eyes burned with pure determination. Misha pulled away.

"I gave up everything for you!" Misha cried as she pushed her husband away. "I did whatever you asked of me. I gave it all up!"

"Baby, please, hear me out. . . ."

"Hear you out? Patrick, that's all I've done is hear you out and do what you fucking say. And you cheat on me because of your own fucking insecurities." Misha could feel the anger reaching maximum levels. "I could have, you know. I could have easily fucked off on you. I've had chances, plenty of them."

"So is that what you need to do?" Patrick stood in front of her, unwilling to let her pass. "You need to go out and sleep with someone?" He had to force the words out of his mouth. "Because if that's what you need to do, go do it. Just come back to me. Don't leave us. Don't leave our family."

Misha turned her head. She couldn't believe what he was saying. She shook her head. Misha thought about all the fights they had had over the past few months. She thought about all the times she had to make up excuses for why she couldn't go visit Carmen because of his issues with her past. Misha shook her head and huffed. The right side of her mouth curved upward.

"You see, Patrick, the thing is, now I don't need your fucking permission anymore." She pushed him again, but her words had cut him to the point where he didn't fight anymore. Shocked by her statement, he let her pass.

Misha walked out the door, unsure if she wanted to ever return.

Denise opened her front door. Cooley stood there, leaning against the wall. Denise opened the door all the way for her obviously drunk friend.

Cooley stumbled in, finding a seat at the kitchen table, while Denise brewed her a cup of expresso.

"Where have you been?" Denise asked.

"The club." Cooley stared at Denise's back. She had never felt so horrible in her life. She wondered if she should tell her or if she should take the mistake to the grave.

"I see you had fun." Denise turned toward her friend. "Hopefully, not too much fun."

"Nah. Well . . . no, not too much."

Denise poured the cup of espresso and walked to the table. She sat down across from Cooley.

"I didn't mean to come down on you so hard. You know I'm always on your side, and being on your side means I need to let you know when you are doing something that could affect you. . . ."

"It's cool. I know." Cooley sipped the hot brew, which burned her tongue. She thought about taking it to the head and letting the cup burn her mouth. Maybe it would burn the essence of Lena out of her mouth. "Where's Farih?"

"At some event or something. Man, are you okay? Talk to me."

"I don't know what I am right now, Dee." Cooley lowered her head. Denise was her best friend, and the thought of hurting her was killing her. "Dee, I need to tell you something."

Chapter 32

The cab pulled in front of Lena's house. She saw Misha's car sitting in the driveway. Lena's whole body began to tremble. She now regretted giving Misha a key. She paid the cabdriver and stumbled to her front door. She found Misha sitting on the couch with a bottle of wine, which was almost completely empty.

"What are you doing here?" Lena's voice cracked as she used the wall as a guide into her house.

Misha didn't respond. She continued to stare at the TV, which was playing songs on the R & B and soul music station.

"Misha." Her call went unanswered again. "Misha, um, sweetie, what are you doing here?" Lena didn't know what to think of Misha's frozen state. Was it possible for Misha to find out that quickly? If Cooley had told Carmen and Carmen had told Misha, it was possible she was already screwed. "Um, well, I'm going to my room. I can't really stand straight."

Lena walked to her bedroom. Her mind raced with what she might say if Misha ever confronted her about the situation. Lena sat on her bed. She could hear Misha's footsteps headed toward her bedroom. With each step Lena's heart pounded harder and harder.

"Lena . . ." Misha's voice trembled. "Lena, I . . ."

"I'm sorry, Mish." Suddenly emotions swept over Lena. Tears flowed from Lena's eyes.

Lena's response startled Misha. Had Patrick already contacted her?

"I just don't know what to think," Misha said and ran to the bed as the first tear fell from her eyes.

"Don't think anything. It was a mistake." Lena sobbed.

"I'm just in so much pain. I never thought in a million . . ." A familiar scent entered Misha's nose. She sniffed again. Misha's eyes widened. She knew the smell was a bit too familiar, and it covered Lena's dress. "Lena, who have you been with tonight?"

"Huh?" Lena's doe-eyed expression hit Misha like a ton of bricks. Lena was confused. How could Misha ask her that when she already knew? "Wait, what are we talking about?"

"You smell . . . you smell like . . . Carla's cologne." Misha folded her arms. "God, tell me Danni doesn't wear that too."

Lena's eyes shifted. "Misha, wait. What have you been talking about this whole time? What happened?"

"I was talking about Patrick. . . ." Misha looked at Lena. "Wait, what did you think I was talking about?"

Lena's eyes widened like those of a deer caught in the headlights. "Mish . . ."

"No . . ." Misha couldn't take her eyes off of Lena who looked like a deer caught in headlights. Her Spidey senses tingled. Her mind scanned the words that had come out of Lena's mouth. "You said you were sorry and it was a mistake, yet you don't know about Patrick."

"What about Patrick? Misha, what happened with Patrick?" Lena struggled to change the subject.

"What are you sorry about, and what was a mistake, Lena?" Misha was on full alert mode. Another strong whiff of the familiar scent hit her nose. She took two steps back from the bed. "And why do you smell like Carla's cologne?"

Lena knew she'd been caught. She tried to speak, but the words couldn't escape her mouth. Tears swelled in her eyes as she watched Misha's whole demeanor change in front of her. Lena had no control over her body. Putting two and two together, Misha threw her hands up and rushed out of the room. Lena's flew after her.

"Misha!" She ran, grabbing Misha's arm as she picked up her keys and purse. Misha snatched her arm away.

"You know what? I don't even want to know what you did, but knowing Cooley I already know."

"It isn't what you think. We didn't . . . just . . . we were at the club and—"

"And what, Lena? You danced? You talked? You what?" Misha screamed.

"It was one kiss. It was a mistake, a terrible, horrible mistake." Before Lena knew it, Misha had pushed her into the wall.

"How the fuck could you, Lena? With Carla? How fucked up of a person are you?"

The words smacked Lena. Misha was fuming and had every right to be. The tears continued to flow down Lena's face. Misha didn't cry; she was too pissed off to cry.

"I don't know how it happened. We were both drunk, both sad. It was quick, meant nothing, and we both felt terrible after it. It was a mistake. I would never want to hurt you or . . ." Lena thought about Denise.

Misha took it all in. She stood looking at her pathetic friend. "You know what, Lena? All this time I thought you were this confused chick who just needed to find herself. No, you are fucked up in more ways than one. You're a selfish, spoiled bitch!"

Lena fell to the floor. She hit the back of her head against the wall. She didn't want to hear what Misha was saying, but she couldn't stop listening.

"And you probably wonder why Carmen and Cooley told Denise to leave yo' ass alone. You are wishy-washy, and you don't give a fuck about anyone but yourself."

Lena looked up. She couldn't believe Carmen had told Denise not to be with her. "I'm not."

"You are! You take everyone on this Lena emotional roller coaster, and you wonder why Terrin wasn't willing to be your fucking friend. She was smart. She knew keeping you in her life would lead her to a lifetime of heartache, because Lena never is going to make up her mind. She doesn't have to!" Misha picked up her purse.

"Misha, please, I can't lose your friendship," Lena cried. "Please don't leave me."

It was déjà vu. Lena's voice transformed into Patrick's right in front of her. Misha felt the room spinning. In one night her whole world had turned upside down, and she had no one to turn to. Misha felt nauseated. Patrick had cheated, and now her best friend had fooled around with the only woman she had ever truly loved.

"For once I come to you, needing my fucking friend, and you somehow manage to still make everything about you. You deserve to be miserable. Lord knows, you've made enough people miserable. I have real problems to deal with, and losing a fake-ass friend isn't one of them." Misha walked out, slamming Lena's front door.

Lena's body was quivering. She fell against the wall. In one day her whole world was crashing down around her.

Chapter 33

Denise didn't move. Cooley stared at her friend, who was sitting as still as a statue in front of her. Denise's eyes were fixated on Cooley. For the first time in her life, Denise had Cooley nervous.

"I'm telling you it was a big mistake. We had both had a crazy amount of liquor. Both fucked up and—"

"So the liquor made you fuck Lena?" Denise pushed the chair back and walked away. She could feel her blood boiling, and if she stayed so close to Cooley, they would end up fighting.

"Whoa, we didn't fuck, Denise. Listen to me, man. We didn't fuck, didn't come close to fucking. There was no fucking involved. It was just a kiss."

Denise had tuned Cooley out. Her head was shaking. "So now you finally got to add Lena to your list. How does it fucking feel, you selfish son of a bitch!"

Cooley stood up. She had braced herself for Denise's anger, but her assumption that she fucked was a bit much.

"Denise, I didn't have sex with her. It was a quick kiss, which we both immediately regretted. Man, I am sorry."

"You're right about that. Sorry-ass muthafucka. You need to get the fuck out of my house before I do something I'm going to regret."

Cooley looked at the front door. Suddenly the conversation from earlier entered her mind. She hit the table.

"You know what, Denise? I know what I did was wrong, but you are taking this shit to another level. You act like I fucked her. It was a meaningless kiss."

"No, Cooley, that's your fucking problem. You don't care about shit. You don't care about any of the women whose hearts you've broken over the years, and you don't care about Sahara and the pain you keep putting her through."

Cooley felt the anger rising. "The pain I put her through? You know what? Fuck you, Denise!"

"Fuck you!"

"No. You know what? I'm not apologizing for shit. You know what? You think you know ever fucking thing, but you don't know shit. Denise, you act like your shit don't fucking stink. Why the fuck am I sitting here, apologizing for a fucking kiss with a girl who has never been yours to begin with!"

Denise's head jerked around toward Cooley. Cooley stood her ground. Cooley was fuming.

"Yeah, I said it! I told you over and over again to lock that shit down with Lena, but you never did. She was never your girlfriend, Denise. You had chance after chance to have her, but you were too afraid to do anything about it."

Denise rushed up, pushing Cooley against the wall. Cooley pushed Denise back.

"You don't know shit!" Denise shouted.

"Oh, I don't? How many times did you have to get Lena? You could have stopped her wedding if you wanted, but you didn't. She came to New York for you, and you sent her away. You picked Farih, remember? That's who you wanted. Now you want to be salty 'cause I kissed a bitch that was never yours to begin with."

Denise's right fist connected with the right side of Cooley's jaw, causing Cooley to fall. Shocked, Cooley looked at Denise, who was standing over her.

"Lena is, has been, and always will be mine. That's all you need to fucking worry about." She watched as Cooley stood back up. Denise stepped back. "You know, all these years people have questioned why I would be friends with such a heartless asshole like you. You don't give a fuck about anything or anyone. I always knew you were a cold muthafucka, I just never in a million years thought you would be that cold muthafucka to me. Get the fuck out of my house!"

Denise didn't wait for Cooley to leave. She walked to her bedroom, leaving her friend standing there speechless. Holding her jaw, Cooley opened the front door to find Farih standing there with a stern look on her face. Knowing there was nothing she could say, Cooley walked past her.

Denise sat on the side of her bed. Lena appeared in her head. She picked up her phone. She had never wanted to curse someone out so bad in her life. She looked at her keys. She didn't want to curse Lena out over the phone. She knew she deserved a face-to-face tongue-lashing. She headed back to the dining room, almost hoping Cooley was still there so she could punch her again.

Denise froze. Standing with her hand on the kitchen table, looking down was Farih.

"Oh, I didn't hear you come in. I gotta go take care—"

"Going to Lena or to Cooley?" Farih didn't look up from the kitchen table. "I'm guessing Lena, since you already told Cooley how you feel." Farih looked at Denise. "Lena's always been yours? Did I hear that correctly?"

Denise's hands fell to her sides. She didn't have anything to say; there was no way to explain that. She knew

Farih deserved some type of explanation, but she was too angry to focus on anything but Lena and Cooley.

Farih shook her head. "You know what? It's all good. I'm not even mad."

"Farih."

"I mean, it was what it is, Denise. Finally, you were real and said how you felt. Too bad it wasn't to me."

Denise watched Farih do her regular routine. She put her purse down, walked into the kitchen, and grabbed a wineglass and poured herself a glass of Riesling.

"I am sorry," Denise muttered.

Farih shook her head. "No, you aren't. Denise, you aren't sorry about this, because this is how you truly feel. You still love her, and I'm not going to attempt to understand why. I've known for a long time. You think I didn't know the love was gone from our relationship?"

"You think I don't love you?" Denise walked to the kitchen entrance.

"I know you love me, but you just aren't in love with me. We haven't been in love for a long time, Denise. It's time to just be real about it." Farih took a sip of the wine. "But I'm not willing to throw away all we've worked for over it. We have careers to think about."

Denise's head tilted. She walked into the kitchen. She looked at her beautiful girlfriend. As usual, Farih looked stunning, like a doll whose face never changed.

"I get it now." Denise put her hand on the sink. "All this time you talked about making it work wasn't because you wanted to be with me. It was because of your career."

"Of course it was, Denise. We have a lot invested in this. You think I would have put up with you and your lovesick antics with that whore all this time for nothing?"

Denise couldn't help but smile. "So how long have you not been in love with me?"

"Since the day of my audition, when I found your phone on the couch and saw Lena's missed call."

Denise remembered her phone going missing. She'd managed to locate it by its ring after Farih dialed her number. Farih must have found her phone on the couch when Denise stepped out of the room and hidden it between the cushions, then pretended she had no idea where it was. Denise couldn't help but laugh. She shook her head.

"So this whole time we've been going through all this shit because of you and your career."

"It's both of our careers, Denise. You think the world is going to give a fuck about a single Denise Chambers? They don't love you. They love *us! We need* each other. You can have your whore. I don't care. But we aren't going to ruin our careers over silly, childish feelings."

Denise walked closer to Farih. She knew Farih was dead serious. She was willing to let Denise do whatever she wanted as long as they preserved their professional image as the happy black lesbian couple.

"Farih, being with you, meeting you back then was amazing. I love you, I've loved you for years, and I truly loved having you in my life. But the thing that has always been different between us is that you care about all of this." Denise threw her hands up. "I don't. I could care less what people think about me, and if being true to myself means that I won't work on another movie, then so be it."

Denise walked out of the kitchen. She grabbed her keys. Farih realized what Denise was saying. She followed her.

"Denise, please, you can't leave me." Farih grabbed Denise's arm. "I won't have anything if we break up.

They wanted me on the show only because of our relationship. They won't want me if we break up."

Denise pulled Farih close to her. She kissed Farih on her forehead. "Our relationship might have got you in the door, but it was your personality and your knowledge that got you the job. You are amazing, and you will be just as amazing with or without me. I'm here for you whenever you need me always, but I can't continue to be with you. It's not fair to either one of us."

"Denise, think about this before you do it. Are you sure you can give *all* this up?"

"Farih, listen to yourself. What happened to the strong and independent girl I fell in love with? Now you let these people make you question yourself to the point that you are willing to stay in a loveless relationship just to have a job. Fuck, Farih, come on. You are better than this. Is your career worth being miserable for the rest of your life? We have been miserable, Farih. Don't you want to be happy—completely happy—again?"

They stood in silence.

Farih shook her head. "I'm willing to do whatever I have to do to be successful."

Denise's head fell. She felt like she was talking to a brick wall. "Then I truly feel bad for you." Unable to listen to any more of this, Denise walked out of the house.

The punch to the face had sobered Cooley right up. Denise had never hit her before, but she knew she deserved that one. The cab ride home was quiet, leaving Cooley with her thoughts. She had possibly lost one of the only people she truly loved. No matter what, her friendships with Denise and Carmen meant more than any money or any other women, except for Sahara.

She didn't know if Sahara was inside the house. She knew she had some major apologizing to do after her latest blow up. Cooley wondered if she had finally gone too far. She cringed at the thought of the things she'd said to Sahara. Cooley was already in hot water, she knew she couldn't come clean about Lena. She wondered if the left side of her face would be throbbing like the right side by the end of the night.

She opened the front door. A glass came flying toward her face. She ducked just before it hit her instead crashing into the wall. Sahara stood in front of the door, fuming. She rushed up on Cooley and began beating her. Cooley blocked the blows with her arms.

"Sahara!"

"Fuck you, you sorry son of a bitch!" Sahara continued to beat on Cooley's arms and chest. Cooley took each blow; she knew she deserved it. "I hate you. I fucking hate you for making me feel like this!"

Cooley pulled Sahara into her arms. Sahara tried to fight her off, but Cooley held on tight, not letting her go.

"I'm sorry. I'm sorry," Cooley repeated over and over.

"Fuck you," Sahara cried as she collapsed in Cooley's arms. "Why, why do you do me like this!"

"I'm sorry. Please, baby." Cooley held on tight. She wanted Sahara to feel the emotions she was feeling. She loved Sahara and wasn't going to lose her, not after all they had been through.

Cooley picked Sahara's sobbing body up and carried her to the bedroom. She put her in the bed without letting go. Cooley pulled Sahara to her. She continued to apologize while Sahara cried until they both fell asleep.

Chapter 34

Lena didn't know how she had ended up in her bed. She turned over and jumped when she saw Carmen standing over her with a serious expression on her face.

"Carmen."

"I don't even know what to say to you right now." Carmen's voice was low. Lena could hear the hurt in every word. She sat up in her bed.

"Carmen, please, please just listen to me—"

"My wedding is in two weeks, and you've ruined it." A tear fell from her eye. "How could you? Do you even realize what you've done?" Carmen walked out of the bedroom. Lena followed, having déjà vu from the night before with Misha.

"Carmen, no. Please, I've already lost Misha. I can't lose you too. Tell me what to do. What can I do to make this right?"

Carmen stood still. "I don't know. Cooley and Denise got into a fight, and they aren't talking. My two best friends, two girls that have been friends since middle school, aren't talking to each other because of you. And Misha . . . Lena, you broke the little piece of Misha's heart she had left."

"I didn't mean to. Oh my God, I'm so sorry." Lena grabbed Carmen's arm. "I don't know what is wrong with me. I don't want to hurt people, and I keep hurting everyone I love. You, Mish, Denise."

Carmen wanted to be mad, but she couldn't. Lena was sobbing uncontrollably. Watching Lena gave her clarity on her friend.

"Lena, you know what I just realized? What I just realized is you might have been put in mature situations, but in the end you are still just immature. But that's to be expected. You are only twenty-three."

"Carmen . . ."

"It's true, Lena. You were engaged at eighteen, out of school at twenty, had a baby at twenty-one. But the thing is, Lena, you have to start taking responsibility for yourself and your actions."

"Carmen, I will do anything. Just tell me what I need to do to fix this. I don't want to ruin your wedding. I won't show up, if that's what is needed. I'll just give you the keys to the Hamptons house, and I'll stay away. I'll do anything."

"Just start taking more responsibility for your actions. And make up your mind. You need to come to some decisions. Hell, Lena, you don't even know if you are gay or not."

Lena knew Carmen was right. The truth was, she didn't want to face the truth. She didn't want to think about figuring out what she was, because she was afraid of what the truth might be.

"I have friendships and a wedding to save. Do some soul-searching, 'cause I don't want this Lena at my wedding. I want the girl I met at school, who was confident and cool. So in the words of Tamar Braxton, you need to get yo' life, honey." Carmen hugged Lena and walked out the door.

Misha felt like a fugitive. Patrick and Lena wouldn't stop calling her phone. Unable to take the ringing, she chucked the phone out her car window. She had no place to go. She knew her husband was smart, and the first thing he would do was check her credit card to see where she was staying. She pulled up to an ATM and took out five hundred dollars. Misha drove until she saw a Residence Inn. The extended stay would be perfect, since she had no idea how long she would have to be there.

She woke up the next morning still numb. The comfortable bed had done nothing for her body, as she ached from head to toe. Sleeping alone was something she hadn't done in over four years. The events from the night before played over and over in her head. In the midst of her issues with Patrick, she couldn't stop thinking about Lena and Carla. She didn't know why one kiss bothered her so much. Misha remembered the talk she had had with Carla at Centennial Olympic Park. Sahara had done the ultimate, but all Lena did was kiss her ex while in a drunken stupor. Why couldn't she forgive and shake it off?

Her thoughts drifted to her son. She suddenly wanted to die. She had done what she had always said she would never do: she had let herself rely completely on someone else. She was nothing more than a housewife. She depended on Patrick for everything, and without him she had nothing and would have to start from scratch.

Misha couldn't get out of bed. She couldn't force herself to move even if the world depended on it. She had no way out, just a son, a cheating husband, and a best friend who she couldn't stand. Misha was lost, and she knew it.

***

Cooley woke up and instantly realized Sahara wasn't lying next to her. She looked up. A dresser drawer had been left open, and it was empty.

"Sahara."

Cooley ran into the living room. Sahara's assistants stood in the living room, next to her luggage. Sahara looked at them. They grabbed the bags and walked out.

"Baby, please, don't do this."

Sahara could see the anguish in Cooley's eyes. She pulled her shades off. Her eyes were still bloodshot. She had obviously been crying that morning as well.

"Carla, I can't do this anymore. We aren't good for each other."

"No, Sahara, we are. I was fucked up. Seeing you with her, you with anyone, just . . . it just hurts so bad."

"Carla, I know. I know that I hurt you and you hurt me. But we both know there's no way you are ever going to be able to be okay with that leaked stuff. And I'm not willing to take the abuse anymore."

Cooley grabbed Sahara's hand. "Wait." She didn't know what to say, but she couldn't let go. "Remember back when we broke up before? You told me then that you weren't giving up. I'm not willing to give up. I can't give up on us. You are my world."

"Carla . . ."

"I can't lose you."

Sahara held on to Cooley's hands. "I couldn't get that song by Emeli Sandé out of my head. Maybe we have to finally stop pretending that we aren't both hurting and we don't keep hurting each other. Maybe our time has come."

Cooley let go of Sahara's hand. She couldn't listen to any more. Her pleas were falling on deaf ears. Sahara was leaving, and there was nothing she could do about it. Cooley grabbed Sahara by her forehead. She kissed her forehead, letting her lips linger, not wanting to let go. She pulled away and walked back to her home office, unable to watch Sahara walk out the door.

Carmen sat next to Denise in Denise's hotel suite. There were no words. They sat in silence. Carmen had pleaded the case for Lena and for Cooley. Denise listened, not saying anything during the whole time.

Denise turned her head to face Carmen.

"I'm sorry, but I can't. Not now, not yet."

"What about my wedding? I need my best friends. It's no wedding without both of you."

"I'll be at your wedding, I wouldn't miss it for the world. But as far as Cooley and I . . . I'm sorry, Carmen, but I'm done."

Denise stood up and walked back to the bedroom. Carmen knew from the sound of Denise's voice that she was for real.

It was an end of an era.

Chapter 35

Lena watched Danni unlock and pulled the door to the side of the birdcage elevator. Lena nodded in approval. Danni's New York loft was something out of a decor magazine. It wasn't as lavish as the Atlanta home and was much more minimal, with just a few pieces of furniture. Japanese shades covered all the walls in the bedroom, making Lena wonder what Danni's silhouette would look like behind them.

"Welcome to my little home." Danni took Lena's bag to the bedroom. "Make yourself comfortable."

Lena sat down on the brown sofa. The seat felt cool to her legs. She leaned back, resting her head. She had had to get away from Atlanta. She had called Danni, who was more than happy to have her come to New York.

"So to what do I owe this pleasure?" Danni said as she jumped over the arm of the couch and plopped down next to Lena.

"I just needed to get away." Lena cuddled in Danni's arms. She felt safe and secure from the drama facing her in Atlanta. "It's been a hard couple of days."

"What's wrong, boo?"

Lena sighed, and before she knew it, the events of the past few days started spilling from her lips. She couldn't stop herself. She sat there while Danni listened to everything with a straight expression, not taking her eyes off of Lena.

It felt good to get it all out. She told Danni about Denise showing up at the house and all the things that had happened afterward. Lena's eyes filled with tears as she thought about Misha and the loss of their friendship. Danni didn't move or say a word; she listened with her hand on Lena's thigh. Lena looked for traces of emotion from Danni when she mentioned the kiss with Cooley, but her face never changed.

"So do you hate me too?" Lena lowered her head.

Danni sat back on her couch and sighed. "Nah. Why would I hate you?"

"Because of the kiss. I mean, I really never meant to, and I don't want to mess up anything between you and her."

"Why would you mess up something between us?" Danni asked, curious. Her eyes widened. "Oh, okay, I get it. Lena, we aren't together. I don't care what you do or who you do it with."

The words slapped Lena across her face. It was the honest truth. She was single and free to do what she wanted in Danni's eyes. The revelation upset her.

"Well, I just figured with how we have been lately . . ."

"We have been doing us. I mean, as far as your friends go, yeah, that was some messy shit you did, but as far as I'm concerned, I could care less." Danni stood up. "But I will say that I'm a little pissed about the reason why you are actually here."

Lena's head rose. "What?"

"Lena, I'm up here thinking you are coming to spend time with me, but really, you are using me to escape the mess you created at home. That's not cool." Danni began to walk to her bedroom.

"No, it's not like that. . . ." Lena struggled to find the right words, but she couldn't.

"Yes, it is." Danni's voice carried from the bedroom. "It's like you didn't listen to your friends at all." Danni walked back out of the bedroom, holding Lena's suitcase. "Both Carmen and Misha called you on your shit, but you still did the same damn thing. You aren't taking responsibility for the hurt and pain you caused. Instead you run up here to take you mind off of what you've done. That's a punk move, sweetheart." Danni walked over to Lena's suitcase and picked it up.

Lena folded her arms. "So you are putting me out?"

"Pretty much." Danni put the suitcase next to Lena. "Look, boo, I really do care about you, which is why I'm doing this. Don't take what I'm about to say the wrong way, but you need to stop acting like a fucking child, grow some balls, and deal with your shit."

Lena was furious. "You don't know what I'm going through. You don't know anything!"

"What don't I know, Lena?" Danni's voice rose. "I know you won't take responsibility for anything. You admitted that you were confused when you were messing with Denise. Well, when will that stop being the excuse for everything? You are a grown-ass woman, so start making some hard decisions before you lose all your friends."

"So because I made a mistake, I'm a child?" Lena stood up.

"You're a child because, like a fucking toddler, you walk around allowing everyone else to clean up your messes. Instead of trying to be there for your friend and begging for forgiveness, you bring your ass to New York so you don't have to deal with the shit you did. And let's not mention your status. Tell me, Lena, what are you? Are you gay, bisexual, or are you taking the punk-ass road and continuing to say you don't know what you are?"

Lena couldn't look at Danni. Her harsh words were breaking Lena down, but she didn't want to show it. She stood still, not blinking her eyes, because she didn't want any tears to fall. Danni walked closer to her. She stared into Lena's eyes.

"So tell me, Lena, what are you?" Lena tried to turn away, but Danni grabbed her by her arms so she couldn't move. "Don't fucking run for once in your life. What are you?"

"I don't know!" Lena fought and freed herself from Danni's hold. "And you are an asshole for trying to make me—"

"Make you what? Come to a fucking decision about something in your life? Sorry, boo, but I'm not Denise. I'm not going to allow you to flip-flop your way in and out of my life. And as long as you want to deal with me, I'm going to call you out when you are doing something wrong, and, Lena, you are dead fucking wrong for the way you are treating your peeps. You should be in Atlanta, helping Carmen with her wedding and being there for your friend Mish. Fuck the bullshit. That girl is going through shit a lot bigger than you, and you acting like such a punk ass, you can't even be there, 'cause of a stupid-ass kiss."

"She doesn't want me there."

"How do you know? Have you called? Have you tried to see her?"

Lena couldn't respond. She had called Misha a few times but was always sent to voice mail. She couldn't bring herself to call again for fear of what Misha might say to her when she actually answered the phone. Danni's words sank in. Lena was being a coward when dealing with her issues. She fell down on the couch.

Danni knew she had been hard on Lena, but she didn't care. She sat down next to Lena and put her arm around her, pulling her to her chest. She ran her fingers through Lena's soft short hair.

"I'm not trying to hurt your feelings, boo. I just want you to wake up and do what you need to do. Make some decisions, and go do right by your crew."

Lena sat up.

"I'm going to go see when the next flight to Memphis is." Danni left Lena in the living room to face the music. Lena had some decisions to make before she lost the only real friends she had ever had.

Cooley sat in her empty place. Nothing seemed real. She didn't want to face the fact that she had lost her love and her best friend. She sat in her oversize chair, staring at the wall. Her mind raced with ideas on how to get Sahara back. She had put Sahara through hell and didn't know how to even begin with her. The insane amount of flowers and gifts she'd sent had all gone unanswered, until Sahara finally sent a message to her saying that she needed time and to please leave her alone. Cooley couldn't bring herself to erase the message.

Cooley needed something, but she couldn't put her finger on it. Liquor didn't have the numbing effect it usually had. She tried to dive into work but couldn't concentrate for long periods of time.

Carmen walked into the house. She was worried. Cooley's face was dull and dry, and she hadn't fixed her hair since Sahara left. Carmen picked up the empty wine bottle sitting next to Cooley.

"What are you doing here?" Cooley whispered.

"I'm checking on you, my friend." Carmen smiled, hoping to lift Cooley's spirits.

"So I have one person left in my life. Thanks." Cooley ran her hand through her hair.

Carmen sat down on the couch, across from Cooley's chair. She couldn't take it anymore.

"I could kill you, Carla! You and Lena!" She jumped up. "How could you do this to us, to our family?" Angry tears rolled down her face.

"I don't know!" Cooley screamed. "If I could take it back, I would, but I can't."

"Carla . . ."

Emotions flooded through Cooley's body. "I'm dying over here, Carmen. I feel like someone ripped my fucking heart out of my fucking chest, and the fucked-up thing is I know it was me who did it. Sahara won't talk to me. And Dee . . ." Cooley's voice cracked. Her best friend entered her head. She looked away from Carmen. She didn't want anyone to see her. Carmen watched Cooley break down in front of her. Cooley covered her face as she broke completely down. Carmen wrapped her arms around her friend, and Cooley sobbed in her arms.

"Carla, it will be okay. You know she's not really gone."

"Yes, she is. She will never forgive me. Sixteen years."

They both knew the truth. Although Cooley was hurting over Sahara, the truth was she had lost someone who was even more important than any girlfriend. She had lost her best friend, her family, and without Denise a piece of her was missing. Through all the women, and all the ups and downs, the only thing that had ever been stable in her life was her friendship with Denise.

"Carla, talk to her. Go to her and tell her that you are sorry."

Cooley shook her head. "I can't, because honestly, C, I don't blame her. She stuck by me through it all, even when I didn't deserve it. What I did . . . Hell, I wouldn't even forgive me." Cooley stood up. "I don't think I should come to the wedding."

"No!" Carmen jumped up. "You guys' drama is not going to ruin my wedding. My own mother won't come celebrate my day. And if you aren't there, I won't have my other family, either. I didn't do anything to deserve this, and you and your guilt are not going to fuck up my day!" Carmen pushed Cooley. Carmen grabbed her bag. "Fix this shit, or I'm calling my wedding off. And that can be something else you can add to your guilt trip." She walked out, slamming the door behind her.

Chapter 36

"Come in," Misha yelled from the hotel bed. She had found solace in a *Love & Hip Hop* marathon on TV. The one thing she could say about reality TV was that it could be an escape from your own reality.

"Don't kill me, but I have a wedding to save," Carmen said as walked in the mini apartment. She moved out of the way, revealing Lena standing behind her.

Misha turned her head from the door. "What is she doing here?"

"She is here to apologize to her friend, who she misses very, very much," Lena said as she walked closer to Misha. Lena sat on the edge of the bed, while Carmen leaned against the wall. "Misha, I'm so sorry. I haven't been a good friend, and I apologize from the bottom of my heart for that."

"Do you even know what you are apologizing for?" Misha folded her arms.

"I'm apologizing to both of you for taking advantage of our friendship. This is bigger than the stupid kiss. You guys have been there to help me with all my issues, and instead of being thankful, I took advantage of the fact that you would always be there for me. I don't want to lose either one of you." Lena looked at Misha and then at Carmen. "You're my best friends."

Misha knew Lena was being genuine. She sighed. "For the record, I didn't really care about the kiss. . . . Okay, yes, I did, but it was just, Lena, I needed you that night."

"You did, and I should have seen that when I walked in the door. But I was just feeling so guilty for what I did. I didn't know what to do, and my guilt blinded me from seeing that you were obviously going through something."

Misha nodded her head. "My life is falling apart. I'm living in a freaking extended stay. I have nothing, you guys. Patrick owns it all."

"Mish, that's not true." Carmen sat on the other side of the bed. "You have us, so you have whatever you need."

Tears fell down Misha's face. "Am I making the right decision? Should I leave him for good?"

"Sweetie, that's something we can't tell you." Carmen rubbed Misha's leg. "But I know you aren't the Misha that I met. You haven't been happy for a long time. If you leave, don't let it be because of the indiscretion. Think about everything as a whole, and make a decision from there."

"And come stay with me," Lena interjected. "You know Jaylin and you can stay at my house as long as you need to."

"Thanks. I might take you up on that, but right now I need to think." Misha held her hands out. "I love both of you, even Lena's crazy ass."

They all laughed as they held hands. Misha knew one thing: in the end everything would be okay as long as she had her girls.

Chapter 37

Lena walked down the long corridor toward Danni's condo at the W Hotel in Atlanta. It had been a week since the falling-out with Cooley. She hadn't really talked to anyone. Misha was in her own shell, and Carmen couldn't talk about anything but wedding details. She had wanted to ask about Denise, but Carmen had made it very clear that the subject of Denise was completely off-limits.

Denise and Farih's breakup had finally hit the news. They had released a statement that they were ending their relationship but still loved and cared about each other. Lena had watched Farih's show that morning, hoping for some insight into the breakup. Farih had kept it classy as ever.

"I love Denise. She is an amazing woman, and I feel very privileged to have her in my life. But sometimes people grow apart not by the fault of anyone. We started as friends and will always remain friends."

Farih was praised for putting on such a brave face in front of everyone. She was hotter than ever, even without Denise.

"Hey, you." Danni kissed Lena as soon as she opened the door. "Damn, you look good, but that's nothing new."

Lena walked into the condo. Danni's sexiness was messing with her from the jump, making it even harder to say what she wanted to say.

"I was thinking we could go to the Cheesecake Factory. I know that's so lame, but I really have been craving some Ultimate Red Velvet Cake Cheesecake."

"Danni."

Danni turned around to see that Lena was still standing by the door. She walked back over to Lena.

"What's wrong?"

Danni sending Lena away from New York had been the wake-up call Lena needed. Because of Danni's tough love, Lena had her friend back. The last-minute wedding details had Lena in a blissful mood. She knew she owed it all to Danni.

"I don't want to do this anymore." Lena fidgeted with her hands.

"Do what, boo?" Danni noticed how nervous Lena was.

"In New York you said some things to me that really hurt, but you were right, and I needed to hear them. I went home and really did what you told me to do. I started thinking about Lena and what Lena wants." Lena began to pace the floor. "I really do like you, and I love what we have, but I want more. I fooled myself into believing that I was okay not being official, but I'm not. I am not a random chick. I want it all or nothing at all."

Danni tilted her head. "Lena, I've told you before, you aren't random. . . ."

"I'm also not your girlfriend. I'm not trying to come in between what you do professionally. I only want to enhance it. You are what I need in my life, and I know I can be what you need."

"Lena." Danni took a step back. "I love the new confidence . . . but I was honest with you when I said I don't want a girlfriend. That hasn't changed."

"I know you don't want a girlfriend, but I know the reason why. You talk about me being a punk, but you aren't being one hundred, either. You are damaged from Farih, and maybe it's time to finally put that behind you for something real. Let's not punish each other for what happened in our pasts."

Danni thought about Farih. She looked at Lena. "You are kidding me, right?" Lena looked at Danni with a confused look on her face. "You are standing here, telling me about getting punished by the past, when you have past baggage too. Fuck outta here, Lena, with that shit." Danni was angry and didn't care if Lena knew it.

"Do I care about Denise? Yes. I will probably always care about her. But I am standing here, telling you I want to commit to you and you only. I want to be your girlfriend, Danni. But you can't even consider what I'm saying to you, because of your own hang-ups about the girl who got away."

"The girl didn't get away, Lena. The bitch left!" Danni's words flew out like fire. "She left me when I worked my ass off to give her the career she wanted. I made her ass, and she left me! I almost gave up everything for ha' ass, all over some fucking pussy. I'm not doing that shit again. Not for you, or anyone else!"

"I'm not Farih!" Lena yelled. "I don't need you to give me a goddamned thing! I only want you to open your heart to me. I want us to try. Danni, don't you want to at least try?"

"You don't know what you want, Lena. Get real right now. You don't know shit. You don't even know if you are gay or not."

"I know that I am not willing to be your weekend lover anymore. I want more."

Danni crossed her arms. "I can't give you more. I won't. You knew the deal when you got into this. Now, if you aren't cool with it anymore, I'm sorry, but I am who I am, and I'm not changing. If you don't like it, there's the door."

They stared at each other for a moment. Lena could tell Danni was hurt, even though she wouldn't let on about it. Even angry, Danni was sexy. Lena's body craved her, but her heart was telling her to run.

"I'm sorry, Danni. Thanks for an amazing time and for helping me to find myself in many ways. But I can't do this." Lena turned to walk out of the condo. Danni called her name, causing her to pause.

"I'm sorry for snapping out on you. It's just that this wasn't what I was expecting today." Danni walked closer. "I expected to have the girl that I care about in my arms, making love to her until the sun comes up. Are you sure that you want to give up what all we have?"

Lena's legs tingled at the thought of Danni and her. Her body wanted to stay more than anything, but her soul wouldn't let her. "I'm sorry, Danni, but I deserve more, and so do you."

Danni knew she couldn't change Lena's mind. "I hope we can still be friends. You are one of a kind, Lena, and I'd hate to lose you in my life for good." Danni wrapped her arms around Lena. She could smell Danni's intoxicating cologne. Lena forced herself to pull away.

"Always." Lena smiled and walked out the door. She hoped Danni would show up like before, pull her out of the elevator, but she didn't. The doors closed on their relationship. Lena had made up her mind, and it didn't work out for her. She didn't have anyone, but for once she didn't feel bad about it. She was open to all possibilities.

Chapter 38

Misha walked into her broken home. A musty odor hit her as she walked in the kitchen. She rolled her eyes. Dishes were piled up in the sink. Patrick obviously hadn't done a thing since she left.

Patrick appeared in the doorway.

"I guess cleaning wasn't an option." Misha put her purse down.

"Sorry. My mind has been elsewhere lately." Patrick walked into the kitchen. "Thanks for coming."

"Patrick . . ." Misha stood tall, trying not to break down. "We can't do this. I can't do this anymore."

"Wait . . . Mish . . ." Patrick rushed closer. He stopped in his tracks when Misha raised her hand, indicating he should halt.

"Patrick, I have been thinking about this for this whole time, and although the idea of you cheating hurts like hell, I really can't blame you for that." Misha sat on a kitchen chair. "You were right. I wasn't completely here, and I haven't been completely here for a long time."

"Misha, we can fix this. Counseling—"

"Patrick, we can't fix everything. I love you, but I don't want to be married to you." The words hurt both of them. Patrick's pained expression changed to anger.

"And this has nothing to do with the fact that you're heading to New York in a few days, where *she* will be?"

Misha sighed. She shook her head and stood up. "See, that's it right there. There is nothing I can do to make you not think Cooley, or any other woman, is a threat."

"Well, what am I supposed to think?"

"You are supposed to realize that your wife loves you and is devoted to you. I am not a cheater, Patrick. I wouldn't cheat with a man or a woman. But you can't see that. You never have been able to see it. Face it, Patrick. You can't be happy with me."

"Yes, I can."

"No, you can't. Because no matter what, you are always going to think I'm going to leave you for a woman." Misha didn't realize how loud she had become until that moment. She took a deep breath. "I can't change my past, and I don't want to. But I can change how my future will be. I can't be with someone who doesn't trust me."

"Wait!" Patrick felt his world crashing down. "I *can* trust you. I *do* trust you. Misha, what about our son?"

"Patrick, I love you. I've loved you since I was in the seventh grade. I never would want to lose you as a part of my life, or your son's life. We just can't be together."

"So you really want to do this. You want to give up everything we have?" Patrick shook his head in disbelief. "What are you going to tell Jaylin?"

"*We* are going to tell him that we love him very much, but Mommy and Daddy won't be living together anymore. . . ."

"This is bullshit." Patrick punched the wall. "I'm sitting here saying, 'Let's at least get counseling,' but you aren't willing to even try to save our marriage. I'm not stupid, Misha. I know why you don't want to try. You know what! Fine! If you want to go, then go. But you aren't taking our son. I won't have him around that filth!"

Misha's motherly instincts kicked in. "Patrick, if you want to be a child about this, then by all means, do what you gotta do. I'm trying to remain an adult and be civil about the situation, but if you threaten me about our son, so help me God, I will use every resource at my disposal to make your life a living hell."

"So you're threatening me now?" Patrick laughed. "That's funny, Misha."

"It's not a threat. It's a promise. I'm leaving, but you better think long and hard about how you want this divorce to go." Misha picked up her purse and walked out the door. She wanted to cry, but she held it together. She knew Patrick wasn't going to go down easily.

She had to prepare for the fight of her life.

Chapter 39

Lena left Danni's place and went straight to the airport and jumped on the first flight to Orlando. Within a few hours she was sitting in her parent's villa at the Disney World Animal Kingdom Resort. She knew there was only one thing she needed. She held on to her daughter, hugging and kissing her. She didn't realize how much she had missed her little girl.

She couldn't believe how her parents looked. Her mother and father both had on matching Mickey Mouse T-shirts. They sat in the lavish Disney hotel suite while Bria modeled her Princess Tiana dress from *The Princess and the Frog*.

"So, honey, do you want to go with us to Animal Kingdom?" Her father's deep voice sounded funny given that he was wearing a purple T-shirt.

"Sure. Why not?"

"You know, I really expected you to join us a lot earlier," Karen remarked.

"Well, I had a lot of things to sort out at home. I'm doing some redecorating, and Carmen's wedding coming up has kept me very busy."

"Papi, I wanna wear my other dress."

"Well, let's go find the dress you want to wear." Bria pulled her grandfather's hand as they headed into the other room.

Lena smiled as they walked out of the room. As soon as the door closed, she noticed the look on her mother's face.

"Yes, Mother?"

"I heard about Denise and her girlfriend." Her judgmental tone irritated Lena. "Is that the reason for this unexpected visit?"

Lena rolled her eyes. "No, Mother, it's not. I wanted to see my daughter."

"And it took you two months to want to see her? Tell the truth, Lena."

"Oh my God, Mother, why don't you just tell me what you want to hear?"

"Who is Danni?" Karen asked, not taking her eyes off of her daughter.

"Where did you—"

"Your daughter mentioned a person named Danni. Who, or should I say what, is Danni?"

Lena couldn't take it. She stood up. "Danni is a woman, Mother. Isn't that want you want to know? Yes, she's a lesbian, a sexy-ass lesbian who I have spent the majority of this break with, having the most amazing sex ever—"

"Lena Jamerson!" The deep voice echoed throughout the room, causing Lena and Karen to jump.

Lena turned to see her father's stern face staring at her. Bria walked out of the room, wearing a Cinderella dress.

"Jessica, take Bria to get some ice cream at the restaurant," her father ordered. Jessica quickly ushered Bria out of the hotel suite. "What did you just say to your mother?"

Lena knew there was no turning back. Her heart raced. "I'm sorry, but I can't continue to lie to either of you. Dad, when I was in school, I fell in love with my roommate."

"So this is the reason you and Brandon split up?" Lena's father was still as a statue.

"No, we had more issues than just Denise."

Karen stood up. "So you blatantly lied to me when you said you were done with that girl?"

"No, I didn't lie. I was done with Terrin, and I didn't know if I was done with women or not, but I can't continue to act like I don't like what I like. I like men, but I love women." Her eyes began to water.

"Lena, so you standing here, telling us that you are a . . . homosexual?" Her father's voice cracked. That crack broke Lena's heart.

"I'm standing here, saying . . . I'm saying that I like women, and that isn't going to change. I am still Lena. I'm still your daughter. But I can't lie to you, or myself, anymore."

"And here, we thought you were mature. You need to grow out of this phase," Karen told her.

"It's not a phase, Mother. It's me. This is me."

"This is all that girl's fault," Karen protested.

"Stop blaming Denise. This isn't her fault. She never came on to me. She rejected me when I approached her. This is not her fault. It just happened. It is what it is."

There was an awkward silence in the room. They couldn't look at each other. Lena's father walked up to her. He put his big hand on her shoulder.

"Are you sure this is what you want, Lena?"

"I'm so sorry I hurt you, Dad. I wish I could fight it, but I can't."

"As long as you are sure this is what you want, then who are we to have a problem with it?"

"Derrick!" Karen shouted.

"Karen, this is our daughter, and if she so happens to be gay, then we just have a gay daughter. I don't know about you, but I'd rather she be happy with a woman than be unhappy with some guy."

Lena couldn't believe her ears. She wrapped her arms around her father. Her mother sat down, shaking her head in disbelief.

"Now, your daughter wants to go to Animal Kingdom, and I want to go to Animal Kingdom. So I'm leaving. Who's coming?"

"I am. . . . Mom?"

"No, go without me."

Lena looked at her father. They walked out of the suite, leaving Karen sitting on the couch. She knew it was going to take more time for her mother to accept the truth, but for the first time Lena felt free.

Chapter 40

Denise looked for the bus stop for the Hampton Jitney. She had signed a few autographs and had avoided the press as best as possible at JFK, but they had followed her all the way. She wanted to get to the house just to get away from the press, but the thought of being in the same house with Lena and Cooley almost made her want to continue dealing with the press.

She noticed a car service. Denise quickly remembered she was rich, and for once she decided to use her money and have a town car take her all the way to the Hamptons.

Her mind was consumed with Lena and Cooley the whole flight and car ride. She hadn't seen either of them in almost two weeks and wasn't looking forward to seeing them or staying under the same roof. She thought about calling in a favor to Melanie, asking to borrow her Hamptons place, but Denise knew she had to go to the house. There was unfinished business that needed to be taken care of.

The town car pulled up to the house. It was smaller than many of the houses around it, but it was still bigger than any house she'd ever want to own. She paid the driver, and he proceeded to take her bags to the front door. Carmen ran out of the house. She threw her arms around Denise.

"I'm so happy to see you."

"Okay, Carmen, you're cutting off my circulation." Denise noticed a curtain moving. She looked up to see Cooley's face briefly. "She's here."

"Yeah. Please, just don't fight the weekend of my wedding."

"I won't. And Lena?"

"She's flying in from Orlando. She went to see her daughter for a bit. She came out to her parents."

Denise's head jerked around. "No shit?"

"Yep."

"And . . . ?"

"Her dad was cool, but her mom is . . . Well, you know how her mom is."

"Damn, well, good for her." Denise wanted to be happy for Lena, but the anger set back in quickly.

"Hey, hey," Nic said as she walked out of the house. "Carmen, the chef has some questions for you inside." Carmen excused herself. Nic looked at Denise. "Walk?"

"Yeah, let's."

They headed to the beach, and Denise watched the waves crash into the sand. They sat down in two beach chairs.

"Soo . . . how does it feel? You are about to be married."

Nic smiled. "It feels the same, actually. I committed myself a long time ago to Carmen. This is just saying some words."

"Ahh, man, that makes it sound special," Denise joked.

"What can I say?" Nic looked around. "But I will say, if I had to get married, this is the way to do it." They both looked at the ocean.

Denise looked at Nic. "What do you think about Cooley?"

"I think that she did something stupid. But we all do stupid things when we are hurt. And I can tell you, that chick in there is hurting."

"I heard about Sahara."

"This has nothing to do with Sahara. She's lost her best friend." Nic and Denise looked at each other.

Denise walked into the living room to find Cooley sitting at her computer. Cooley turned when she heard someone enter. She saw Denise's face and immediately turned back to her computer.

"Can't give up work even on a vacation, I see," Denise joked, hoping to lighten the mood.

"Well, I gotta take care of business, even if my clients hate me."

Denise sat down at the table. She closed Cooley's computer. Cooley couldn't look at Denise.

"I don't hate you. I think you can be a total asshole, but I don't hate you," Denise confessed.

"Dee."

"You were wrong for what you did, but you were also right. Lena has never been my girl, and so I technically have no claim. . . ."

"Nah, fuck that. You have every right to claim her, and I was dead wrong. I let my emotions get the best of me. That and Patrón and champagne mixed don't make for a rational Cool."

"Carla."

Cooley looked up. It was a rare occasion when Denise called her by her real name.

"Yeah, I said 'Carla.' I said it because you aren't Cooley anymore. You aren't the playboy, the 'I don't give a fuck about anything' chick that you were years ago. You have changed, and that's a good thing."

"You think so?"

"I know so." They gave each other daps.

"Man, you know, even after Sahara leaving me, the thing that killed me most was the idea of not having you in my life anymore."

"You can't get rid of family." Denise looked at Cooley. They hugged, both getting emotional, causing them to laugh.

"See, this shit right here, this isn't cool." Cooley laughed. "Got me all open and shit."

"My guys!" Carmen squealed as she ran in and wrapped her arms around both of them. "I'm so happy now!"

"Carmen! Wit' yo' emotional ass." Cooley let Carmen hug her.

That moment the front door opened. They watched as Lena walked into the house. She froze. She knew it was going to happen, but she didn't expect to be hit with Cooley and Denise as soon as she walked in the house.

"Umm. H-hey," Lena stuttered. She looked at Denise.

Denise wanted to say something, but she couldn't. She stood up and walked out of the room. Lena's head dropped. Carmen quickly came to her.

"Come on, girl. I figured out which room was yours and didn't touch it."

They opened the door to Lena's bedroom. It still looked like it had when she was sixteen years old. The pink walls made her want to throw up. She knew she would never do that color for Bria.

"She hates me," Lena muttered.

"Just give it time. Where's Mish?"

"Had some stuff to deal with. She'll be here later," Lena informed her.

"Cool." Carmen hugged Lena. "I'm gonna head back down. See you soon?"

Lena nodded, but she had no intention of leaving her room for the night.

Misha watched as Patrick walked out of the house. She grabbed Jaylin's overnight bags out of the car. Jaylin ran into his father's arms. Patrick hugged Jaylin like he hadn't seen him in weeks. Jaylin ran into the house to get the gift Patrick had told him was waiting inside.

"Hey," Patrick said as he took the bags from Misha.

"All his stuff is in here."

"You know, he still has clothes here."

"Yeah, but his Spiderman pj's are his favorite. He won't sleep without them on." Misha closed the back car door. Patrick grabbed her hand.

"Misha . . ." He lowered his head. "I'm sorry about last time. I was tripping. A man kind of loses it when he realizes he's losing the only woman he ever loved."

Misha's palm touched Patrick's face. "You aren't losing me. We are just changing our relationship."

"But it's hard for me to want to change it."

"Me too. But it's for the best. You know it, Patrick."

Patrick sighed. He hated to admit it, but she was right. He knew in his heart that he would never be able to completely forget her past. He dropped Jaylin's bags and wrapped his arms around Misha.

"I'm not going to fight you. I love you too much to bring you any more pain. We will work everything out."

Misha breathed a sigh of relief. She wrapped her arms around his strong torso and hugged him tight.

"Thank you, Patrick. Thank you so much." They hugged each other, neither wanting to let go. Misha finally pulled herself away.

"I have to catch this flight."

"You want us to drive you?" Patrick asked. "At least then, you don't have to pay for parking."

Misha smiled. "That would be great."

Patrick headed in the house to get their son. Misha could finally see the light at the end of the tunnel.

Chapter 41

Lena could hear the laughter coming from outside. She could see the flames from the fire pit. She felt like a prisoner in her own home. She wanted to go outside, but the idea of being around Denise, and ruining Carmen's day, made her stay in her bedroom.

There was a knock at the door. The door opened. Lena's eyes widened as Misha walked in and closed the door.

"So you are going to hide in here all weekend?" Misha's famous curly 'fro was bouncier than normal.

"When did you get here?"

"About an hour ago."

Lena sighed. "I just don't want to ruin anything."

"Oh, and making people feel bad that you are stuck in your room isn't going to ruin anything?" Misha sat on the side of the bed.

"She wouldn't even look at me, Mish."

"Maybe you should make her."

"How am I supposed to do that?"

"Girl, you two have been playing this cat and mouse game for years. Maybe it's time for someone to finally to give in." Misha gave Lena a hug and stood up.

"You and that hair."

Cooley's voice sent chills through Misha's body. Misha turned around to see Cooley smiling in the doorway, her deep dimples inset.

"Don't you flirt with me. I am still mad at you."

"You are mad at me?" Cooley walked into the room. "Okay, I'll take that. You know it was a mistake, right?"

"I know that you and your loose libido probably got caught in the moment. I do know you well. When you are mad, you do fucked-up things. Bad habit, Cooley. You need to work on that."

"Oh, I am, trust me." Cooley couldn't look at Misha. She thought about Sahara. "My anger lost me both the women I ever loved and almost lost me my best friend."

"Your anger didn't lose me, Cooley. We just weren't meant to be." Misha sat next to Cooley. "I've thought about this a lot, and I think that in the end, it's always been her."

"So where is your boy?"

"At home with our son, and he's not my boy anymore."

Cooley's eyes widened. *What?*

"We are getting . . . divorced." It was still hard for Misha to say the word out loud.

"I'm sorry to hear that, boo." Cooley put her arm around Misha. "I know you loved him."

"I still do love him, but some things just aren't meant to be."

Sahara entered Cooley's mind. "I guess you're right about that. I guess me and Sha just weren't meant to be." Cooley smirked. "But can't say I didn't see you and him ending. You were *way* too good at eating pussy to give that shit up."

"Shut up, asshole." They laughed as Misha playfully pushed Cooley, but Cooley's smile quickly faded.

"Misha, I really thought she was the one. Hell, I know she was the one. I've never felt that way about anyone. I just . . . man, I . . ." Cooley felt herself getting choked up.

Misha put her hand on Cooley's leg. That gesture caused Cooley to break down. Tears flowed from her eyes.

"I feel lost without her."

Misha wiped Cooley's face. "Don't worry, Carla. It will work out. If it's meant to be, it will be. Please stop crying. It's freaking me out."

Cooley couldn't do anything but laugh. She hugged Misha. They embraced as Misha consoled her in the way she needed, by laughing and cracking jokes.

Lena woke up in a hot sweat. She looked at her clock. It was 3:00 A.M., and the house was completely silent. Her stomach rumbled. She tiptoed out of her room and downstairs.

The old hardwood floor let out a loud creak when her bare foot hit the bottom step. She looked up, hoping that no one had heard her upstairs. She walked into kitchen and opened the fridge door. She grabbed an orange and closed the door.

"Shit!" Lena jumped out of her skin, dropping the orange on the floor when she saw the dark figure in the doorway. The figure walked into the room. Lena's heart dropped as Denise's face appeared. "Denise." Lena slowly picked the orange up off the floor.

"Why, Lena?" Denise leaned against the wall.

"I don't know what to say. It was a terrible mistake."

"I'm not talking about Cooley, although that was some fucked-up shit. I'm talking about me and you. Why, Lena? Why could we never get this shit right?" Denise walked closer. The room was silent. Lena swore she could hear Denise's heart beating in the silence.

"I don't know. I ask myself that question all the time."

"I guess I just wasn't enough." Denise turned her head.

Lena looked at Denise. She didn't feel sad; she felt irritated.

"You weren't enough? Fuck out of here, Denise!" Lena put the orange down.

"Fuck out of here?" Denise couldn't believe Lena had just gone New York on her.

"I fucking came to you. I left him. I left him pregnant to come to you, and you pushed me away. And you have the nerve to stand here and act like this was all my fault? Please! You had plenty of chances to get me. You chose not to."

"Because you aren't any good for me, Lena. You are like a fucking drug. I lose all grip on reality when you come into my life."

"Well, it takes one to know one!" Lena picked her orange back up and headed to the door. "I came to you, Denise. You pushed me away, more than once. I know I did some fucked-up things, but so did you."

"So maybe this has all been a big mistake since day one," Denise mumbled.

"Maybe." Lena shook her head. "All I know is that I'm not that same girl that you saw when you came to my house last time. I'm not allowing you to be fickle when it comes to me." Lena turned away from Denise. She couldn't look at her anymore. "I left him. I left him for you. But you didn't give me a chance. But I don't need it anymore." Lena walked away, feeling stronger than she had ever felt before.

Denise was speechless. Lena was right. She couldn't blame anyone but herself. She looked down and smirked.

"Fuck out of here. Did she really say that shit?" Denise shook her head in amazement. That wasn't the little Lena she'd roomed with. She was so much more.

Chapter 42

The decorators had the back of Lena's beach house looking amazing. An arch covered with bright blue orchids stood in the middle, with the ocean making the perfect backdrop. Carmen stared at the decorations from the window.

"It's time to put on the dress, Carmen," Lena said as she and Misha stood in the doorway.

Carmen turned around. They could see the pain on her face, even though she tried to hide it.

"What's wrong, honey?" Misha patted Carmen on her back.

"Nothing. Everything is just so beautiful. I just . . . I just wish my mom wanted to come, and Nic's family."

"Well, Nic's people were going to come, but—" Lena stepped closer.

"I know. Her mom is too sick to travel."

"We are sending a perfect video of the whole thing. And if we have to go to L.A. and do the whole thing all over again, we will." Misha smiled.

"Carmen, it's your day. You should be happy," Lena said.

"I am. I . . . I am."

There was a knock at the door. Denise and Cooley walked in, both holding presents in their hands. Lena tried not to look at Denise, but she looked too good in her white suit, with her hair perfectly pressed and hanging down her back.

"Baby girl, we have something for you." Cooley handed Carmen her box. Carmen opened it to find an old garter belt. "Your mom gave this to me to give to you." Carmen's eyes widened. "She said she couldn't come, but she couldn't let you go down the aisle without it."

Tears flowed from Carmen's eyes. "Oh my God, this belonged to my grandmother, and my mother wore it too." Although her mom hadn't come, that item let her know things would be all right in the end.

"This is from me." Denise handed her the familiar blue Tiffany box." Carmen opened it to find a beautiful diamond-encrusted hair clip. "It's your something new."

"And . . ." Lena handed Carmen another box. She opened it to find a pair of sapphire earrings. "This is something blue."

"And something borrowed." Misha put a silver bracelet on Carmen's arm. The Chi Theta letters were engraved on it. "It's the bracelet you gave me when we crossed."

"Thank you, guys. I don't know what to say." Carmen couldn't stop blubbering.

"You can stop crying so we can get you ready." Misha blotted Carmen's face with a tissue.

"We are going to check on Nic and make sure she hasn't changed her mind," Cooley joked, lightening the mood in the room.

Lena and Denise caught glimpses of each other, and neither wanted to turn away. Denise gave a quick grin before walking out of the room.

The friends stood around while Carmen and Nic stared deeply into each other's eyes and the preacher gave words of encouragement and inspiration for their lives together.

"And now the couple would like to say their own vows."

They could see the tears forming in Nic's eyes.

Carmen held Nic's hands. She struggled to get the words out. "Nicole, I love you so much. When there were times that I didn't know what love was, you loved me. When I didn't love myself, you loved me. And in times that I didn't deserve your love, you still loved me. My life didn't start until you entered it. And I'm ready to spend the rest of forever with you."

A single tear fell from Lena's right eye. Misha held Lena's hand, while Nic wiped the tears from Carmen's face.

"Carmen, you are the most amazing, fantastic, irritating, wonderful woman I have ever met in my life." The group chuckled. "I knew from the moment I saw you, I wanted to spend the rest of my life with you. Was it easy? No. But nothing worth having is ever easy."

Nic's words echoed in Lena's head.

Nic went on. "I fought for you, for our love, and I promise here and now that I will never stop fighting for us. I love you, and life is complete with you in my life."

Misha's, Carmen's, and Lena's makeup were ruined as the tears flowed from Nic's eyes and their own. Cooley found herself getting choked up. In moments there wasn't a dry eye in the group.

The preacher said his final remarks. "And by the power vested in me and by the state of New York, I now pronounce you wife and wife."

Cooley couldn't help but shake her head at the preacher's choice of words. They clapped and cheered, throwing orchid petals on the couple as they kissed for what seemed to be an eternity.

"I's married now!" Carmen yelled out as she threw her hands up. They all laughed as she turned around. She threw her bouquet in the direction of Misha and Lena. Lena caught it. She looked up to find Denise staring at her.

The group headed to one of the local bars to party the night away. Carmen and Nic danced in their wedding attire. Carmen refused to take off the dress that she so loved. People congratulated them, even pinned money on her dress.

The group finally headed back to the house. Cooley and Denise walked together to the front door.

"So, I guess you will be next," Cooley joked.

"Yeah, right."

"Well, the chances of you finding someone before me are pretty obvious."

"Are you sure about that?" Denise nudged Cooley and pointed to the front door. Sahara stood on the patio in a beautiful white and peach sundress. Cooley looked at Denise, then back at Sahara.

"I thought you two needed to talk," Misha said as she walked up behind Cooley and Denise.

Cooley blinked. "You?"

"You want something, go get it, Cooley." Misha smiled. Cooley hugged her.

"You are amazing," Cooley whispered.

"I know. I know." Misha smiled as she and Denise watched Cooley run to Sahara.

There were no words. They just embraced, locking lips like it was the first time.

"I think I'm going to go to the beach." Denise smiled. She walked off toward the back of the house.

Lena got out of the car and watched Denise until she disappeared from view. Nic's vows entered her mind. Something came over Lena. She pulled her shoes off and ran to the back of the house.

The beach was dark. If it wasn't for the lights from the houses, it would have been pitch-black. Lena felt the sand covering her feet. She thought about her dream. It was now or never.

"We never really tried," Lena yelled.

Denise turned around to see Lena headed toward her.

"Lena . . ."

"We never really tried. Neither one of us. Denise, when you wanted me, I didn't try to make it work. When you told me to leave your room, I shouldn't have taken no for an answer. And that day in your apartment, when I found out I was pregnant, you shouldn't have let me go. You shouldn't have told me to go back. We never truly tried, Denise. We both gave up at the first sign of trouble."

"Lena, I know but . . ."

"But I want to try."

Lena didn't care. In that moment she didn't want another day to pass when Denise was not hers.

"Denise, I'm standing here, letting you know I want to try. I want the chance we always deserved. I don't care about anything else. I want this, and I'm begging you to please just give it a try."

"So much has happened, Lena."

"And I'm sure more will happen. But don't you think we deserve to give it a shot? We owe it to each other to at least try."

Lena stood in front of Denise. There were no tears. She was determined.

Denise stared at Lena's face. She didn't know what to say. Had too much happened? Was there too much baggage for them to even attempt to be more? Denise lowered her head.

Lena watched as Denise's head dropped. She felt her knees go weak. "Oh." Lena couldn't breathe. She turned around. She had poured her heart out again. It had never occurred to her that Denise just didn't want her anymore. She tried to move, but her legs were frozen. She mustered every bit of might in her to make her right leg move forward.

Denise watched as Lena slowly walked away. The cold waves crashed into her legs. She hadn't realized how close she was to the surf. She looked back up at Lena.

"Lena!"

The call caused Lena to halt. She turned around to find Denise standing directly behind her.

"Lena, I don't want to try." Denise's words caused Lena's legs to tremble. Denise stared into Lena's eyes. In that moment nothing else mattered. "Lena, I don't want to try. Fuck trying. There's nothing to *try* to do."

"Fine." Lena turned, but Denise grabbed her arm.

"I don't want to try, because I just want to do it. It's always been you, Lena. We don't need to try. It's always been."

Lena let out a sigh of relief. The tears poured forth as she threw her arms around the love of her life. Denise picked her up. They kissed the kiss they should have had years before. Every breath, every moment, every tear, and every heartache had led to this moment. Lena's feet hit the sand, but it felt like clouds.

"Are we insane?" Lena smiled.

"No, we just are." Denise leaned in, placing another kiss on her love's lips. "I love you, Lena Jamerson."

"I love you, Denise Chambers."

Epilogue

CHOICES MADE TWO YEARS LATER

Bria's nose pressed against the tinted window of the black limousine. It had been pressed against the window ever since they'd entered the long line of limousines.

"Bria, honey, sit back."

"We're almost there, Mommy!" Bria squealed.

"Back, child." Lena pointed at the seat. Bria frowned but did what her mother said. Lena glanced over at Denise, who was in her own world. Lena put her hand on Denise's thigh. "Are you okay?"

Denise's head rose. She smiled. "Yeah, I'm just a bit nervous when I have to do these things."

"You will be wonderful." Lena kissed Denise gently on her lips, causing Bria to make a swooning noise.

Bria could hardly contain herself as they prepared to leave the limo. Lena reminded Bria how important it was that she be on her best behavior for Denise. Bria agreed as the door swung open and cameras began to flash. Denise stepped out to the screams of fans and the flashes of the photographers. She smiled and waved at the fans holding posters of her and the other actors. She had landed the role of Aqua in the summer's biggest movie, based on a teen novel series that was an overnight sensation. Denise knew in that moment that her life would never be the same.

"Denise Chambers. Or shall I say Aqua?" said the reporter from E! as Denise walked to the network's booth. "This must be a little crazy to you."

Denise smiled. "It's insane, but I love all the fans, and I loved the character Aqua."

"How did you get into the books?"

"My girlfriend is actually a huge fan. When she found out I was up for the role, she wanted me to do it, but her daughter insisted that I do it."

"And is this the little agent?" The reporter motioned for Bria and Lena to join them. Bria strutted to the booth. Denise reached for Lena's hand.

"Yes, I'm going to run everything by her from now on," Denise quipped.

Lena smiled, finding it hard to contain the true emotions she felt. It was the first time since they'd been together that Denise had publicly referred to her as her girlfriend. After the very public relationship with Farih, Denise didn't want to subject their growing relationship to any media scrutiny. The gossip blogs blamed Lena for the breakup of the black Ellen and Portia. Even though Farih and Denise had remained good friends, the beginning wasn't so easy, as Farih, being the fame seeker that she was, never confirmed or denied that Lena was the cause for the breakup. Farih wouldn't admit it, but a piece of her loved seeing Lena's photo on MediaTakeOut and Sandra Rose, next to descriptions of her as a home wrecker.

Brandon was another person who didn't take the news of Lena and Denise's relationship too great. It was one thing for Lena to be gay in private, but having a serious relationship with a woman while raising their child didn't work for him. It took a sit-down between them to finally air out all the past issues he had with the woman who had essentially turned his ex-wife gay.

Denise, Lena, and Bria made their way into the busy theater after finally making it down the press hall. Denise greeted various members of the film's cast and other celebrities, never letting go of Lena's hand. Lena found it hilarious how Denise schmoozed with people, knowing the whole thing made Denise very uncomfortable. They both breathed a sigh of relief when they saw familiar faces.

"Hey, Aqua," Cooley joked as she approached with Sahara. She held up a poster with Denise on it, covered in her blue makeup. "Can I get your autograph please?"

"Shut up." Denise grabbed the poster and rolled it up.

"This is so exciting," Carmen squeaked as she ran up and hugged Denise. "I'm so happy for you. Oh my God, Jada Pinkett is here!" Nic shook her head as Carmen snapped photos of celebrities, who had no idea they were being photographed by her excited wife.

Bria pulled Lena toward the candy bar that had been set up for the children attending the premiere. She watched as Bria filled her swag bag with the various sweets all covered in advertisements for the movie.

"Lena, how you enjoying it all?" Lena turned around to see Sahara walking up to her. Sahara ordered a glass of wine for herself and Cooley at the real bar next to the candy bar.

"It's sort of surreal."

"Surreal?"

"On the one hand, I've been to so many premieres in my lifetime that this doesn't faze me at all. I feel like I've done it all. Then I see her." She looked at Denise, who was talking it up with their friends. "And I remember that this is nothing like anything I've ever experienced. It's so much more." Lena smiled.

Lena and Sahara headed back, with Bria in tow, to join the women they loved. Lena placed her arm around Denise's back.

Denise smiled. "What's all this?"

"Did I ever tell you thank you?"

"For?" Denise asked.

"For catching me." Lena smiled.

"Catching you?" Denise was confused.

"Yes. For catching me back at Freedom when I almost fell off of the chair. I just wanted to say thank you for catching me."

Denise smiled. "Well, in that case, thank you too."

Lena looked at her loving girlfriend.

"For catching me that day as well." Denise kissed Lena on her forehead.

Notes

Notes

Notes

ORDER FORM
URBAN BOOKS, LLC
78 E. Industry Ct
Deer Park, NY 11729

Name: (please print):_____

Address: _____

City/State: _____

Zip: _____

QTY	TITLES	PRICE
	16 On The Block	$14.95
	A Girl From Flint	$14.95
	A Pimp's Life	$14.95
	Baltimore Chronicles	$14.95
	Baltimore Chronicles 2	$14.95
	Betrayal	$14.95
	Black Diamond	$14.95
	Black Diamond 2	$14.95
	Black Friday	$14.95
	Both Sides Of The Fence	$14.95
	Both Sides Of The Fence 2	$14.95
	California Connection	$14.95

Shipping and handling-add $3.50 for 1st book, then $1.75 for each additional book.

Please send a check payable to:

Urban Books, LLC

Please allow 4-6 weeks for delivery

ORDER FORM
URBAN BOOKS, LLC
78 E. Industry Ct
Deer Park, NY 11729

Name: (please print):_____

Address: _____

City/State: _____

Zip: _____

QTY	TITLES	PRICE
	California Connection 2	$14.95
	Cheesecake And Teardrops	$14.95
	Congratulations	$14.95
	Crazy In Love	$14.95
	Cyber Case	$14.95
	Denim Diaries	$14.95
	Diary Of A Mad First Lady	$14.95
	Diary Of A Stalker	$14.95
	Diary Of A Street Diva	$14.95
	Diary Of A Young Girl	$14.95
	Dirty Money	$14.95
	Dirty To The Grave	$14.95

Shipping and handling-add $3.50 for 1st book, then $1.75 for each additional book.

Please send a check payable to:

Urban Books, LLC

Please allow 4–6 weeks for delivery

ORDER FORM
URBAN BOOKS, LLC
78 E. Industry Ct
Deer Park, NY 11729

Name: (please print): _____

Address: _____

City/State: _____

Zip: _____

QTY			

Shipp... for
each
Pleas

Pleas